REAPER

CRADLE : VOLUME TEN

WILL
WIGHT

HIDDEN GNOME PUBLISHING

HIDDEN
GNOME
PUBLISHING

PROLOGUE

Information restricted: Personal Record 8154.
Authorization required to access.
Authorization confirmed: 008 Ozriel.
Beginning record...

Ozmanthus Arelius looked up into the ash falling from the sky and knew he'd failed.

His descendants had died in droves, trusting in him. Techniques flashed through the air from miles away, and the earth trembled beneath his feet. He had done what he could to protect the innocents, but there was no bringing them back now. He could only break things.

And once again, he hadn't broken the right things quickly enough.

He almost left the world immediately, abandoning what remained of his family to clean up after his failure. But he had not yet finished his work in Cradle. He needed to leave something behind.

He looked down in his hand, where a small barrier in the shape of an orb contained a fragment of his power. To the mortal eye, it resembled a black hole contained in a glass bead a little bigger than his thumbnail.

This marble carried his parting message to his family. So far, no one had listened to him.

But he could try again.

One last time.

RECORD COMPLETE.

第一章

CHAPTER ONE

With his Remnant arm in a scripted sling, Lindon stood motionless on a Thousand-Mile Cloud. This one was rust-red, similar to the one he'd used when leaving Sacred Valley for the first time.

This time, he tried not to dwell on all the devastation below him.

"This is not very dignified, young one," Elder Whisper protested.

Lindon had the giant five-tailed snowfox bound up in wind aura and floating behind him. Now it looked as though the sacred beast was being carried in a giant invisible fist.

"Apologies, Elder. I'm not certain I could transfer us directly with any precision, so please bear with the indignity for a short time."

"I don't see why I could not have ridden my own Cloud."

Lindon had another Thousand-Mile Cloud, and could make one easily enough, but he didn't trust Elder Whisper to stay in place. Lindon could see through illusions now, but he was still exhausted. He didn't want to spend his every second staring to prevent the elder from sneaking away.

"We're almost there."

Gripped by air though he was, the white fox still had

enough control to stretch his head further and whisper into Lindon's ear. "I offered you the secrets of Monarchs, young Lindon. They are not for just anyone to hear."

"I'm not bringing you to just anyone."

Lindon's red cloud drifted upwards toward a much larger island of blue cloud madra with a blocky castle-like slab of stone on it. Ziel's unnamed cloud fortress.

As soon as he set down on the edge of the cloud base, another cloud zipped up to him. This one was no bigger than his fist, and it was driven by an ocean-blue woman about a foot tall. She glared at him, and her voice was like the clatter of dropped pans.

Lindon dipped his head to Little Blue. "Forgiveness. I didn't want to disturb you."

She would have known that he was fine and generally where he'd gone, but that didn't mean she enjoyed being left behind. She leaped off the cloud onto his shoulder, chattering at him not to forget her again.

"Your Sylvan Riverseed has power similar to your own," Elder Whisper noted. "So that's how you expanded your pure madra to catch up to your peers."

Little Blue shot Whisper an indifferent glance, then ignored him.

Lindon released the elder so they could walk up to Ziel's home together. There were scripts all over the territory to protect them from being spied on by the spiritual senses of others, but Lindon carried a ward key. Mercy and Ziel were still recovering, and the biggest surprise was that he didn't feel Eithan at all.

When he entered the plain gray house, Yerin was already standing in the entry, looking down at him. Her red eyes were filled with worry.

"Thought you'd be gone for longer than two and a half seconds."

Her concern brought up the reality he'd been trying to avoid. A purple mass of spiritual power rested at the base of his skull, weak and unclear.

Dross. Or what was left of him.

Those thoughts were razor-sharp, and Lindon stopped handling them before they cut him too badly. "Whisper is one of the elders of my clan," Lindon said, gesturing to the fox behind him. "He had information about the labyrinth that he wanted to share. And after that...I have something to show you as well."

She looked confused, but nodded to Elder Whisper. "Whisper, huh? You that quiet?"

Another Elder Whisper appeared behind her, resting his jaws on her shoulder and whispering into her ear. "I can be when I wish."

The original Elder had made himself invisible to complete the illusion, but she kept her eyes on him. "Not much to it when you look hard enough, is it?"

Elder Whisper sighed and dropped the illusions. "I am nowhere near advanced enough to deceive eyes of your caliber."

"And yet..." Lindon began, but he cut the sentence off before he said, *"And yet you held the Sword Sage's private void space open for years."*

"Some things are not included in what we traditionally call advancement," the fox said. He followed Lindon through a door and up a nearby set of stairs, and together the three of them walked into an open room at the top.

This was the control room of Ziel's cloud fortress, and it was smaller and dimmer than Lindon's. The one on *Windfall* resembled the common room of a house more than a cloud-ship control room, complete with a couch and chairs, but this one was just a wide panel of scripts and precisely one window on each wall.

Yerin shut the door and Lindon sent his spiritual perception through the ship, making sure the scripts protecting them were active.

"We shouldn't be overheard here," Lindon said.

"We wouldn't have been overheard back at the Tomb," Whisper pointed out, and Yerin glanced at Lindon.

"As I said, I'm not the only one that needs to hear this."

Little Blue chimed out, asking about Eithan. Her name for him sounded like a cheery whistle.

"Does anyone know where Eithan is?" When no one responded, Lindon went on. "Then he'll have to catch up."

Eithan *would* catch up, Lindon was certain. Usually, it was Lindon trying to catch up to him.

Whisper settled onto his haunches. "This story would go a lot easier if we had some fish..."

"Apologies, but I'm not sure Ziel has had time to restock." It had been only a day since an all-out battle against the Dreadgods, and they had ferried a number of refugees from Sacred Valley in that time. Many of them had been hungry.

Even if Ziel did have food left, Lindon didn't know where to find it.

"Then I suppose I must go without." Five white tails lashed at the air, and Elder Whisper looked from Lindon to Little Blue to Yerin as though doubting their credentials. "As I told young Lindon here, I can lead you toward one of the truths of this world: how to kill the Dreadgods."

There was a stretch of silence before Yerin audibly scoffed. She waited longer than Lindon had expected.

"You a Monarch in disguise, are you?" Yerin asked.

"I am old, and I have lived above the labyrinth for almost my entire life. There are secrets within that make the Monarchs tremble."

Lindon wanted to bring out the canister marked with the symbol of House Arelius, but even behind their scripts, he worried it would attract distant attention.

"The maze beneath us is the birthplace of the Dreadgods," Elder Whisper went on, "but it is far more ancient even than they. Secrets creep out from time to time, where those with insight can collect them."

Lindon wanted details, but first he had to see if Whisper's knowledge was worth anything. "How do we kill the Dreadgods?"

"You cannot simply disassemble them physically. You

must destroy them on a fundamental level. Sever the origin of their existence."

Lindon looked to Yerin, whose scowl was melting into a thoughtful expression. They'd heard terms like this before: when the Abidan was describing Penance.

A weapon that had instantly slain a Monarch.

"I do not understand the mechanics well myself," Whisper said. "These are ideas I have stitched together from fractured memories and broken whispers. But as I see it, any who could kill the Dreadgods directly have already moved on from this world. Even the Monarchs combined could not do it.

"However, there is something anchoring the Dreadgods to life. If you remove it, they will be made mortal." One tail pointed to Lindon. "No weaker, you understand. But mortal."

"What is this anchor?" Lindon asked.

"And *where* is it?" Yerin followed, with a tone as though she already knew.

Little Blue gave a chime expressing her reluctance to fight another Dreadgod whether it was mortal or not.

Elder Whisper looked to Yerin. "He waits at the bottom of the labyrinth, deeper than anyone has gone in years uncounted. Your master contended with his will, and it was that which weakened him beyond even the field suppressing his power."

Yerin stiffened, but Whisper had already moved on to Lindon. "*He* is the first product of the experiments that resulted in the creation of the Dreadgods. In the myths that tell of his existence, he is sometimes called the fifth Dreadgod, and sometimes the first. The Father of Hunger, some call him. The Slumbering Wraith. But I have seen notes from his observers calling him Subject One."

Lindon's mind flicked back to the old notes he'd once studied with Fisher Gesha, wishing Dross was here to help him sort his thoughts.

He had questions, but the elder had turned to Little Blue. "No one should look forward to fighting Dreadgods. It is not a pleasant task, but they cannot be allowed to rampage forever."

Lindon and the others had done battle with the Wandering Titan at its weakest, and it had taken everything they had just to convince it to trample someone else. It was the equivalent of curling up and letting an opponent whale on you with their fists in the hopes that they tired themselves out and walked away.

For the moment it had worked, in the sense that the Titan had chosen not to bother with them anymore. It could come back at any time.

But there wasn't much left in Sacred Valley to defend.

"Can we get into the labyrinth?" Lindon asked.

"There is a way inside. The Sage of the Endless Sword took advantage of it, and so can you."

Lindon stared into the distant clouds outside the window and thought. His arm could use repairs, and there were countless people from Sacred Valley that lacked protection and guidance. He was concerned about Orthos, the whole team needed rest, and he needed to get his family—and his own cloud fortress—back from Moongrave.

From his pocket, he pulled out a clear marble with a single blue candle-flame burning at its center. He turned it in his fingers.

It seemed forever ago that Suriel had given him that marble, but at the same time, like almost no time had passed at all. He had expected his task to take him the rest of his life.

Now it was over. Sacred Valley, or what was left of it, was saved.

He wasn't sure whether to consider it a success or a failure, but either way his mission was done. He had started to climb a mountain, expecting it to take decades, only to suddenly find himself at the peak.

Maybe it was that realization that helped him feel how tired he really was.

He had time now. Time to rest, time to spend with Yerin, time to practice Soulsmithing, time to learn what it meant to be a Sage. Time to get to know his family again, though he wasn't quite sure how he felt about that.

But there was one concern that outweighed the rest.

Dross.

Eithan had said that Dross might come back on his own, but Lindon couldn't sit by and wait to see what happened. He would learn as much as he could.

At least now he had the time.

"There should be plenty of Soulsmithing records inside the labyrinth, right?" Lindon asked Elder Whisper.

The fox shot him a look. "It is a repository of ancient truths, as well as the home and workplace of the greatest Soulsmiths in history. You could study there for the next five hundred years and never reach the depths of their understanding."

"Gratitude. Then I intend to learn whatever I can from the labyrinth, but we still need to discuss our next actions. Together."

Elder Whisper raised his eyebrows in an expression that wouldn't have looked out of place on a human face. "I expected more commitment from you."

"There are too many questions left. For one thing, if *you* know about this, why haven't the Monarchs taken action?"

"I have had...dreams."

Lindon blinked at the fox's abrupt change in topic, but Elder Whisper only continued. "Once in a long while, when the heavens allow, I can catch a glimpse of Fate in my dreams. And when I dream of seeking out Monarchs, I see death. My death, always. Sometimes also the death of our home."

"What causes it?" Lindon asked. "Which Monarchs?"

"I regret to say I cannot tell, but much is unclear to me. The Monarchs should not need me to petition them in any case. They should know much more about the contents of the labyrinth than I do, and yet they have refused to move. This is one of the answers you should seek in the depths."

"I will," Lindon said. "But I'm not going by myself."

Yerin gave him a decisive nod.

"Numbers are of limited use in the labyrinth. You may..."

Elder Whisper continued speaking, but his words faded to the back of Lindon's awareness. Something invaded his consciousness—a message, but deeper and softer than words. Impossibly distant.

He felt regret. Apology. Someone urging him to do his best, and to survive at all costs. If he had to interpret the message in words, he would have bet it said *"I'm sorry. Hold on."*

He stretched out his spiritual perception, looking for the source of the message, and Yerin noticed. Her spirit sharpened as she prepared herself for battle.

"We about to bleed somebody?"

"No, I...I'm sorry, did you sense something a minute ago?"

"Before you jumped like a dog trying to fly?" She raised an eyebrow. "If there's anything here, I'm blind to it. And I'm not leaping to fight invisible enemies today, I'll tell you that. Ask me tomorrow."

He shook his head. It had only been a vague impression, and it had passed anyway. "Apologies, I think I'm on edge."

"Can't imagine why."

Lindon rolled Suriel's marble in his fingers again. Somehow, the message had felt like the feelings that radiated from the blue flame. And the comfort that usually came off the transparent orb seemed somehow weaker than usual.

Another sign of his own anxiety, surely. Unless...

There came a thunk as the door on the first floor swung open, interrupting Lindon's thoughts. A voice echoed up from below.

"Oh no, I missed something!" Eithan cried. "Quickly, repeat your entire conversation before you forget a word!"

Deep in the labyrinth, Reigan Shen withdrew a drudge from a pouch at his belt and set it free. He had cobbled this one together specifically for this mission, and it was made to exist in this low-energy environment.

The construct unfolded from a pocket-sized rectangle of compressed madra into something resembling a mechanical dog, then began to sniff around an ancient laboratory.

The room was large enough to contain a flight of dragons, but was decorated like an expensive study. Lots of polished wood and plush cushions, with empty windows that would probably once have displayed illusionary scenery of the outside.

Around the center of this laboratory were empty cages of scripted glass, which would certainly once have contained experimental subjects. Time-shriveled husks that had once been dreadbeasts remained in some, while others had been broken from the outside. Or from the inside.

The laboratory had long waited in disarray, with desks destroyed, papers scattered, and holes scorched in the walls. There were preservation scripts on everything, but most of them had failed, leaving odd scenarios where one half of a sheet of paper might have been aged and yellowed into illegibility while the other half looked as though it had been scribed that morning.

Papers and scrolls were of limited value to Reigan Shen, though he scooped them all up anyway. He was looking for ways deeper into the labyrinth, so unless he found a map, there wasn't much here that could help him.

Here and there, his drudge spotted what he *was* looking for: dream tablets. It brought the treasures back in its teeth, dropping the stones at his feet. Some resembled hand-sized gemstones while others were more like dull slabs the size of his face, but he could see their dream aura as a purplish chaotic haze.

Ordinarily, his spiritual perception would have crashed over this room in a wave, and anything he sought would fly to him on wings of wind aura. But the deeper he went, the more effect the suppression field had on him.

In some ways, the Monarch Reigan Shen was now weaker

than if he had never trained in the sacred arts a day in his life.

But he had his own methods.

A gray-white ghost oozed up from the floor in front of him, its arms dragging the ground, its jaw hanging loose. Empty eye sockets sought him, and it groaned in pure hunger.

It resembled a Remnant, but was actually a Striker technique carrying enough will of its own that it acted more like a spirit. An attack from the Devourer itself, the Slumbering Wraith. Subject One.

With his power suppressed, Reigan Shen still might have enough authority to disperse the technique. But power he lost down here would be difficult to regain.

Historically, most of those who had explored this labyrinth had done so by staying inside only a short time. That would be Shen's preferred approach as well, but every time he left and re-entered the labyrinth, he risked discovery once again.

So he had prepared to stay longer than anyone had since this place sealed itself so long ago. He'd brought tools.

Reigan Shen unclipped another construct from his belt. This one unfolded into a shining orange-yellow launcher that wrapped around his wrist. He pointed it at the ghoul and triggered the binding.

The launcher construct was Herald-level, and thus powerful enough to reduce this huge room to ash and cave in the structure of the surrounding building. After being carried around in the labyrinth for so long, it merely disintegrated the spirit.

With businesslike motions, Shen folded up the launcher again. If the weapon hadn't remained in a scripted container for so long, it would have faded away already. It was only due to its faultless construction and some binding scripts that it worked at all.

He would have greatly preferred to store his weapons in a void space, but those were difficult to open in this place, so he preserved energy by strapping script-sealed devices all over him.

If everything went according to his plan, he would only have to open up his void space once a month. That would last him more than long enough to reach the bottom.

He would empty this place if it took him a decade. Because in the end, he would do what no one else had ever done, and seize control of the greatest weapons ever created.

The Dreadgods.

All five of them.

After the retreat of the Wandering Titan, the Bleeding Phoenix had retreated north.

Akura Malice had regrouped, gathered her power, and followed.

She met the Bleeding Phoenix as an equal, striking it with her bow like a staff. The blow landed on the Phoenix's oozing red body, and the Dreadgod shrieked.

The sound carried enough hostility that Malice had to brace herself against it, even as a bloody red dragon burst through the Phoenix's body. Northstrider's attack. The Bleeding Phoenix responded with a simple Striker technique—a lance of light from its open beak wider than a river.

To others, the attack would appear large enough to swallow cities, but Malice threw herself in front and blocked it on her shoulder.

The pressure on her amethyst armor increased, straining her spirit, and causing her to push more madra to keep the gemstone structure stable. But she spared Northstrider from having to deal with it, and he had taken the opportunity to appear behind the Dreadgod and tear another chunk out of it with a blow that blasted out the air for miles.

The Phoenix's eyes shone, and it screamed again. This time, Malice's heart tightened.

They were playing this close. Not only would they run out of power faster than the Dreadgod would, but if they damaged it too much more, its brothers would show up. The Titan was nearby. And if they managed to kill it, the situation would get even worse.

She reserved a bit of her fury for Reigan Shen, who had forced her to fight a Dreadgod in her territory. Again. For the second—no, third!—time in five years.

If only there were another arrowhead around to deal with him too.

Northstrider had taken quite a beating from the Phoenix already, so he was only too happy to back up and let Malice trade blows with the Dreadgod in her towering armored form. She landed a few lighthouse-sized arrows of crystalline blue madra before the Phoenix's simple brain got the message.

This prey could bite back. It wasn't worth it.

This was how fights between Monarchs and Dreadgods normally proceeded. One of the great beasts would wander somewhere inconvenient, and then whoever owned that territory would fight until the Dreadgod decided the fight wasn't worthwhile and wandered somewhere less valuable.

But it was such a delicate balance to strike.

The Dreadgods hit at least as hard as any Monarch, and they were sturdy enough that Malice could never kill one alone before having to flee herself. It was a bit like a Copper driving off a fully grown bear with a whip.

It was better than pushing them to the brink, though. If they pushed them too far, the Dreadgods would join forces… or worse. They could awaken.

Malice had not been a Monarch during the Dread War, but she had seen the memories of others.

So now, when the Phoenix gave another irritated cry and retreated north, she stopped and let it happen. The crimson sky rolled away, and she relaxed. Let the Tidewalker Herald deal with the Dreadgod for a change; he had supported Reigan Shen too much in the past, and now he would pay for it.

When the Bleeding Phoenix was no longer visible, even to

her, she let her armor fade into great clouds of shining violet essence that rose into the clouds. She hovered in the air, stretching her arms and spirit at once. She got far too little exercise as a Monarch, and her armor was a serious burden. At least against a real opponent.

Northstrider appeared next to her, clothes rumpled and golden eyes scowling.

"Good thing I was here to help," Malice said. "You look terrible."

He looked the same as always, unshaven and unkempt, with scavenged clothing. Like a homeless king. But what she *felt* from him was another story.

His spirit was strained and weak, and she was sure his mind was on the verge of collapse. He had fought bitterly.

Northstrider ground his jaw, and she detected the heat of real anger. "Do you know what you were risking, letting those children face the Titan?"

"May I remind you that one of those children is my own?"

"You were supposed to *replace* Yerin Arelius in driving off the Dreadgod, not *join* her."

"I thought things were proceeding quite well, until..." Malice's voice gained an icy chill with all her hatred boiling behind it. "...*he* stuck his *paws* where they were not wanted."

Northstrider crossed black-scaled arms. "If anything, that proves how high the stakes are. Now we know for certain he can rouse and direct the Dreadgods, and he revealed that card to get rid of a pack of Lords."

"He has been claiming that ability for years now. I suspect that show wasn't for us."

By moving the Phoenix, Reigan Shen had not only threatened to remove valuable members of the next generation—including Malice's own daughter—but he had proved his claims to the neutral Monarchs. Northstrider and Malice had been forced to spend their own time and energy, so he had exhausted them at no cost or risk to himself. A fine move.

This was exactly the sort of price she had expected when she gave up Fury. For a while, she would be vulnerable.

But she could endure, and when she did, she would be in a better situation than ever.

"Take care of those children," Northstrider said flatly, which pricked her pride.

"Do you think *I*, of all people, need a lecture from you on how to protect my own family?"

His perception stretched out into the distance. "Perhaps you need lessons in spatial transfer."

She reached out on her own, and with shock felt Yerin almost immediately. Mercy, Eithan, and Lindon were all there too, their presences a bit fainter than Yerin's.

Had they just arrived? Yerin may have taken the Moonlight Bridge back, if it had recovered its full capabilities, but how had the others returned so quickly? The Void Icon had a good connection to spatial abilities, but if Lindon had taken them all this way unaided, he was a prodigy the likes of which the world hadn't seen in millennia.

She realized the truth after only a few more moments of examination. Reigan Shen's anchor.

Malice spared another moment of anger for the lion. Even his *belongings* were opposing her now.

"Hmmm...I suppose I should return their cloudship," Malice said, more lightly than she felt. "Leave them to me, and concern yourself instead with Shen's next move."

Northstrider looked into the horizon where the Phoenix vanished, and his reflective black orb appeared over his shoulder. It flashed with madra as it communicated with him.

"I'm going into seclusion again," he said after a moment. "Fate has been moving...erratically."

Malice nodded. She could only agree.

She had far more talent in reading the future than he did, the Shadow Icon being more connected to Fate than any of his, but he had his own means.

"I put what forces I can spare at your disposal. The Wastelanders have agreed to protect the Blackflame Empire in my absence, and the Beast King and his fellow Heralds will help you keep the cults in check."

"So gracious of you." Fury had driven off the Dreadgod cults, but not too far. They were drifting around her territory, behaving themselves for now, but she had to keep her eye on them.

If Northstrider was vanishing again on one of his projects, then she would need help to protect herself from both the awakened Dreadgods and their cults. The unaffiliated Heralds who occasionally answered to Northstrider would go a long way toward helping her maintain stability in the continent.

"How long will you be gone this time?" she asked.

"Difficult to say. The more I can refine my oracle codex, the better odds I have of removing Shen myself, and the more clearly I can see the future." Gold eyes turned to her. "Unless you can share more details than you already have."

She smirked at him, letting him know she enjoyed having sight where he was blind. "As I said, the Dreadgods loom larger than they have before. All other possibilities are scattered and unpredictable. Too vague to lean on."

He grunted. "You may call me if the worst should occur."

"Oh, do I have your permission? I will keep an eye on the future and the other Monarchs, while I maintain my cordon on the labyrinth entrances. He won't be able to act without us seeing him now, and time is on our side."

The Dreadgods would run out of energy soon, if they kept up this level of activity. The cults were expending energy without gaining any back, and Malice was slowly absorbing the half of the continent the gold dragons had once ruled.

The longer this stalemate went on, the more territory she would claim. All she had to do was wait.

"We'll see," Northstrider responded.

Then he tore open the fabric of the world and flowed into the Way.

"Always so rude," Malice murmured. Then she stretched her awareness out for hundreds of miles around her. There was no one who mattered.

She didn't like to do this when she wasn't fully secured,

but Northstrider had her wondering.

So Malice slipped into the World of Night and summoned shadows of the future.

CHAPTER TWO

INFORMATION RESTRICTED: PERSONAL RECORD 0013.
AUTHORIZATION REQUIRED TO ACCESS.
AUTHORIZATION CONFIRMED: 008 OZRIEL.
BEGINNING RECORD...

In the legends of the ancient Rosegold continent, long forgotten by the current inhabitants of Cradle, there is a mythical location that contains all the secrets of the sacred arts. A buried city of infinite insight. A child's tale. Anyone who finds the city and walks its streets will gain secret techniques of surpassing power, will never face any bottlenecks when advancing, and will understand secret wisdom of the heavens that will allow them to ascend.

There is no historical precedent for this location. It's purely a myth.

But at one point on the Rosegold continent, it was a common topic of discussion. If you sought easy advancement, or tried to refine your Path, it was said that you were "Seeking Arelia."

Ozmanthus, a boy named after a flower, was said to be seeking Arelia from the time he was a child. From his earliest years, he ran through the tunnels of the mountain in which he was born, looking for secrets in those dark caves.

Even at the initial stages of advancement, later known as Copper, he had discernment and understanding far beyond his peers. He astonished his tutors with questions about the nature and origin of vital aura, questions they were nowhere near advanced enough to answer. His control of madra made him a prodigy in his own right, so there was no lack of teachers competing to take him as a student.

This was a relief to his mother, who had no money to subsidize the advancement of a powerful sacred artist.

At Copper, Ozmanthus was celebrated for his skill. He was popular not just among his tutors, but among those his age.

At Iron, Ozmanthus became famous in his generation. He designed and perfected his own Iron body, and was once again said to be seeking Arelia. Everyone expected great things.

It was at Jade that Ozmanthus began to notice a problem.

The others his age were still Copper.

That wasn't entirely true; some of those from wealthy families, or from organizations that focused exclusively on the sacred arts, had been sponsored directly to Lowgold. But the ones he'd grown up with, those who had only recently been his friends, were two entire stages down from him.

He could no longer play games with them, as he would win. He couldn't study with them, as he had already outstripped many of their teachers in theory. And they began to avoid him.

For Ozmanthus, it was only a minor grief. His Path lay ahead of him, full of possibility, and everyone told him what wonders he would accomplish. With his spiritual perception now open, there was a whole new world bared to his mind.

He had decided the details of his Path by Lowgold, refining it during endless hours in the library. He chose techniques of pure destruction. Why settle for inefficiency?

That led to another troubling trend for Ozmanthus. The sacred arts in Cradle tend to focus on combat applications because of the never-ending competition for resources, but soon, there was no one under the Lord realm who could compete against him.

He was not shunned for this. Far from it; his master and those from his homeland were ecstatic at this young genius.

But he was always alone. When he went into the wilderness seeking spirits or natural treasures, it was easier to go himself. Someone else would just slow him down.

While Ozmanthus was not entirely content with his solitude, he knew it was only temporary. He couldn't be the greatest genius in the world. Somewhere, he would find someone who would keep up with him.

Until then, he would slow down. He gave up his spear for a broom, but he didn't mind that. He liked being the only sacred artist in the world to fight with a broom. It had style.

After reaching Underlord, he grew in knowledge, and insight, and power. He studied the nature of soulfire and proved its connection to deeper truths by manifesting an Icon of his choice in front of a panel of renowned scholars.

The Broom Icon.

Rather than impressed, the scholars were crushed. Ozmanthus had made their entire lives into a joke, publicly humiliating them. No less than three of them killed themselves within a week.

This greatly disturbed Ozmanthus.

In addition to advancement, Ozmanthus also turned his genius to other aspects of the sacred arts. He became known as a reliable refiner and one of the greatest Soulsmiths of his generation. He was more satisfied with this avenue of progress, and he began investigating the great Soulsmiths of the past.

This was the path for him, he decided. He would become known as a creator, a researcher. One who built.

His Path was most suited for creating weapons, which did not bother him. He never lost his admiration for those who kept the world clean, and one of the most hideous plagues in the world was the population of dreadbeasts that roamed the countryside, feeding and spewing out more of their kind.

With his weapons, he would clean the countryside.

He found an ancient labyrinth, built by the original Court

of Seven before their ascension. He researched their under-standing, growing in knowledge and power. And he built weapons.

To better understand his creations, he sought knowledge of death. He even created a device that would kill and revive him.

He did not realize what a catalyst that would be. As the creator of the world's deadliest weapons, when he killed and revived himself, he instantly manifested the Death Icon.

Not what he had sought to achieve.

Ozmanthus found it now even easier to create deadly weapons. Too easy. He could create reality-warping weap-ons on the level of the Abidan before even ascending from the Iteration.

And with his every accomplishment, he grew more alone. No one could match his accomplishments, no one could face him in battle, and no one could understand his insights into the world beyond.

He abandoned his weapons. He focused on another of his talents: his sight. When he advanced to Monarch, he devel-oped the bloodline ability to *see*.

Ozmanthus was so relieved that he wept. This was the ability that he wanted to define his legacy. And he would leave his descendants with the ability to see as he did, to one day catch up to him.

He named his House after the city he had always sought. The Arelius family should always seek greater insight.

And when he finally ascended, he left a beacon behind, a measure of his power like a black hole sealed in a transparent barrier that resembled glass. When someone appeared from his family with enough talent to join him, they would ascend with the marble, and he would know.

He expected to wait a generation, perhaps two or three.

But he was certain that very soon, House Arelius would be a dynasty that spread to the heavens themselves.

Record complete.

Lindon shouted Northstrider's name into the sky. He begged, he pleaded, he bargained, and he even threatened. Politely.

The Monarch never responded.

Without his help, Lindon's chances of repairing Dross fell significantly. But Lindon could try again. Until Dross awakened, he had time to research.

In the meantime, he brought Yerin to the Sword Sage's void space.

Lindon had expected Yerin to follow him out of curiosity, but the more he hinted that he had something to show her, the more reluctant she became. He dropped several hints, expecting her to sprint ahead of him. Instead, the more she learned, the slower her feet moved.

It was as though she dreaded finding something her master left behind.

Lindon marched into the half-destroyed Tomb, a chunk of its roof caved in and one of its pillars cracked. He had to pick his way around pieces of debris that looked like they had been deposited here by a hurricane.

Yerin paused at the entrance, at the top of the stairs where she had once fought her master's Remnant. The cold wind grabbed the lock of red hair over her eyes, which she hadn't had all that time ago.

"Is this gonna kill me if I don't see it?" she asked.

Lindon stopped. He moved back to her, gently placing his hand on her arm.

She didn't tremble, but her spirit did.

"We don't have to do this now," he said. "We can come back later."

"It's not his...body, is it?"

This was the first time he had seen her hesitate over a dead body. Even when she'd removed her master's sword from his corpse, she hadn't seemed disturbed.

Then again, he hadn't known her well back then.

He hurried to reassure her. "It's not. It's just some things he left behind." Lindon had waited to tell her exactly what he found because he had expected her to be eager to see for herself, but he had been wrong.

"Do you want me to tell you first?"

Yerin squared her shoulders. "Nothing to be scared of, is there? He didn't leave a Dreadgod tucked away."

Lindon thought of a shriveled, gray-white mummified hand and hesitated to respond. Yerin saw that.

"Bleed and bury me, if he really—"

"No, no, nothing threatening. But there's no hurry either."

"Doubt either one of us wants to come back into this script longer than we have to. Let's do what we're going to do and be gone." The suppression field hung heavy on them both, and it hadn't been long since they'd escaped it the first time.

Lindon searched her face, but took her at her word. He focused his will on a barely-sensed indentation in space at the back of the room.

Then, using a finger of Blackflame madra as a medium, he cut through it.

"Open," Lindon commanded.

The Sword Sage's private void space expanded in front of them. They looked through a rift into a large room filled with collected treasures.

Most of the collection seemed to be organized in sections—refining equipment here, training area there—but you could find artwork and swords anywhere. Landscape paintings hung over a rack of nicked wooden swords, while a dancing sculpture of light fluttered beside an Overlord-level sword of condensed venom madra.

Lindon had expected Yerin to gasp, or to exclaim, or to make a sound of some kind. Instead, she was silent.

When he focused, he realized she had stopped breathing entirely.

Her red eyes were wide, her face pale. As a Herald—if a partial one—her body and spirit had a unique relationship to one another, one that he didn't quite understand. But even her spirit felt faint, as though her soul was on the verge of dissipating to essence.

Lindon stepped in front of her, blocking the view behind him. She continued to stare.

"Yerin?"

"I need...I need to..." She swallowed. "Come in with me?"

Silently, Lindon followed her inside. She drifted from one section to another like a wild Remnant, from a rack of training manuals to the portrait of a woman Lindon recognized as the Winter Sage.

For more than ten minutes, Yerin just floated around, absorbing memories. Finally, she slowed as she approached a rack of black training clothes. Each of them were shredded on the edges, as though they'd been dragged through a thicket of thorns.

She ran her fingers over the shreds. The ones she had left herself on these robes as she trained the Endless Sword and lost control.

"Used to say I'd be ready when I stopped cutting my own clothes. He was going to have me a sword made, like his. And I...I lost his sword. I broke it."

That was when her tears started to flow.

Lindon didn't say much. He just held her as she cried.

"I wasn't allowed in here," she muttered after a few minutes. "He'd take out what I needed when I needed it. Thought I'd never see these again. Should be dust in the wind."

With another moment surveying the space, she turned to Lindon. "I want it."

"I would never leave a scrap behind." He hesitated. "Unless you wanted to, of course."

"My key's not big enough for everything, but we've got space in the house. We can carry it the old way."

"No need for that," Lindon said immediately. He had prepared to come back here. Yerin's void key wasn't big enough to hold everything, and neither was his.

Fortunately, he had spares.

There was only one thing they didn't pack up: a small metal cube, marked with a crescent moon, that Lindon knew from experience contained the hand of Subject One.

Lindon also held in his palm a small purple-black jewel that had caught his eye. It was clearly a dream tablet of some kind, and he suspected it was a composite gemstone used to hold pieces of several memories instead of one complete experience.

Dross could have told him for sure.

Without him, Lindon had to spend a few minutes scanning through the memories. After a few glimpses and brief words, he was certain.

And far more excited.

He handed it over to Yerin while he explained. "Your master prepared before he entered the labyrinth. These are some records from other teams who explored the labyrinth first."

Yerin's eyes widened as she skimmed the dream tablet herself. It would bear further study, but Lindon had come to some conclusions already.

First, almost every explorer had gone in alone. Those who did have teams treated them as support crews rather than partners.

This made sense, based on the other things he had seen. You had to have some degree of control over your willpower to navigate the labyrinth's environment, and the more advanced you were, the harder it was to find companions of equal ability. At least, those who wouldn't betray you.

Indeed, one of the memories he glimpsed was a three-man group of Archlords who had bickered and betrayed one another after finding a treasure. Only one survivor had escaped, forever spiritually scarred, to leave a dream tablet behind.

Yerin noticed the same thing, because she grimaced. "Can't say I'm blind to why my master went in on his own. Not that it's a shock. My hair would have fallen out if he ever worked with a team."

"Look at the last memory." It had stuck in Lindon's mind, clear enough that it was like Dross had replayed it for him.

A man with short, blond hair and a cropped golden beard sat behind a desk, speaking to the person leaving the memory. There were few thoughts attached to it, only his appearance and his words.

His looks—like an older version of Eithan—and the lightning crackling behind his blue eyes had made Lindon assume at first glance that this was Tiberian Arelius.

"You have the backing of House Arelius to study the labyrinth," the Monarch in the memory said. *"But I expect you to keep that quiet except at great need. I cannot trust any Sage or Herald under a Monarch's protection, and I'm certain you understand why."*

"That's clear as new glass," said the man leaving the memory, and his casual drawl made Lindon think of Yerin. Lindon wished he'd recorded more of his thoughts, because this had to be a personal record of the Sword Sage himself.

"Since you're going deeper into the labyrinth than you planned, you might consider taking a team. Just be sure you're only bringing people you trust."

The Sword Sage laughed. *"I was going alone before I heard a word from you. If you've got a list of people who can keep up with me, can be trusted, and are itching to run off across the world on my say-so, I'd love to see it."*

Tiberian's posture sagged, and he rubbed his forehead. *"I take your point. If I had so many subordinates who were capable, trustworthy, and unified in purpose, I would have no need to employ you. But please, don't risk yourself. My advisors and I are simply testing a theory. We should have many years left before this becomes urgent."*

"Wouldn't that be a treat," the Sword Sage muttered.

Lindon could see when the memory faded from Yerin, because her eyes focused and she scowled into empty space. "Well, isn't this a nest of snakes?"

"We'll need a good plan," Lindon said. Based on his quick glimpse, it felt like half of those who had gone into the labyrinth had failed because of a lack of information. "But first," he continued, "I think we should take a quick look inside."

"Not going to get our faces bitten off for a peek, are we?"

Lindon slipped the dream tablet into his void key. With some study, he might even be able to make a partial map out of those memories.

"Let's find out," he said.

They left the Sword Sage's void space open and readied themselves for battle, facing down the circular stone door leading into the labyrinth.

"Open," Lindon commanded once again.

His working crashed against the door...and fell apart.

Yerin relaxed her grip on her sword. "Try it harder?"

"This part isn't supposed to be difficult, I'm certain. It's just the outer door. There are outer entrances that Underlords can open, and some that open themselves at set times."

Lindon considered for a moment, then spread his spiritual sense out as far as he could under the suppression of Sacred Valley. He received a clear impression of the underground labyrinth; like a turtle that had entered its shell.

"It's locked down."

"The Titan, you think?"

"It must be. We'll have to check with Elder Whisper."

Lindon stared at the outer door, wondering if he could break through it. It would be stupid to try; even if he succeeded, he would only be exposing Sacred Valley to whatever was inside. But he felt like they had begun a race, only to stumble at the first step.

"Huh," Yerin said. "That's a kick to the face."

Elder Whisper whipped his tails in agitation as he stared at the sealed labyrinth door.

"I have read of this reaction," he whispered. "And I have seen times when the Nethergate refused to open on time, or when the labyrinth seems to...sulk, if you wish to put it that way. The cause is almost always beyond my understanding."

"Not so much this time," Yerin said.

"Yes. One does assume that the labyrinth has locked itself to prevent further intrusion by the Titan." A white snout turned in Lindon's direction. "What else could it be?"

That question bothered Lindon greatly.

"Can we use the hand?" he asked.

Whisper shook his head. "That tool allows you to borrow the authority of the Slumbering Wraith, and thus command the layers of the labyrinth that he himself controls. If he controlled the outer gates, he would long ago have released himself upon the world."

"At least this gives us time to prepare," Lindon said, reluctant as he was to give up on entering. "I don't think any of us are ready to fight another battle yet, and we can put together all the information we can about what's inside."

Elder Whisper sighed. "Poor timing in one sense, but fortunate in another. The Dreadgods have been driven off, for the moment, and we need time to settle our people. At least for now, there is no disaster looming over us."

"Not that we know," Yerin muttered.

Lindon evened his breathing, hoping Elder Whisper was right. The Dreadgods were stirring, but taken care of for the moment. There was no reason to assume anything disastrous would happen at least for the next few months.

Their luck couldn't be *that* bad.

ITERATION 001: SANCTUM

Suriel connected to the network of Abidan all over existence. They didn't control nearly as much territory as they did before, and the Way was disrupted by chaotic interference everywhere.

But she spread her message as widely as she could.

"Ozriel," Suriel called. "We need you."

None of the Judges had ever done this before. Such an

open call could be intercepted by anyone, assuming they were in a world that was still connected to Abidan control. Making this broadcast was as good as telling the entire cosmos that Ozriel was gone. That the Court of Seven had misplaced their greatest weapon.

If they hadn't figured it out already, they never would.

"Wherever you are, I know you can't see what's happening. You would have returned. Unless you really are dead, and then..." She sighed. "I wish you would have trusted me more."

That was too personal for a public broadcast, but it was hard to care. She could see the lights that represented Iterations turning gray one by one as the Vroshir extended farther than they ever had before. Tightening the noose on Sector 11. On Cradle. On the Abidan.

"They have your Scythe. If you could see what they're doing with it, it would break your heart. Come back, and tell us what you saw. Because if you saw this, and you left anyway..."

It wasn't the optimal thing to say to lure Ozriel back, but Suriel had to say it. Her voice went cold.

"...then I'll execute you myself."

She canceled the connection, and a construct of light like a sapphire spiderweb vanished from in front of her. Her message now traveled through the Way Between Worlds, where it would be received by every Abidan and every world still connected to reality.

In theory. In practice, the amount of chaos the Vroshir were introducing meant she had no idea how far this message would spread. Maybe it still wouldn't reach Ozriel.

But there weren't many other actions she could take.

She wasn't wearing her armor, there not being much chance of combat here in Sanctum. She wore a simple white uniform that her Presence materialized for her as she waited here, in the headquarters of the Phoenix Division of the Abidan.

All Divisions were currently stretched to their absolute limits, but there was a special pressure on the Phoenixes right now. This massive headquarters, with its gleaming white domes the size of a mountain range, was the greatest hospital in existence. There were few things they couldn't heal quickly, so they rarely needed to house many patients. The building's size reflected its importance and the number of staff.

Now the huge edifice was practically empty. She was in her personal quarters at the peak of the central dome, but she was almost the only Abidan in the entire place.

Phoenixes weren't just in charge of healing, but rebuilding. Of the ten sectors the Abidan still firmly controlled, not one of them had escaped damage. Members of her Sixth Division were even now restoring lives, fending off corruption, and reconstructing entire continents. Where worlds had cracked under spatial assault, her people knitted them back together.

She could have joined them, as the most capable of their order, but that would require turning her back on the greater wound.

The nine hundred and ninety sectors they had abandoned.

[Correction: many of those sectors are still within bounds of safe recovery, after the Vroshir incursion ends,] her Presence reminded her. The ghost of gray smoke hovered next to her, and she may have imagined a slight admonishment in its tone. [Also, the vast majority of those Iterations were sparsely inhabited pioneer worlds. The situation is bad enough without embellishing reality.]

Of course, the Presence was right. Most fully corrupted worlds ended slowly; there would still be trillions of lives left to save after the Vroshir retreated.

Arguing with your personal Presence was an exercise in futility, but Suriel countered by summoning images all over her room. Windows opened onto many realities, covering the walls, images projected from reports that were delivered to the Abidan even now.

Each of these was from the perspective of an Abidan agent somewhere calling for assistance. Each an image of devastation.

An orbital barrage, shown from the ground, as deadly orange light rained from a steel sky.

A deluge of once-human monsters swarming up the side of a fortress, the army conducted by a hovering figure in a silver crown.

A desperate blur of combat as an Abidan from the Wolf Division held off a warrior whose spear-strikes leveled mountains.

The Mad King manifesting into reality, holding a black Scythe.

That last image was only shown for a moment before an overwhelming tide of blue light as the Abidan delivering the report escaped, but even in that brief flash less than a second, Suriel could see the sky behind the Vroshir—and the entire Iteration—crack.

There were a thousand of these, and they covered the room. Suriel faced her Presence, though she knew the construct could hear her every thought.

"What can we do?" she asked.

[You cannot leave this Iteration until Makiel is restored,] her Presence reminded her. [With that restriction, you are limited in what you can accomplish alone.]

In her mind, the Presence spooled out a list of how she could resolve each of these emergency scenarios...except for the appearance of the Mad King. That was beyond her.

"And if I'm not alone?"

[Your highest probability of success comes from cooperating with the other Judges in the tasks they are already performing.]

Her Presence gave her brief glimpses of possibility. Razael, the Wolf, would never leave the battlefield. Joining her would mean putting two of their seven greatest assets in the same place...but it would also make Razael far more capable. Together, they could potentially cut off the advance of the Mad King, though still not oppose him directly.

Telariel, the Spider, wouldn't risk his own life even in the event of total system collapse. He was currently coordinating

Abidan efforts on all fronts, and with Suriel's support, he would have an easier time pushing past chaos. Not to mention more willing to take the field, with the greatest healer backing him up.

Zakariel, the Fox, was more selfish even than Telariel. She had a lot in common with the Angler of the Crystal Halls, and each considered the other something of a rival. If it didn't benefit her directly, she usually didn't do it, and she was currently raiding Iterations under Vroshir assault to scoop up any valuables before the world fell. Though any Silverlords that encountered her had no chance of escape.

Suriel might persuade the Fox to act for the good of the Court, which would open coordinated rescue efforts.

Suriel could work together with any of the other Judges and accomplish great things. But not enough. None of them could stop the advance of the Vroshir.

All predictive models showed the same thing: the Mad King cementing his isolation of Sector Eleven, then moving in for the kill. Once Sector Eleven was in ruins, he would retreat before even he was cut off by the chaos he'd left in his wake. Then he'd leave the Abidan to clean up after him.

No two Judges could stop him. Without Makiel, no two could even fight him.

But what about three?

"What are my odds of getting two other Judges to work with me against the Vroshir directly?"

[Not high.]

Suriel preferred her Presence to answer numerically where possible, even when regarding scenarios that were technically incalculable. When it didn't, that meant the scenario was truly uncertain.

[It is a shame that those who rise to become Judges tend to be unusually individualistic,] her Presence continued. [Forceful. Difficult to persuade, even with objective facts.]

Suriel stroked the ghostly gray correlation lines that ran from the back of her skull to her knuckles like strings of smoke. "It will be difficult to get them to abandon their individual pursuits, but not impossible. Is there any other chance of victory?"

[If you define victory as preserving as many of those under our protection as possible, then a defensive engagement has the highest probability of success. Taking conservative actions and retaining territory until the Vroshir incursion ends gives us the best chance of reclaiming as many worlds as possible almost one hundred percent of the time.]

"And what if I define victory as forcing the Vroshir incursion to end early?"

[It is a shame that those who rise to become Judges tend to be unusually individualistic,] her Presence repeated. [Forceful. Difficult to persuade, even—]

"Connect me to the Titan," Suriel interrupted.

With a faint sigh, her Presence obeyed.

第三章

CHAPTER THREE

Within the corrupted lands of the Desolate Wilds, there were only a few livable pockets in which the dreadbeasts and the blight of venom aura had been pushed back. A few years ago, Lindon had found an alliance of five factions formed around the emergence of the Transcendent Ruins, but that had only been temporary.

The town in which the residents of Sacred Valley found shelter was called, quite simply, Refuge. It had started off as a temporary camp, but that had been years ago. Recently, it had been home to thousands, and some homes had housed families for three generations.

But that was before the attack of the Wandering Titan.

Now, the town was half-empty, and signs of battle against the tide of dreadbeasts marred the walls and littered the streets. The buildings had only survived thanks to their own good fortune; attacks from Dreadgods or Monarchs had carved new ravines into the territory all around.

The townsfolk, though, were anything but grateful for their survival. Everyone had lost someone, many had lost homes, and now they were facing an influx of refugees from their west. As Lindon had expected, they would have violently rejected the people from Sacred Valley.

Would have, except that the most advanced experts in the region were Truegold. Even Jai Long could toy with the most powerful people here. Not only did they keep their complaints down, but they would do anything to keep the mighty strangers here. There was a sense of security from curling up next to the strong.

So far, it was within Lindon's expectations. But once again, he wished he had Dross to talk to, because he had begun seeing strange flags pop up everywhere in and around Refuge.

And he was afraid he knew who was responsible for them.

"Where did these flags come from, Eithan?" Lindon asked the air.

A few nearby people shot him strange looks, but they kept about their business. They hadn't met him yet, and once again they couldn't sense anything through his veil.

Eithan could hear him. He was close enough, and Lindon knew he was paying attention.

The flags came in many colors, but they all had one symbol: a starburst with one half red or orange and the other half blue. Both halves were melded roughly, as though they'd been fused together. He hadn't paid much attention to it at first, until he overheard a name attached to the symbol.

The Sect of Twin Stars.

"Eithan, what's the Sect of Twin Stars?"

A girl his own age came to a stop when she heard him speak. She was a Lowgold with a blue hurricane Goldsign swirling around one wrist, and she zipped over to him as though he'd called her by name.

Too late, he saw that she was wearing the same two-colored starburst symbol newly sewn onto her robes.

"Are you interested in the Sect of Twin Stars?" she asked excitedly. "They'll take just about anyone, you know. It doesn't matter what Path you're on. And they have teachers you wouldn't believe! The sect founder is a *Sage!* I don't know what he's doing here, but they say if you're a loyal member of the sect, they'll take you east with them when they leave."

Lindon felt like he was trapped in some kind of bizarre illusion, but he still responded automatically. "Gratitude. Where did you learn about this sect?"

"Oh, they're telling everybody! You can go see for yourself. There's a big blue cloudship to the north where you can go and apply, and if you're accepted, you'll get an elixir right away!"

She straightened herself and said proudly, "With their support, they say I can make Truegold in a year. And..." She darkened as she added, "...and we won't have to stay around here anymore."

"I see." He dipped his head. "Apologies for taking up your time."

He didn't ask her name because he didn't want to give his own, but he marked her face. He didn't know if Eithan was serious about taking these people away from Refuge, but he would make sure she at least got a spot.

When he arrived at the north side of town, his suspicions were confirmed. Sure enough, the blue cloudship was *Windfall,* with Eithan's portion of the island—the part covered in crops—angled toward Refuge.

A huge crowd had gathered at the edge of the giant blue cloud, encircling a few young men and women who were proudly displaying sewn-on badges of the Twin Star Sect.

Standing on the top of the cloud, half of his body still wrapped in bandages, was Eithan.

"Stand proud, new acolytes of the Twin Star Sect!" Eithan cried. He sounded more energetic than anyone so injured should be. "We have chosen you to receive training from the best of the best, so that you may reach heights undreamt of!"

The crowd applauded, and the new recruits looked smug, but Lindon was starting to wonder if this was all some elaborate prank on Eithan's part.

He activated the Soul Cloak for just a moment, kicking off and soaring over the crowd. When he landed next to Eithan, the Archlord swept a very stiff bow to the people down below.

"Now I must bid you farewell, as the time has come for me to confer with our founder and Patriarch: the Sage of Twin Stars!"

Eithan ushered Lindon toward Lindon's own home as the crowd cheered below.

"What?" Lindon asked.

"I feel like you've already pieced it together accurately," Eithan said. He sagged down onto his personal Thousand-Mile Cloud, groaning as he did. He made a gesture as though to brush hair away from his face, but grimaced as he found his hair short.

"You created a sect in my name."

"That I did. It was something of a bluff, but you know how it is. Sometimes these things get away from you."

"I don't know how to lead a sect!"

"I, of course, considered that you might feel that way. Not a problem at all. I would just like to borrow your image as a figurehead. That might work even better, in its own way; you could be the enigmatic mysterious expert backing our operations from the shadows."

Lindon gave Eithan a sidelong glance, but the man looked perfectly sincere.

"Apologies, but I thought you would try to trick me into doing it."

"Lindon! Lindon. *Lindon.* How dare you say something so hurtful and yet so accurate."

Lindon continued staring at him, and Eithan's usual smile faded a bit. "Believe it or not, I had intended to consult you first. I had a plan for a grand reveal and everything. You do like tiger meat, don't you? Anyway, events got ahead of me, and I had to work quickly to bail out of a complicated situation. I do apologize."

Lindon shook his head. "No need."

"What?"

"This is *perfect.*" Lindon's mind was whirling. "We had to keep borrowing the name of House Arelius or the Akura clan, but now we can act on our own. You know what we can

REAPER   ○   39

do with an organization behind us? Besides..." He winced as his enthusiasm was too much for his fractured Remnant arm. "You taught me my cycling technique and guided me in my pure madra techniques. You have more right to the Path of Twin Stars than anyone but me. And Dross."

Eithan looked from his own bandages to Lindon's sling. "If I hugged you right now, would that put an awkward strain on our relationship?"

"It would certainly strain our injuries."

"Then just know that I embrace you in spirit." Eithan settled down on his cloud. "As you can imagine, many of the people around here no longer have anywhere to belong. And no one in several hundred miles has ever had a *real* sacred arts education. We need teachers, and refiners, and more resources...but most of all, we need somewhere to settle that doesn't have the word 'desolate' in its name. Or Dreadgods lurking nearby."

"I assume we'll use whatever portal you brought *Windfall* through." That hadn't even struck Lindon as odd. When he'd seen the cloud fortress appear out of nowhere, Eithan's presence had been the only explanation Lindon needed. Clearly, Eithan had set up some kind of transportation between here and Moongrave, or had bartered with the Monarch.

Eithan became interested in his own fingernails. "As... eager as I am to claim credit for that, it actually crawled out of a shadow without warning or explanation. I begin to wonder if Malice has some kind of grudge against me."

"Why? Sending the fortress back was a favor."

"It was *my* shadow that it popped out of."

Presumably Lindon's family had been aboard; he could sense them nearby. Not that their presence was entirely a relief. They would have been perfectly safe in Moongrave.

"They should have room for us in the Blackflame Empire," Lindon said. "Naru Saeya suggested the Emperor was very pleased with us."

Eithan sighed. "Yes, it does, and just between you and me and any Monarchs that happen to be eavesdropping on us, I suspect they'll be sending some cloudships for us soon. They won't have missed a Dreadgod's rampage, and they know we were involved. Naru Huan has an opportunity. But we would be the most powerful beings in the Empire by a huge margin. Our presence could change the entire landscape of the nation, not to mention their relationship with the Akura clan."

Lindon chewed on that for a long moment. If he wasn't qualified to lead a sect, he *certainly* didn't feel qualified to give his opinion on international politics.

Then again, he was a Sage now.

"Moving to the Empire solves our problems," Lindon said at last. "If they want us to leave later, we can. But there are too many people here, and even clean water is expensive. We have to move."

"We do, but relocating into the Blackflame Empire will cause much to change. There's no telling how everything will fall out." Eithan paused. "I withdraw my objections. That sounds exciting!"

They were only a few steps from Lindon's house, but instead of drifting up to the door, Eithan led his Thousand-Mile Cloud to the edge of the floating island. He looked down onto the twisted green-and-black trees of the Desolate Wilds.

People were camped everywhere, crammed into shacks, hasty walls and scripts protecting them. The protections didn't look like they would survive a stiff breeze in the night, much less an actual attack.

Of course, if there *was* an actual attack from anything less than a Monarch, Lindon would sense it coming from miles away and take care of it before any of those below were in any real danger. But he couldn't be everywhere all the time.

"This is what a sect is for," Eithan said. "We can't do everything. At some point, they have to protect themselves."

Lindon watched an Iron man from Sacred Valley bowing to a Lowgold child from the Wilds, and he nodded. Without someone around who was Underlord or better, the first Truegold-level dreadbeast to attack would tear through this crowd like a wolf through sheep.

And he could sense the tension quivering in the air like a vibration in the vital aura. These people had all lived through a Dreadgod rampage, and they never knew when it might return.

The only ones who looked confident were those wearing the Sect of Twin Stars logo. They belonged to an organization that would survive. One that could protect them.

"I see," Lindon said.

"I thought you would."

Orthos hovered over the black, corrupted trees of the Desolate Wilds, just outside the camp the refugees from Sacred Valley were using for shelter. The turtle was suspended on flows of vital aura, scripts directing life aura to him to regenerate his wounds.

Lindon looked up from the shadow as the giant sacred beast blotted out the sun.

Orthos rotated in the air, one smoldering red-and-black eye rolling to see Lindon. "Tell these children to lower me to the ground. I can stay still myself."

A team of sixteen Truegold elders—the best the region had to offer—sweated and labored over scripts and natural treasures. They stared at Orthos with fear, but toward Lindon they demonstrated only polite respect.

They could sense how powerful Orthos was, and at the moment, he was almost half the size of a Dreadgod. He could roll over and crush a town.

As for Lindon, if he didn't remove his veil, they couldn't feel his power at all. As far as they knew, he may have just been a Jade. But his powerful friends treated him well, so they followed suit.

Lindon controlled wind aura to levitate up to Orthos so they could speak eye-to-eye. He looked down to survey the

Truegolds, who were slightly more impressed now that they had seen his skilled control of aura. Although this was nothing a Gold on a wind Path couldn't do.

"They're working under Eithan's instructions," Lindon pointed out. "I doubt they'd listen to me unless I forced them."

Orthos grumbled, which sent a covey of startled birds fluttering into the air. "It's good luck for them that I'm not in a bad mood. If I broke this formation, I'd squash them."

Some Truegolds went pale and stepped back. Orthos couldn't keep his voice down when he was big enough to swallow cloudships.

"Now that you're awake..." Lindon hesitated, unsure how to phrase his thoughts properly. "I've heard of giant sacred beasts, and I knew you were going to transform. But how..."

Orthos laughed, and several of the Golds lost their feet. "Bigger than you expected?"

"I thought you'd be a dragon," Lindon admitted.

"What do you call someone who violates their own soul?" Orthos asked. "What do you call a trash human who does something that no one with a conscience would ever consider? You say they're *inhuman*, don't you? It's your actions that determine what you are on the inside."

He raised his head proudly. "I'm more a dragon than any of those proud gold dragons who ambushed you like cowards. And I gained this control over my body when I accepted that I was in the form that suited me best."

"I am grateful to have you back in any form," Lindon said. "But I do admit, I was afraid I wouldn't recognize you."

"The lot of you need a shell more than you need fangs and claws." Orthos glanced down at himself. "But...hmmm...I didn't realize it would take so much soulfire to grow. And just as much to shrink."

Lindon had a little experience in the subject, and he could recall information more efficiently thanks to Dross' presence. Even if Dross himself was unconscious.

"That's because you did it so quickly, and without practice. You strained your channels and your body. If you practice changing and do it gradually, you'll lessen the strain and the cost."

When Orthos looked at him, he felt compelled to add: "At least, that's what it's normally like for sacred beasts who take human form."

He had absorbed memories from many dragons, and while he left the sorting of most memories to Dross, he had seen his share. But dragons almost exclusively adopted human form, which was the smoothest body in which to advance.

"I'll find out for myself, now that we have time to practice."

Orthos obviously felt something in their spiritual connection, because he eyed Lindon again. "We *do* have time, Lindon."

"There's still so much to do. The Dreadgods are still around, I've barely scratched the surface of what a Sage can do, the people from the Valley need somewhere to settle, and Dross..."

"A hunter doesn't catch its prey by dashing at full speed all the time. You need a lair, Lindon. Even the most powerful dragon curls up and rests."

Lindon glanced in the direction of *Windfall.*

"That's a base," Orthos rumbled. "But it *could* be a home. If you made it one."

Lindon sighed and placed his hand on the wall of leather that was Orthos' skin. "Gratitude. I'll try. But I do plan to take a look inside the labyrinth. At least the outer edges, for now."

"Maybe the greatest challenge I could give you is to keep your feet still for a month." Orthos snorted out great plumes of smoke. "At least take us with you."

"I'm not sure you'll fit."

"Then you'll have to wait for me, won't you?"

"Not just you. I don't plan on going alone."

Orthos grunted. "You should check the condition of the others, then."

Lindon felt the turtle's concern in his spirit. "Mercy?"

"She still hasn't woken up."

Mercy had suffered significant spiritual injuries after the Wandering Titan had shattered her bloodline armor, but even the attention of Little Blue hadn't been enough to restore her. Her madra channels were connected to her Book of Eternal Night in a unique way that Lindon still didn't understand.

If her life had been in danger, he would have contacted the Akura clan already. Even as it was, every hour that passed threatened the appearance of Akura Charity.

Now, the time had come for a more thorough inspection.

"I'll take a deeper look," Lindon said. "Heal well, Orthos. Don't scare the Golds."

Lindon flew off.

Left behind, Orthos twisted in the air. He reached out and munched into a pile of boulders the humans had piled up for him nearby. To his current size, they were little more than a handful of nuts.

As he crunched, he murmured aloud.

"Too big..."

The tears had long dried on Mercy's cheeks. She shivered as she pressed her body against the cold stone wall, trying to build up the courage to peek around the corner.

In fact, the wall wasn't stone. It was more like condensed madra with properties like stone. Nothing in this spiritual space was real, physically speaking.

But it was real enough to make her fingers tremble against her bow. She hadn't come here consciously, so she hadn't been able to bring Suu with her. Instead, she had Forged her own bow and arrows out of Strings of Shadow.

It was the only thing that protected her here, deep inside her own soul.

In the fifth page of the Book of Eternal Night.

This whole place was built from shadow and nightmares, and the Dream of Darkness technique hung like mist in the air. Every time she let her guard down for an instant, her spirit was flogged with terror.

And she wasn't alone.

One by one, pale fingers slithered out of the darkness to grip the edge of the corner in front of her.

She raised her bow instantly, but something cold brushed the back of her neck at the same time. Mercy screamed and turned, coming face-to-face with one of the pale demons that haunted this nightmare world.

Its face was made of white clay, except for its teeth, which gleamed like sharpened and yellowed bone. Its milky eyes bulged.

"Ours now," it whispered.

Her arrow took it in the chest, and it didn't notice.

"Ours now," came a whisper from the other side.

Mercy bolted, but she'd been caught before. They weren't here to tear her to pieces, but to feed on her fear and her fading will. That should have relieved her, but it didn't. Not at all.

Their touch, and the very air of this place, struck her deepest horror and trauma. They could inject pure fear into her.

So when she fled, she trembled until fingers grabbed her. Then she screamed.

"Oh! Apologies," Lindon said.

She whipped her head around to stare at him in shock.

He was glancing around with open curiosity. "This is *fascinating.* I'd heard of spiritual spaces, and of course we're here only in spirit, but it seems like it should be possible to enter this place in a body. Have you ever come here physically?"

"Lindon! Are you...real?"

The Dream of Darkness couldn't be used to manually create illusions, but she had found that she had a hard time separating imagination from reality here. She'd hallucinated rescue before.

But this felt very different.

"It's just my soul, but I'm interested that we don't look like Remnants. I wonder if this is an effect of our perception, or if the Book itself makes us look like we do on the outside." He took a deep breath, as though savoring the scent of the cavern. "Dross would love it here."

Out of habit, Mercy looked over her shoulder for her stalkers. She saw none, but she felt eyes on her from the shadows. Or at least she imagined she did.

"How did you get here?"

Lindon rubbed the back of his neck, and between the gesture and his size, he reminded her of her Uncle Fury. "I do apologize; I was reluctant to interfere with the mechanism of a Divine Treasure created by a Monarch without Dross' guidance, but you weren't waking up."

"How long has it been?" Mercy asked, a lump in her throat. If he had gotten worried, then she had to have been gone more than just a night.

"Three days."

Mercy sagged in relief. "Oh, good. It only felt like a few hours to me." If it had really felt like three days, she might have gone insane.

Lindon was about to respond, but the aura pressed in on Mercy again, forcing her to push against it. Pale fingers reached out to Lindon, and she raised her bow to defend him.

Lindon's eyes turned to blue crystal with circles of white where his irises had been. Blue-white pure madra pushed out from him.

The creatures hissed as his Hollow Domain pushed against them, and they fled like rats from a fire.

As the Domain passed over Mercy, she felt a burden lift from her. Her knees went weak, and she collapsed, but Lindon caught her and steadied her before she hit the floor.

"There's not much spirits can do to me in a spiritual realm," Lindon assured her. "But, if you don't mind me asking, where exactly are we?"

"Inside my Book, but you knew that. This is the fifth page. The home of the Dream of Darkness technique."

He nodded as he looked around. "Ah, so that's why there's Overlord-level madra here. So why did you end up here when your armor broke?"

"I had it open too long."

This was embarrassing to admit, but he was standing literally inside her soul at the moment, so it was only fair that she open up a bit.

"After the tournament, you and Yerin advanced. I had to lean on the book to fight Sophara, and the more practiced I got, the easier it was to keep the page open. That's how it works when you're close to advancing. So I just...kept it open."

She shifted, not meeting his eyes. The unnatural fear that had gripped her had faded, and now she was just tired. And a bit ashamed.

As expected, Lindon caught her meaning immediately. "Your advancement wasn't stable."

Mercy nodded. When she had faced down the Titan—and *that* was a memory fresh enough to send another tremble of fear through her—it had crushed her armor quickly. Too quickly.

Her unstable spirit had collapsed, and the Book had filled in the gaps. Unfortunately, the imbalance resulted in her consciousness being tied more to the fifth page than to her own body.

"Apologies. I should have left this conversation for later." He extended a hand to her. "Let's leave."

"I'm not sure you can just—"

"Release," Lindon commanded.

The Book vomited her up instantly at his order, and her eyes snapped open. Her body ached, real air harsh in her lungs, and she saw Lindon sitting peacefully at the side of her bed. They were aboard Ziel's cloudship; all the rooms in it looked alike.

"That was fascinating," Lindon said eagerly. "With your permission, I'd love to study your Book more closely."

Mercy put a hand to her chest. Inside, her Book was recharging from its expenditure of madra, and the burden on her spirit had greatly lessened now that she was released.

And now that she was only an Underlady again.

She could feel heat in her face, and her shoulders drooped. "I'm sorry. I thought I couldn't help you unless I could keep up."

"I would welcome it if you did advance, of course. But whether you do or not, we're planning on exploring the labyrinth. I'd love to have you with us."

Lindon looked as though he understood, and she suspected he did. She gave him the weak shadow of her usual smile, and Lindon returned it more heartily.

Then, after a little more chatter in which he made sure she didn't need anything further, he left her alone.

She couldn't stop wondering if they *really* needed someone who couldn't even reach Overlord.

Mercy was not used to being self-conscious about her lack of advancement. Quite the opposite. As a girl, she'd regularly wondered why she was so much faster than her peers.

Now, she wasn't sure she could advance if she needed to. That bothered her more than she wanted to admit.

Only then did the full impact of Lindon's proposal dawn on her.

Explore the labyrinth?

That meant defying the law of the Akura clan, which had declared this territory off-limits. Lindon and Yerin had been granted substantial liberties, but this was a decree directly from Mercy's mother. There had to be a reason for it.

Mercy started to sweat again. She kicked off the sheets.

Not only did she need to work on her advancement, but she had to throw her Aunt Charity off the scent. The Heart Sage could smell lies.

So she would have to be very, very careful not to lie.

Ziel's spirit hadn't felt truly *comfortable* in years, but these days, it was like he was borrowing someone else's madra. Sparks ran along his madra channels, fresh from the latest stage of the Pure Storm Baptism, and he was still recovering from the effects of the suppression field around Sacred Valley. Not to mention the exertion of a fight against a Dreadgod.

He planned on staying inside his house aboard his cloud fortress, motionless, until he had healed.

He had spent no effort on decorations or customizing his housing, so his bedroom was a room with a bed in it. That was all. If he needed to keep his belongings somewhere, they could stay in his void key or sit on the floor.

Likewise, he lay on his bed and stared up at the ceiling and waited for the discomfort to fade.

Or so he intended. But he grew bored.

He rummaged through his void key with his perception, but he found nothing that could entertain him. The best he had kept were dream tablets demonstrating scripts or techniques.

Ziel had once told his students that if they had a spare moment to themselves, they should spend it cycling. He cursed himself. There were immersive tablets that would allow him to experience any kind of dream he wanted, and all of them would beat lying there staring up at his ceiling.

He wished for any distraction, and then he heard a knock at the door.

Ziel revised his wish.

Any distraction except a visitor, he thought.

The person knocked politely but persistently, and Ziel finally reached out and felt their spirit. When he sensed who it was, he dragged himself to his feet and out to the front entrance, where he opened the door.

Lindon loomed outside, his broad frame taking up the entire doorway. He ducked his head and his wintersteel badge dangled in front of him.

"Apologies for bothering you, but do you have a moment to talk?"

"I'm busy."

Lindon started to apologize again, which pricked Ziel's conscience. Lindon was too earnest, to the point that it made Ziel feel guilty lying to him.

"Never mind, I was lying," Ziel said. "Come in."

That should be enough explanation. He turned around and left the door open so Lindon could follow him.

"Gratitude. I don't think I've been on a proper tour of your fortress."

Ziel braced himself for polite compliments about his bare, boring house, but then Lindon continued.

"Does yours have the same foundational scripts that ours does?"

Ziel considered that it would be downright rude to refuse a curious student's question. "Mostly. It was solid enough—the Court does good work—but I had them add another layer of concealment. Then I laid an encryption circle of my own around the whole cloudbase."

It was the first and only modification Ziel had made to his home. If he kept the Ninecloud Court scripts as they were, then the Sha family would have ward keys to all his security.

That shouldn't be a problem, since he had never been an enemy of the Ninecloud Court in the first place, but he wouldn't allow them the ability to deactivate his cloud and let him plummet from the sky if he could help it.

Granted, any Monarch could do that regardless of what scripts he had in place, but that he *couldn't* help.

Lindon squinted at the floor as though he could see the buried scripts below. "Fascinating. Do you mind if I..."

Ziel gestured his agreement, and Lindon extended his own perception to admire the scripts. Strictly from a security perspective, Ziel ought to have prevented anyone from seeing the exact layout of his protective scripts, including Lindon.

But it came back to a similar situation to that of the

Monarchs. If Lindon really wanted to kill Ziel, he could, and an extra layer of encryption wasn't going to slow him down.

Lindon muttered to himself, and Ziel expected him to pull out a pad to take notes. Or to summon that mind-spirit of his.

Then Ziel remembered that Dross was gone, maybe for good, and his heart squeezed out one small drop of pity.

"Gratitude," Lindon said at last. "I appreciate the chance to learn from a master."

"Scripts are great. My food stays fresh and my house is warm in the winter. But ask me what good my scripts did me against the Weeping Dragon."

"It was a script formation that weakened the Titan enough for us to drive it off," Lindon pointed out.

"Yeah. *That's* the work of a master. You want to learn from someone, learn from them."

"That's what I came here to talk to you about," Lindon said, and suddenly it was as though Ziel could see the future. He saw exactly what Lindon was about to ask him.

"I'm not coming," he said.

"We would very much appreciate your expertise."

"I said I wasn't going to fight the Dreadgod, but I did that. I've done my part."

"I'll scout it out myself first. But if we're going to make any progress, we need—"

"Stop. I like you, Lindon. I was a lot like you when I was your age, except weaker and not so crazy. But I'm not part of your team."

Lindon looked vaguely hurt, but that wasn't enough to slow Ziel down. It would only be more painful the more he let this play out.

"I will fulfill my obligation to Eithan, and then I will go my own way. Don't rely on me for help."

Lindon's gaze dropped. "I didn't mean to cause you any inconvenience. If we find anything to bring back, would you mind taking a look from here?"

Ziel shrugged. "Sure. As long as it isn't too much effort."

Lindon's unhealthy obsession with advancement had paid

dividends, and he was far stronger than anyone his age had any right to be, but he was still young. He needed to find a life to live before it was too late, and Ziel hoped this would remind him that there were people in the world who didn't care about the sacred arts to the exclusion of all else.

Then Lindon looked back up, and Ziel felt a chill. Lindon's eyes changed color often, and this was nothing so overt.

But something had changed nonetheless.

"One more thing, if you don't mind. You say you're not part of our team. I say you're the only one who thinks that."

"You're not even really a team," Ziel said dismissively. "You're not a sect, and two of you are only part of the Arelius clan in name. Mercy's going to go back to her mother the second she calls, and if you think Eithan cares more about you than about what he can get of you...well. You're not that naïve."

That might have been going a little too far, Ziel reflected, but it was best that Lindon hear it early.

Somehow, though, the chill Ziel felt from the depths of Lindon's black eyes had deepened.

"Anyone who fights a Dreadgod by my side is on my team," Lindon said quietly.

Ziel didn't have much to say to that.

"You can call us what you want," Lindon went on. "But whether or not you consider yourself my ally, I am yours. You have only to call on me."

That was hardly fair. It turned out that Ziel had more than just a drop of pity left, because now some guilt was seeping out of his long-dry heart.

Lindon stood to leave, but before Ziel could say anything, Lindon spoke again.

"I know you have far more experience than I do, so I apologize if I'm overstepping my bounds. But I think you've seen what you can do on your own. We're going farther. And I want you to join us."

Finally, Ziel realized where that chill was coming from. He wasn't talking to Lindon anymore.

That was the Void Sage.

The door shut before Ziel found his voice again, and then he took a deep breath. The pressure he'd felt in that moment was difficult for him to even process.

Ziel flopped back down on his bed.

"I knew I shouldn't have opened the door," he muttered.

第四章

CHAPTER FOUR

Only days after Eithan had predicted it, a fleet of cloud-ships arrived from the Blackflame Empire. Lindon sensed them coming before he saw them, and he flew as high as he could on his own personal cloud to get a better vantage point.

Past the rolling hills and blighted forests of the Desolate Wilds, Lindon could see in the distance the desert that took up most of the western Blackflame Empire. Patches of the sand were red for miles, and Lindon wondered if that was some natural phenomenon created by aura or if those were marks left by the Bleeding Phoenix.

Above that sand, dozens of ships traveled on clouds of every color, growing closer by the moment.

Lindon's perception met another Overlord's extended toward him, one on a Path he recognized. That gave him a shock.

Naru Huan, Emperor of the Blackflame Empire, had come in person.

His relatives, Naru Gwei and Naru Saeya, were aboard the same cloudship. They stood out as presences of powerful wind madra among the mostly Gold crew.

The aura here was thin, and their cloudships were relatively weak, so Lindon estimated they were about a day out. He considered spreading the word, but Eithan had certainly felt them coming and taken action before Lindon.

So Lindon focused on preparing his own household.

There was plenty of room on *Windfall* for his family, so he set them up in a wing of his own house. His mother spent most of the day out with the people of Refuge, his sister trained with Jai Long or Jai Chen, and his father...well, his father was the problem.

Lindon sat across a table from Wei Shi Jaran and, for at least the fifth time, tried to explain the procedure.

"I'm not replacing your eyes," Lindon said.

He *could* do that, but that would be as much a surgical procedure as a spiritual one, so he would need to find an accomplished healer.

"I am going to *layer* a pair of construct eyes over your own. These will allow you to see as Remnants do, but I selected the Remnants carefully. It will be very similar to ordinary sight. You will rarely notice a difference."

Jaran folded his arms. "I've known warriors with Remnant eyes. It's even odds that you go mad, and the others are little better than blind."

"That's because they did it *wrong*," Lindon explained again.

"Your mother performed some of those procedures herself."

"I'm...sure she did the best she could. She was working under very difficult conditions."

"So you think you could do better?"

"Yes!"

"Just get me to Jade, if you can do so much. That'll fix my eyes."

"It *will*, but you'll never see as well as you would if we addressed the problem first."

"My spiritual senses will make up for it."

Lindon immediately suppressed his desire to tie Jaran with constructs and perform the procedure anyway. They had run this topic around in circles, and they couldn't get over one fundamental problem: Lindon's father didn't trust him.

"Perception is very useful," Lindon allowed, "but you can't sense anything that doesn't have spiritual power."

"It's better than I could do now." Jaran gestured with his cane as though he'd just scored a winning point, though Lindon couldn't see how that was a victory from any perspective.

Lindon brought out a scripted wooden box and a small pair of goldsteel tongs. "I have the tools in front of me. Your Path made the compatibility issue easy to solve. With your cooperation, we could be done in an hour, and it will be completely painless."

"Painless?"

Lindon had been away from home too long. He only realized he had made a mistake when he saw the stubborn clench of his father's jaw.

"You think I'm afraid of a little pain?" Jaran rolled up his sleeve and pointed to a scar that ran the length of his forearm. "This is where a Kazan spearman ran me through, and I didn't make a sound." He pulled his collar down and showed a small burn scar. "Acid burn from the Li clan." He gestured to his leg. "I'm in agony with every step. I know you've seen the world now, and you think you know everything, but enduring pain? That's *real* experience."

Lindon's fist slammed down on the table.

The table didn't break so much as it *disintegrated*. A deafening explosion filled the room as splinters sprayed across the floor. Jaran yelped and leaped backwards, toppling over in his chair.

He would have fallen—and with his Iron body, he would have been entirely unharmed—but Lindon caught him with a cushion of wind aura anyway.

Lindon squeezed his fury down, trying not to even *think* of Blackflame. The prosthetic eyes he had worked on for days now rolled across the floor, motes of essence slowly drifting up from them.

"Do what you want." He summoned another box out of his void key and shoved it into his father's chest. "There's a pill in there that'll take you to Jade in ten minutes."

Jaran gripped the box harder. "What was that sound? Did you break something?"

"I can sponsor you through Truegold. That's as far as you'll go. I'll come back when you've finished with the pill."

"Did your sect leader give you this?" Jaran opened the box and smelled the pill inside. "Is this what they used on you?"

"No," Lindon said. "I found this on an Underlord after I killed him and devoured his spirit. He was planning on throwing it away because it was defective."

"You want me to take a defective pill?"

"Any pill that only advances you to Jade is a defect. If you don't want it, throw it away. Now, pardon me, but the Emperor is coming to see me and I have to prepare."

Outside his house, as Lindon was taking deep breaths to steady his spirit, he was unsurprised to sense his mother approach.

She had a bag over one shoulder, which was filled with Forged toys and tools that must have been the work of Gold Soulsmiths in town. Her brown hair was tied behind her, and for once she wasn't followed by the floating fish drudge that she had used since he was a child. It must have run out of energy when she used it while shopping.

Wei Shi Seisha came up behind her son, but he turned to greet her before she called out to him. "Apologies," he said. "I was...catching my breath for a moment."

"Hmm. It was my understanding that Overlord bodies didn't have such weaknesses."

"It's not a physical weakness so much as a mental one."

She slipped the bag from her shoulder and leaned it against the wall of the house; lights of every color shone from inside. "Your father can be a demanding opponent."

Lindon gave her a brief version of the conversation, and she listened without a word until he finished.

"He won't take that pill now," she said with certainty.

"You've wounded his pride. I'll be impressed if he hasn't thrown it away already."

Lindon sighed. "That's all right. It's not expensive."

"Don't be wasteful. I'll use it myself, once I'm ready."

Seisha had decided to correct her study of the Path of the White Fox before she advanced any further, to prevent any possibility of problems later. Technically she was right to do so, Lindon knew, but it wouldn't matter much so long as she fixed her Path before Lowgold.

"Pardon," Lindon said, "but one scale from me could hire a refiner to make these pills for the next ten years."

That might have been an exaggeration, but not by much.

"Oh." For a moment Seisha wilted, overwhelmed by the scope. Lindon had seen her react that way many times over the last several days, and at last she shook it off and smiled again. "Amazing. I still have much more to learn."

"Can you talk him into taking the eyes?"

"I'll do what I can, but he's..." She hesitated. "If you're right, then he's been living a lie his entire life. It's hard for him. For both of us."

Lindon thought he understood, but at the same time, he wasn't sure he did.

When he found out there was more to the world, he had been astonished, but he had also been delighted. He had been *glad* to learn that the ceiling he'd lived under his entire life was only an illusion.

"I dropped the eyes on the floor, if you could take care of them. I really do have to go prepare. The Emperor's coming."

"The Emperor of the...Blackflame Empire? And where is he?"

Lindon pointed to the east.

His mother squinted in that direction. "You can sense him from here?"

"I can *see* him," Lindon said quietly.

That was a *slight* overstatement. He could see the cloud-ship, and knew Naru Huan was aboard, but the Emperor was actually below deck.

Dross would have corrected him.

Seisha missed a breath. "I...I see." She braced herself. "I'll talk to him, but this is a new world for us. Please be patient."

Lindon promised to try.

Lindon paced on the edge of *Windfall,* wearing the best clothes he owned: the black-and-red sacred artist's robes that Eithan had prepared for him long ago. A red turtle emblem blazed on his back, and he had hoped the real Orthos would be with him as well, but the turtle's spirit was still weak.

"You really are too worked up," Eithan pointed out. The Archlord was lounging on the corner of Lindon's roof, a book in one hand and a drink in the other. "It's not like you haven't met Huan before. You should take Yerin's example."

Yerin wore her normal black robes and was playing a game of darts with sharpened blades of grass. She kept reinforcing them with a spark of soulfire and then hurling the blades far off the side of the cloud.

"He's the one who ought to shake meeting me," Yerin said, closing one eye to take aim. She let the grass loose.

"What are you aiming at?" Lindon asked. He had looked down into the forest, but he couldn't even tell where her makeshift darts were landing.

"I'm trying to draw a little face with knocked-over trees. Hard to do, though. The grass drives right through 'em."

She put more power into the next throw, and Lindon saw this one land. It exploded as it hit the trunk and sent half a tree flying into the air.

For the tenth time that minute, Lindon glanced east at the Emperor's approaching fleet. He could hear the musicians playing a march as they approached, and madra filled the skies like a rainbow-colored sunrise to herald the Emperor's approach.

"Best thank the heavens they don't pull the Titan back with that much noise," Yerin muttered.

Eithan waved his drink dismissively. "If this much would attract the attention of the Dreadgods, we'd all be dead. And they are, of course, taking the current location of the Titan and the Phoenix into account."

"Do you not like this?" Lindon asked Yerin. He had grown up in the Wei clan, and he respected the showmanship.

Yerin brushed her hands clean and stood next to him. "Don't like it when they break their spines to impress me. The flashier the right hand is, the more I look for a dagger in the left."

"I'm surprised *you're* entertained, Lindon," Eithan said. "They can't hold a candle to the Ninecloud Court."

Yes, even the most casual display of the Ninecloud Court was brighter and more impressive than the best the Blackflame Empire could do. Lindon had been honored in front of the entire Akura clan as well, and the scale there was a thousand times greater than this. By comparison, it was almost like watching children imitate their parents.

Lindon still found himself drawn in as waves of color and sound emanated from the Emperor's cloudship. "That's what I enjoy about it. It was easy for the Ninecloud Court, but the Empire has to do this with Golds."

Yerin drummed her fingers on the hilt of her sword, Netherclaw. Lindon could see an idea dawning on her face.

"Could be I was going too easy about this. Now I think of it, he *is* an Emperor. Shouldn't we welcome him ourselves?"

"Well well *well*, that's what I like to hear." Eithan snapped his book shut and made it vanish, then drained the rest of his glass. He snapped his sleeves in the air. "You're absolutely right, Yerin. In many cultures it would be considered rude to host an Emperor without a welcoming ceremony of our own."

Eithan and Yerin began cycling their madra.

Lindon's gut tightened. "Wait a minute. This is going to look like we're trying to outdo him. Or scare him off."

He was also concerned that a display of their overwhelming madra might come across as an attack.

"Don't worry, I know Naru Huan well. He will appreciate this."

Something in Eithan's tone made Lindon look closer at his face. "Will he really?"

"The word 'appreciate' can have so many definitions, don't you think?"

Wei Shi Jaran shaded his new eyes as he watched the flying ships approach from the east. Only long years of practice allowed him to keep up his stoic front.

He could *see* again. Even the pattern on the bark of a tree was fascinating to him now, and this display...he couldn't believe he had almost missed half the sky changing colors, like a dozen different flavors of sunset.

He almost regretted not taking his son up on the offer of new eyes immediately. Almost. But in the end, he had been right to avoid the risk.

Whatever advancement Lindon had achieved, he was still an amateur. Jaran had been reluctant enough to allow his own wife to attach the Remnant's eyes to his, and he had only allowed *that* because advancing to Jade would fix any problems the eyes caused.

Not that he had noticed any problems so far. Lindon, it seemed, had been right that these Remnant eyes worked roughly the same as human ones. They glowed a soft white-pink and didn't look natural, but Jaran had never cared what others thought about his appearance.

All in all, he had been correct to wait. He was glad to have eyes now, but his son was too impatient. Endurance and fortitude were the way. Lindon would learn that when he realized he'd ruined his own future advancement with his impatience.

Ribbons of green wind madra spiraled around the entire fleet of these foreigners, and Jaran leaned on his cane to get closer to his wife's ear. "The Blackflame Empire, you said?"

She nodded absently. Her drudge bristled with sensors, and she checked some flashing scripts on its back, writing down some readings. Analyzing the patterns of the madra used for the display, no doubt.

"That's supposed to be the Emperor and his entourage. Seeing this, I can believe it."

"And how big is this Blackflame Empire?"

"Very," Seisha said quietly.

Jaran didn't give any external sign of how much that thought disturbed him. He wasn't stupid. He had picked up Orthos' stories, and heard others talking since leaving Sacred Valley. Even if you took out the parts that were obviously exaggeration, the Empire dwarfed Sacred Valley and the surrounding lands many times over.

"How advanced is he?" Jaran asked.

"Overlord."

He frowned. "Overlord. That's..."

"Yes, like Lindon," she said, in a long-suffering tone that put him on edge. "I *told* you."

"Can't be that impressive," he grumbled. Lindon was an Overlord, and he wasn't even twenty yet. Either this Blackflame Emperor was only a child, or Lindon's advancement was inflated.

Probably the second one. There was no way to advance... what was it, six stages? Six stages or so in only three or four years, without harming your own spirit. He had seen young warriors push up to Jade too quickly, before they were ready, and they were always weaker than their peers.

Suddenly a thousand golden stars burst from a cloud over their heads, and Jaran looked straight up in shock. A large, dark blue cloud hung over them, and he hadn't given it much notice. It seemed everyone outside the Valley used Thousand-Mile Clouds for transportation, and there was nothing to attract his attention to this one compared to the Emperor's fleet.

Nothing except, now, the golden stars that burst out and flew around the cloud in a complex web. It shone like a firework that never ended, like one of the festival displays that required all the Wei clan's Jades to coordinate, and that was only the beginning.

Red light burst from the top of the cloud in a column that stretched toward the sky, a flash of crimson that outshone even the Empire's celebration. After a few seconds, the vibrant beam burst, and a shower of crimson lights fell like needles down to the earth below.

Jaran's body felt great pressure, as though this technique pushed on his muscles directly. He may not have been a Jade, but his hand still clenched on his cane as he sensed this attack.

The needles burst into harmless essence at once before they struck the treetops, red sparks fading into the sky.

A low whistle came from Seisha's drudge, and she stared around her in shock. "That level of control..."

"They must have scripted it," Jaran said, but without certainty. If Seisha was impressed, she had reason to be.

"That was controlled directly," Seisha said. "And it was one person."

Jaran stared at her, looking for signs of a joke. That technique had covered the sky and dwarfed the entire spectacle coming from the Blackflame Empire, and theirs was *clearly* the work of many sacred artists.

But she wasn't joking, and there was more.

Above the Thousand-Mile Cloud, more clouds began to whirl in the air. These were clouds of dark flame.

Kelsa had described Orthos to him, and Jaran had heard about his son's Path. But it was something else to see a hurricane of black fire swirling overhead, a burning vortex. Stinging hot wind blew down on him, though he couldn't guess how many miles away the fire really was.

The golden stars that had been spinning around the cloud fortress were now joined by stars of dense blue-white energy. Dark balls of flame fell from the spiral overhead, and they danced with crimson sparks that shone somehow silver.

The colors of madra wove a complex pattern with one another, and then rushed out toward the Emperor's fleet.

From the way the music faltered, Jaran felt the hesitation of the sacred artists aboard the incoming cloudships. If he had been standing aboard one himself, he would have assumed he was about to be bombarded by a volley of Striker techniques.

But these stars spun around, encircling the fleet, forming a sort of tunnel. After slowing slightly, the cloudships passed through, accepting the invitation.

"How many were responsible for that?" Jaran asked.

"Three," Seisha said after consulting her drudge. "But there were four types of madra. I think the gold light was from a construct."

"Were they all Overlords?"

"One of them was Lindon."

Jaran grunted and shifted his weight off his wounded leg. He understood the truth that Lindon had been forcibly advanced, but he couldn't help but think it was a waste. What could someone else have accomplished with those same resources?

He wondered if Orthos could intervene on Kelsa's behalf. If Lindon could do as much in only a few years, Kelsa would shock the entire world.

On the lead cloudship, a figure rose up on shining emerald wings. He looked like a powerfully built man in ornate green robes, though Jaran couldn't make out his features in any detail. But from the shining crown he wore, and from the visible distortion of air around him, Jaran assumed he must be the Emperor.

A moment later, he revised that assumption. No Emperor would press his fists together and bow his head to subordinates in his own territory.

The voice of the majestic figure boomed out, easily audible to everyone.

"The Blackflame Emperor greets his three esteemed guests. We are gratified to count you among our allies. Let all our Empire show respect to Archlord Eithan Arelius."

There came a booming sound of cheering and music from the fleet of cloudships.

Before it had faded entirely, the Emperor spoke again.

"Let all our Empire show respect to the Uncrowned Queen, Yerin Arelius."

Another, even louder cheer shook the ground. Even the people of Refuge began to cheer, though Jaran was certain that at least those who came from Sacred Valley had little idea what was happening.

"Let all our Empire show respect to the Sage of Twin Stars, Wei Shi Lindon Arelius."

A final wave of sound came out from the fleet, no softer than the last, but Jaran barely heard it.

The show had kicked him in a place no one's words had reached. It was one thing hearing about how powerful Lindon had become, and reluctantly accepting that someone had made Lindon powerful.

But seeing here, with his own eyes, a display that would have shaken all of Sacred Valley...and to have it directed to *his son...*

Seisha looked at the expression on his face and sighed.

"I did tell you," she said.

Lindon stood on the edge of *Windfall,* each passing second convincing him that he was supposed to do something.

After greeting them, Naru Huan had remained hovering in midair, his head still bowed. He was clearly waiting for a response, just as Lindon was waiting for Eithan to give him one.

Yerin scratched her neck. She wasn't going to bother saying anything, and if she did, it wouldn't be for everyone's benefit. She would probably wave to Naru Huan and tell him to come over. This was Eithan's job, so where was—

Eithan was grinning an idiot's grin while staring straight at Lindon.

Lindon wasn't as surprised as he felt he should have been.

He stifled a sigh and rose on a Thousand-Mile Cloud he summoned from his void key for this purpose. He drifted over to face the Emperor, and only when he felt the Ruler technique around Naru Huan did he remember to manipulate the air around him using soulfire to magnify his words.

"We are humbled to be visited personally by the Blackflame Emperor," Lindon said formally. And too stiffly. He wished Mercy were here to do this instead, but she was occupied with some family obligation. "We are grateful to be allowed into your territory."

The Emperor was a handsome man who appeared in his forties, with a square jaw and neatly trimmed beard. Every time Lindon had seen him before, including in the depths of battle, he had looked like someone who was always in possession of himself.

So Lindon knew he'd made a mistake when he saw surprise flash briefly across the Emperor's face.

"Not at all," Naru Huan boomed out. "It is our honor to host you for as long as you wish to stay."

Lindon didn't know where to go with the conversation, so he steered it in a direction he understood. If this were a normal visit, he would invite his visitor inside.

"We could use a guide to your Empire. Please, step inside for a moment and provide us your wisdom."

That can't have been *too* wrong, because the Emperor dipped his head again. "It will be our pleasure. With your permission, our cloudships will land and begin distributing refreshments to the people."

That was the loudest cheer Lindon had heard so far.

He expected Naru Huan to drop the formalities when he arrived on *Windfall,* so he was surprised to see the Emperor go to one knee the second he touched down.

"Naru Huan greets the Sage and the Herald. Forgive me if I have offended you with my lacking manners in the past, and allow me the chance to make up for it in the future."

Lindon and Yerin exchanged a look.

"No eyes on us up here, so you can stand up," Yerin said.

"Please," Lindon added. "It would put us at ease."

Naru Huan straightened up, but he still didn't meet their eyes. "Your words are more generous than I deserve. Please, tell me how I or my empire might serve you two."

Eithan pointed to himself. "I can't help but feel like someone is being intentionally excluded."

Naru Huan's head slowly turned toward Eithan. "I'm sorry, Uncrowned Queen, but does this Lord speak for you?"

"You know my name," Eithan protested.

Naru Huan didn't correct himself.

"Pardon, but I thought you two were friends," Lindon said. An idea occurred to him, and he said, "We wouldn't mind if you spoke candidly about him. Would we, Yerin?"

"He's harmless," Yerin agreed.

"I would prefer to be called *gentle.* Maybe 'tender.'"

"Of course, I intend no disrespect to the Archlord," the Emperor said stiffly. "I simply thought it was appropriate to greet the Sage and Herald first."

"Come on, Huan! We're closer than that! I thought we were friends."

Naru Huan's gaze snapped to him. "I wanted a *friend* who would keep me informed! My sister sent me word from the Uncrowned King tournament as soon as she could, but I heard nothing from you. The Akura clan sent me congratulations and didn't even explain why."

"That's quite rude of them," Eithan said, but Naru Huan kept talking.

"I was aware the Titan was going to wake up, but then there was a *second* Dreadgod, and then *Monarchs* fought on my western border. And I hear you fought as well! Successfully!"

"In fairness, I didn't know about the Phoenix either."

"Sometimes I wonder why I play at ruling, when everything that matters is decided by the games of the truly powerful."

"If it makes you feel better," Eithan said, "everything turned out great!"

Naru Huan looked to Yerin. "You will go down in history as a hero of the Blackflame Empire. Saeya hasn't stopped talking about your battles since she returned. And to you..." He turned to Lindon with awe and pain clear in his expression. "If you could give me just a word of advice, I would be grateful for the rest of my life. Reaching Sage at Overlord...I didn't know it was possible, truly. For a moment of your time, I will give you anything within my meager power."

Lindon didn't feel like it was the time to mention that he had first summoned an Icon when he was an Underlord.

Eithan raised a hand. "May I point out that I trained these two?"

Naru Huan breathed in for a solid five seconds, and then exhaled even more slowly. He strolled over to Eithan and put a hand on the Archlord's shoulder.

"I know, Eithan. I do know. You have done more for the Empire than anyone since my mother, but you make it so hard to be grateful. If only you weren't so...infuriating. All the time."

"*All* the time is a little harsh." A little more humanity cracked Eithan's smile. "I will allow, though, that I can be a unique experience."

"Let him kick you," Yerin suggested. Everyone looked to her—Naru Huan's face had grown substantially brighter—but she didn't back down. "You want to show you're sorry? Let him kick you."

Eithan's eyes narrowed suspiciously. "I'm a little disturbed at how quickly you came to that suggestion."

"I dream about it every night."

Naru Huan controlled himself, but Lindon could see that he was holding back excitement. "I would like that very much."

"Well, if I'm not going to defend myself, I would prefer if you took it easy—"

He didn't.

The Emperor's kick contained all the madra, aura, and soulfire of an experienced Overlord. The sudden detonation of air would have leveled Lindon's house if not for the scripts and his own protection. As it was, air surged out from *Windfall* for miles, even buffeting some landing cloudships.

Lindon watched as Eithan flew as a rapidly vanishing speck to the west. "I think he might make it all the way to Sacred Valley."

Naru Huan clapped his hands and shouted. "Bring me a blank tablet!" His escort of Golds on the neighboring cloudship scurried to obey.

Lowering his voice back to normal, the Emperor spoke to Lindon and Yerin. "I need to record this memory while it's fresh. I can never forget this."

Indeed, he looked like he'd been injected with a good night's sleep in an instant.

Kicking Eithan. Lindon would have to try that.

第五章

CHAPTER FIVE

Lindon didn't need to do much to load the people of Sacred Valley onto the cloudships. He didn't have a role here other than to supervise; in fact, he could have left on *Windfall* and delegated everything to the subordinates from the Blackflame Empire.

But there were a few things he needed to see to himself.

Orthos was healthier than he'd been since the fight with the Titan, but Lindon only knew that through his bond. He hadn't visited yet today, so when he landed, he was surprised not to see Orthos. Normally, even an Iron could see Orthos from miles away. It was hard to miss a flaming turtle literally the size of a hill.

He found a handful of Truegolds still packing up the intricate script-circle and other tools they'd used to see to Orthos' safety for the last several days. All the bustling action in the area stopped when Lindon arrived, as everyone bowed.

Lindon was getting used to that. At least enough to not let it slow him down. "Continue with what you were doing. I'm just here to see Orthos."

He looked into the forest where he felt Orthos, and would have expected to see him even at normal size. Apprehensively, he asked, "Did everything go...well?"

Little Blue whistled her concern.

An old Truegold woman cleared her throat. "We are assured by Lord Orthos that the process was completed according to plan, but the ways of soulfire are unknown to us. You will have to assess his condition for yourself, honored guest."

"Lord Orthos?"

"He told us to call him that himself. Should we address him by a different title?"

Lindon supposed Orthos *was* a Lord now, so he reassured the Golds that they had done well, passed them a scale—which they regarded with awe—and then leaped across the clearing and into the forest.

"How are you?" Lindon asked. He knew Orthos could hear him.

"Well enough to devour some enemies," Orthos said. "But not so well that I want to fly. You're a Sage now, just move us there."

Lindon heard Orthos' voice, and based on that and his spiritual presence, Orthos should have been right in front of him. He saw only a red glow in some bushes, and an odd thought came to him: had Orthos buried himself in the ground?

Then the bush shook, and Lindon saw Orthos emerge.

At about the level of Lindon's ankle.

Orthos snapped up a bee that had crawled along the ground too close to his mouth. "Don't give me that look. My spirit is as strong as ever."

Lindon knew *that*. If it hadn't been, he would have sensed the change immediately.

But now Orthos was the size of an ordinary turtle. Maybe a baby one. Lindon was having trouble reconciling the sight, but Little Blue wasn't.

She gave a flute's whistle of pure joy and leaped off Lindon's shoulder. When she landed in front of Orthos, she chattered about how happy she was to see him and threw her arms around his shell.

Orthos spat out a mouthful of insect. "Stop it! You'll get burned!"

But Little Blue was sturdier than she had ever been, and the glowing red plates of Orthos' shell didn't harm her at all.

Lindon knelt, though he didn't need to get any closer for a clear view. He was starting to feel like he was the awkward one for being so tall. "Did something go wrong with the soulfire?"

Orthos snorted smoke. "I told the Golds everything was fine. We're going into the labyrinth, aren't we? Well, now I can fit anywhere. *You're* the one who might get stuck."

He lifted his chin proudly, as though being less than a foot long was his life's greatest accomplishment.

Little Blue sat cross-legged on top of his shell, the ocean blue madra of her dress draping over his sides. She chittered about how he should stay this size all the time.

"What happened to your voice?" Lindon asked.

"Nothing," Orthos rumbled.

"That's what concerns me." Shouldn't Orthos' voice be higher pitched? Or at least fainter.

Orthos raised his head proudly. "I have a wonderful voice. I see no reason to change it."

Little Blue peeped her agreement.

Lindon tried and discarded a number of responses. He eventually settled on "As long as you're happy. We can get you some more soulfire whenever you want to change back."

"It won't be soon," Orthos assured him. "Transformation is exhausting. And you can keep me in your void key while we're flying, so I won't feel it. Let's get going."

Orthos began marching back toward the fleet of cloudships as Little Blue rode happily along.

Lindon straightened to join them. He was a little worried about his stride, though Orthos could use the Burning Cloak. He'd keep up.

But no sooner had Lindon taken one step than he heard a deep clearing of a throat behind him.

"Carry me," Orthos demanded.

"Are you sure? I thought you would consider it... demeaning."

"If you had a shell, I'd ride on it. You owe me."

That was true, and it wasn't as though Lindon found it embarrassing. The thought of carrying Orthos was just very, very odd. Like him carrying a horse on his shoulders to market. He was strong enough to lift a horse easily, but that didn't mean it wouldn't look strange.

He lifted Orthos, cradling the turtle in his arm, but Little Blue protested. She patted her own shoulder.

"On my shoulder?" Lindon asked.

She chimed once in agreement, scrambling over to his right shoulder and taking her usual seat.

Orthos didn't object, so Lindon settled him on his left shoulder. He was a little worried that the turtle would wobble off, but claws gouged into Lindon's skin as Orthos got a grip.

That wasn't enough to puncture an Overlord's skin, so Lindon merely waited until Orthos stopped wiggling around.

"Comfortable?" Lindon asked.

"Better than flying. Next time, I'll try sitting on your head."

Lindon walked back to *Windfall,* feeling very peculiar. He was also certain that, if Dross were around, he would have joined the other two. If Lindon wasn't careful, he was going to end up with some sort of reputation as a Sage who kept tiny pets.

Unless, he thought, he had such a reputation already.

Lindon shuddered.

Below the deck of one of the larger cloudships, Jai Long swept his spear through Kelsa's torso.

Her body vanished, the Forged illusion dispersing into essence of dreams and light. The aura around him trembled, and his sight wavered; for a moment, his vision started to flip upside-down.

With a flex of soulfire, he burst the incomplete Ruler technique and whipped the butt of his spear toward Kelsa's throat.

She held up her hands in defeat before collapsing onto the deck. Wei Shi Kelsa was tall and broad, if not so large as her younger brother. She had enough reach to be a match for him with her own training spear, if only she were advanced enough to do it.

Now she panted in exhaustion, covered in sweat from a hard day's training. He pulled his spear back, grounding it against the deck.

For him, this level of sparring counted as a break.

"Gratitude," Kelsa said between breaths. "I still can't... switch techniques."

"Not quickly enough. Any of my teachers would have recommended focused technique training."

By repeating one technique over and over, and practicing it under many different conditions, one could greatly improve their mastery of a technique. It tended to help those struggling to unleash their techniques more efficiently.

But, of course, that was for Gold students.

He didn't say it, but Kelsa sighed as she heaved her way to her feet. "I will advance soon, I promise. Lindon offered me a pill already. But I don't even have my balance as a Jade yet, and I know stability is important."

It *was*. Technically. But Jai Long had seen plenty of sacred artists adjust fine to skipping Jade entirely. If Lindon or Eithan Arelius had insisted she stay a Jade, he wouldn't have argued, but he would characterize their attitude as similar to his own.

While she was right about stability being important, the difference was so minuscule at Jade as to be negligible.

But everyone had to travel their own Path, and it wasn't as though he'd taken her in as a disciple. So he gave her a nod and went to pick up a 'heavier' training spear.

This one wasn't physically much heavier at all, but it was scripted to be similar to a parasite ring. It became harder to move madra through it, which allowed him to refine his madra, exercise his channels, and practice his weapon Enforcer techniques at once.

Kelsa settled into a chair nearby and watched him as she drank from a bottle of water. She didn't rest her perception on him directly, which would have distracted him, but she did observe him closely. Determined to take only one step at a time she may have been, but she never passed up an opportunity to learn.

This training didn't take much concentration, and she knew it, so after a few minutes of watching him she picked up their earlier conversation.

"So you think I should advance to Gold, then?"

"I wouldn't delay too long." He swung his spear vertically, leaving a trail of light that hissed like a snake before quickly dissipating. When it did, he swung again.

"I'm...not sure how I feel about taking someone else's Remnant into my spirit," she admitted. "Even if there are plenty to choose from."

Sacred Valley had been littered with Remnants after the Dreadgod's rampage, many of which were from the Path of the White Fox. They would be little help in advancing to Gold, though, since they could only be Jade at best.

"There are other compatible Paths," Jai Long said, focusing on his spear. "It's difficult to integrate their techniques into yours, but it can be done." She would have an easier time at Lowgold than he had, no matter what she did.

At least her Remnant wouldn't be trying to eat her from the inside out.

"Your brother didn't take a Remnant at all," he pointed out.

"No, but he had Orthos. I suppose there is Elder Whisper... but if he hasn't chosen a contractor by now, I can't see why he'd want me."

From what little Jai Long had heard of Elder Whisper, he

doubted anyone should *want* to contract with him. The fox couldn't be trusted.

"No point worrying about it," Jai Long said. This time, he slashed through the ghost of a snake he'd Forged out of his own madra. "If you run into any problems, you can get your brother to solve them."

Kelsa took another drink of water. "You don't like him."

"I wouldn't say that."

In fact, if Jai Long had to choose whether he felt positively or negatively toward Lindon, he would give Lindon a passing grade. Lindon had gone out of his way to help Jai Long and his sister more than once.

But he *had* killed Jai Long's closest friend, even if the circumstances were understandable. And...

In the quiet of his own heart, Jai Long could admit that he was jealous.

Lindon had started out so far behind, and had overtaken Jai Long so quickly. What could Jai Long himself have done with Lindon's opportunities?

Jai Chen would be safe for life, that would be certain. And he himself could pursue...the sacred arts, he supposed. He wasn't actually sure what he would do if he attained unrivaled power. His training had always been driven by necessity and the existence of enemies greater than he was.

If he was in Lindon's position, he couldn't even imagine what he'd do.

He had been quiet for too long, and had given Kelsa time to read his body language. Not his face, because that was still wrapped in bandages.

"You keep calling him my brother," she pointed out. "You call *me* by name."

"If he was here, I'd use his name."

"Not his title?"

His strike stopped in the middle. That was an accurate, if painful, point. Even if you set aside Lindon's status as a Sage, he was still an Overlord. Jai Long should be respectful.

He resumed his training, this time letting soulfire leak into his techniques. A small colorless spark infused one of the snakes that he produced. He couldn't infuse his techniques with soulfire while they were inside him—his body and spirit still couldn't handle it—but he could refine techniques with soulfire as he used them.

It was clumsy compared to what a real Underlord could do, like trying to paint while holding the brush with his toes, but at least there wasn't much any other Truegold could do to him.

He decided to turn the conversation back on Kelsa, at least to regain momentum. "It's hard for me to reconcile the Lowgold I knew with the Sage and Overlord he is now. It must be even more difficult for you."

"It's frightening," she said simply. "Not just what he can do, but that he only stumbled on the truth by chance. What if he hadn't made it? What if no one had ever left? We would never have known what the real sacred arts were like, and when the Dreadgod came..."

Jai Long was more than aware. If no one had come to warn the people of Sacred Valley, they would have all died.

"We would still have saved you," he said, though he wasn't sure why. He wasn't even certain it was true.

As soon as he said it, he'd known she wouldn't let the statement go unchallenged. She liked things to be as objective as possible.

"Would you have had the chance to come west? Would we have met if not for Orthos sensing you?"

No to both, he was certain, but he kept quiet.

Her lips quirked up into a smile. "That was still nice to hear."

Jai Long wished he hadn't said anything.

"So what about now that we *have* met?" Kelsa asked. "What are you going to do now? Are you going to head out into the Blackflame Empire?"

The Empire was probably the *worst* place for him to blend in, especially the west. And they were heading to Serpent's Grave. A city he had once helped Jai Daishou to attack.

"Jai Chen likes it here." She was taking her role as one of the founding members of the Twin Star sect seriously. Too seriously.

"I was asking about you."

"I can think about the rest after I reach Underlord, now that I have an actual chance." He had long given up on Underlord...or so he thought before Lindon and Yerin showed up, having casually brushed past the barrier where he had remained stuck for years.

Now, if he didn't at least break into the Lord realm, he wouldn't be able to hold his head up.

"What if it doesn't fix..." Kelsa gestured to his face.

Jai Long had, of course, told her why his head was wrapped up all the time. It was the first question he had to answer if he ever wanted to work with anyone.

Most people understood. Many sacred artists had strange Goldsigns or disfiguring scars. Kelsa had wanted to see immediately, but he had refused. The advancement to Underlord should fix him, or at least get it under his control. That was another source of motivation; Lindon looked like he had aged five years in the best way, and Yerin had lost all her scars. That gave Jai Long hope for himself.

But no one knew what exact changes the soulfire transformation would cause. It could make things worse, and he had been honest about that with Kelsa.

"If Underlord doesn't work, then I will continue as I always have. And I'll hope that Overlord heals me."

Overlord was a legend, and one that he would never have dreamed of reaching before these last few weeks.

Kelsa was staring into his mask so intently that he had to re-focus on his spear. "Just advancement, huh. Seems boring."

Jai Long sensed someone in the hall heading their way and it provided him an easy escape from the conversation. "My sister's on her way."

Kelsa accepted that, leaning back against the wall. But she kept watching him.

For a long, awkward minute and a half.

Just as she said, "Is Jai Chen really—" the door burst open. And *two* people walked in.

His sister, Jai Chen, wore a set of sacred artists robes trimmed in blue and burnt orange: the colors of the Twin Star sect. She wore the emblem proudly over her heart, and she moved as though it gave her endless energy.

She bounced into the room beaming, and even her companion spirit danced around in midair as though he'd inherited the mood. Fingerling was a serpentine, finger-sized pink dragon that was the manifestation of Jai Chen's power. To Jai Long's spiritual senses, he felt like an extension of her power.

But there should be as many as three other souls next to her, and Jai Long had felt nothing.

Lindon ducked as he passed through the doorway, a looming physical presence without the spirit to back it up. From a boy that had looked like he was spoiling for a fight, he had grown into a real Lord. If Jai Long hadn't known better, he could have been convinced that Lindon was a hundred-year-old expert. Even with his pale right arm bound up in a sling, he looked like he could fight everyone in the room without using any madra.

On one shoulder was Little Blue, bouncing up and down on her seat as she chattered to Jai Chen. That wasn't unusual, but on his other shoulder was a tiny red-and-black turtle that resembled Orthos. Did Orthos have children?

That idea wasn't nearly as strange as the fact that Jai Long hadn't sensed them coming.

He stiffened up, and Lindon noticed. The Overlord gave Jai Long an apologetic look.

"Apologies; I've been working on my veils. It's easier when people don't drop to their knees every time they sense me coming."

The turtle on Lindon's shoulder grunted, bringing up a plume of smoke. "You don't have to veil me. I've been hiding my own power since before your grandfather hatched."

That voice. Jai Long stared. That was *definitely* Orthos.

Kelsa looked as stunned as he felt. "Orthos?"

At the opposite extreme, Jai Chen was delighted. "Right? It's really him! I can't believe it!"

"This is nothing. I have many more...stop, what are you doing? Get away!"

Fingerling was bobbing around Orthos, and Jai Long couldn't tell if the spirit was happy to have recognized an old friend or if he was gloating that the turtle was his size now.

Lindon dipped his head to Kelsa and Jai Long. "Pardon us for disturbing your training. I only wanted to see if there was anything I could do to help."

Jai Long was immediately torn. On the one hand, he might have a chance to learn from an Overlord and a Sage.

On the other hand...well, Jai Long had been the one to cut off Lindon's other hand.

Kelsa stood up immediately and pressed her fists together, bowing to him. "This one would be grateful for your attention, Overlord."

Lindon's cheeks colored. "Please don't do that."

"If you're going to train me, then I need to treat you as my teacher." Kelsa wasn't playing around, and Lindon knew that just as well as Jai Long did.

But Lindon adapted in an instant. "Then I've decided that the title you should use to address me is my name."

"You're the highest-ranking person on this ship. We have to keep a clear—"

"Are you questioning me?" Lindon asked quietly.

Lindon still hadn't released his veil, but every muscle in Jai Long's body froze up as though he were staring down the jaws of a massive beast.

Kelsa straightened her spine. "No, sir!"

"Then my name is Lindon."

"...fine." Kelsa blew out a breath and scratched the back of her neck. "I can't win against you at all anymore, can I?"

The tension had vanished like an illusion, and Lindon gave her a sheepish smile. Orthos was the one that answered.

"Of course you can't. A hatchling shouldn't try to bring down a whole flight."

Little Blue crossed her arms and gave a ring that somehow managed to sound smug.

Jai Chen grabbed Lindon's arm and pulled him forward, which seized Jai Long's attention. When had they gotten that close?

"You said you could teach all of us at once, right?"

Lindon coughed. "Ah, actually, that was Little Blue who said—"

"Come on, I know you can do it!"

He glanced from Jai Long to Kelsa, looking uncomfortable, but Kelsa looked intensely interested.

When he saw that, Lindon sighed. "Okay. Everyone go sit by a different wall and start cycling, if you don't mind."

Kelsa and Jai Chen ran off immediately, leaving Jai Long standing alone. This was stupid. Even tips from someone more advanced than him wasn't worth this. This was just giving Lindon a chance to show off.

Lindon looked to him again, and Jai Long suddenly thought that he didn't have anything better to do anyway, so he might as well follow instructions.

When all three of them were cycling, with Lindon standing in the center of the room, Lindon's veil slipped. Just a little.

His spiritual perception filled the room like an overwhelming tide. Jai Long's whole spirit shivered, but only for an instant.

"Jai Chen, you've been focusing on using your techniques with your contracted spirit as a medium. You don't have to do that; not all your madra is taken up by him anymore. I'll give you four basic techniques you can work on, and you can refine them on your own, but for now start cycling your madra separately from your dragon."

Jai Chen looked startled, but Lindon had already turned to Kelsa.

"You're practicing the techniques I gave you correctly, but you're too slow. Don't learn to walk by taking one step and stopping to evaluate. Walk. You could spar against some clan elders, but for now..."

He whispered something to the blue spirit leaning against his neck, and then Little Blue hopped down from his shoulder and walked up to Kelsa.

"...she'll be your opponent."

Little Blue put hands on her hips and whistled a challenge.

Kelsa looked like her brother had told her to kick a baby off a cliff. "Uh, Lindon..."

"Blue."

The spirit shoved her palm forward. A Forged blue-white handprint manifested in front of Kelsa's body and slammed into her midsection, driving the air from her lungs and blasting her back into the wall. Her spirit was disrupted at the same time, and Jai Long winced. He'd been on the receiving end of that technique before.

Kelsa's body crumpled to the ground and she groaned.

Little Blue gave a deep flute note of concern.

"She's fine," Lindon said. "Just wait for her to get up. Now..."

Finally, he turned to Jai Long.

"Why haven't you advanced yet?"

Jai Long stopped himself from saying something he would regret. Lindon could talk like advancing to Underlord was so easy, but it was a barrier that stopped virtually every sacred artist in the entire Blackflame Empire.

"I have not received the necessary insight," Jai Long said stiffly.

Lindon didn't scan him with spiritual perception, but Jai Long felt as though he were being examined thoroughly nonetheless. "What have you tried?"

"Tried? I have isolated myself, I meditate on the nature of my madra every morning, and Jai Daishou ran me through a number of personal trials."

Lindon nodded as though he'd expected as much. "He didn't know what the Underlord revelation was, did he?"

Jai Long didn't even understand the question. Everyone knew that every Underlord's transformation was triggered differently. It had something to do with insight into your own Path, but some people achieved the knowledge in battle while others needed isolation, or even conversation.

"He was enlightened when he visited the birthplace of the Path of the Stellar Spear," Jai Long said. He didn't know how else to respond.

Lindon rubbed his chin. "I wonder why this isn't common knowledge. The Underlord advancement is caused by an understanding of what started you on your Path in the first place. Why did you start practicing the sacred arts?"

"Because I was one of the most gifted in my clan," Jai Long said immediately.

Of course, no transformation began. He hadn't expected otherwise.

"It's easier to sense in an environment with stronger vital aura. I'll give you some treasures. You'll want to open yourself to the resonance of aura while you try and discover what your original motivation was."

Lindon's gaze grew distant. "It's not as easy as it sounds."

It sounded pointless, but Jai Long had attempted less likely things when he was first trying to reach Underlord. He could give this a shot, especially if it came with free natural treasures.

"I'll try it."

He was being sincere, but Lindon seemed to sense some skepticism.

"This is the way it works."

"I believe you."

"You have to give this your full attention."

"I will."

Lindon still seemed doubtful.

A crash echoed as Kelsa slammed into the ceiling, and then another as she fell back to the ground, groaning.

Little Blue warbled a question, pointing at her, and Jai Long somehow understood it perfectly. She was asking *Are you sure this is okay?*

"...maybe take it easy on her," Lindon allowed.

第六章

CHAPTER SIX

On *Windfall*, Lindon had finally finished construction of a new building. It was a large, wooden, one-roomed structure that resembled a barn, and he had carved an intricate set of protective scripts into the foundation.

This was his Soulsmith foundry, and for the most part it stayed empty. He kept his tools and materials in his void key.

But now he and his mother were together in the center as he very delicately pulled Dross apart.

While Dross hadn't responded for weeks, he was still alive in Lindon's spirit. Just...faded. Lindon had cycled plenty of madra to him, and still Dross hadn't recovered.

Now, Lindon had manifested him as a spinning purple ball almost as big as Lindon's head. With great care, Lindon controlled the madra that made up Dross' form in order to view his insides.

This wouldn't harm him, though Dross would have been disturbed to see it. Spirits generally didn't rely on a specific physical structure to remain alive. If all their parts existed, they should be fine.

Though that didn't mean that Lindon couldn't cause problems by accident. He was reluctant to mess with Dross' internal configuration, but he needed a better look.

Dross expanded, his external layer of "skin" vanishing. Now he looked like a mass of organic rings, all spinning in time with one another. Between these interlocking circles was a recognizable system of madra channels, the hazy dream madra moving in gradual loops.

Seisha's brush froze in her hands as she was about to take notes. Her drudge gave a whistle that Lindon thought sounded hopeless.

"I've never seen anything like this," she breathed. "It's like a Remnant with another unique, independent spirit of its own. I can't even begin..."

Lindon's one hand was occupied with directing Dross' madra—his right arm still in its sling—so he split his attention to summon a brief spark of fire aura to point out a specific part of Dross' soul. One of the major rings at the top was faded in a particular spot, as though it had broken and begun to return. "This is one of the connections that broke when he exhausted himself. I was thinking if I could reinforce it—"

She cut him off with a look of wide-eyed horror. "What? You want to splice another spirit inside him?"

"Oh, apologies, that's not what I meant. I'll graft purified dream madra into him and let his own spirit rebuild itself."

"It's doing that already."

"Yes, but if I let it continue, it will be like he's being born all over again. There's no telling who he'll become."

At his core, Dross was a compilation of many minds and spirits that had been pieced together and then developed into an individual over time. But on some level, he was still a memory spirit. Just *remembering* who he had been might be enough to make him that person again.

Or it could start him over from the beginning.

Seisha looked completely overwhelmed. "Okay...let's say you can do that. What happens next?"

"Well, improving the connection in that ring would hook over to *this* one, which would accelerate its regeneration. That's my biggest concern. If I could make all the repairs at one time, I'd get Dross back as he was. But fixing one link in the chain starts a cascade I can't predict."

Lindon could tell his mother was only following him on the most theoretical level. He had hoped her years of experience would make up for her faulty education, but then again, this was a unique spirit. Perhaps the only expert in the world was Northstrider.

And the Monarch had never responded, no matter how many times Lindon called his name.

"So if you were to repair him, you'd either be bringing him back to life...or killing him."

That phrasing hurt, so Lindon focused on the job. "Technically, he *should* be functional now. Just without much personality or most of his memories. That's what I'm trying to bring back."

"I see," Seisha said faintly.

Then she corrected herself.

"No, I don't see at all. But I will."

With determination, she began sketching Dross' internal structure. Her drudge bristled with sensors and flew all around.

To his mother, every new mystery was an opportunity to learn. That was something he'd always been proud of.

But he *had* hoped she would know an answer that would help him now. Just waiting to see if Dross recovered went against everything he wanted to do.

He wanted Dross back.

Lindon released Dross, letting the purple loops fade back into a ball at the back of his spirit. "For now, he needs time. He'll stabilize slowly, which will give him better odds of recovery. I hope."

Seisha placed a hand on his shoulder. "I'm sorry. All we can do is our best, and the rest is up to the heavens."

Lindon clenched Suriel's marble in his hand and nodded.

"Not fair," Yerin said, immediately upon catching sight of Lindon.

Little Blue and Orthos had finished supervising Kelsa's training for the day, and now they were sitting on his shoulders again.

"You could raise a spirit of your own," Lindon pointed out. "There are Sylvan Riverseeds forming out by the pond."

"You ever spent time chatting with a sword spirit? No, because they're always cutting. And blood spirits are..." She shuddered.

Lindon had interacted with some blood-aspect Remnants, and even their dead matter tended to act as sadistically as possible. Then again, the only real blood spirit he had spent any time with was Ruby, and she was an exception in most ways.

Little Blue gave a little chime of sympathy and ran down, leaping off Lindon's sling and over to Yerin. Yerin caught her, looking pleased.

"You are a peach and a half. You don't have to ride him around all the time, you know. You're invited to stick to me."

Little Blue whistled that she was sticking with *both* of them, and if anything, Yerin looked even more touched than before. Lindon thought she might cry.

"Aren't you a gem. You know how to pick 'em." Yerin nudged Lindon's shoulder. When she jostled his arm, she noticed his sling again. "Still can't piece that together?"

Lindon sighed. "The underlying structure of the binding is damaged. No matter how much hunger madra I add, I can't fix it." In fact, the problem was essentially the opposite. He had *flooded* the arm with madra of a higher quality than he could handle when he'd Consumed energy from the Wandering Titan.

At this rate, he'd have to replace it, but he was holding back. He needed to find hunger madra of a higher quality, and there was only one source for that. Without it, he could potentially get the binding working temporarily, but it would be a patchwork fix at best.

Yerin hesitated, stroking Little Blue's hair while she searched for the right words. "Not taking a side myself, understand, but why don't you grow a new arm? Like, one with skin."

"I don't want to lose the technique. Consuming power is the fastest shortcut I have for advancing."

Most people didn't have the option of regrowing body parts, and they needed a Remnant prosthetic. But most people didn't have Sages and Monarchs who owed them favors. Lindon was certain he could get his arm back if he wanted it.

But he didn't. The new one was more convenient, and his sense of touch was even returning with time. When he advanced to Herald, he expected it to be just as good as his old arm would have been.

Of course, when he advanced to Herald, that would make him a Monarch.

"You planning on fighting one-handed all the way to Monarch?"

"I could fix it after that, I suppose."

She broke into a crooked grin and leaned into him. Little Blue gave a tinkling laugh.

"Just thought hitting Monarch wouldn't take long, didn't you?"

Lindon cleared his throat. "Not exactly..."

"Can't lie to me. My dream techniques are too powerful."

"Well...without Consume, I will definitely be slower."

Yerin leaned deeper into him until he wrapped his arm around her. "Wouldn't mind trying that myself, for a change. Dragging our feet, seeing the sights."

Lindon was reminded of a blood-spirit who had been excited to see the world with her own eyes. Ruby. He glanced at the red streak of Yerin's hair and wondered how much of that longing remained.

People had been telling Lindon to slow down for years, but he had never felt like he could afford to. Now, though...

Yerin went on. "Most sacred artists are advancing for something. Keep a home, take over a sect, kill a rival...bake a cake, I don't know. Not saying that's for you and me, but I just thought...maybe we could try it for ourselves, since we've got the chance. See through their eyes for a while."

As much as Lindon ached to *do* something, he was beginning to think she might be right. The Dreadgods were loose out there...but they weren't about to kill him, and they weren't his responsibility anyway. He couldn't explore the labyrinth yet, he couldn't fix Dross yet, and he couldn't advance yet.

All he had left to do was cycle normally and investigate his Sage powers.

And just...live.

"I guess we could try that," Lindon admitted. "For a while, at least."

The caravan of cloudships were not as advanced as those provided by the Akura family to reach the Uncrowned King tournament. They took three months to get from the Desolate Wilds to Serpent's Grave, landing regularly to refuel their constructs from ambient aura and their store of scales.

Over the course of that journey, everyone went on with their lives.

Naru Huan sparred against Lindon more than once, making Lindon glad that he wasn't an enemy. He was quite practiced in fighting against Blackflame, possessing several sacred weapons designed explicitly for that purpose, and he himself was a powerful and crafty opponent.

Not that he was able to win. Lindon himself had more madra than he did, even if he didn't use any Sage authority. Not to mention his other special advantages. If Dross had been able to give him a combat report, Lindon thought he could beat Naru Huan every time even if he limited himself to only his pure core.

Not that he told the Emperor that.

Naru Huan spent the rest of his time either dealing with the administration of his territory, visiting his family, or with Eithan. Officially, he was looking for advice on advancing to Archlord, but Lindon thought he might just be enjoying the chance to spend time with someone who saw him as a friend and not an emperor.

As for the rest of the Naru clan, Captain Naru Gwei saw entirely to the leadership of the Skysworn and was never on the same cloudship as Eithan at the same time. Naru Saeya, by contrast, had become much friendlier than Lindon realized she could be.

She trained the other Underlords from her Empire, sparred with Yerin, sought advancement tips from Eithan, and even challenged Lindon to a duel. Once. He thought she was enjoying this trip as a sort of pleasure cruise, and was glad someone was enjoying themselves so much.

If anyone else was having as good a time, it was Little Blue. She had grown addicted to training Kelsa, and was now seeking out fights with the other Jades and Golds on the ship. She mostly used the Empty Palm, which she could Forge to make big enough to interact with a human body, but she could also partially manifest the Hollow Domain and even accelerate herself with the Soul Cloak.

Her battles with Jai Chen's spirit, Fingerling, were especially entertaining to watch, as she would quickly become tired of using techniques and just wrestle instead.

After introducing his tiny form to everyone, Orthos was true to his word and spent most of the trip inside the Dawn Sky Palace stolen from Sophara. Lindon kept expecting him to get bored, but he insisted that bored was better than elevated.

The other person who longed for boredom was Ziel. He kept trying to rest, but wherever he went, the Sect of Twin Stars found him.

They always found him.

Someone had given Ziel the title "Master of the Training Hall," and any students who needed specialized training hunted him down. Ziel tried his best to scare them off, but he was prevented from outright refusing by the oath he'd made to Eithan in return for the Pure Storm Baptism.

The sect quickly figured out that he didn't mean all the harsh things he said, and that became part of his charm. They sought his advice on everything from scripting to advancement to technique training to roommate squabbles.

Every time he was asked to rule on which Jade most deserved to eat lunch first, or whether a Lowgold's new Goldsign was really making his snoring worse, Lindon was certain he'd summon his hammer and knock someone into the horizon.

He never did, though, leading Lindon to wonder if he didn't mind as much as he pretended.

Mercy, meanwhile, was perhaps the busiest aboard the fleet. With Fury absent, Charity and Malice were the two remaining pillars of the Akura family. And Mercy had sworn to take on their burden, so she had been taken away by the Heart Sage to help lead their clan.

For about a week.

Charity brought her back, haggard and worn, with a pile of work that could be completed on the ship. Lindon was starting to appreciate how much effort and expense went into such spatial travel, even for only one passenger, and was surprised that Charity had allowed it at all.

When he saw Mercy's state of living death upon her return, he also wondered why Mercy had returned. Surely she could have visited them once they arrived in Serpent's Grave.

But just chatting with him about the day's training, or playing with Little Blue, or dragging Yerin along to visit the other ships, gradually brought her back to life. She was like a plant absorbing life madra, going from wilted to healthy in an instant.

A few weeks later, Charity returned to pick Mercy up one more time, and she took a deep breath before diving back in.

This repeated several times, with the Akura clan sapping her will and time with her friends restoring it. Lindon imagined how Pride must feel, seeing the situation from the opposite side, and the thought amused him.

The trip to Serpent's Grave was a great improvement to Lindon's mood generally. Since leaving Sacred Valley, time to relax was scarce. Not that he knew what to do with himself when he wasn't working, as every single person he knew pointed out at every opportunity.

But even life with his family had grown easier, which Lindon suspected had to do with his parents witnessing not only his sacred arts but the general deference everyone else showed him. Having an Emperor ask for pointers during training didn't hurt his reputation.

He and his mother practiced Soulsmithing, which started as him showing her what he'd learned and ended up with her grilling him constantly for information.

With his father, he didn't have much in common, but the restoration of Jaran's eyes had helped his attitude. Lindon pushing both his parents to advance to Jade had helped as well, even repairing the shape of Jaran's long-twisted leg.

He no longer needed a cane, a fact that seemed to amaze him every day. But he still limped occasionally, when he wasn't paying attention. Everything physical had been cured, but after so many years, he had to learn how to walk properly again.

Kelsa, meanwhile, had advanced to Lowgold.

Lindon spent a few weeks nurturing up a White Fox Remnant he'd taken from Sacred Valley. He had to cleanse it with his own pure madra, then supplement the Remnant with White Fox madra he'd refined until it met his quality standards.

Once he considered the Remnant advanced enough for his sister, she had no trouble bonding it whatsoever. Jai Long had been very concerned about that, which Lindon supposed made sense, considering the man's own abnormal advancement to Lowgold.

Lindon had the materials for another Heaven's Drop, and

some of the refiners onboard were skilled enough to help him make one, but Kelsa had a much more difficult time adapting to the control over her Gold madra than he had.

At first, he had assumed she was suffering from the effects of spending so long in Sacred Valley, or from practicing low-quality cycling techniques for so long. But it turned out this was common, even in those with flawless foundations. Some people just didn't have a good sense for madra control.

She would gradually adapt, but it left Lindon surprised. He had intended to forcibly advance his entire family to the peak of Truegold immediately, and had expected Kelsa to break through to the Lord realm without much trouble.

He wondered aloud if maybe not everyone could advance as quickly as he did, even given the chance.

Yerin had stared at him for five straight minutes when she heard him say that, while Eithan laughed himself sick and then stored the memory in a dream tablet to share with others.

Lindon still didn't see why it was funny.

Eithan, as usual, was everywhere.

He hopped from ship to ship, keeping an eye on everyone—though he could have done that without moving—and popped up randomly to give advice to every guard, soldier, servant, deckhand, and fighter in the fleet.

Lindon wondered once again when Eithan found the time to work on his own advancement. But then again, the cloudships had never been cleaner.

Eithan ate dinner with Lindon and Yerin almost every night, regaling them with stories from all over the fleet, often including stories that he hadn't been privy to and that the subjects would probably object to sharing.

His greatest contribution to the trip was undoubtedly giving Lindon and Yerin tips on their advancement.

As it turned out, there were reasons beyond the mystical why Heralds found it difficult to comprehend Sage techniques, and vice-versa. They required almost entirely opposite training methods.

To become stronger as a Herald, Yerin had to push herself to the limit and accumulate power. It took a mind-boggling quantity of resources to push one to the peak of Herald, which was the way to maximize the chances of a successful advancement to Monarch.

She had to cycle diligently, take every elixir she could afford, and fight often.

Yerin found that an easy road to travel.

But to advance as a Sage, Lindon had to meditate on his Icon, and take actions to "align himself conceptually to its deeper meaning." Lindon began to wish he had another Icon, because "aligning himself" to the Void Icon meant long hours of reaching out toward it and trying to *empty his thoughts.*

Yes, it was boring. But Lindon found it easier and easier to gather his willpower and exercise his authority, which made the boredom much more bearable.

Reaching Archlord, Eithan said, would come to them with time. Advancing to Archlord required insight into their future, which Lindon and Yerin had already glimpsed by touching on Sage and Herald respectively.

As for how exactly Eithan knew how to train Heralds and Sages to become Monarchs, despite spending so many years stuck at Underlord, Lindon had asked him almost immediately.

"The sacred arts aren't as reliant on personal experience as people think," Eithan had responded. "There's an underlying structure that can be comprehended, if you look at things the right way."

He wouldn't elaborate any further, saying that Lindon was already on the right track to see for himself.

Honestly, Lindon was just happy to have gotten a straight answer out of him.

As for Yerin...there had been other times that they had lived together for months at a time. The Blackflame Trials, working for the Skysworn, even not so long ago in Ninecloud City, between rounds of the Uncrowned King tournament.

But in each one of those, they had been working together toward one purpose. Now, they were just living.

When Lindon was younger, learning enough sacred arts to live a normal life had seemed like a distant adventure, ambitious beyond his reach. This ordinary daily life with Yerin gave him a taste of that dream.

Lindon found that he enjoyed it.

When they arrived in Serpent's Grave, the Emperor arranged another elaborate welcoming display on the scale of a city-wide festival. During this one, Lindon had to make a public appearance. Not only was he an adopted son of the Arelius family, but he was from *this branch* of the Arelius family. From a certain point of view, this was a huge honor to the current Patriarch, Gaien Arelius.

Lindon had never met the man before, but Gaien was quick enough to bask in reflected glory.

Serpent's Grave was a city built from ancient, giant dragon bones. Almost every building was either carved into a towering rib, supported by yellowed fangs, or resting inside a skull. When Lindon had last seen the place, it had just weathered an attack from the Jai clan, and he was taken away by the Skysworn.

Now, Arelius family colors were everywhere. Their crescent moon symbol stood out from each street, and their banners flew dark blue, black, and white.

Gaien Arelius was therefore very important here, but Lindon didn't care much for the aging Truegold. He had far more respect for Gaien's son, the next heir to the Blackflame branch of the Arelius family: Cassias Arelius.

Cassias sought out Lindon and Yerin after the major welcoming ceremony, his curly hair shining golden. He held a long, thin silver saber at his hip, and he bowed gracefully before the two of them.

"I hoped I would be able to welcome you back someday," he said. "But I never dreamed it would be like this."

Lindon was happier to see Cassias than he had expected.

Windfall settled over the city. At first, Lindon intended to stay only long enough to get the refugees from Sacred Valley started in their new lives. But there was always someone who wanted the opinion of the Void Sage, and Cassias was dealing with some rivals who had been sabotaging his operations in neighboring cities.

Once Yerin took a casual stroll in the streets of those cities without using a veil, the obstacles to the Arelius family quietly disappeared.

All in all, there was always something else to do.

Windfall went from waiting in the sky, ready to depart at a moment's notice, to sitting on the ground inside the city walls. Before long, a camp of the Twin Star sect sprouted around it.

And the seasons slid slowly by.

Reigan Shen tore through a crowd of slavering ghouls made from hunger madra with a sword that blazed like the sun.

His body was so weak as to be worthless, and he had lived among the suppression field for months. He was panting and sweaty, caked in filth.

But Reigan hadn't always been a Monarch. He had fought his way up, just like the others. And he had forgotten nothing.

The ghouls hungered for his blood essence, for his madra, for his lifeline, for his authority, for his soulfire—for any source of energy he had on him or in him. He gave that energy to them in his attacks, flooding them with power from the edge of his blade, slicing them in half with a weapon of golden sunlight.

He left chunks of hunger madra dissolving on the ground behind him. Some of the other half-formed spirits stopped to feed on the essence flowing out of their comrades.

Reigan Shen finally found his way to a stretch of wall.

This had once been a door, but centuries ago, it had been filled in and sealed off. Never intended to be opened again.

There was no key to this door any longer, and the wall was almost indestructible.

But *almost* indestructible was no obstacle.

Shen deactivated the sword, noting as he did that the red-gold blade was starting to warp under the strain. Using powerful sacred instruments in this environment was terrible, and his heart ached at the waste.

There was almost no such thing as a true Monarch-level construct. Monarchs died so rarely that weapons formed from their bodies or Remnants were considered final life-saving treasures. There might even be more Abidan artifacts on Cradle than Monarch weapons, though no one would be able to prove that.

But this sword had been made by a Monarch and intended for use by Monarchs. It was a work of art, and outside of this maze, it could cleave mountains.

He placed the tip of the sword against the wall with great reluctance. The prize was worth the cost, but that didn't make the cost easy to pay.

"You will be used for a great purpose," he said to the weapon.

Then he activated the binding at full power. At least, the full extent of power it could manage down here.

The Song of Falling Ash shone with fire, light, and destruction. Its bright light filled the hall, illuminating the stone...but failing to pierce through.

The walls here had been invested with authority to make them inviolable, but this sword was the true product of a Monarch, made in the Soulforge and imbued with his will to break.

And, weakened though he may have been, Reigan Shen was a Monarch as well.

"Begone!" Reigan Shen commanded.

The authority on the wall shattered...and then the wall did.

A wave of flaming power dissolved the broad stone wall, leaving a hole big enough to pass a cloud fortress through. The Blade of Falling Ash was twisted and half-melted, its physical shell now leaking madra.

Reigan Shen sheathed it anyway. He could repurpose its material, and the masterpiece of a Monarch Soulsmith deserved more than to be thrown away.

Then again, this labyrinth might be the *best* place to dispose of such works. No one knew how many genius Soulsmiths had put their life's work into this place.

And nowhere was that more evident than in this room. Behind the wall, he found a massive chamber filled with blue crystals. But perhaps "crystals" was the wrong word; though they seemed to be solid, they flowed like rivers over every inch of the walls and floor.

This was madra Forged naturally and infused with aura for years. This material would be perfect to make priceless treasures, but Reigan Shen couldn't afford to open his void space more than necessary. He would risk destabilizing the rest of his collection.

In the center of the chamber, several hundred yards from the entrance, was a shining sphere the size of Shen's entire torso. It looked like a perfectly round sapphire, and it emitted a thick beam of blue energy into the air.

Inside that ball of blue, lightning crackled every few moments. When it did, corresponding sparks flickered through every river of crystal in the entire room.

Reigan Shen felt the envy grip him as he watched the sphere at the heart of the room. The Storm Core. The impossible treasure born from the Weeping Dragon's power.

Just taking this for himself and leaving would solidify his status as one of the greatest Monarchs in history. But, of course, he wasn't content with just being *one* of the greatest Monarchs. And if he left this project half-finished, he would be forced out of this world in a matter of weeks.

He had to be quick.

For this exact purpose, Reigan Shen had prepared a special container. He pulled a rectangular metal case off his belt and approached the Core. The case was empty, having been designed solely to carry this item.

Just like any other spatial artifact in this environment, it would decay quickly every time he used it here, but that was no problem. It was disposable.

This container only had to open twice: once to put the Core in, and once to take it out again. Then its purpose would be fulfilled.

Reigan Shen had his perception stretched out as he approached the Storm Core, but he felt no hostile presences among the overwhelming power of water and lightning.

Not until a blue lightning bolt crashed down on him.

Weakened as he was, the Striker technique should have killed him instantly. Instead, a golden shell of earth and destruction madra appeared over his head, taking the brunt of the attack.

The shield was made to last, and should have taken ten to fifteen such blows, but it shattered after only one. The ring that hosted that binding went dim on his finger.

This place truly devoured treasures.

The shield ring had bought him enough time to see his opponent: a huge stormcloud, crackling with sapphire lightning, with two limbs molded to resemble a pair of thick arms. A natural spirit, formed from the Storm Core's power.

And no doubt guided by some script buried here to protect the room. The people who sealed this place off had never intended to return.

Those ancient Soulsmiths were more than capable of crafting living weapons that could do battle with Monarchs, so if this thing could exert its full strength while Reigan Shen was veiled, he would have been annihilated in a breath.

But the suppression field was an even-handed curse. No one could escape it.

Thus, the spirit was only on his own level. And no opponent of the same level could defeat the Lion Monarch.

Drawing a pair of launcher constructs, one in each hand, Reigan Shen began the battle.

⬡

Far above the battle in the labyrinth, the Holy Wind School had begun to return to the slopes of the mountain they called the Greatfather.

When they felt the mountain begin to shake again, some panicked, thinking the Wandering Titan had decided to return. Others dismissed it. They were only aftershocks.

When the shaking died down in mere hours, this crowd felt themselves vindicated.

The very next day, a Copper child sent to fetch water said that Greatfather's Tears were lower than they should be. No one listened to her.

Three weeks later, when they discovered that the Dragon River was starting to dry up, they blamed the change on the Dreadgod's attack. The Valley had been reshaped by that monster, and besides, at least they were better off than the Golden Sword school. *Their* mountain was still intact.

So they continued their lives as the power in their water faded, day by day.

The Sage of Red Faith was not the most precise when it came to spatial transportation under his own power. He preferred using a tool, and this was one more benefit of his cooperation with Reigan Shen: the lion had plenty of tools to spare.

A gatekey brought him back to the cloud fortress that was Redmoon Hall's mobile headquarters. The massive ship hovered over mountains somewhere in the western Ashwind continent; he couldn't be bothered to determine their location any further.

He strode across the dark wood of the deck as Emissaries and agents of Redmoon Hall saluted him. Men and women in dark robes marked with a red moon. Most of them had their Shadows wrapped around their weapons, and with a few here and there keeping their Shadows in the form of a sacred beast or twisted monster.

Red Faith didn't acknowledge those who saluted him, and they were wise enough to move out of his way. A young man with a Shadow in the form of a bushy-tailed crystalline fox bowed with fists pressed together, and Red Faith could feel sincere gratitude.

This was one of their most recent recruits, a young Truegold who had reached Underlord quickly thanks to Red Faith's tutelage and sponsorship of his Shadow. Not long ago, Red Faith would have valued him highly, thinking of him as an investment in the research.

Now, he was useless. They were all useless.

Red Faith chewed on the knuckle of his thumb to calm himself down. They *weren't* useless. They still had utility.

Anything could be used if it brought him closer to Yerin Arelius.

Lower-ranking agents ushered him down past the top few decks to the ballroom-sized audience hall where Red Faith's Blood Shadow held court. Like a puppet pretending to be a king.

The entry to the audience hall was tall and wide enough to make one forget it was inside a ship, and the two agents on the doors hurried to open the towering double doors before Red Faith had to trouble himself.

But he was in a hurry, so he simply ordered them to open. They swung inward, pulling away from the hands of the agents.

The audience hall was cavernous—a waste of space bent to satisfy the arrogance of their sect's other leader. The Herald of Redmoon Hall had developed a disastrous ego that fully blinded himself to practicality.

For instance, the Herald insisted on being referred to as "Redmoon." How needlessly confusing. It made far more sense to adopt a title, as Red Faith himself had done.

The Herald hunched on a throne at the end of the hall, an inverted mirror of the Sage, scarlet where he was pale. While Red Faith had lost color in his skin and hair, his former Blood Shadow was all red. Bright scarlet hair trailing down his back, pink skin, and crimson eyes. The only spots of white on him were his Goldsigns, rivers of white trailing down from the corners of his eyes as though he wept milk.

Red Faith's own Goldsigns, bright like trails of blood, made far more sense. And were certainly more useful for intimidating and disconcerting the masses for a psychological advantage.

The Herald had dismissed several Emissaries when he felt the Sage coming, and those Emissaries saluted with their red-covered weapons before they left the room. Red Faith barely saw them. He was fixed on his opposite. His failed clone.

"You're wasting your time on this farce?" Red Faith demanded as the doors shut behind him. "That you remain here instead of hunting for Yerin Arelius, as I have done, only proves that you do not deserve the independence you stole."

The Herald, Redmoon, cocked his head to one side. "That you believe searching on your own is more efficient than leveraging an organization establishes to me that you should have ceded to me in our union. The body should always be subordinate to the mind."

"*I* am the mind! *You* are the body!" Red Faith wanted to scratch his own eyes out. "The *Sage* advances through understanding, and the Herald through brute force!"

"Such shallow understanding for one who calls himself a Sage. You were born flesh and bone, while I was born from the spirit. My origin is that of the mind and the soul, and if I were allowed to lead our union, it would be Reigan Shen who begged our support rather than the reverse."

Red Faith bit into the skin of his hand, letting the taste of blood and the flow of aura calm him. "Let us at least agree that the perfect fusion is our highest priority."

"She is living proof of the validity of our research. Your opinion of me cannot be so low that you think I would abandon our ambition."

It was *his* ambition, which the former Remnant Redmoon had only stolen, but Red Faith didn't quibble over semantics.

"Good. Then, since you have such faith in the Hall, tell me what you have learned."

Redmoon stared at him and began chewing on a fingernail. Red Faith left him to think. After a long pause, the Herald finally spoke.

"She is not hard to locate with spiritual perception, so we found her weeks ago, but I instructed my Emissaries not to approach."

Red Faith's jaw slowly dropped. He wasn't sure which would win in the confrontation between his astonishment and his rage.

"I knew it," he whispered. "You sabotage our efforts."

Redmoon spat a bit of fingernail onto the floor. "If you believe you are the mind in our relationship, then it should not trouble you so much to *think*. What will Yerin Arelius do if we approach, or anyone approaches her on our behalf?"

She would inevitably not cooperate, and with the Moonlight Bridge, it would be difficult to find her once she fled. Especially for the Herald, who could not follow through space as Red Faith could.

Though, granted, it would be complex to track her even for him.

"You would let shadows of possibility stop you from attempting to attain ultimate power?"

"We could kidnap Lindon Arelius or Eithan Arelius and hold them hostage in exchange for her cooperation. I suppose that is what you would do, short-sighted as you are."

Red Faith's entire frustration came from the fact that he *couldn't* simply threaten a hostage and force Yerin to obey. He needed her to work with him willingly; it would be too easy for her to deceive or harm him otherwise, unless she was positively wrapped in soul oaths.

Even that was not a viable option. He intended to fuel her advancement as part of his experiments. Who would freely sharpen a weapon that could turn on its user's throat?

"That you think my view is so narrow only proves that your own vision is lacking," Red Faith said. "She is one who hated her Blood Shadow, hated us, hated the Phoenix, but who carefully cultivated a clone Shadow because she recognized its potential for power. She will be persuaded by the promise of more, but only if we *find her* and make that promise!"

Identical scowls clashed as Sage and Herald glared at one another from opposite sides of the hall.

Both of them calmed down and thought for a moment of silence. Red Faith thought about the situation. He considered Yerin's perspective, and how he thought they should act.

He considered what Redmoon would say to that, and examined his arguments. He presented some of his own. All in his head.

Across the hall, his clone did the same.

When they were both finished, Redmoon spoke. "She will return to the Valley when we begin."

"So we will follow Shen's instructions," Red Faith agreed. "For now."

Unwittingly, the Monarch had positioned them exactly where they needed to be. For they were instructed to return south, soon. To Sacred Valley.

Where they would inevitably find Yerin Arelius.

Red Faith nodded. "We will have leverage on her then. She will join us with gratitude, and it will be in her own best interests to support the research. Very well. We will wait."

"As I said all along."

Red Faith snorted, but allowed the Herald his hollow victory. At least they were unified now.

As they should have been all along.

第七章

CHAPTER SEVEN

It was Cassias' habit to stroll the streets of the city every night after dinner. It was a pleasant way to cycle, helped him to get a sense for the city, and reassured his employees—who often started their work when the sun went down—that he was around and watching.

And, of course, Eithan had done this back when he was in charge.

He had very often shirked his normal responsibilities, but whenever he had been in the city, he had walked its length and breadth. He intervened in problems, no matter how minor, and made sure the Arelius presence was felt.

Cassias didn't have Eithan's talent in using their bloodline legacy, but he was still an Arelius. He saw more than anyone else could.

So he stepped aside gracefully as Eithan plummeted from a rooftop above him.

The Archlord landed gently, as though he'd merely stepped off a stoop, but he still clicked his tongue in disappointment.

"Were you trying to land on me?" Cassias asked.

"I was going to land on your shoulders. Then I was going to make a joke about how it was your turn to hold me up, but now it's dead."

"That doesn't sound like a very good joke."

"Well, the moment's gone, isn't it? You ruined it."

Despite his words, the smile on Eithan's face looked more genuine than usual. He took a deep breath of the cool night air as he spread sapphire sleeves wide.

"You ever have a night when you're just glad you don't have to fight to the death?" Eithan asked.

"Yes. Every night."

"Every night? Really? What do you do if you're not fighting for your life?"

"Literally anything else."

"Huh. Well, sometimes even I prefer not to have the pressure of the world on my shoulders." Eithan looked at Cassias' shoulders and sighed in regret, no doubt thinking of the missed opportunity for his joke.

Cassias glimpsed something in the strands of power constantly radiated by his bloodline, and looked off to his left. Two streets over, someone was creeping along an alleyway outside a restaurant. A quick scan showed that their spirit was veiled. A robber?

They were walking *away* from the restaurant, but there were houses that way. Cassias was about to leap over the house and confront the sneaking man when Eithan manifested a ball of madra between his fingers. A tiny Striker technique.

He closed one eye, aimed for a moment, and then hurled it into the sky.

It came down on the same man Cassias had been watching, driving into the man's spirit and tearing through his veil. He yelped. An employee of the restaurant came out furious while wiping hands on her apron.

"Thief?" Cassias asked.

"He dined without paying." Eithan shook his fist at the sky in mock outrage. "Not in my town!"

Then he strode down the street, whistling.

They didn't foil any more crimes that night, though Eithan shouted encouragement to a girl trying to work up the courage to dance, then led Cassias up to a bird's nest on top of a chimney. Cassias had expected them to be dread-beasts or hostile sacred crows or something, but no, Eithan had just wanted to show him some sparkly eggshells.

Eithan then climbed to the top of the highest tower around—if you could call soaring from floor to floor with one tap of the foot "climbing"—and trusted Cassias to follow.

With a lot of grumbling and much more physical exertion, Cassias eventually made it up.

He found Eithan sitting on the edge of the roof, staring out into the night. Usually, his hair would be blowing in the breeze, and Cassias was glad he'd seen sense and kept it short. Long hair could be a liability in combat.

Although Cassias reflected on that as he sat down by Eithan. That was true in combat between Golds, but Eithan was an Archlord now. How could an opponent getting a grip on his hair possibly inconvenience him? And he couldn't be blinded by it fluttering into his eyes.

"What a beautiful city," Eithan sighed. "Then again, I've found that most cities are beautiful, if you have the right perspective."

Cassias shook himself back to reality. He had just gotten distracted thinking about *hair.*

Eithan would be proud.

"I don't often find you in a contemplative mood," Cassias said. These days, he mostly didn't find Eithan at all. The Archlord was in high demand.

"I contemplate all the time! Truly, my deep machinations make Monarchs and emperors tremble."

He waited a beat, then added, "I am shocked that man on the third floor can eat so much fried meat at once. Truly shocked. It's not his Iron body or anything, I think he's just... very hungry."

Cassias wasn't paying attention to the man on the third floor of the tower, as he was studying Eithan. The Archlord had leaned back on his palms, his feet still dangling off the edge, and was now staring up at the stars with a small, content smile.

"You look happy," Cassias observed.

Eithan responded without looking away from the sky. "I'm always happy. Haven't you noticed how much I smile?"

"Then you're doing well?"

"My new haircut suits me, so I suppose I'm doing wonderfully."

Cassias nodded and leaned back himself, looking up at the stars. Eithan would answer seriously soon, or he never would.

After a minute or so of silence, Eithan spoke. "Sincerely, I am content. Better than I have been in...a long time."

Cassias thought back to the beaten, battered, and burned Underlord that had come through the Arelius family portal about nine years ago. Since then, as long as Cassias had known him, he had been searching for something.

"I'm glad you found what you were looking for," Cassias said.

Eithan seemed to know what he meant, because he nodded. "Everything's finally—"

With a slap to his own mouth, Eithan cut himself off. The slap made such a loud explosion that Cassias shot up, cycling his madra against an attack.

Eithan gave a heavy breath of relief. "I almost said 'Everything's finally perfect.' Can you imagine what a mistake that would have been? I can't afford to tempt fate like that."

Cassias was happy for him, he really was, but he still kicked Eithan off the tower.

It felt just as good as the Emperor had promised.

Reigan Shen coughed up blood, which wasn't as bad a sign as it seemed.

Nine flying tridents wove around him each glowing with the soft green flame of death madra. He directed the

Nightstone Spear Formation according to a method passed down for generations on the Iceflower continent.

They swept through in a complex pattern, butchering the army of blood spirits that filled this massive chamber. He had to fuel their flight by scattering his own natural treasures, given the lack of wind aura here, but their performance was worth it.

The Blood Core's prison looked identical to the one that had held the Storm Core, except instead of being covered in flowing blue crystals, this one was filled with semi-liquid beings that hungered to consume flesh. The second Reigan Shen had blasted his way in here, he'd been flooded by a tide of blood spirits.

The rich blood aura was too much for his weakened body, especially combined with the half-formed Ruler techniques of this host. Blood oozed from his eyes, from the smallest of scratches, and pooled in his chest.

Perhaps a human would have died. Reigan Shen didn't know. He wore his human form like a cloak.

And lions were not so fragile. He maintained his concentration, focusing his will on the nine tridents as they wove a complex web of green death throughout the room.

In seconds, there was silence except for the red liquid spattering to the stone floor.

The pressure on Shen's veins eased up, and he wiped off his lips with the back of one hand. The Blood Core sent a crimson pillar of light up to the ceiling. If not for the suppression field, its power would have blasted through the entire mountain and pierced the sky.

Then again, if it weren't for the suppression field, the Blood Core would have no reason to be here.

Shen readied the second of the four silver containers he had prepared. He'd chosen the order of this operation very carefully.

If he had removed the Titan Core to the west, the golden beam currently streaming into the sky would have been interrupted. Everyone in a hundred miles would notice.

Likewise with the east. When he removed the Silent Core from beneath Mount Samara, its ring would begin to fade within a day.

He had spent almost a year living here, in his own personal Netherworld of private torment, taking his time at every turn. He had mapped and cleared the routes between all four peaks, disabled countless scripts, and even tampered with the great script-circle that maintained the suppression field. All to allow this.

When the locals noticed, it would only be a matter of time before the other Monarchs did as well.

This was the last step he could perform slowly. Soon, the race would begin.

Reigan Shen seized the Blood Core, as large around as his own midsection, and shoved it toward the opening of a silver, rectangular case small enough to fit in one hand.

Space distorted as the Core was slurped inside, like water draining.

He could rest now, catch his breath, take his time. Only when the next step began would he have to rush.

For now, he simply had to take the Blood Core to the south and return it. To where it had always belonged.

Lindon strode through the school building that the city had given him, watching the rows of students wearing burnt orange and pale blue.

There were about forty of them, all younger than Lindon himself, most Copper or Iron. They had gone through the training to cleanse their madra, returning it to a pure state— if they had been too advanced, it wouldn't have worked.

Now they had their eyes closed, cycling clumsily according to a spiritual Enforcer technique that Lindon had taught them.

The Heart of Twin Stars.

Lindon had to point out mistakes here and there, but for the most part, their madra control was more than good enough for the technique. And they weren't splitting their cores today; this was only a cycling technique to prepare them.

Under Lindon's supervision, they should have an easier time than he himself had. But his stomach rolled as he sensed them.

What if he was wrong? What if they messed up under his guidance, and damaged their own spirits? What if he hadn't eased the way for them as much as he thought, and the spiritual pain was too much for them?

It was gut-churning, being responsible for someone else advancing safely. He preferred when it was only his own safety he risked.

Little Blue patted the back of his ear and quietly whispered encouragement to him. It did help. He was confident in his theoretical understanding, though he would be *more* confident if Dross were still around.

Lindon flexed his right arm. He had stitched it together with hunger madra he'd gathered from dreadbeast cores, though the limb was barely functional. It looked like it was covered in painted-over cracks, which from a Soulsmithing perspective was roughly what he'd done.

He could use the Consume technique again, and he did. But he was careful every time. With a less-functional arm and no Dross, the burden on the Heart of Twin Stars technique was increased. He had to take much longer to sort the various powers he absorbed.

Therefore, Lindon's comprehension of Heart of Twin Stars was higher than it had ever been. He *should* be completely confident in teaching it to others. There was only one person Lindon knew of who might understand the principles of pure madra better than he did.

As if summoned by Lindon's thoughts, Eithan swooped in through the window at that exact moment.

He straightened his pink-and-yellow clothes once he

landed, then smoothed back his hair, which was all reassuringly normal behavior. But he stared off into the distance with a distracted frown on his face.

The students all bubbled at his entrance, their cycling forgotten. Some called questions, while others whispered his name.

For his part, Lindon swept his spiritual perception over the students again, suddenly frightened that Eithan had sensed a problem or cycling deviation that he'd missed.

But while he panicked internally, he kept himself under control outwardly so he wouldn't disturb the students. Strong emotion could disrupt the Heart of Twin Stars.

"How can I help you, Archlord?" Lindon asked.

"Did you sense anything just now?"

Lindon followed Eithan's gaze. The Arelius was staring through the western wall.

Why was Eithan coming to *him?*

Surely if there was anything he could sense, Eithan would already have seen it. And if it were a matter of spiritual perception, Yerin's could extend the furthest among all of them.

So it must be...

Lindon aligned himself to the Void Icon. It had become easier this year, though it was still strange. While he touched the Icon, he felt everything around him as vessels that could be drained, material that could be consumed.

But he sensed no authority challenging his own.

"Nothing," Lindon said, though he didn't release the Icon.

Eithan tapped his own lip. "I'm not sure I did either...it's nothing, I'm sure. Almost sure."

That didn't give Lindon much information, but he tried to stretch his perception even farther. They were hundreds of miles from Sacred Valley now, but that was the direction Eithan was looking, so he reached.

He passed through an uncountable sea of powers, madra and aura of every aspect, and here and there a will that might have been strong enough to affect something.

An ordinary population, in other words.

"What am I looking for?"

"I don't know." Eithan gave Lindon a brief embarrassed shrug. "Perhaps it has been too long since I've lived without a crisis. I shouldn't have disturbed you."

But his frown deepened, and Lindon's forehead broke out into a cold sweat.

Eithan was being both serious *and* uncertain.

"Students, I need to have a word with the Archlord. Cycle with your parasite rings for an hour tonight, but don't activate the Heart of Twin Stars. Wait for my supervision. All right?"

They murmured their agreement, but most of the students weren't in a hurry to leave. They filtered out with many a glance backward. Some hid beneath the windows, hoping to hear something.

Lindon even felt some spiritual senses brushing up against the building; some students must have gotten their parents or older siblings involved. And quickly; they'd only left seconds ago.

But there was nothing for them to sense yet.

"So you had a...premonition?" Lindon asked, keeping his voice low.

"A bad feeling. Intuition." Eithan tapped his chin, still staring to the west. "It's like all the aura in the world suddenly shifted, like a loose tile. But when I looked closer, everything was as it should be."

"Sacred Valley?" Lindon asked.

"I hope not. I'm not in a hurry to return."

Lindon appreciated Eithan's implication that he would immediately rush toward the source of trouble.

If Eithan was this serious, then Lindon couldn't brush this off as a feeling. He sat down in a cycling position, where a student had sat only a moment before, and cycled his pure madra. He opened up his perception as broadly as he could.

All the while, he stretched out to the Void Icon. Emptiness, hunger, and nonexistence.

He didn't sense anything that alarmed him, but he didn't give up right away. Better to be safe.

Reigan Shen stood beneath the Greatfather once more, at the heart of the chamber filled with oozing blue crystals.

He had gone through great battles, suffered indignities, and lost weapons of incalculable value these last few days. But now there were no obstacles remaining.

He raised the silver container at his belt, the one that had been stained red. The Blood Core was overpowering its case.

Fortunately, he didn't need it anymore.

Reigan Shen steadied himself, cycling his madra, stilling his heart and focusing his will. This was it. When he placed the Blood Core back where it had belonged, he would be flipping the hourglass.

Then the whole world would be against him.

For a time.

When his mind was steady, Shen summoned the Blood Core. The huge red sphere streamed out of the tiny flask, and he placed it on the altar from which he had first taken the Storm Core.

Instantly, red light poured upward. And the room changed.

The liquid-looking crystals all over the walls and ceiling turned from blue to purple in an instant, blood madra flowing through them. The lightning now crackled red.

Originally, this chamber had been made to hold the Blood Core. The Cores had been scrambled long ago, their placement swapped, to help change the function of the script they powered. In a sense, Reigan Shen was setting something right.

The power of storms had built up in this room over centuries of exposure to the Storm Core, leaving these remainders, but that would be cleared out soon.

Now, for the first time in memory, this place would serve its true purpose.

Shen didn't linger. He dashed out of the room, pitting his willpower against reality to push him *faster,* faster than his body could normally handle. Even the air swept around him, guided by his soulfire control.

Hunger madra focused on him. He was spending too much power in the labyrinth, but he had no choice.

The clock had begun to tick.

One of the elders of the Holy Wind school dipped her hand into Greatfather's Tears to take a drink. The water level had fallen after the attack of the Titan, but over the last few days, it had risen again. But it was no longer as crystal-clear as before.

An instant after tasting the water, she spat it out. The Greatfather's Tears had been corrupted. This coppery tang was unmistakable; it was blood.

She drew herself up, shouting in fury for the guards. If their most sacred place had been defiled with violence, then her entire school had failed in its duty. There might even be a body at the bottom of the spring.

She marched away, furious, as bit by bit the water darkened further.

The door slamming open interrupted Lindon's meal, though both he and Yerin had sensed Eithan coming from a mile away.

They both looked to him in equal irritation. They had specifically taken time away from training and anyone else but each other, and booked an entire restaurant. Lindon had even gone to see a barber on Eithan's desperate pleading.

Yerin's sword-arms stretched out, but she deliberately pulled them back in. "You had a chance to keep your skin in one piece, and you left it at home."

"It happened again!"

Lindon exchanged a look with Yerin. It had been weeks since Eithan had felt his first premonition of danger, and both had kept their eyes out. But neither had sensed anything like what Eithan had described.

They still took it seriously.

Yerin frowned and her perception rushed out of the restaurant in a river. She might have a chance of reaching all the way to Sacred Valley, if that was indeed where the problem had come from, but she still wouldn't be able to push past the suppression field.

Lindon reached out to the Void Icon. He still spoke as he did. "This is bad timing, Eithan."

"It could have been worse!" Eithan pointed out. "Believe it or not, I do know when people can be interrupted and when they can't."

Lindon's cheeks heated, and he focused on his spiritual sense to avoid meeting Eithan's eye. Again, he felt no foreign authority in the area. There was no influence that reminded him of the Void Icon, nor any powerful wills working against them.

Yerin's ruby eyes snapped open. "Not a sniff or a hair. I'd be red-hot if I thought you were just poking at us, Eithan, but I don't think you are. You've got me shaking."

Lindon had a similar feeling. The longer this went without passing as one of Eithan's jokes, the more disturbed he became.

Eithan scratched furiously at the side of his head, disturbing his short hair. "It's *something*, but...if only I could...maybe if I fly..."

He mumbled to himself as he left, leaving Lindon and Yerin staring at the door in shock.

"He didn't even try to pull up a chair," Lindon said.

Yerin leaned over to look out the window. She didn't watch the street, looking instead to the sky.

"What are you looking for?"

"Just checking to be sure the moon's still there. The longer he does this, the bigger the problem's gonna be." She fell back into her chair and speared a chunk of eel.

She looked at it, then replaced it without eating it.

"Maybe we should take a cloudship out west," Lindon suggested. "I do think he sensed something."

"That's why I'm shaking."

The shattered remains of Mount Venture still vomited up yellow light. It was fainter than it had been, the Core having been fed upon by the Titan, but it would work for Shen's purposes.

There was no guardian spirit in this chamber, which was filled with jagged blades of golden stone. Most likely, one had formed here, but the Wandering Titan had annihilated it without even noticing.

Another palm-sized silver flask came off his belt, and he absorbed the Titan Core. The yellow light vanished.

It had been flickering off and on since the Dreadgod had consumed most of its power, so Shen could only hope this would go unnoticed for a while.

He pushed himself. Faster.

Lindon found Eithan standing on the edge of *Windfall's* cloudbase, looking west.

"Strange feeling?" Lindon asked.

Eithan's clothes were rumpled, and he had worn the same thing for three days straight. Given that Eithan normally changed at least twice a day, Lindon thought he might be on the verge of death.

"Every time I turn around," Eithan responded. "If I didn't know better, I would say it was just...nerves. Anxiety. Overactive imagination."

"So what is it?"

Eithan threw out his hands in frustration. "You think I know and I'm holding out on you?"

"Apologies if I'm overstepping, but...what would Tiberian Arelius' advisor say?"

Eithan closed his mouth. He brought his arms around and crossed them, thinking. To Lindon's discomfort, he found traces of someone he didn't recognize in Eithan's expression. Just flickers, like the shadow of another person passing through the man.

"There are three possibilities," Eithan responded eventually, and all playfulness was gone from his tone. "One, there is a problem with me. A working of will or authority that I cannot detect, which is compromising my senses. Two, I could be sensing authority at work. If I'm close to Sage—especially the Oracle Icon, which I was once considered a prime candidate to manifest—then I could be picking up hints of another Sage or Monarch's working. It could be a working you are too inexperienced to recognize, or something too far away from the realm of the Void Icon."

Lindon didn't take offense at the slight to his abilities. It was a reasonable possibility. He only listened.

"Three..." The businesslike Eithan hesitated, and Lindon saw the usual man again. Although an uncertain one.

"...you're going to laugh."

"I usually don't."

"That's true. It's of great concern to me. The third possibility is...fate."

Lindon didn't feel like laughing. In fact, he sought out the warmth of Suriel's marble for comfort.

She had spoken of fate. Reading it, changing it, altering its flow.

"Fate, or destiny, or the will of the heavens...it's a real force. Dream artists contact it once in a while, and some Monarchs are more attuned to it than others. As an Archlord with no dream abilities, I should have no ability to see it. So that's a distant third possibility."

Lindon didn't think it sounded distant. If he were to bet based on this conversation, he would put his chips on fate.

But that would be a bet he'd be happy to lose.

"Pardon, but I hope the problem is with you," Lindon said.

"I would be delighted."

When Reigan Shen placed the Titan Core in the north where it belonged, the mountain the locals called Yoma erupted in stone spires.

Even Irons wouldn't miss a sign like that. Shen flew down the halls of the labyrinth's upper layer, supported by blue strands of energy emanating from a construct at his belt. The construct wouldn't last long, but this was the fastest and most economical way of traveling for now.

Subject One's attacks had intensified, and now there were traps of hunger madra placed in his way, Forger techniques strung across the halls like webs.

If he had been less skilled, he might have fallen for them. But they still slowed him down.

As soon as the pillar of light from the western peak had vanished, he'd put himself on a time limit. And it would only run out faster and faster.

He reached the eastern chamber, buried beneath Mount Samara, and detonated another powerful weapon to carve through the wall. This chamber had been influenced by the Silent Core for hundreds of years, so it should be a trap of powerful light and dream madra.

He could *sense* that it was, but he couldn't see anything. Beyond the hole in the wall, he saw only a chaotic jumble of spinning images.

Even his aura sight was useless here, though that had more to do with the suppression field than the complexity of this dream working.

Shen placed a pair of spectacles over his eyes, which should show him the path through this dream formation.

Unfortunately, he saw immediately that this wasn't a formation so much as a mess. There was no path through; the strong and weak points of the illusion shifted with every second.

So he had no choice.

Reigan focused his willpower again, hating how long it took him, and how weak his authority felt here.

"Flee," the Monarch commanded.

The fog of deceptive madra and aura parted like a forking river. He dashed through, scooping up the purple-white Silent Core now that he could see it clearly. He had to be quick; there were undoubtedly spirits that had formed inside this environment as well.

He placed the Storm Core on its altar, then ran away as the clouds of dream madra began to flash with lightning.

From this moment, the ring of the mountain ahead would start to change.

This was his last step, and then he could proceed into the true depths of the labyrinth.

Reigan Shen flooded his madra through his flight construct, shattering it almost immediately. Three of the four Cores had been returned to their proper places. Once he placed the Silent Core in the chamber, all of Sacred Valley would change.

No, the *world* would change.

The messenger constructs finally returned to Lindon. Most were shaped like butterflies of various colors, though some resembled birds, clouds of sparks, or mechanical flying machines.

Some of the faster ones had returned already, but he'd sent them out at roughly the same time, so he expected them to arrive more or less at once.

He listened to each message. Some constructs bore recorded messages from human scouts, others pinged yes or no to tell him if they'd seen what he'd sent them to look for, and still others gave their own rudimentary opinion like a Remnant's.

When they finished, Lindon summarized the information and brought it to Eithan.

He found the Archlord waiting right outside of Lindon's house on *Windfall.*

"You could have deactivated the ward against me," Eithan pointed out. "Then I would already know what you have to say."

"Apologies, it...slipped my mind." That was a lie that fooled no one; Lindon didn't want to set a precedent of allowing Eithan to spy on his home. "There's so much activity in and around Sacred Valley, it's hard to pinpoint anything. There's a new entrance into the labyrinth, some strange Remnants have popped up with aspects no one can recognize, the orus trees on Mount Yoma have started to wither, a tribe of outsiders from the south came into the valley to conquer but left as soon as the suppression field set in..."

Lindon spread his hands. If he had to rely on notes, he would have waved them in the air. "I don't know what to look for. There's too much."

Eithan frowned into the distance. "Keep going."

"Dreadbeasts are gathering outside the valley. Some people say Samara's ring is dimmer, or its light is less consistent. Almost certainly damage from the—"

Eithan cut him off without a word. His entire aspect had become cold. "The ring around the mountain to the east? Did they report a change in color? Sparks?"

"Sparks, yes. One report said the light "crackled" now. But color, I don't know. We'll be able to see for ourselves tomorrow, though."

Windfall had been heading back to Sacred Valley for several days now. Eithan's premonition was too disturbing to ignore, but he still wasn't certain it had anything to do with Sacred Valley, or they both would have rushed over.

Eithan extended a hand over the edge of the cloud fortress, and a golden light shimmered. *The Bounding Gazelle*, his high-speed cloudship, materialized from sparks of gold over the edge.

"We need to see for ourselves. Send a message to Yerin just in case."

Lindon did, launching a purple-and-white butterfly after Yerin's spiritual signature. The technique dispersed into the aura, where it would make the journey to Serpent's Grave in hours instead of days.

Thanks to her Moonlight Bridge, Yerin could meet them anywhere at any time. She had stayed back in Serpent's Grave to train a new batch of students and keep Mercy company, who was in between jobs for her family at the moment.

Lindon joined Eithan aboard the cloudship as it shot off, leaving the lumbering *Windfall* behind. He was feeling left behind himself.

"Eithan, what would it mean if Samara's ring changed color?"

"The suppression field needs a power source," Eithan said, still icy. "The ring around the mountain should be a side effect of housing such a source." He was looking westward as though heading to meet a blood enemy.

Lindon picked up on the implication. If it was changing color, that meant the aspects of the power had changed. But the only thing he could think of that might cause that was the Titan's attack.

"I would find it more alarming if the ring really was fading," Lindon said. A loss of power to the suppression field might call the Dreadgod back. Or all of them, this time.

Eithan glanced to him, but Lindon followed the train of logic before the Archlord said a word.

"Unless...the power source was altered." He spun out the scenario in his mind. "If it just ran out of power, we could replace it. But if it changed, that means someone else has already done that. So someone could be messing with the labyrinth from the inside."

Eithan didn't respond, but he flooded the propulsion constructs with madra. So much pure madra would make the ship run faster *now,* but it would dilute the network of constructs that ran it, so the cloudship would require extensive maintenance and repair later.

Lindon didn't comment. They did indeed need to move faster.

They flew through the night, covering in hours what should have taken them days if not weeks in a slower vessel. Eithan began reporting before the Valley was visible to Lindon.

"Clear distortion in the ring, but I don't see much change in color. I suspect it may not be as bright as it was. I *don't* see the pillar of earth madra to the west."

"It's been unsteady since the Titan fed on it," Lindon reported. "It isn't unusual for it to vanish for days at a time."

Eithan nodded, but he remained silent—watching—as they blasted through the skies.

Only when Lindon could see Samara's ring with his own eyes did Eithan let out a breath of relief. His normal self leaked back into him.

"I'm not ashamed to admit that I was frightened for a while there. It seems I may have thought too much."

"Better too much than too little. But, if you'll pardon me for saying so, you were frightening in your own right."

Eithan flinched. "I have heard that before. I do apologize. Take it as my reaction to..."

He trailed off. The pillar of light on the western end of Sacred Valley had returned, but now it wasn't golden-yellow. Now it was a soft white; a color that reminded him of Samara's ring, in fact.

That was strange, but sometimes certain aspects of madra changed color as they lost power. Still, it was better to be safe, in case someone *was* tinkering with the structure of Sacred Valley.

Lindon extended his perception and opened himself to the Void Icon, reaching out to the Valley. He wouldn't be able to feel anything past the border, but he could still get a sense of the surrounding aura.

Which, he realized, was changing before his eyes.

The chaotic powers of vital aura spun like a churning sea. He traced the sensation back, expecting his senses to weaken as they approached Sacred Valley.

But they didn't.

"Lindon, stop!" Eithan shouted.

Eithan grabbed Lindon's shoulder and his madra flooded into Lindon's spirit, but they were both too late. A wave of power gushed out of Sacred Valley, rushing out in all directions, sweeping over their cloudship in an instant. A pure white aura that felt to Lindon's senses like an endless, gnawing greed for *more.*

Hunger aura.

Power blotted out Lindon's senses, and he was swallowed by blinding pain.

第八章

CHAPTER EIGHT

Akura Malice had submerged herself in a world of silhouettes. Her World of Night technique. Shadows and dreams moved around her, vague shapes she could make out only distantly.

But they came with impressions. As she saw the outline of a woman with a staff, she wouldn't necessarily be able to identify it with her eyes. But her spirit felt Emriss Silentborn. The Remnant Queen would be involved in her future soon.

Close by, drifting in the emptiness, she found the shadows of a ruined city. There would be a battle here, but she felt as though the battle hadn't included her. So she would travel to this place in the aftermath of someone else's battle.

These hints and clues were difficult to piece together, but the World of Night was the best technique Malice had to interact with Fate. In these recent years, the future had been even more obscured than usual.

She had seen no hint of the Bleeding Phoenix rising, for instance, and usually the Dreadgods were as difficult to spot as sharks crammed into a bathtub. But this made twice within half a decade that she had failed to spot one.

Someone was meddling with her perception, or with the flow of the future. Fate, as she understood it, was only a tendency for things to happen a certain way. Just as you could stop an object from falling by catching it, so you could take action to prevent certain outcomes.

Most of the time.

Malice scanned these suggestions of the future, trying to piece them together, and realized she couldn't. Some events seemed even to contradict one another.

Something strange was going on. She had immersed herself into this world several times over the last few months, spending every ounce of her attention to try to unravel the future. She couldn't allow herself to be caught unawares again.

Moments after thinking that, she was caught unaware.

Four shadows suddenly loomed up in her World of Night, surrounding her, like black statues that had sprouted from the ground. A bird, a shelled warrior, a tiger with a halo, and a dragon accompanied by clouds.

She didn't need her spiritual sense to recognize the Dreadgods.

They lurked in the distance forever, threats that always existed somewhere in the world, but now they were here. Right now. Looking down on her.

And with every passing second, they grew larger.

Malice tore the technique apart and stepped back into the real world.

"Dreadgods!" she called, and while terror coursed through her soul, her voice was that of a majestic queen.

Carried by her will, those words echoed throughout Moongrave. Everyone heard as though she stood before them.

And the entire city rushed into action.

They did not panic. They had prepared for this. Shelters were opened, powerful sacred artists were awakened, emergency constructs were wheeled out of treasuries, and messages flew all throughout her territory.

Malice herself reached out to Charity, who had contacted her at almost the same time.

Her granddaughter's voice rang in her mind. *"It's the northwest, Grandmother. Mercy's still there."*

"Then bring her back," Malice ordered. "And move our people into position."

Lindon sat up with his head and spirit screaming.

He had been brought to the second floor of his house on *Windfall* and lain on the couch. He had never entirely lost consciousness, but he didn't remember much. Just the blinding sight of so much *hunger*, washing over the land in a wave.

If he hadn't been open to the Void Icon at the time, it wouldn't have been so bad, but he had his aura sight *and* his perception *and* his Sage senses open wide.

Even now, he was finding it hard to focus his vision. He kept sliding between seeing double, seeing blurs, and seeing only the colored wash of aura.

A fuzzy mass of red that Lindon was sure was Yerin broke off from talking, appearing at his side in a blink. "Whoa, steady there. Don't rock the boat. Can you drink?"

A cup was lifted to his lips, and Lindon took a sip of water. Something waved in front of his face.

"Still got your eyes? How many arms do I have?"

Lindon peered at her. "Eight."

She chuckled, and so did Eithan, who was apparently still in the room. They must have thought he was making a joke about her sword-arms, but he really saw four of her, each with a pair of hazy human arms.

"You'll be fine after some rest," Eithan assured him. "You were looking right at the field when it dropped."

That spiked Lindon's alarm. "The suppression field! The Dreadgods..."

He started to move, but Yerin had him by the shoulders.

Eithan made a sound of reassurance. "Don't worry, they aren't coming. This wave of power is contained to the valley...so far."

"Is the labyrinth still locked?"

"It is not," Eithan said, grinning.

"Then we have to move," Lindon said. "This is our chance!"

The door swung open, and two blobs of color came in that Lindon eventually identified as Mercy and Ziel.

"My mother's—oh, Lindon's awake! How are you feeling?"

"How did you get here?" Lindon asked.

"The whole clan's being mobilized," Mercy said. "They set up a network of emergency gatekeys to take people west, to cordon off Sacred Valley. I snuck in, but Aunt Charity will figure out I'm here very soon."

Lindon slipped away from Yerin and stood. At least his feet were steady, even if his vision wasn't. "We have to go in. Now's our chance."

"Go *in?*" Mercy repeated.

There was clear hesitation in Yerin's voice too. "That's a shaky bridge to walk. We're not ready to go into the labyrinth yet, but you want to head in now that a Monarch's getting ready to slam the lid on the whole thing?"

"The suppression field is gone," Lindon said. "What do our preparations matter now? We'll have our full powers inside."

"Not our *full* powers," Eithan corrected. "It is the domain of hunger madra, after all. It will slowly chip away at us as we remain inside, so we should keep this to a quick operation."

The blob of white and black that Lindon had determined was Mercy spun toward Eithan. "You're *for* this?"

"I'll put it to you this way: if none of you come with me, I'll head in by myself. Well, Lindon and I will. This is a unique opportunity that we won't miss."

Yerin pondered silently, and Lindon could practically hear her thoughts. She was skeptical about risking their lives for no reason, but then again, the labyrinth was a hiding place for all sorts of treasure. And if Eithan and Lindon were going...

Mercy turned behind her, looking for support.

"There's a way to kill the Dreadgods in there?" Ziel asked.

Lindon nodded.

Ziel sighed. "And I'm part of the team?"

Lindon nodded again.

Ziel sighed again, more heavily. "And I still have some time left in my contract. Ah, well." He walked out the door, leaving the other four of them behind.

"I don't..." Mercy's voice shook. "I can't...Lindon, my mother...if she shows up and we're still inside, she could...I don't even know. She could seal us inside, but it might be worse if she didn't. She'll have our heads for this."

There was something worse, something that no one had brought up yet, but Lindon remained silent.

Eithan slid up to his side and elbowed him. Lindon shifted away but remained quiet.

Yerin looked at the two of them, leaning close enough that Lindon could make out her face, and then she sighed as though she'd seen something in Lindon's eyes.

"What?" Mercy asked.

"Somebody turned off the field," Yerin said, speaking for all of them.

Lindon was certain that was the case, but he still protested. "It *could* have been natural decay after the damage from the Titan."

"But it wasn't," Eithan followed up. "Someone modified the function of the labyrinth with intention. Now, they may not have intended to deactivate the suppression field, but they certainly intended to change something."

"How do you know?" Mercy asked.

Lindon answered that. "The power shifted beneath the valley. Samara's ring is now fueled by different aspects of madra than it was before. You could automate that, but there wouldn't be any reason for it. If it was just damage from the Titan breaking the field, then we would have expected to see the suppression weakening before that. And Eithan..."

Eithan picked it up. "If I was indeed sensing a disruption

in Fate, as now seems likely, then it must have been caused by someone. By every popular theory, natural cause and effect should not change Fate."

Mercy let out a heavy breath. "How many people could get down there and make changes in the script formation?"

"I can't see anyone below Sage or Herald having the ability to both survive and alter its workings," Eithan said.

"So we've got a real fight coming," Yerin said.

"Only if we go in," Lindon said, fixing his gaze on Mercy. He tried to make his eyes clear. "I've gone through an abandoned laboratory before, and I was alone. Orthos was too injured to help. We have a limited window here, and I want the whole team with us."

Mercy straightened, and even with Lindon's compromised vision, he could see her brighten up. "We're a team?"

"Of course we are," Yerin said immediately.

"Eithan said he and I would go in alone," Lindon continued, "but I don't want to do that. We've only got one shot at this, so let's make it our best one."

Mercy paced anxiously, tapping her staff on the floor with every other step. "I don't want to go up against an unknown enemy *and* the Dreadgods *and* whatever's in the labyrinth *and* probably my mother."

"That sounds like an adventure!" Eithan said.

Mercy's voice was grim. "There's no way this ends well. No way. Even if we get what we're after and make it out, the Monarchs will punish us. Do we all know that?"

"You'll have to walk me through how that's different than now," Yerin said.

"That was a worthy warning, Mercy!" Eithan declared. "Let us count the cost before we dive headfirst into one of the most dangerous places on the planet."

Lindon thought longer before he answered. He could easily see the Monarchs taking a closer look at him than he wanted.

Though that was a normal consequence of gaining more power. The higher you climbed, the more eyes were on you.

"I understand," Lindon said at last.

Mercy clicked her tongue. "Fine, then let's get going. Maybe if I'm with you, my mother will hesitate before she locks us all inside."

Or maybe she won't, Lindon thought. He remembered Malice's attitude toward Mercy in the Uncrowned King tournament.

But he wasn't callous enough to say that out loud.

Belatedly, he realized something he'd forgotten. "I should have let Orthos out! He needs to hear this."

"Can't he hear every thought that goes through your head?" Yerin asked.

"No, he just gets impressions. He's not Dross." Lindon realized something even as he spoke. "...and we need Dross."

He had waited for the better part of a year. Dross was as stable as he was going to get. Lindon had hoped for Dross to wake on his own—or for Northstrider to contact him—but without those things, there was only one thing he could try.

Without waiting for anyone else, Lindon opened his void key. He summoned a scripted box of stable, Forged dream madra that he had prepared. With his hunger arm mobile now, he didn't need his goldsteel tongs.

And he had prepared for this operation for a long time.

Eithan's eyes widened. "Decisive! Best of luck to you."

"You're not going to try and fix him *here,* are you?" Mercy sounded horrified.

Yerin gripped his shoulder, lending him strength. He reached into his own soul and found the slowly spinning purple orb at the base of his skull.

As he had done with his mother months ago, he projected Dross' internal structure into the air. Purple rings expanded until they spun in midair around them all.

The largest ring was still thinner in one section than any-where else. Lindon took a deep breath to steady himself, and another. Then he grabbed a loop of dream madra from the chest and, in one motion, fused it to the ring from Dross' spirit with a lick of soulfire.

The change was immediate.

Purple light flashed through the ring, and then in the smaller rings around that one. It moved through the entirety of Dross' spirit in a chain reaction, faster and faster. Lindon couldn't slow down his breath any longer. His heart pounded.

The enlarged loops of dream madra collapsed as Dross returned to Lindon. *Something* was changing and squirming inside of him, and Lindon couldn't fully understand what.

Finally, the dream-spirit inside Lindon slowed and stopped spinning. Lindon waited to hear something...but after only a few seconds, he could wait no longer.

"Dross?"

At the sound of that word, power spun out of Lindon's spirit. A purple blob appeared in midair next to him...but it wasn't as dark a purple as before. It was pale and washed-out, almost gray.

[Ready to comply,] Dross said in their heads.

Lindon's heart stopped.

Everyone stared at Dross in shock.

Lindon's joy overwhelmed his surprise, and he grabbed Dross in his Remnant hand. "Dross! Are you okay? Do you... remember me?"

[Wei Shi Lindon,] Dross recited, [adopted into the Arelius family. You were responsible for my evolution in the Ghostwater facility, and for introducing me to the Monarch Northstrider.]

It was Dross' voice, but just a dry and passionless recital of words. In that way, it didn't sound like Dross at all.

Lindon's excitement sank into his stomach. "How are you feeling?"

[My condition is functional. No significant abnormalities to report.]

Collective sounds of disappointment went up from the humans in the room. Eithan placed a hand on Lindon's shoulder.

"His personality could still recover," Eithan said sympathetically.

Lindon agreed, but he wasn't optimistic. "There are adjustments we can try...but the more we change, the less time we have."

"This labyrinth contains tools from some of the greatest Soulsmiths of all time," Eithan said.

"Good. We'll look for anything that might help."

Lindon turned to Dross and focused, the blur in his vision retreating for a moment. "I'm going to fix you," he promised.

[Unnecessary. I am largely operational.]

"Don't you remember what you used to be like?"

[I recall. My idiosyncrasies were left over from the component spirits used to construct me. They added nothing to my function, and I think you will find my operations significantly improved.]

Dross' form was the same as before—one large eye, one mouth filled with sharp-looking teeth, and two boneless pseudopod arms. The only difference was the pale gray cast to his skin.

But his expression was blank. He spoke like a construct reporting exact words.

It gripped Lindon's gut with grief, as though he'd lost Dross all over again. But there was still hope, so he kept his words clipped and straightforward.

"The idiosyncrasies were important to me," Lindon said. "If you come up with a way to restore them, tell me immediately."

[Acknowledged.] A faint frown appeared on Dross' face. [I will attempt to reconstruct my persona in accordance with my memories.]

"You do that." Lindon looked to the rest of them, and he could almost see them. "In the meantime, let's get ready to leave."

"Not much to get ready," Yerin said. "Got my sword, got my void key."

Mercy dashed for the door. "I do need to get ready! Give me two minutes!"

"Someone probably ought to catch Ziel," Eithan noted.

Lindon was still watching Dross, looking for a shred of the individual he used to be. "I'll tell Orthos and Little Blue. In the meantime, Dross, what do you know about the labyrinth?"

[Information requested: history of the western labyrinth,] Dross intoned.

But nothing happened. Usually, when Dross spoke like that, Lindon's mind was taken over by a vision.

[Error: synchronization denied. No access available.] Dross shook himself. [I apologize. That was very strange. I will rely solely on my own memory.]

That statement piqued Lindon's curiosity. "Were you not always relying on your own memory?"

[I...do not believe so. My apologies. My memories are more fragmented than I realized.]

Lindon renewed his resolve to fix the spirit.

[What you call the labyrinth is also known as the western labyrinth, the Dreadgod labyrinth, the First Tomb, the forgotten maze, and several other titles that may or may not apply to this location. It extends all over the world, but its largest—and presumably most central—hub is located under the land you call Sacred Valley.

[Records of its purpose and contents are incomplete and often contradictory. It is called the birthplace of the Dreadgods, but other claims dispute this, suggesting that it was a place where samples of the Dreadgods were studied. Records seem to agree that it *was* the birthplace of the lesser copies known as dreadbeasts.

[Studies refer to an entity sealed in the labyrinth known as Subject One, though this individual's true identity is unknown. Subject One is referred to alternately as "it" and "he," implying it to possess intelligence and identity of some kind. He is always referenced in conjunction with hunger madra, and is either its source or its first host.

[Inside, we should find creations of hunger madra, as well as relics and security measures left by the Soulsmiths of old, many of which will be extraordinarily dangerous. I am reminded of the Ghostwater facility, only I will have no map and no security access. And this location is known as a labyrinth primarily due to its impossibility to navigate.]

As Lindon absorbed this information, he looked over to Eithan. "How long will it take us to get there?"

Eithan paused a moment before gesturing to the massive windows. "We're here. We don't want to head any further into Sacred Valley in case the field reactivates."

Yerin leaned closer to look into Lindon's eyes, but Lindon didn't acknowledge his own blindness. He was recovering anyway.

"All right, then let's go," Lindon said. "Without the suppression field, we should be able to move quickly. The sooner we're in and out, the better."

With luck, they could move full speed in the labyrinth. They might even be able to make it to the bottom and back up in less than a day.

Though Lindon doubted it.

[Yes, by all means let us rush headfirst into danger,] Dross said. [There is no way that it will result in all of our deaths. Ha ha.]

The delivery was so dry and toneless that it made Lindon shiver.

"Dross, you can stop that."

[I was emulating my previous persona.]

"I know. It's...unnerving."

[Acknowledged. Next time, I will attempt a more accurate impression.]

第九章

CHAPTER NINE

INFORMATION RESTRICTED: PERSONAL RECORD 1126.
AUTHORIZATION REQUIRED TO ACCESS.
AUTHORIZATION CONFIRMED: 008 OZRIEL.
BEGINNING RECORD...

The Abidan didn't know what to do with Ozmanthus Arelius.

Even his initial compatibility tests came back with unprecedented results. He had maximum potential in six of the seven Divisions. It quickly became clear that he could inherit the Mantle of any Judge.

Except one: Suriel. He had no compatibility with the Phoenix at all, as though his very existence was in opposition to the concept of restoration.

Naturally, Ozmanthus was not satisfied with these results.

He dedicated himself to fixing, building, creating, healing, and restoring. He couldn't join the Phoenix Division, but he worked with them as closely as possible. He thought that surely his skill in crafting and engineering would be his pathway forward, but when that never worked, he branched out.

He learned the arts of many worlds, took on ancient riddles, repaired governments and relationships. He lived for a time as a pacifist monk wandering the streets of Sanctum, though he quickly grew bored with that.

No matter what he did, the nature of his origin didn't change.

Not that anyone else from the Abidan minded. Warriors and killers could both be put to work in the service of order, and if Ozmanthus didn't want to bring death, there was always his other great talent of detection.

The Spider of the Abidan works to find instances of chaos and disruption among the Iterations, and to bind the Abidan together with communication. Ozmanthus joined his Third Division and was declared the successor to Telariel in record time.

In this capacity, he continued to have a special fascination with the Phoenix Division, as they were those who could do what he could not. He struck up a friendship with a woman expected to succeed the Mantle of Suriel.

She advised him not to ignore his talents. A true Phoenix would contribute to the greater cause of restoration however they could.

He kept that in mind when he and his fellow Spiders encountered a Vroshir trap.

It was an ambush intended to wipe them out. The enemy had taken over an entire Iteration, then cut it off from the Way when the Abidan arrived to investigate. Upon entry into the world, his entire team was eradicated.

Except him.

He escaped, but the disparity bothered him. With a weapon on the level of a Judge, he would have been able to defend his team, but such weapons were highly restricted and forbidden to create.

Ozmanthus began to gather materials.

He stole, unearthed, or recovered weapons of absolute destructive authority. Obsolete Judge weapons, like the prototype Razor of Suriel, and the Shears of a previous Makiel that had once snipped threads from Fate. Weapons that had been used against Judges, like the Bane of the Titan—made by the Vroshir to kill the second-generation Gadrael. Even the greatest weapons used by the Vroshir: Sha'irik, the absolute curse, and Auctarius, the Blade that Sundered Heaven.

Finally, he added his own original creation. An improved version of Penance, his old creation, the arrowhead of absolute death.

He bound these together in the depths of the Void, so far from the Way that even Fiends could not last long, in a zone of pure nonexistence and annihilation.

He forged them in the energy of a stolen Worldseed, with enough power that it could have birthed an entire Iteration.

By doing so, he indeed created a peerless weapon: a Scythe that would let him fight like a Judge. But he did not expect the recognition of the Way.

He became the avatar of true Destruction, the opposite of lost Creation. And when he was taken into custody by the Court of Seven for his creation of the Scythe, the Court was in awe.

Unwittingly, Ozmanthus had achieved a goal that the Court of Seven had pursued since antiquity. He had manifested another absolute aspect of reality. He had become the Judge of Destruction.

With the exception of Makiel, who urged that Ozmanthus be executed, the other Judges agreed that Ozmanthus should be given the mantle of the Reaper and raised up as their peer.

He was even granted a new name: Ozriel.

RECORD COMPLETE.

Back in the Ancestor's Tomb, Lindon faced the door marked with the symbols of the four Dreadgods. He still had a headache, but his vision and spiritual sense had largely returned. In fact, this was the clearest his perception had ever been in Sacred Valley, now that the suppression field was gone.

He could sense panic all over the Valley. Their spirits were weak, and their populations were depleted, but they scurried everywhere. He could sense techniques of every aspect and Path used from here all the way to the remainder of Mount Venture in the west.

Including a presence cloaked in light and dreams. Lindon turned from the door to face Elder Whisper as the fox dashed up, five tails lashing.

"What have you done?" Elder Whisper demanded.

Mercy, Yerin, Eithan, and Ziel stared at the fox. Even Orthos and Little Blue, on Lindon's shoulders, faced him down.

None of them were intentionally threatening—Eithan was unsurprised at Whisper's appearance, while Little Blue gave a little gasp, and Mercy waved—but Lindon could see the realization dawn over Elder Whisper as the sacred beast realized he was facing down a group of sacred artists far more advanced than he was.

That must have been a serious adjustment to make, after centuries of being the strongest in many miles.

"Apologies," Elder Whisper said quietly. "If you don't mind telling me, I would be grateful to learn what happened to the suppression field."

He was holding back his urgency, but he still gave a little dip of his forelegs in what could be considered a bow.

Dross manifested on Lindon's shoulder and spoke to everyone. [This is Akura clan territory. Legally, you are not obliged to answer him. In fact, with Akura Mercy here, execution would be within your rights as a Lord.]

"Why would I *execute* him, Dross?"

Dross gave a long, slow blink with his one eye. [That was a joke. Ha ha.]

Elder Whisper sank lower into the stones.

"Apologies, Elder Whisper. My mind-spirit is not himself right now. We believe someone has tampered with the structure of the labyrinth, and we're going to investigate now. But we don't expect to return until we've found Subject One."

Whisper's tails began to drift back and forth again. "That's... good. Very good. Gratitude. You have the key I gave you?"

Lindon produced the silver box containing the shriveled hand.

Elder Whisper looked from the case to Eithan's clothes, which bore the Arelius clan symbol. "I notice this one has the same symbol on his robes."

Only then did Lindon realize they had never told Elder Whisper about House Arelius. Before he could explain, Eithan swept a bow.

"Eithan Arelius, at your service," he said, though he'd met Elder Whisper before. "I am a humble scion of the ancient House Arelius, which is the symbol I bear. This key that you have shared with Lindon was once the property of my clan's leader and Monarch, Tiberian."

"Elder Whisper, we believe there may be someone else in the labyrinth," Lindon said.

Elder Whisper watched the door carefully. "I saw no one enter or leave this labyrinth since the attack of the Dreadgod. And several of these too-curious children have tried. But I cannot guard every entrance, especially now."

"Do we have time for this?" Ziel demanded. He had been dragged back from going off on his own, but every second he seemed more and more likely to walk away again.

"We don't!" Mercy said.

"Then I will leave it to you," Whisper said. "Please do what I could not."

Lindon focused on the door. "I will try. **Open.**"

He felt weaker as his will passed out of him, but the stone carving slid inward. Ziel entered without hesitation, though the power emanating from within caused everyone else to hesitate. It was the same all-consuming hunger that reminded him of the Void Icon. Identical to the aura that had flooded out the night before.

Hunger aura.

As Ziel walked inside, Yerin drew her black sword. "Oi, fox. How long does it take for a trip down there?"

"The labyrinth constantly shifts. The hand can allow you to reach the center, and it is said that those who mastered its patterns could reach the heart in a day. Those I have known spent months or even years down there, and never reached the heart. If they made it out at all."

Yerin nodded briefly. "That's about what I would have bet." She followed Ziel inside.

[The Sword Sage made it out,] Dross pointed out to Lindon. [But based on his records, he must not have gone very deep. He was also weakened severely enough to be killed by Jades.]

The suppression field is gone now, Lindon said.

[For now. And how much of his weakness was the suppression versus the constant effects of being fed upon by hunger madra?]

The yawning mouth of the labyrinth was more ominous now than it had been a moment before. Mercy took a deep breath and dove in.

Where do you put our odds of survival? Lindon asked Dross.

[It's impossible to accurately calculate odds of survival without a statistically significant number of prior examples. Under these imprecise conditions, I would say that we have better than fifty-fifty odds of making it out alive as long as we retreat before we reach the bottom.]

This isn't cheering me up.

[Was that the goal? Then cheer up.]

The complete absence of mirth in Dross' voice did not help Lindon's spirits.

Eithan threw an arm around Lindon and began to walk with him into the labyrinth. "I believe we have all been appropriately cautioned against leaving this door open for too long. Even more so since the field is down, I think."

Orthos glanced down at Eithan's arm. "*You* were eager to dive into this madness. What kind of plan do you have?"

"Plan? My plan is the same as it has always been. I planned to build up a team of those who can walk into situations like this, together, and solve the problems that no one else could." Eithan took a deep breath as they crossed the threshold into the musty air of the labyrinth, then released Lindon. "As long as we all survive this, no matter the outcome, I will consider this a successful team-building exercise."

Lindon pulled the door shut behind them. The stone slammed into place, completing a script that suddenly flared white.

Now they were sealed in.

Little Blue burbled that she didn't feel well, and even Orthos grunted. "I think these waters may be too deep for the two of us."

"Nonsense!" Eithan said. "Lindon, protect them."

Lindon had been about to open up the Dawn Sky Palace void key and hide them away when he paused. "How?"

"The same way you learned to veil them. Let your will flow along the connection of your contract, and extend it to them. Simply intending to protect them should focus the spiritual pressure of this place on you."

Lindon did as directed, and to his surprise, found it easy. Little Blue gave a relieved whistle, and Orthos examined one of his feet as though looking for signs of damage.

"That's amazing," Lindon said, sincerely impressed. "How does that work?"

"You three are bound together on an existential level. In essence, the universe considers you connected. You can work your will through them almost as easily as you could through yourself."

Lindon noted the implications of that, but the others were moving deeper into the labyrinth, so he simply nodded his thanks and moved deeper.

This room was a long hallway with rows and rows of polished wooden cupboards. All of those Lindon could see were closed and locked, but he felt nothing inside.

He still investigated a few, finding nothing useful. Some had copper rings or wooden hilts, but whatever they had once been attached to had dissolved long ago. Lindon recognized the pieces of what had once been sacred instruments; swords or spears or other devices that had rotted away.

Mercy kept her voice low, so it wouldn't echo in the long space. "We have some records of the outer layers of the labyrinth. This looks like one of the armories where the Lord-level weapons were kept."

Lindon's heart clenched at the thought of what they might have found, and even Yerin gave a disappointed sigh as she pulled off one of the doors and found nothing within.

"Too bad about that field," Yerin said in regret. "One Underlord spear would have ruled Sacred Valley for generations."

Lindon suspected that the few good things that had made it to the Heaven's Glory school had come from inside this place in some way. Even if they hadn't once been hidden in these cupboards, random junk from the people who built the labyrinth would be treasures in Sacred Valley.

"We *should* be deep enough to try the key," Eithan pointed out.

Lindon wasn't quite as optimistic. "Let's get into the next room." He wanted at least one more layer between them and the outside world before they revealed Subject One's hand.

He had to use his authority once again when they reached the end of the long hallway, and another door swung open to allow them to pass.

This time, the room more closely resembled what Lindon had expected of the labyrinth. They entered a huge sphere of smooth stone, with only three exits: the door they'd come from and two others.

Over the door they'd come from, a symbol of a sun was carved into the rock. The other two entrances also had a symbol above them. One was a hammer, identical to the one on the Forger badges. And the other...

Upon seeing it, Lindon's eyes shot to Eithan. So did Yerin's. Mercy gasped as she, too, looked to Eithan.

Only Ziel didn't immediately spin to Eithan, because he had been the first through the doorway and had been staring at Eithan the entire time.

The symbol over the second hallway was a curved crescent and the ancient characters indicating great power, just like the Arelius family crest. But there were two key differences.

For one thing, the crescent was *over* the words, instead of to the side. For another, the crescent was connected to a line running down the side. Now, it didn't look like a crescent moon at all.

It looked like the blade of a scythe.

Eithan's brow furrowed. "How unexpected," he said, in a tone that suggested it wasn't unexpected at all.

Lindon looked to the silver cube he held, which was marked with the symbol of the modern House Arelius. "Eithan. Did the Arelius clan build this labyrinth?"

[Unlikely,] Dross responded. [The ancient foundation of this facility predates the founding of the Arelius line by at least several centuries.]

"That it does," Eithan said. He drew something from his pocket and flipped it into the air so that it caught the light, which shone down from a script on the ceiling of the circular room.

It was his own marble, which contained darkness just as Suriel's contained light. It had been passed down through generations of the Arelius family.

From Ozriel. Their founder.

"Ozmanthus Arelius, the original Patriarch of our clan, was known as the greatest Soulsmith of his day," Eithan explained. "Perhaps in history. *That* was his personal crest, which was eventually adapted into the symbol of our House."

"Did you know he'd signed his name down here?" Yerin asked.

"I had hoped we'd see something of his, though I'm surprised we came across it so soon. It's my understanding that he left his mark on most Soulsmith relics of his era all over the world. He was a busy man."

And Lindon knew that he'd stayed busy even after ascending, becoming the Abidan known as Ozriel. Judging by the message he'd left in Eithan's marble, Ozriel at least seemed to be an ally to Suriel, though Lindon couldn't be sure about their relative ranks.

"Let's see what he left," Mercy said, but Lindon stopped her by speaking.

"We should check with our key first. Prepare yourselves."

He had to calm his own spirit as he focused on the case he held. Exposing the hand before had been an overwhelming experience, and he was frightened to do it here in the labyrinth.

Yerin's red-tinted sword-arms spread out behind her, and Mercy shifted Suu into the form of a bow. Ziel opened his void key—which, strangely, seemed to take longer than usual—and withdrew his massive steel hammer. Eithan began playing with his pair of dark fabric scissors.

Orthos cycled Blackflame, and Little Blue punched her left palm.

"Open," Lindon commanded once again.

The silver metal bloomed like a steel flower, revealing a gruesome, mummified left hand of chalk-white flesh.

Worse was the aura that boiled out. It made Lindon feel like he was starving, like he was empty, *lacking* in every sense. The air warped, twisting like they were at the center of an invisible whirlpool. Even the walls bent inward.

Everything faded, leaving the hand as the only real thing in the world. It was a fragment of another will, the strongest existence here, the pulsing heart at the center of the labyrinth. Subject One.

Lindon forced his will against the hand, controlling it as he would a construct. But unlike a construct, the hand fought back.

Its fingers squirmed and lunged, trying to escape his grip, and a high-pitched howl echoed through the stone halls. The hand tried to command the labyrinth to take it away, to escape.

But Lindon was in charge.

If it were the full Dreadgod, he would have stood no chance. Over a long-separated hand, though, Lindon's willpower won out. The fingers went limp as the hand gave up... and then Lindon felt his authority expand.

It wasn't the same as his relationship with an Icon; it felt more like his bond with his Remnant arm. Like a new part grafted onto his spirit. Except instead of a prosthetic limb, it was a piece of the labyrinth.

He could feel this hallway, and the rooms ahead. He sensed the flows of power, and which way led forward.

"This way," Lindon said.

Then Subject One's anger crashed into him, and he staggered. The imprisoned Dreadgod was distant and weakened, but Lindon felt its will. It was furious that someone had dared to usurp its authority...and now it wanted to make them prey.

The ground erupted beneath their feet.

Gray-white hunger madra lurched upward from the stone, grabbing for ankles. They all reacted at once.

Yerin leaped upward as her sword rang out, shredding the hands. Mercy's feet were covered to the ankles by greaves of purple crystal, and she spun her bow around her in a blurring circle. Pure madra rushed away from Eithan's feet, brushing away the hands like water clearing away paint. Ziel simply let them grab his ankles, then Forged a ring of shining green runes around him. A moment later, force crushed the hands against the stone as though gravity had been increased.

Lindon's attention was taken by the hand, but he still extended the Hollow Domain around him. A sphere of blue-white madra pushed several feet out from his body, dispersing the spirits of hunger madra. Including their true bodies, which waited underground.

Around everyone but Eithan and Lindon, bodies followed the hands. These were skeletal ghouls of hunger madra, their jaws hanging down to their chests. They howled as though trying to inhale their meals as they rose from the stone, lunging for everyone else.

They were still outclassed. This was only a distant projection of Subject One's anger, a disdainful slap. The deeper they traveled, the more control the imprisoned Dreadgod would have.

Everyone in the room handled the ghouls in a moment, even as Lindon sealed the desiccated hand back into its silver casing.

When the brief battle was over, hunger madra dissolved all over the room. Lindon initially intended to collect this madra to rebuild his arm, but none of this had been properly Forged. These were effectively Striker techniques given mobility and the faint will to feed.

Yerin scuffed her shoe on the stone and spoke scornfully. "Not much security."

"Recall that they would normally be acting against victims under the effects of the suppression field," Eithan pointed out. "They would be suppressed as well, but when both sides are down to Jade, losing even a bit of your madra can be deadly. Speaking of which, how are you holding up, Ziel?"

Lindon had noticed the same thing. By letting one of the animated techniques touch him, Ziel had given up part of his power. The ghouls were some version of his own Consume technique, so they would drain more than madra.

Ziel looked disgusted more than weakened. "Lost a little madra, a little soulfire, maybe some blood aura. Feels gross."

"One brush shouldn't be too bad," Lindon said. "But it will add up. If they can move through the walls, we should protect ourselves."

Glowing script-circles appeared around Ziel's ankles, and he heaved the hammer onto his shoulder. "Great. Now that we know what we're up against, let's pick up the pace."

Lindon moved his spiritual perception forward, just like everyone else. It wasn't too far to the next room, and while he couldn't pierce the walls with his senses, he had no problem feeling the next room.

Lindon nodded.

As one, the entire group vanished.

From the other side of the continent, Malice felt power erupting from the western labyrinth.

She sent messages to her forces arrayed all around the Blackflame Empire. She had people closer than anyone else. She'd be in control of the situation before anyone else could sense it and react.

Not long after, her agents began speaking her name with intention. Their will focused on her, drawing her perception. She couldn't exactly hear what they were saying to her—she wasn't an Arelius—but she felt their desire to contact her and a touch of their desperate anxiety.

She abandoned Moongrave.

When she stepped out of the Way a moment later, she was within sight of Sacred Valley.

And what she saw made her livid.

The island of the Silent Servants, with its shining white tree, drifted just outside the eastern mountain. Both shared a white halo of crystallized light madra, though other aspects had been sneaking into the one around Mount Samara.

Beside the northern peak floated the great ship of Redmoon Hall, the pyramid of Abyssal Palace rolled in on flying stones to the west, and a serpentine raincloud held the Stormcallers to the south.

The four cults loomed over Sacred Valley. Many of them still bore marks of their fight with Fury—Abyssal Palace had a huge chunk missing and was listing to one side—but their leaders were still in fighting shape. Malice's perception was somewhat blunted by scripts inside the Redmoon Hall vessel, but she thought she sensed Red Faith in there as well.

These cults arriving so quickly meant they *knew* this was going to happen. They *knew* the suppression field script around the Valley was going to be inverted, meaning they had one of their most advanced sacred artists inside the labyrinth. Maybe Shen himself.

Instead of a desert of aura, Sacred Valley now *gushed* with power...but so much of it was hunger. Dreadbeasts would be born or empowered every second. The land around the labyrinth was like a slowly erupting volcano.

"I have to thank you," Malice whispered into the air. The newly refreshed aura carried her words to the cults. "It's not so often I'm given such a fine excuse."

She drew her crystalline bow and used its binding to Forge a matching arrow onto the string. Air rippled as the fabric of the world was warped by the power she invested into the arrow, and she let it loose casually in the direction of Abyssal Palace.

See if their Herald could stop that. Even if he did, there were more arrows where that one came from.

An arrow flew from the island of the Silent Servants, striking her own in midair.

The collision of the two missiles created a thunderous detonation of light, which whipped up a hurricane and darkened the sky. Even the island was pushed back.

Malice's mood soured even further.

"What a wonderful veil you have," she said, and this time she didn't enhance her voice with aura at all.

Miles away, a blonde woman in golden armor strode out onto the edge of the Silent Servants' island. Larian of the Eight-Man Empire rapped her knuckles on her own breastplate. "Wish I could take credit for it, but I'm more about hitting things with sticks from very far away."

"So you have chosen to side with the beasts, then. Curious. I thought you liked being on the winning team."

Larian leaned on her bow, which looked to the mortal eye to be made of twisted gray driftwood. "The 'human versus beasts' line doesn't work without the dragon around, you know. It's not like all of us are human anyway. Besides, you know why we're doing this." Her voice sharpened. "The Monarchs are the only ones who benefit from the system the way it is. It's about time we shake things up."

Malice itched to beat some sense into this shortsighted

Sage, but no one on the Path of the Eightfold Spear traveled alone.

Sure enough, seven other presences removed their veils all around Sacred Valley. The Eight-Man Empire was here in full, surrounding Sacred Valley.

"You think Shen is going to change things?" Malice asked softly. "He will never do anything that costs him power."

Larian shrugged. "We're not like the rest of you; we don't need an ironclad plan before we'll put one foot in front of the other. Any change is better than none."

"Beautiful. So noble of you to be involved to change the world, and not for any sordid material motives."

"Malice, he paid us so *much*." Larian staggered under the invisible weight of a fortune, only her bow keeping her upright. "We were going to say no at first, but then he just kept bringing out *more* and *more*. I felt bad! I said, 'Reigan, how are you going to feed your people if you give us all this?' He didn't even say anything, he just kept dumping treasures into this big pile.

"Priceless art? Right onto the pile. Gold? Pile. Scales? Weapons? Natural treasures? Pile. By the time he was done, I swear on my heart, it was taller than my head. Best day of my life."

Larian sighed fondly. "So anyway, we can't let him down after all that, right?"

From the lands all around the valley, war-bands of the Eight-Man Empire raised their banners. Not crude constructions of cloth and wood, but projections of symbols made of Forged madra. Ghost-Blade, Nine-Hands, Flame-Gift, Blood-Chorus...each of the eight wandering mercenary armies that made up the Eight-Man Empire's workforce was arrayed against her.

Malice had sensed them already, but without closer inspection, had taken them to be the forces of House Shen. The war-bands averaged one Archlord, a handful of Overlords, and two or three dozen Underlords apiece, so only when they were gathered in one place could they possibly face down a Monarch's forces. Just like the Eight-Man Empire themselves.

But this only stoked her rage hotter, because the presence of the Empire's armies meant two things. First, that Reigan Shen had devoted staggering resources to bring so many people so far. Second, that House Shen was still unaccounted for.

He had presumably kept his own forces in reserve to defend his territory, but she would know soon. Her subordinates were on their way to the Rosegold continent already.

Malice gave the gathered horde an icy once-over. "To think he would empty his treasury to bring such an army here."

"I told you! He's invested." Larian pulled her bow from the ground and gestured with it. "So are you going to let this happen, or do you want to make us earn our keep?"

Miles behind Malice, the unaffiliated experts of the Wasteland received her transmitted message and removed their veils. Three Heralds, a Sage, and five ancient Archlords. From the other side of Sacred Valley, Charity cycled her own madra, and several Herald-level spirits shone like bonfires as well—living weapons of the Akura clan.

At a glance, Malice's own forces were lacking. She had fewer Sages and fewer Heralds.

Then again, the Eight-Man Empire couldn't really be counted as a collection of Sages and Heralds, but as one Monarch. And these were Malice's lands. Not only could she draw upon more forces than the enemy, she had other resources to play.

And she could call Northstrider.

Larian sighed. "I don't suppose you'd consider settling our differences with a series of duels, would you?"

Malice tapped her bloodline legacy so that her eyes shone, and she radiated shadow aura to blacken the sky. "Invaders, hear me! You have trespassed on Akura lands. Withdraw, or your blood will flow like water."

"Guess the fight will come down to Golds, then," Larian said. "At least it is a good cause, in the end." Then she shed her casual appearance and adopted a manner more befitting a self-respecting Sage. "Long-Sight!"

The Long-Sight war-band, beneath their banner of a bow and an eye, gave a shout and a pulse of spiritual power that shook the ground.

Far away, a different voice shouted. "Ghost-Blade!"

The Ghost-Blade war-band answered their leader, and another cry went up from another member of the Eight-Man Empire.

"Blood-Chorus!"

"Flame-Gift!"

"Green-Stride!"

The war-bands of the Eight-Man Empire sounded like the footsteps of the Wandering Titan as they answered their leaders.

And soon, if Malice didn't stop them, they would hear the Titan's *actual* footsteps once again. Reigan Shen had often claimed he wanted to call the Dreadgods together to destroy them and make them into weapons. Even if that were true, it would ruin her lands.

So she would crack open this formation and destroy Shen's plans, even if she had to drown them in blood.

第十章

CHAPTER TEN

Lindon could best describe the next room as a "hall of hammers."

It was a stone cellar, and very recently, the walls had been lined with wooden shelves and racks. He had to piece that together, because now the room was strewn with splinters. Someone had clearly done battle here, and recently, though the stone of the walls was unharmed.

Before that battle, the racks and walls of the room had been filled with hammers. Lindon was certain only because some pieces remained.

As they entered, he had to step over a hammer with a head that looked like it was made of dark purple glass. It still leaked sparks of pink essence from a crack. A pile of broken hammers lay in the corners, where they had been discarded, and a few had been crushed while still strapped to a rack.

Those same racks were all over the room, empty, and Lindon noticed evidence that they had been occupied recently.

"Dross," Lindon said aloud.

[Yes?]

"...what do you think about this situation?" Lindon had thought that question would go without asking.

[This room was recently the repository for sacred instruments. All, or most, hammers. Most likely the intact instruments were looted after the battle.]

Yerin nudged a pile of rubble aside with her foot. "Wake me when we find a room like this for swords."

Orthos had already hopped off of Lindon's shoulder and started munching at a defunct hammer.

"Stop that," Lindon said. "That could be a thousand years old."

Orthos met Lindon's eyes and deliberately took another bite.

Eithan skipped to the middle of the room, then twirled in place. "Ah, I see, I see. Well, this is a disappointment. This is all quite ancient by modern standards, of course, but none of it dates back to our first Patriarch. They must have removed any of his relics when they first arrived."

[I know little about the Arelius founder. You should tell me more, so that I may form a more accurate picture of our situation.]

Lindon knelt for one of the hammers and ran his fingers across it. He could sense its madra composition just as easily standing, but there was something more immediate about feeling it himself.

"These aren't hunger madra," he noted. He had hoped to find some materials to upgrade his arm here. As it was, he was reluctant to use the Consume technique at all, since the binding was always on the verge of breaking again.

Eithan slapped his forehead. "Ah, that's right! I forgot we had neglected that aspect of your education. You see, these are Soulsmith hammers."

Lindon stared blankly around the room. He had used hammers in Soulsmithing before. They were only used to physically batter certain stubborn types of dead matter into place, or to crack open a Remnant's carapace.

There didn't seem to be any reason to store a massive variety of sacred instruments for such a simple task. And all those that remained were broken, so there wasn't much else to learn.

"Oh," Lindon said. He stood, ready to move on.

"I hear from your lack of enthusiasm that you don't know what that means. Well, ahem, you see, there is a *reason* why hammers are often associated with Soulsmiths besides the use of hammers in more mundane smithing."

Mercy hopped from one foot to another. She looked between the three exits in the room. "Yes, this is fascinating, but don't you think we could scoop everything into a void key and move on?"

Ziel jerked a thumb toward her. "We can have the history lesson on the way. I don't know why we would...what do you have there?"

Orthos had pulled a huge pile of wood and debris away from the wall, then ignited a smoky red flame so he could examine something around the base of the wall.

Ziel edged closer, and they both examined what appeared to be a barely visible line of inactive script.

"So this goes to the outer boundary of the room..." Ziel murmured, tracing a line of script with his finger.

"What does it do?" Orthos asked.

Lindon longed to go over and take a look for himself, but Eithan was gesturing him over to the other side of the room to show him a mostly intact hammer.

"Once upon a time," Eithan said, "the tool you used for your Soulsmithing was as important as the material you used. It was said that our Patriarch could make a weapon fit for a Sage with just his hammer and a Gold Remnant. The hammer is used to inject your will into an object, shaping its function according to your intentions. And each hammer has its own specialty, some being better for crafting weapons, some made for altering dream tablets, and so on."

Pink sparks flew up from the cracked hammerhead as Eithan spun it between his fingers. Lindon examined it, intrigued.

"So what did this one do?"

"Difficult to tell now, but you can sense the dream madra as well as I can."

Lindon had the vague sense that this hammer had once been used to shape memories. If he had to guess, he would say that it was made to alter dreams from their natural form, modifying them.

As Lindon looked over the collection of hammers, he started to understand. And new libraries of possibility opened up to him.

"I see. It's only useful to Soulsmiths who can directly manipulate their willpower. So only Lords."

As Lindon was lost in the possibilities of Soulsmithing, he overheard Yerin talking to Mercy. "You think we should pick a hallway and leave them behind?"

"We *really* don't want to get lost in here. But if we stay in here too long, that's what's going to happen!"

Lindon dragged himself out of his trance and snatched up the most intact hammers. He tossed them into his void key... which took a moment longer than usual to open. He would have to check its script.

From his pocket, he withdrew the case containing the white hand.

"Apologies. I'm ready to go."

"It's a pity," Eithan said, as Lindon readied the hand. "I was really hoping to find some Arelius relics here. But if there were any, they were taken."

Everyone present knew that someone had fought in here, and it was probably the same one who had deactivated the suppression field.

There were no traces of the intruder's madra left, or at least none that could be sensed compared to the leaking and broken hammers. This battle had taken place days ago, or maybe weeks.

If everything went according to plan, they would eventually run into this person. So there was no point speculating.

It was time to move on.

This time, when Lindon revealed the hand, all the uncontrolled power in the room flowed toward him immediately as the hunger devoured it. The hand twisted in his grip as it fed, and a howl echoed through the room.

Instead of ghouls rising through the floor, this time strands of Forged madra—like Mercy's Strings of Shadow technique—shot from each wall and webbed up the entire room.

In the first instant, they were all on their guard. Each of them dodged or blocked strands shooting out from the walls, and they ended up separated by webs of hunger madra.

For a breath or two afterwards, they all waited for the next part of the trap.

Finally, Eithan cleared his throat. "I guess this one is free."

The borrowed authority of Subject One pulled Lindon toward the door on the left wall, so he sealed the hand back in its metal case before unleashing a Hollow Domain with a wisp of soulfire.

The blue-white sphere filled the room, wiping out all the hunger madra. Each strand resisted a little, holding a small amount of will behind it, but the entire room was clear in a moment.

"Ten scales if somebody can tell me what the point to that technique was," Yerin said.

"I don't think that was a conscious attack," Lindon responded. It was just a gut feeling, but he thought he was probably right.

Orthos grunted. "It feels like something stirring in its sleep. I don't like it."

Little Blue shuddered as she made a tinkling sound in agreement, snuggling closer to Lindon's neck.

"I suspect these are indeed instinctive defensive reactions," Eithan said. "Like scratching at an itch while you sleep. But attacks of this level would never trouble someone like the Sword Sage, even taking the suppression field into account."

Ziel pushed himself up from the ground, rolling up a tiny scroll. He had copied some of the runes himself. "It's definitely going to get stronger. Let's get deeper while we're still fresh."

"Thank you!" Mercy cried. "Whatever we do, we need to *move*."

Lindon nodded and led the way to the tunnel the hand had indicated.

Until the tunnel vanished.

He sensed something, and it felt similar to the substance he pushed through to create a portal. Like he was feeling the fabric of space itself.

Now there was only a blank stretch of wall where a tunnel had been a moment before.

Everyone except Lindon and Eithan put their guard up at the sudden shift, including Little Blue. Lindon looked around for the entrances; if they had *all* vanished, they were going to need to find a way to break through this stone before they died here.

There were still two entrances left. The hall they'd come from had vanished, just like the one they had been headed into. Now there was one entrance against the right wall, and one in the *ceiling.*

The ceiling tunnel was marked with the image of a coiled, serpentine dragon, and the entrance in the right wall bore another symbol of the Arelius Patriarch.

Ziel leaned against his hammer and sighed. "They can manipulate space. Great. I should have known."

"Think of it this way," Eithan said. "We have so much to learn!"

Once more, Lindon brought out the hand.

In the headquarters of the Twin Star Sect, on the edge of Serpent's Grave, Jai Long completed his morning cycling. This aura chamber was perfect for him, having once belonged to the Jai clan; it was filled with glowing blades that saturated the air with the power of light and swords.

He couldn't replenish the animating force of the snake that brought all his techniques to life, but that resource seemed inexhaustible. Jai Long only wished it would one day leave his madra, no matter that his entire fighting style was now based around it.

He wrapped the bands of scripted red cloth around his face with practiced motions before he unlocked the chamber door, and found Wei Shi Kelsa waiting for him on the other side.

Just like the rest of her family, she was tall and intense, but where Lindon tended to look like he was contemplating a murder, Kelsa gave off the impression that she was always giving you one hundred percent of her attention. No matter what was happening.

"Kelsa. Is something wrong?"

"I thought you might want to train together," she said. A fox's tail of purple-white foxfire lashed behind her. Her Goldsign.

She saw him glance at it, and her gaze darkened. "I still hate it."

"It could be worse," Jai Long said.

"It's not practical, even if it can burn people. Snowfoxes have claws and teeth. I could have gotten those."

Jai Long began to walk away from the Stellar Spear aura chamber, and she fell into step beside him. As every morning, there was a decent-sized crowd on the path leading to the various aura chambers. Morning cycling was a common practice.

"Not every Goldsign is practical."

"Why not? It isn't fair that some people should have extra weapons growing from their body, while others have useless decorations."

"Even without Goldsigns, some people have longer reach with their swords, or learn techniques faster. The world isn't fair."

Jai Long had bitterly resented the unfairness of Goldsigns for years, so he had accepted the truth of it more thoroughly than anyone else.

Kelsa scowled about it, though she didn't argue. It was a mark of her familiarity with him that she was complaining about this to his face at all; shortly after her advancement, she hadn't said a negative word about his Goldsign for fear of offending him.

He didn't mind. If anything, having the worst Goldsign in the world made him empathize more.

"You didn't answer me," she said abruptly. "Do you want to train together?"

"Why do you have to make it a formal invitation? It doesn't make much difference if we train together or separately." There was enough of a gap in their advancement, and enough of a difference in their Paths, that there weren't many benefits they could offer one another.

"It's romantic," she responded. Jai Long missed a step, but she gave him a confused look. "What? I told you I was interested in you."

"People don't normally do that," he said. Not just say exactly what they meant with zero subtlety, but also express interest in him. No one had done that since he had botched his advancement to Lowgold when he was a child.

"Most people like to waste time."

Jai Long had a knot of complicated emotions to untangle, but he knew how to control himself under pressure. And he *was* interested. Potentially.

"If you wanted to spend some time together, we don't have to train. There's a new—"

"What do you mean?" she interrupted. "Training together is romantic."

Jai Long stared blankly at her. Training was boring and repetitive work.

As he did, he felt a light touch brush across his perception, and he realized there had been a web of madra strands observing him for a while.

He glanced to his left and saw his sister smiling as she walked up to him. Fingerling was coiled onto her shoulder. She dipped her head as she reached Kelsa.

"Apologies," Jai Chen said, which made Jai Long think they'd been around the people of Sacred Valley for too long. "I didn't mean to eavesdrop."

Kelsa looked from her to Jai Long, studying his eyes. "Your brother doesn't think training together is romantic."

"It isn't," he said.

"Jai Chen, what do you think?"

His sister cupped her chin and gave the question far more consideration than it deserved. "I could see that, I think. It's personal, intimate. One-on-one. You'd have to be with the right person, though."

Kelsa looked to him triumphantly, but now he only thought they were *both* crazy. He may have been out of his depth with this subject, but he had observed others. Training was just...work.

Unwittingly, he thought of Lindon. The twenty-year-old Sage who used his free time to train more.

Maybe something ran in the family.

Jai Chen gave a sharp gasp, and he immediately stretched his perception out to her. Even with the support of the sect, she'd had a difficult time reaching Lowgold. There weren't any Remnants with her unique blend of aspects, not to mention any appropriate scales.

But since she had, her detection web had become easier to use and far more efficient. As a Truegold, his spiritual perception was naturally far beyond hers, but she could sense physical changes far faster than he could.

It didn't take long before everyone saw what she had. A thin pillar of shadow stretched into the sky behind Jai Long. He couldn't feel it with his perception—it was veiled somehow, or maybe just beyond his ability to detect—but he certainly felt the power of the one stepping through it.

Underlord.

So this was a portal of some kind. Without discussion, the three pushed toward the black beam stretching into the sky. Of course, they weren't the only ones.

And a moment later, that was proved unnecessary, as a Truegold woman in the green armor of the Skysworn drifted up on a Thousand-Mile Cloud. The Underlord, whoever it was, remained on the ground.

A green construct flashed in front of the Skysworn's mouth, and her voice echoed over the crowd. "By the order of the Blackflame Emperor, and with the support of the Akura clan, every combat-capable sacred artist of Lowgold or higher is commanded to report to the Skysworn immediately for inspection and possible transfer to battle."

Jai Long felt a chill. The pillar of shadow was still there, which meant they might see combat *today.* A small army of clerks and administrators from the Blackflame Empire was flooding out of the portal now, already shouting orders and organizing those they could reach.

He straightened his spine. "Stick with me. They'll evaluate us together."

He was certain the other two wouldn't pass the Empire's examination. They were both newly advanced to Lowgold, neither were ranked on any of the combat lists, and they both had Paths better suited to support.

It was easy for those in a large clan or powerful sect to forget, but most sacred artists were not dedicated to combat and advancement. A practitioner of illusion techniques, like the Path of the White Fox, was far more common as a teacher, artist, or messenger than a fighter. Not only was raising a real warrior a commitment of time and difficult training, but it was expensive.

As expected, most of the Lowgolds—and even a large chunk of the Highgolds—he saw lined up in front of the Blackflame clerks were quickly turned away. But not as many as he expected.

It was an hour before they were seen, and Jai Long didn't even get an examination. A Lowgold sensed his power and the soulfire in his spirit, bowed, and presented him with a chip of cheap metal that had 'Peak Truegold' stamped on it.

"Sect, school, or clan?" the clerk asked. He was respectful, but it had the tone of a question he'd asked a thousand times already.

"Sect of Twin Stars," Jai Long said. Those words sounded strange to his own ears.

The clerk dutifully marked it down before asking for his name, age, and Path.

"As a peak Truegold, you'll be a squad leader," the clerk explained. "Wait in the designated area for your squad to be assigned to you. It's usually three Highgolds and five Lowgolds, but it depends on who we get."

Jai Long saw a squad matching that description pass into a nearby tent from which no one had returned. Another portal, presumably. "Loading us out quickly."

"Emperor's orders." The clerk clearly wanted him to move on, but Jai Long looked over to Jai Chen and Kelsa, who were being examined nearby. A woman was poking Fingerling with a drudge shaped like a spiky ball while a man watched Kelsa demonstrate her techniques.

Jai Long pointed to one, then the other. "*That* is my sister, and she's not a fighter, so I want her off the list. *That* one is, but she's an illusion artist, so I want her in my squad."

The clerk scribbled a note. "If your sister passes the examination, she'll be fighting, I'm sorry. But I can arrange to have them both assigned to you, unless there's someone higher-ranked who wants them."

"Underlords won't be fighting over Lowgolds."

The clerk, a Lowgold himself, chuckled nervously at the words of a peak Truegold. "Heavens know that's true."

"Where are we fighting?"

As expected, the clerk didn't know.

To Jai Long's dismay, his sister passed the examination as a fighter. As did Kelsa, but he had expected that. If she had claimed to be an entertainer or even lamplighter, they would probably have believed her, but she would have certainly asked to fight.

He was assigned three Highgolds and another pair of Lowgolds. At first scan, none of them were impressive.

But they all stood stiffly and silently as he watched them, frightened of his attention. Except for his sister, who looked terrified—just not of him—and Kelsa, who scanned the situation herself with unrelieved intensity.

"Can we not tell our families where we're going?" she asked him, voice low.

"You can leave a message with one of the clerks," Jai Long told her, "but I've never seen anything like this before. If it's such an emergency, why do they need so many Lowgolds?"

This kind of rushed recruitment reminded him of a clan scraping up all its disciples to defend against a sudden raid, but that was only necessary when the experts were already occupied. The Emperor—an Overlord—could obliterate every Gold here with a wave of his hand.

Which meant that, wherever they were headed, the most advanced sacred artists were either absent or countered.

Their squad was waved through quickly, and he found them ushered into a tent taken up almost entirely by a shimmering doorframe that led onto another bustling camp far away.

He couldn't tell *how* far, but the woman sweating and loading scales into the doorframe was an Underlord. And she wasn't Forging the scales, either; they were coming from a scripted case at her side, and the madra shining from the purple-black scales was so intense that he had to close off his spiritual sense.

A Truegold attendant waved them through, and as the leader and most advanced member of his party, he stepped through first.

His heart dropped in an instant.

Even surrounded by a crowd of strangers, he recognized where they were immediately. The trees were black, the buildings were temporary, and the mountain looming in the far distance had a halo around its peak.

"We can't get away," Jai Long muttered. "There is no escape."

They were heading back to Sacred Valley.

This time, when the labyrinth shifted, the tunnel opened over Lindon's head and pointed straight upward. There was no ladder, but it wasn't as though Lindon needed one.

He and Yerin leaped. They didn't know exactly how high it was, but it didn't matter much. If they started running out of momentum, they could leap off the walls.

It didn't come to that. Lindon's jump carried him into a huge, empty room that reminded him of an arena. Yerin hit the ceiling, far overhead, and had to push off. Orthos grumbled about the trip and demanded that Lindon put him down, while Little Blue cheered at the thrill.

Mercy was right behind them, pulling her way up with Strings of Shadow, and Ziel hopped up on discs of Forged runes.

To Lindon's surprise, the last one up was Eithan. He pulled himself up the last few feet rather gracelessly, but he salvaged it by striking a pose when he made it all the way up.

"This isn't fair," he said. "You all know Enforcer techniques are my weakness. That, and fine imported silk."

[These weaknesses have been logged for future reference,] Dross said dutifully.

Eithan looked startled.

Lindon had already started glancing around the room. What he had first taken for rows of seats were coffins, each carved with the image of a dragon. They were all very different in appearance—from four-legged dragons with wings spread to serpentine dragons with claws—and each was set with colored gemstones that would likely have matched what color the dragon was in life.

He sensed very little power coming from inside any of these coffins, but several had been opened, presumably to remove any treasures. He glanced inside, just in case, but found only a dragon's skeleton.

Ziel only examined the script-circles around the room for a second before he said, "Death aura."

Lindon had assumed as much. There were only a few reasons to collect corpses in a place like this labyrinth, and "honoring the dead" was probably the least likely. This had once been the place to generate death aura and funnel it away to some project.

Though, like all the other aura in the place, it had been consumed by hunger.

Lindon started to open the hand, ready to move on, when Eithan stopped him.

"There's no exit," Eithan pointed out.

Lindon saw he was right. The only way out was the entrance through which they'd come.

"All right," Mercy said, "back down!"

She made as though to leap down the hole, but Lindon had unraveled the case around the hand already. Hunger filled the room, and he sensed immediately where to go. It was a hallway sealed behind a blank stretch of wall.

No enemy techniques struck at them this time, but it still left them in a quandary. Yerin sat down immediately, arms crossed.

"Bet my sword against a fingernail there's about to be a door there."

Mercy took several deep breaths, calming herself. "You're right. I know you're right, but...we're going so *slow.*"

"I'm just as worried about going too fast," Lindon said. "We want to know what we're walking into." He didn't mind the chance to explore the room some more, so after packing away the hand, he immediately checked the entire room. By looking to Eithan.

Instantly, Eithan pointed to a corner of the room. "An unfortunate previous explorer. Left some records. Could be a map."

Lindon crossed the space in one leap, landing on the highest tier around the outside wall. A skeleton huddled there, in between heavy stone coffins that had been dragged around to make a makeshift fortress. Old scripts had been painted around him, though they were faded with time.

Orthos scurried up to the skeleton, pulling out a scrap of paper that had been tucked away in the would-be tomb robber's clothes.

Lindon focused his perception on the rest of the body, trying to sense anything with even a trace of power, but either the years or other explorers had taken everything of value.

Meanwhile, Orthos was reading the paper.

"He was writing a warning to a team coming after him," Orthos rumbled. "He warns against a guardian. He says it has powers beyond his understanding, and calls it...a baby Dreadgod. The Tomb Hydra."

Unwilling to rely solely on his spiritual sense, Lindon had been flipping through the dead man's pockets with his hand. After he flipped open the front of the man's robes, his fingers stopped.

The skeleton was wearing a badge. A white badge.

Unlike Lindon's, this one was carved with the symbol of a cloud, but quick inspection revealed this to be winter-steel-plated bronze. If Lindon understood Eithan's history lesson correctly, that meant this man had been a Sage.

Orthos snorted smoke over the document. "His power was weighed down by the field. We won't be as weak as he was."

Lindon hesitated, halfway between pocketing this badge. Had Orthos not seen it? Did he not realize how advanced this sacred artist had been?

"Orthos..."

"I saw it," the turtle said.

Lindon nodded and slipped the badge into his pocket. There was no need to ask if Eithan had seen it; indeed, the Archlord was already calling out to the rest of the room.

"It seems we're about to reach a guardian known as the Tomb Hydra, powerful enough to cause a Sage to tremble in fear, and likened to a Dreadgod. Probably not without cause, given that somewhere in here is the birthplace of the Dreadgods. Who's frightened?"

Lindon wished he had his right arm at full capacity, but he wasn't *frightened*.

Mercy shrugged.

Yerin brightened, her crimson eyes sparkling. "You're thinking we get a real fight?"

"The suppression field worked on everything," Ziel pointed out. "It shouldn't be able to take us at full power unless it's a *real* Dreadgod. Then we're dead."

Dross materialized in front of Lindon again, his color still too pale and washed-out. [It is good to be optimistic. You will perform better if your spirits are up. But defeat here is not the greatest risk. We should consider the fact that any madra or soulfire we expend in this battle will be difficult, if not impossible, to replace. Our power is finite.]

Everyone grew more grim, except Eithan, who beamed at Dross. "Thank you for reintroducing some tension to the situation, Dross!"

[You're welcome. Ha ha.]

The fake laugh told Lindon that Dross thought he'd told a joke, but Lindon wasn't sure which part the joke was supposed to be.

Space shifted again, and suddenly there was an opening in front of Yerin. She shot to her feet as deadly green-black aura blew out of the tunnel like a toxic wind.

It battered at her lifeline, but Lindon wasn't concerned about her. She was a Herald now; aura of this level wouldn't be able to touch her unless she lived in it for years. He was more concerned for Mercy, and he moved to stand in front of her. He reinforced his protection of Orthos and Little Blue as he did so.

Mercy gave him a grateful smile. "Thanks! I can handle it for a while, but I'd rather be in combat shape."

Lindon nodded back and headed into a tunnel marked with a pair of crossed swords. And toward the monster that waited there.

"Good thing it hasn't attacked us yet!" Eithan shouted.

It immediately attacked.

第十一章

CHAPTER ELEVEN

From deep in the tunnel that crawled with death aura, a beam of pale, sickly green light blasted toward Lindon and the others. It tore through the air, filled with malevolent will-power, pressing heavy against Lindon's Sage senses like one of the Wandering Titan's casual attacks.

Everyone had techniques ready to defend themselves, but Yerin met the attack first. She stood in front, her scarlet sword-arms extended, the black sword Netherclaw in both hands. It shone with a silver-red light as she used the weapon Enforcer technique of her Path: the Flowing Sword.

The beam of condensed death madra crashed into the tip of her sword and splintered, smaller beams breaking off and scouring the walls. Any living thing would be annihilated by that Striker technique, but the stones were not only enforced with authority, but they were also *stones*. The death madra was harmless.

Yerin's lock of red hair whipped in the wind caused by the clash between their techniques, but she didn't take a step backwards. She pushed forward a step, shoving against the enemy technique.

When the beam of death faded, Yerin pulled her sword back.

"See how you like it," she muttered.

And she responded in kind.

A gleaming beam of red-white light shot down the tunnel, lighting everything crimson. Her focused will to destroy pushed against Lindon's mind, and he suspected Orthos and Little Blue wouldn't have even been able to stand this close to the technique without his protection.

From the other end of the tunnel, they heard a monstrous scream.

"Wonder what that was," Eithan said brightly.

It took them two seconds to clear the long tunnel.

The Tomb Hydra waited at the end of the hall, in a room that reminded Lindon of a honeycomb. It was spherical, like many of the other rooms they had encountered so far, but this time virtually every stretch of wall was filled with tunnel after tunnel. You could barely see any wall between all the doors, heading in every direction.

And many of *those* were hidden behind the Hydra's massive body.

It was a wall of gray-green scales that wrapped around the entire room, dwarfing them many times over. Its eyes blazed like lanterns of pale, deadly green...all six of them.

One of the Tomb Hydra's three heads roared at Yerin, clearly enraged by the bloody cut her technique had gouged in its jaw. The other two spread out, leaning their necks around to get a better vantage point on the rest of the party.

But no one was waiting around for that to happen.

Blackflame roared from Lindon's hand, empowered with soulfire. A hail of violet arrows erupted from Mercy's bow. Orthos breathed flame, Eithan called stars down on each of the Hydra's heads, and Ziel's body began to shine bright emerald as he picked up his hammer.

The Hydra sent out a wave of death madra, but it still screamed from three throats as the barrage of techniques tore its body apart.

Not as much as it *should* have been torn apart, though.

Lindon's Blackflame didn't carve the Hydra down to the bone or melt through its scales, but rather scorched it like a superficial burn. Yerin's Endless Sword left deep grooves spraying blood, but didn't sever a head. Mercy's arrows stuck in the scales and did nothing. Eithan's stars passed into the Hydra's spirit but didn't come out the other side, indicating they hadn't speared through it.

And in the same instant, its body uncoiled. It whipped at them, a wall of scales and muscle, forcing them all to take to the air.

One head shot toward Lindon and Mercy, one snapped at Ziel and Yerin, and the third lunged at Eithan.

At the same time, and at the worst possible moment, webs of hunger madra shot out of the tunnels from every direction. There was a distinct will behind these attacks, and Lindon knew they had finally caught Subject One's attention.

Suspended in midair, with no aura to push against, Lindon felt the pangs of panic. If he had been drawing from his pure core, he would have had a better defense, but he was already channeling Blackflame to attack the Hydra. The Burning Cloak appeared around him, and he dodged most of the threads. One landed against his hip with a burning sensation, and he lost a little energy to it before he twisted to break it.

Then Little Blue screamed in his ear like a shattering bell. One of the strands had touched her.

And that was the moment when Lindon took the enemy seriously.

He dropped Blackflame and switched to the Path of Twin Stars. Little Blue cleansed her own channels at the same time, snapping the thread, but she was already weaker.

He surrounded himself with the Hollow Armor, letting the death madra wash over him, and landed on the body of the snake.

Then he slammed his palm down on its scales.

An instant later, a Forged hand bigger than his body followed the motion of his own palm.

Pure madra coursed into the Hydra, and the light in its six eyes flickered. The others exploded with their own techniques, and Lindon switched back to Blackflame.

He drove a beam of black dragon's breath up through one of the snake's heads.

Yerin sliced off a second as Ziel crushed a third, and then the room was filled with the hiss of rising essence and a tide of death aura.

Lindon grabbed Little Blue, checking with his eyes and spirit to make sure she was all right. She didn't protest in his grip, instead sagging into his hand and whistling relief.

She had been weakened. Substantially. But her contact with his madra was restoring her strength.

"Eithan, you and I handle the Remnant," Lindon called. His pure madra cycled faster.

Eithan was peering in the direction of the Hydra's body. "No need. It's a dreadbeast."

Lindon looked at the creature, unconvinced. "Pardon, but it doesn't look like one."

Even the Dreadgods—at least, the ones he'd seen—didn't look like sacred beasts that could occur in the real world. The Phoenix was made up of liquid blood madra, and the Titan looked to be made of stone.

The lesser dreadbeasts, even those with the power of Lords, had all looked like creatures from a horror story. They were twisted and mutated bodies, broken from the inside out.

"Look for yourself!" Eithan suggested. He gestured to the oozing neck stump.

Lindon placed his foot on the edge of the snake's head, which was bigger than he was, and shoved it aside. Sure enough, lines burned with the pale, spectral green of death madra, running in veins all through the Hydra's flesh.

"This is..." Lindon had dissected his share of dreadbeasts, and it was hard to put into words how shocked he was by this sight. "...it's so *organized*. This looks like a real set of madra channels. And how can *death* madra, of all things, possibly exist alongside real, living flesh?"

Yerin was peering into the severed neck as well. He suspected that she was doing the same thing he was, and blocking off her sense of smell.

"You think this is what the Dreadgods look like inside?" Yerin asked.

Lindon remembered a vision Suriel had shown him, not so long ago. A white tiger the size of a house, strung up and splayed open so that he could separate its spirit from its body surgically. Its spirit had been every bit as intricate as its flesh, with the two layered over and into one another so it was difficult to tell where one ended and the other began.

"We need to find out." Before Mercy could protest, he continued. "I know we don't have as much time as we'd like, but this could end up being the most valuable thing we find down here. It's a chance to study a small Dreadgod! If we come out with nothing else, this could be invaluable."

[I agree,] Dross said. [Master Northstrider's subordinates gathered and studied many dreadbeasts to better understand the relationship between the body and the spirit. They would have been grateful for this opportunity.]

Mercy leaned on her staff, shifting her weight anxiously. She glanced at the ceiling as though she might see her mother's hand descending on them at any second. "I understand, I really do. But please *hurry.*"

Lindon triggered his void key.

It didn't open.

He frowned at it, pulling the bronze key from the thread around his neck and sensing the script. It seemed to be fully intact.

He triggered it again. This time, light slowly zipped open, revealing the entrance to his void space.

"Eithan," Lindon said.

"I saw it. Clearly spatial manipulation is restricted here. I suppose it's to keep certain beings from escaping. Well, that prevents us from easily hiding in a void key."

Lindon glanced to Little Blue. He had considered sending her and Orthos back into the Dawn Sky Palace to avoid the dangers here, now that it was clear that he couldn't fully protect them. If there was a chance for them to get trapped inside, that option was no longer available.

But they were still on a time limit, and Lindon had work to do. He climbed into his void key, fishing around for his Soulsmithing tools.

He withdrew a pair of goldsteel-plated tongs and a knife, though after a moment of thought, he pocketed the knife. He blanketed the Tomb Hydra's body in his spiritual perception, tracing the madra system that nested parasitically within its body.

"Dross, would you locate the binding for me?"

[Of course.]

"Yerin, can you open up the body? From here to about *there*, and I would be grateful if you could leave the madra intact."

Yerin tapped the hilt of her sword with a finger, and the flesh slid away from the dreadbeast's body. It released a cloud of steam and most likely a putrid stench. Lindon didn't know because his nose was still sealed off.

The shining veins of spectral green madra began to release essence, but they were clear and unbroken. Lindon readied his tongs only a moment before Dross said [Binding located.]

A purple light shone about a foot deep in the center of the Hydra's body. Lindon resonated his soulfire and reached out to the blood aura, which hadn't yet been sipped away by the labyrinth's hunger.

With the blood aura, he pulled the flesh apart and revealed the binding. It *grew* from the meat around it, reminding him at the same time of a ripe fruit and a pulsing heart. It was condensed from the power of death, a pale green fire that pumped power into the rest of the body instead of blood.

He seized it with the goldsteel tongs, pointing out to Yerin where he needed incisions, but his instincts said the binding was somewhat strange. It looked more like an Enforcer binding, though the dreadbeast's breath must have been a Striker technique. Striker techniques were usually elongated, with a clear input and output. Striker bindings this round were rare.

Still, he withdrew it and quickly placed it into a script-sealed box. Valuable materials were not to be wasted.

"Any more bindings, Dross?"

[None.]

That was also odd. Sometimes bindings didn't survive the transformation into a Remnant, so you couldn't always recover every technique the sacred artist had engraved into their spirit in life, but the dreadbeast's spirit hadn't become a Remnant. Surely it had more than one technique.

Lindon peeled away some veins of death madra as well—he wasn't about to pass up free dead matter—but that wasn't nearly as valuable as the binding. He only spent a few minutes stripping those lines out and coiling them into the box with the binding before he slammed it shut and slid it back into his void key.

"That's an advanced binding," Ziel observed. "What are you going to make with it?"

"I'll have to see what it does first," Lindon responded, but it was always going to become some kind of weapon. There weren't too many other uses for death madra.

He supposed it should have a hunger aspect, too. He hadn't sensed it, but then again, he hadn't activated the binding. And sensing hunger madra here was like trying to sense water aura in the depths of the ocean.

Now that he'd gotten what he was going to get out of the dreadbeast's corpse, it was safe to use the hand again.

He struggled with the awareness of the labyrinth the hand's authority granted him, trying to unravel it into a map in his mind as the hand itself struggled against him. It shook his concentration and fought against him physically, practically dragging him down a tunnel before he figured out where they needed to go.

And then he wrestled it to a stop, because the hand was trying to pull him in two directions at once. It sprang to his left, but when he approached the tunnel on his left, it would suddenly lunge to the opening on his right.

It repeated that several times until some hungry ghouls clawed their way through the stone, and the others eradicated them. He had to tuck the hand away so it didn't keep calling hostile attention.

"It looks like we have a choice," Lindon said.

On the left, the tunnel was marked with a hammer. The Forger symbol from the Sacred Valley badges. On the right, it bore the scythe symbol. The crest of the Arelius founder. Of Ozriel.

The map had given him the layout, and a sense into the structure and pattern of the labyrinth itself, but very little into what the rooms contained. That was what the symbols were for, and given the choice between an ordinary Soulsmith room and one left behind by Ozriel, the conclusion was clear.

"Easy decision," Lindon said as he led the way into the tunnel. Eithan followed him immediately, but Yerin was stopped by a thrown hand from Ziel.

"Hang on," he said. "The script is diff—"

The tunnel entrance vanished.

Leaving Lindon and Eithan locked inside.

The scripted lights on the ceiling still cast dim illumination over them, but Lindon added to it with his black dragon's breath. It did absolutely nothing, which he had expected.

He could sense the authority hanging over this whole place. It was inviolable.

Lindon drew up his will and prepared to challenge that.

Eithan rested a hand on his shoulder, but he wasn't watching Lindon. He was looking up and around him, tracing his bloodline power. "I can't see through the walls here," he said, "but there's a way around. They'll stay in place. We can loop around and find them."

"Hurry," Lindon said, setting off down the tunnel. "I don't like our odds in here with just us."

Little Blue burbled a reminder in his ear.

"I was counting you," he protested.

[You weren't counting me,] Dross said.

That was true.

"Ah, four and four!" Eithan said. "We've been divided in half. What a...fortuitous coincidence."

Lindon thought about the living techniques that had

tracked them. He looked to the walls, with the authority on them, which required living intention to maintain.

Someone was controlling this place. Subject One.

The Soul Cloak sprung up around him. "Keep up," he said shortly.

Then he dashed into the darkness.

Yerin lowered her weapon as the air still crackled from her Final Sword—or at least, the version of it she could use in here. The stone wall was unscratched.

This was the downside of blood madra. If it didn't have blood, she had a harder time cutting it.

Mercy dropped into a crouch, holding her head. "Okay. Deep breaths. They'll come back for us."

"If they can," Ziel said. He glanced around to the few remaining exits; instead of being full of uncountable tunnels, the room was now mostly bare.

Orthos was pacing impatiently back and forth, but he still shot a red-and-black glare at Ziel. "We have nothing to guide us forward. We should wait here."

Yerin held Netherclaw loosely in her right hand and glanced around. She had a bad feeling about this.

The labyrinth wasn't shifting at random, she was certain. There was a will behind it. And while she had nothing to lean on but her intuition, she felt like it wasn't watching Lindon at the moment. It was watching them.

"Stay sharp," Yerin said. "Swords up."

Mercy had her bow drawn and arrow nocked before Yerin finished the first word. Her back was to the group, and she scanned the darkness. "Did you sense something?"

"The body's still here."

Yerin couldn't feel any hunger madra coming, but trying to sense hunger down here was blinding. She just knew that something was on its way.

Ziel started scraping runes in the Tomb Hydra's blood, which covered much of the floor. Not a bad idea. Might as well build up some defenses, even if they wouldn't last long.

Yerin's spirit screamed a warning, and she activated the Endless Sword.

Half a dozen hungry ghouls that had been rising from the floor fell apart, but the aura was too weak here. Some living techniques survived, and there were dozens more. They flooded up around the dreadbeast's body, forcing the sacred artists to fall back.

As they rose, the ghouls shredded the Hydra. They opened their wide mouths and took chunks out of its meat, devouring madra, aura, and flesh alike.

"I saw some sword-fish feed in a river once," Orthos said in solemn tones. "They stripped a bird the size of a house down to its bones in seconds."

"Do swordfish live in rivers?" Mercy asked.

"Not swordfish. Sword-fish. Their teeth are swords."

"We should back up," Ziel pointed out.

The hunger techniques did their work in seconds, and they did more than just strip the corpse down to bones. Even the bones were devoured, reduced to nothing. Leaving a swarm of pale ghouls made of madra scurrying over the spot where the beast had been, like ants after a feast.

The others retreated, but Yerin didn't. She stood only a few strides from the hunger techniques.

She was feeling weak after that Final Sword, and even the Endless Sword had stretched her since she was using it in such an aura-dry environment. She knew exactly what it meant to spend more power here.

But something was watching her.

A silver-red glow shone around her blade as she activated the Flowing Sword. She only had traces of aura to complement the madra, so the technique wasn't stable. But it was stable enough.

She struck each ghoul with her madra-clad sword, dispersing them to clouds of madra. It took her less than a second.

Puffs of death madra, and aura of every kind, leaked into the air as the ghouls died. They had fed, but hadn't had the chance to return to their source yet. In that way, they were like the bloodspawn of the Bleeding Phoenix.

She didn't like that comparison.

Yerin glared down at the floor. "We're not backing down."

She doubted it could hear her, but it was her actions that should send the message. When she didn't get a response, she turned back to the others. "Huddle up and get our backs to a wall. If we don't get hit again soon, I'll dance a little jig."

"I would be interested to see that," Orthos said.

Ziel frowned into the distance. "You think it will keep sending the spirits after us?"

"No, but if there's no way for a giant dreadbeast to stay alive down here, that means it came from somewhere else. They'll make another one."

"There's no telling how long that will take," Mercy pointed out. "Maybe it takes days! And this could be the last one; they can't have bred *too* many."

"If that's true, you'll get to see my jig. But..."

The walls blurred right on cue, once again making Yerin wonder what the controller of the labyrinth could see.

Now, only one opening remained. On the ceiling.

And another Tomb Hydra dropped from the ceiling.

"...I'm not much of a dancer."

By the time Eithan shouted for Lindon to stop, Lindon had already slammed to a halt. His instincts had warned him just in time, even before Eithan's superior detection could keep up.

But it had been close. A script activated right in front of Lindon's eyes, sending a line of what looked like black glass sliding up ahead of his nose.

Destruction madra.

Eithan gave an exaggerated sigh when he caught up. "I'm not sure that would have been tough enough to break you, but I don't want to be performing emergency medical aid here in an ancient tomb at the heart of the world."

Lindon caught his breath and stilled his beating heart as he examined the script. "Dross, what do you think about this?"

[I think it's a good thing you weren't a little faster. Ha ha.]

Lindon winced.

[...this is a security measure against intruders. I find it strange that we have not seen more such scripts thus far.]

"We'll have to slow down," Lindon said, but he was excited by the trap's presence. Eithan noticed.

"I see you're thinking what I'm thinking."

"The other intruder would have broken this. If we're the first people here in centuries, there might be something left."

And any hint left behind by Ozriel could be a treasure.

"We don't want to make our friends wait too long."

"Oh, of course not."

"But where there's one trap, there could be others. We should move cautiously."

"It's only wise."

Little Blue's voice rang with her impatience.

Passing the scripted trap was easy once they knew it was there, and there were indeed more traps afterwards. They were all lethal; Lindon had expected more illusions or clouds, but he was met entirely with razor-sharp blades or focused beams of heat.

In other words, Lindon and Eithan strolled through.

"How do constructs stay powered around so much hunger?" Lindon asked. The aura here should feed on anything indiscriminately, not even counting the living hunger techniques that traveled around consuming whatever they found.

"They're protected," Eithan said. "Which is fascinating, since anything from the Arelius founder should predate the introduction of hunger madra to this labyrinth. Did he anticipate this, or was he protecting against other threats? A puzzle for you!"

"Pardon, but surely your guess would be better than mine."

Eithan was quiet for a moment as they both dodged a spray of venomous darts. "Making my own guess would be less than productive. Why don't you see if you can guess the thoughts of a genius Soulsmith? Might be good for you."

That didn't make much sense to Lindon, but if Eithan wasn't willing to speculate, Lindon wasn't going to make him.

Especially since they'd made it to the end of the hallway.

The room was less than Lindon had expected from a secret chamber hidden by a powerful expert at the heart of a deadly labyrinth. It was more like a cramped bedroom than a huge Soulsmith foundry, though there was no bed. There were instead wooden tables crammed against the walls, each carrying piles of...

Lindon didn't want to call the objects "random junk," because there had to be more to them than met the eye. But he saw a pearl necklace tossed carelessly on top of a pile of mismatched silk scarves. A quiver full of arrows leaned against a set of fifteen books with titles Lindon couldn't read.

There were eight tables in the room, each with a similar pile. And not one of the objects held any obvious spiritual power...at least, none that remained.

But there were a few spots of dream madra here and there, and the sources were obvious. Tiny crystals had been tied to each object, and Lindon ran his spiritual sense into one such dream tablet.

A stately woman wears the necklace of pearls as she addresses her army. She raises a hand to direct them, and the scene shifts.

She comes onto the deck of a cloudship, and rays of golden light form around her hands. The scene shifts again.

With an icy look on her face, she orders the execution of a sobbing woman who looks just like her. Grief hangs over the scene like a cloud.

Abruptly, the memory cut off.

Lindon was shaken. Compared to most of the other tablets he'd viewed, this one was more chaotic and less complete. And it wasn't entirely clear whose memory it was; it felt almost like a composite of memories from someone else with the noblewoman's emotions layered over them.

But it was clear that this woman, whose name he hadn't caught, had been the owner of the necklace. It had been important to her, Lindon had felt that. She was known for always wearing this necklace, and it had become one of her signatures.

Lindon quickly relayed what he'd seen to Eithan, who nodded. He looked unsurprised, but he also didn't seem to be examining the objects himself.

Then again, he could be scrutinizing everything in the room at once without moving an inch.

Lindon checked another one, a signet ring bearing the image of a winged ship. This one belonged to a water artist who fought across the seas, attempting to create safe paths for humans through sacred beast territory. He lent this ring to his subordinates, and anyone who carried it could speak for him.

From the ring, Lindon finally sensed something. It was subtle, but...heavy. Slightly more real than the objects around it.

It reminded him of a Sage's command. The word carrying authority felt heavier than the others.

Now that he knew what to look for, he sharpened his senses and scanned the other objects on the table. Some of their dream tablets had faded with time, and from most of the objects themselves, he felt nothing.

But a handful gave him a positive feeling, so he separated them into a pile. A quiver of arrows, the ring, a blue silk scarf, and a bronze buckler carved with the image of a chariot in battle.

Only these four gave him any sense that they could be worth anything, but it was difficult to be certain.

"Did you find anything?" he asked Eithan.

Eithan was holding a small dagger, smiling sadly at it as the dream tablet flickered. Its memory must be tragic.

"My sense for these things is not as developed as yours," he said.

"So you know what's special about these?" Lindon had wondered as much, with Eithan being Eithan.

"Just as certain people can exert greater force on reality than others, so too can certain objects," Eithan said quietly. "They are significant because of what, or more commonly whom, they represent."

He tossed the dagger back down as though it were worthless. "It seems that this room is where someone, presumably my Patriarch, kept objects that he suspected might become significant. Most of them failed the test."

Lindon looked eagerly at the four objects he'd separated. "So these are powerful?"

"They can be. This is the highest level of Soulsmithing, and it must be approached with care. The price of success can be higher than the price of failure."

Little Blue tugged at Lindon's hair, pointing toward the room's one exit, but Lindon couldn't let Eithan's remark pass.

"Where did you learn this, Eithan?"

Eithan looked deeply into Lindon's eyes, searching for something. Then he pulled out a marble, inside which a hole in the world hung suspended.

"As I've told you, I became the advisor to the Monarch Tiberian Arelius very early in my advancement."

Eithan had shared several stories from that time in his life over the last few months, and Lindon had hung onto each one. They felt like glimpses into a mystery.

"I have always had a...knack for understanding the records of my predecessors. Not just dream tablets, but their writings. There were patterns that I picked up on that very few have ever put together."

He thought for a moment, seeming to choose his words carefully. "I believed that I could advance my family, and perhaps the world, by revealing these truths. And one such truth I revealed was this."

He held up Ozriel's marble. "His records were hidden among my family for hundreds of generations, and if you know how to read them, they contained insight applicable to more than Soulsmithing. They locked this away and worshiped it instead of following the path it outlined.

"Of course, there *have* been members of my family who have ascended. In the grand scheme of things, it isn't terribly unusual to ascend beyond this world. But none of them picked up the banner he tried to pass them.

"With Tiberian, I thought we had a chance. And then, against my advice, he approached...the other Monarch on the continent."

Lindon's stomach dropped. "You're not saying his name."

Eithan looked into the darkness. "No. No, I'm not."

"There are only a few people who could navigate the labyrinth besides us."

"And perhaps now we are trapped in here with a Monarch. Or...perhaps he is trapped here with us."

第十二章

CHAPTER TWELVE

Yerin sent a wave of razor-sharp madra at the Tomb Hydra while it was still falling from the hole in the ceiling.

Ziel conjured a barrier of force around himself, lifting his hammer. Mercy had already released a barrage of arrows, and Orthos breathed out a bar of black dragon's breath that was now bigger than his entire head.

The concentrated wave of death madra wiped out most of their attacks in an instant.

Only Yerin's Rippling Sword was dense enough to cut through the Hydra's madra, and it half-severed the creature's rightmost head.

But she had to dash to the side and intercept the rest of the death madra, diverting enough of the deadly energy with her sword to protect the others. Or at least Orthos and Mercy. She suspected Ziel would be fine.

The remaining madra from the Striker technique washed over the semi-transparent barrier generated by Ziel's script, and then the Tomb Hydra landed with an impact that shook the entire room. Both heads, with their shining green eyes, lunged at Yerin.

Which was how she wanted it.

She extended her sword-arms and planted her feet, focusing her will. She *would not be moved.*

The teeth of the first head crashed around her, and her sword-arms caught them. She flexed, forcing the jaws apart.

The second head simply rammed into her from the other side, surrounded by a ring of death madra that would burn away her lifeline. She met that with her sword, which shone with her own madra.

By all rights, the impact alone should have torn her to shreds, or pulverized her insides. But instead of popping like a swatted mosquito, she stood her ground.

The Hydra heads reacted like they'd run into a rock. The first head's teeth began to crack, and the second head slammed into her sword and then lurched back, dazed.

Yerin may not have advanced to Archlord yet, but she hadn't spent the last months sitting on her hands.

Her will was steel.

She slashed down with her Goldsigns and up with Netherclaw. Blood sprayed both the floor and the ceiling.

The Tomb Hydra retreated, hissing furiously, but only one of its heads remained alive. It was dragging the other two along as dead weight. Even that remaining head was torn half-off, revealing bone and a few glowing veins of raw madra.

Yerin understood she wasn't getting back the madra she'd spent here, especially if she didn't meet up with Lindon soon. She had a few elixirs remaining, but she never carried most of them. Why would she? Lindon carried enough supplies to start a business as a refiner and a Soulsmith both.

But she was still feeling sunny about her odds. Whatever it cost the labyrinth to make or summon or breed these huge dreadbeasts, they couldn't be free either.

Her mood cracked like an egg when she saw the walls blur again, and a huge tunnel opened up on their left. A second massive Tomb Hydra slithered out, hauling death.

Now fear crept up on her. Not for herself, but for the others. If only one person made it out of here, it was likely to be her.

Three mouths opened, shining with death madra, and Yerin stopped holding back.

Her Moonlight Bridge wrapped her in white light, carrying her to her destination: on top of the Tomb Hydra.

Madra awakened Netherclaw, and it summoned the Forger technique for which it had been named. A massive beast claw formed over her head, constructed strand by strand from bloody madra. It carried her power alongside its own, and the Archlord technique cut down at the Tomb Hydra.

It twisted in place, clashing with its power against her sword, but Yerin wasn't waiting around. As soon as she'd used the binding in the sword, she spun and slammed her fist down on the Hydra's scales with all her strength.

All her strength.

The chamber rang louder than it had when the monster hit the ground. The force of her punch pulverized bones and twisted space. Air tore away from her like a hurricane, and tiny cracks crawled out across the ground in a web.

The snake spasmed, its midsection crushed, and the Netherclaw slashed without resistance.

All three heads were torn off in one swipe.

Yerin leaped off the body, sword in hand. The other snake was still alive, and she had to protect the others.

From midair, she saw the others finish off the first Hydra. The head of Ziel's hammer, powered by a circle of green runes, slammed it into the floor.

Yerin let herself land gently. She burned the gore from her sword with blood madra, and nodded in respect to Ziel. "Nice hit."

He looked as though he didn't believe her. At first, she thought that was just him being unfriendly, but Mercy was staring at her too.

"Yerin," Mercy said hesitantly, "I think I might head back once we meet up with the others."

Yerin forced open her own void key, which seemed to want to stick, and rummaged around until she found one of her few elixirs. This one had been made just for her, as the bottle contained a medicine that specialized in restoring blood and sword madra, but she grimaced as she drank it. It was gritty and tasted like steel and charcoal.

Yerin wiped her mouth, mostly to buy time to think about her response. "Not a bad idea. It'd be safer inside a dragon's mouth than down here. But you knew that when you came down."

Orthos snorted smoke and nibbled at the dreadbeast's body. "We thought there would be something we could do."

Mercy fiddled with black-gloved fingers. "Dreadbeasts like this...to us, one would be a deadly fight. But for you, they're not worth mentioning. I'm not sure what we can do other than get in the way."

Yerin felt hunger spirits rising around the corpse, and she saw the chance to make a point. She hopped up on top of the dead Hydra and looked down on the others.

Then she cycled a little madra to her eyes so they would glow red. For effect.

"We've been friends for a long stretch now," Yerin said. "You think I'd rather be down here alone?" White ghouls began crawling up from the ground, and she released her spiritual pressure.

Yerin glared at the nearest ghoul. "*Mine,*" she said. She was no Sage, but she suspected it would get the point.

Now, there were two possibilities, and either would suit her purpose. Either these mindless techniques would ignore her warning and head for her, in which case she would crush them and show off a bit.

Or they would go for easier prey.

The hollow-eyed ghouls slid away from Yerin even as they bubbled up from below, lurching after the others with surprising speed. Yerin cycled her madra to her Steelborn Iron body and braced herself.

Then she dashed all over the room in a blur of speed. It cost her very little madra; even here, with the hunger aura grinding away her spirit a little at a time, she could keep this up all day.

She sheathed her sword, and severed limbs of animated hunger madra dissolved to essence.

"You'll catch up," Yerin said confidently. "And until you do...what's so bad about letting me carry you?"

Orthos burned so clearly with the resolve to improve himself that Yerin could practically see it. Mercy's eyes welled up, and even Ziel gripped his hammer a little harder.

Yerin felt a smile tug at the corner of her mouth. Not only did she have friends along, but she was in a position where she could protect them.

Ruby would be just as happy as Yerin was.

Lindon paced outside the chamber, waiting as the storm of deadly blades raged. Eithan had clearly indicated this was the way through, but it seemed this room was designed solely to slow them down.

When they approached, they had triggered a script that activated constructs all throughout the room. Swords of madra, clouds of corrosive aura, and needles of blood rampaged through the room in a deadly storm.

Eithan and Lindon could wade through the room untouched, and Lindon had wanted to do that, but Eithan had stopped him.

They'd already wasted quite a bit of madra, and the only way to get through was for them to spend more. Instead, Eithan suggested they simply wait. The room's constructs would run out of power before they ran out of time.

Lindon was impatient. Who knew when the route back would shift?

"We need to get back," he insisted. "As far as we know, there might never be a way back again."

[That would be unlikely,] Dross said, and Eithan nodded in agreement.

"There's obviously some kind of intelligence running this place," Eithan said, "but it can't keep us separated forever. There must be certain patterns, or it could lock all intruders in a room and remove the exits."

"Apologies, but that's weak logic to hang all of our lives on."

Eithan shrugged. "If I'm wrong, then you burn through the walls. With the Void Icon and Blackflame, it should be possible."

Lindon nodded. He wanted to do it now, but that would exhaust him, and he'd be useless for the rest of the trip. Or at least for a while.

Little Blue whispered comfort to him, and Lindon decided to distract himself with another project.

"Dross, can you simulate a Soulsmithing project?"

[Somewhat. My capabilities are not what they were, but as long as we can rely on known information, I should be able to replicate a simple project successfully.]

Once again, Lindon missed the real Dross.

At his request, the binding from the Tomb Hydra appeared in front of him, floating in the air. It shone with the pale, spectral green of death madra, and looked roughly like a human heart the size of a head.

There were several entrances, which resembled broken arteries. Lindon ran pure madra through one, and a weak beam of death emanated from the other end of the binding.

Curious, he moved his pure madra through the other one. This time, a haze of death madra appeared around the heart. A lethal field that, if it were real, would have eaten away at his lifeline and begun corroding his flesh.

"Is this accurate?" Lindon asked.

[As much as it can be without testing. The intensity of the effect, its response to pure madra, and its activation time are all suppositions on my part.]

"But this is really several techniques?"

[Yes.]

That was intriguing. Potentially revolutionary.

Bindings were crystallized techniques, meaning they were each *one* technique. Sometimes Soulsmiths could blend one into the other, but it always created a hybrid technique. It never layered the two techniques on top of one another. If you wanted the techniques to be used together, or in sequence, you had to design your construct to allow it. Usually, that was done with scripts.

But this dreadbeast had only one binding for several techniques. As though its bindings had all organically fused into one.

Lindon fueled the third of the four openings, and a Forged set of jaws appeared, its teeth shining green. It snapped down on nothing, and now Lindon finally felt the hunger component of the binding coming to the forefront. This was how the Hydra fed.

Eithan cleared his throat. "I hate to complain, but it's pretty boring sitting here watching you hold on to nothing."

Lindon remembered that he must look ridiculous, interacting with thin air. "Dross, can you project to Eithan?"

[I can, but that will cost me valuable madra.]

Lindon hesitated. He was doubly reluctant to exhaust Dross after what had happened the last time the spirit strained himself.

"Very well then, leave me out," Eithan said. "I will infer from your conversation what you have been doing: are you testing out the Hydra's binding?"

"It's amazing. Like four bindings grown into one. I've seen dreadbeasts with bindings that had melted into one another, but they never worked well. They always felt like a failure, but this could be the perfected version."

He activated the fourth binding, but nothing happened. He sensed it had been reaching out to the surrounding aura, but there was no death aura nearby, so the Ruler technique hadn't activated.

Eithan tapped his fingers together. "Disturbing implications, but that was always one of the strongest theories about the origins of the dreadbeasts. That they were the failures, and the successes were the Dreadgods."

Lindon examined the binding, turning it in his hands. "So you're saying the Dreadgods have a binding like this one."

"You'd have to kill one to prove it. But I would say it's likely."

Lindon ran his perception through the room ahead. The constructs were starting to slow down, but he still had time.

He could take a closer look at the actual binding. It would help him later, and Dross couldn't model it accurately unless Lindon studied it.

Eithan slowly slid into his line of sight. He was massaging his temples with both hands. "Let me see if I can divine your thoughts. You are tempted to examine the actual binding, but you are hesitant to do so, and...what's this? Please, I know you admire my keen insight, but don't let those thoughts distract you. Focus."

"This might be my only chance at this. I don't want to waste it." A mistake Soulsmithing could damage the binding beyond repair. If Dross learned enough to be able to replicate the binding, then that was fine, but he still didn't want to lose such a valuable material.

"There should be better facilities somewhere here," Lindon went on. "I want to see the effect of the location myself. And if the hammer's as important as you say it is, I want one of those too."

Eithan cupped a hand around his ear. "I need to hear you say it. I need to hear you say *the words.*"

Lindon was lost.

"Say, 'please, Eithan, solve this problem for me.'"

"It's not a *problem,* really. I could examine it now, but I think it's better to wait until later."

"Okay then, say 'If only I had a place to practice Soulsmithing right here!'"

"That would be convenient, but I'm not really looking to make a construct."

"Please say it."

"If only I had a place—"

"*Worry no more, my student!* With my incredible foresight, I have solved your problem long ago!"

With a flourish, Eithan produced a tiny object shaped like an anvil. Lindon could immediately sense that it was a void key, or something similar. Eithan practically forced it into his hand, so Lindon ran his madra through it.

He had to join his will to it and *push* through a faint resistance. Either the labyrinth's suppression of spatial artifacts was increasing, or he was getting tired.

A moment later, a door opened in midair. It led onto a space that was much stranger than most void keys Lindon had seen.

A platform of stones hovered in the middle of an endless starry sky. Each of the stars were larger and clearer than usual, shining brightly from every direction. The stones themselves were large wedges that fit together into a circle about the size of a small room. Each wedge held a symbol that—

Lindon had to look away from the symbols because of a piercing pain in his head. They formed a script, he was sure, but they reminded him more of the runes in Suriel's eyes. There was meaning there that he couldn't pierce.

At the center of the platform of interlocking stones, there was a slab of dull metal. It resembled an altar more than an anvil, or perhaps half of a column. Inside that altar, a blue flame burned, visible through a small window. So perhaps it was more like a stove.

Lindon drew Suriel's marble from his pocket and compared. As he'd suspected, the blue fire in his marble was eerily similar to the one blazing within the altar. Except the one here was many times bigger.

"Lindon, allow me to introduce you to the ultimate Soulsmithing tool: the Soulforge."

Lindon reverently held his breath as he walked inside. He felt the world around him change as he stepped inside, in ways more than the physical. Echoes of creation filled the air. This was a place where wonders were born.

He paced around the anvil at the center, examining the stones, the flame, even the stars in the distance. "How does it work?" he asked.

Eithan beamed. "Why don't you tell me?"

Lindon still couldn't examine the huge paving-stones beneath his feet too closely, because the single rune carved on each of them was too overwhelming, but it was clear that the script-circle was focused on the anvil at the center.

And the anvil, if that's what it was, was clearly the focus of all the creative energies in this space. In a mundane forge, you would heat up metal in the flame to make it malleable enough to shape, but that didn't have much relevance to Soulsmithing.

He approached the center and felt the energy gathered above the altar-like anvil. There was little to see, but the air felt invisibly *focused* there, charged, as though waiting for something.

"I think anything you put there is...altered. Enhanced, maybe." He knelt to look at the blue fire. "This fuels the effect somehow. I assume you have to burn something here? Soulfire?"

Eithan was about to answer, but Lindon cut him off as an idea occurred to him. "No...wait." He pulled out the pearl necklace he had found earlier.

From Eithan's proud smile, Lindon already knew he was right, but he tossed the necklace in anyway. The physical form of the necklace burned to ash in an instant, which dissolved to nothing with a hiss. But the flames strengthened.

Just to test it out, he tossed in some junk with no authority whatsoever. It burned up, but the flame didn't change.

Lindon moved to his feet, full of confidence. "It takes objects with embedded authority and burns them, focusing it on whatever you're making above the altar."

Eithan applauded. "Very good! We say objects with invested authority or willpower are *significant,* but the terminology changes from place to place, so it's not important. You're so right it brings a tear to my eye."

"But what does it do to the Soulsmithing?"

"In traditional Soulsmithing, Archlord artifacts are effectively the peak. There is no higher form of soulfire than that which Archlords produce, and spirits are usually raised past that stage artificially. Beings stronger than Archlords don't often die and leave Remnants, you see.

"Even if you were fortunate enough to get a Herald or Monarch's Remnant, or to raise a Remnant to be equivalent to a Herald, you would still be tempering it in Archlord soulfire. It would be only marginally better than an actual Archlord weapon."

Eithan swept his arms around the Soulforge. "If you *really* want to perform Soulsmithing on a higher level, you need a way to imbue the authority and willpower of a greater existence into the item. That requires tools and locations on a superior tier of existence, which are few and far between. If you wanted to forge a Monarch a sword, for instance, you would want to do it on a battlefield in which Monarchs died, of which there are surpassingly few.

"This was a fairly ingenious solution, I will admit. A portable location that can increase the level of existence of projects worked here, allowing the manipulation of more advanced forces. It's not quite as good as if you crafted a device in a significant location that suited the project, but it has the advantage of being universally compatible and mobile."

Lindon wanted to rub his cheek all over the anvil. He could see exactly how much of an advantage this would be.

But Eithan had used a word that caught his attention. "Did you have a hand in the creation of this Soulforge, Eithan?"

The Archlord sighed. "Sadly not. This was Reigan Shen's design and creation, and he was only willing to part with it because he is capable of building another one. Though it will be expensive, even for him."

Something visibly occurred to Eithan, and he asked, "Why did you ask if I made it?"

"You called it ingenious."

Eithan staggered back, clapping a finger to his chest as though wounded. "I do not like what you're implying, my beloved disciple."

"So this was part of Reigan Shen's bribe?" Lindon looked around the space, jealousy worming his way through his heart. "Why didn't you show me this before? Are you even a Soulsmith?"

"It's rare to find a sacred artist who hasn't at least *dabbled* in Soulsmithing," Eithan protested. "And it so happens that I have been using this facility to prepare the materials for the Pure Storm Baptism that Ziel has enjoyed. I intended to pass this on to you when you were ready, and now that we have been interacting with objects of some significance..."

He left the sentence hanging suggestively, and Lindon was so excited by the space that he was willing to let it pass that Eithan had kept another secret from them. "Does this mean you can make anything—wait just a second, did you say you were passing it on to me?"

"Very soon. Ziel could still use one more treatment, I'd say, but it's best that you start practicing before you inherit this from me."

"Can we use this to fix Dross?"

Eithan cleared his throat. "If it could, I would have revealed it to you earlier. I'm sorry. But you will find a solution for Dross, I'm certain!"

Lindon was overwhelmed. He blinked back tears. "It's too much," Lindon said, though he would already fight a Dreadgod with half a paintbrush over the Soulforge. "You've given me so much already."

Eithan cocked his head as though he didn't understand. "I consider the things I've given you to be the best investments I've ever made."

Lindon straightened up and pressed his fists together, bowing over them in a sincere salute. "Gratitude, master."

"You know, you never call me that." Eithan ushered Lindon out of the Soulforge, though Lindon kept shooting longing glances backwards. "It's probably for the best. I don't want status to go to my head."

"I'm not sure I can pay back an investment like this."

"Oh, you can start paying me back once we're out of Cradle. My investments are *long*-term."

⬡

INFORMATION RESTRICTED: PERSONAL RECORD 3349.
AUTHORIZATION REQUIRED TO ACCESS.
AUTHORIZATION CONFIRMED: 008 OZRIEL.
BEGINNING RECORD...

When Ozriel reaped a world, perfectly eliminating it from existence, the Abidan could colonize nine others.

His work was vital to Abidan expansion, and there were even those who believed him to be the most valuable of the Judges. When an Iteration dies normally, it corrodes, breaking into corrupted fragments that tend to corrupt others and accelerate their own death.

With Ozriel, that no longer happened. He was the machete the Court of Seven used to beat back the wilderness of chaos, rapidly expanding their holdings.

More Iterations became habitable than ever before. It was an unprecedented golden age for the influence of the Way, and even Makiel admitted the utility of Ozriel's Scythe. It was only the man behind the mantle that Makiel didn't trust.

Ozriel's own objections started to grow louder.

If he weren't bound by the Eledari Pact, he could have gone in and saved that world. They had known for centuries that this Iteration was going to be corrupted, and he could have cut the cause off at the root.

That would itself be a deviation from Fate, Makiel argued. In the grand scheme of things, that would lead to an increase in chaos.

But manageable, Ozriel said. They could keep the deviations under control, which would rarely—if ever—rise to the point of having to destroy an entire world.

Unfortunately, while both models had their advantages, neither could be proven conclusively. By the very nature of the problem, there was no looking into the future to see how it would play out. So the two beings most skilled in reading Fate continued to argue.

Meanwhile, Ozriel discovered the restricted records of the Court of Seven regarding the Executor program.

This should be his solution, he thought. Raise up people from the Iterations, not sworn to the Way, who could interfere without compromising their oaths.

But from the records, he could see that it had failed. Again and again. Those who fought corruption inevitably became corrupted themselves.

So Ozriel decided to do some investigation of his own.

He traveled to Haven, the prison-world of the Abidan, where he used his authority as a Judge to gain access to the Mad King, Daruman. Once the greatest of the Abidan Executors.

He asked the Mad King what he thought. Why was the Executor program flawed?

It wasn't the program, Daruman insisted. It was the Abidan.

Being sworn to order made the Abidan too inflexible, too bound to their own thoughts. Creativity and flexibility were beyond them, and the second that anyone started pushing at the boundaries of their rules, the offending party would be condemned.

Ozriel promised change. He wanted to revive the Executor program, but this time, they would be an official division of the Abidan beneath him. They would be unbound to the Eledari Pact, able to intervene in worlds, and personally selected and supervised by him. They would save worlds by eliminating apocalypses at the root.

He would call them Reapers.

And if he could get enough support from the Court of Seven to create his own official Division, he would even recruit Daruman. Ozriel was uniquely able to handle Class One Fiends.

Daruman and Oth'kimeth laughed together.

Mighty as Ozriel may be, as keen as his eyes were, he would never succeed. The Court of Seven could not be convinced, and they would be against him for this.

If Ozriel was really dedicated to his ideals, as he claimed to be, he should join the Vroshir. They, at least, saved human lives.

Ozriel brought his proposal before the Court, and as expected, there was heavy resistance. Only the new, young Suriel would have allowed it—a woman he had known for centuries by this point, as she worked her way up the ranks. And even she had misgivings.

Ozriel pled his case but was dismissed.

He accepted that. He had looked into the future and seen that this would not be an easy task. He would try again, and again.

As long as it took.

RECORD COMPLETE.

第十三章

CHAPTER THIRTEEN

Yerin cycled her last elixir and focused on the layer of red aura around her. The Hydra blood that had caked her robes and splattered on her skin flowed off, leaving her spotless.

The same couldn't be said for Ziel and Mercy. Ziel didn't look particularly bothered by the dark spots that covered him and his gray cloak, but Mercy looked like a rat that had been partially drowned in mud.

Orthos had simply burned the blood away, but he was clearly unhappy. He snorted as he looked up at the entrance overhead. "How many is that now?"

Yerin had been keeping track. "Six. Bleed me like a pig if something's not spitting them out."

Every time they killed one, hunger spirits devoured it. They were repurposing the energy, she was sure.

She had tried to stop them as much as possible, but the hunger spirits were endless, and her power wasn't.

The others were all tired, and she was still carrying the bulk of each battle. But her perception was warning her about what was lurking up above. It felt like the Tomb Hydras, but much deeper. Bigger. It *felt* like a mother, giving birth to each of the dreadbeasts that fell down.

She hoped that wasn't it.

"I'm going up," she said reluctantly.

Mercy threw out a hand like she thought Yerin was going to dash away immediately. "No, wait! We agreed we'd stay here!"

"They're going to grind us like grain in a mill. We stay here, and Lindon will know exactly where to find our bodies."

It was hard to sense anything here, since her perception couldn't penetrate the walls and everything was soaked in hunger madra, but she had still expected to sense Eithan or Lindon by now. Something had delayed them.

Ziel sighed. "You think it's going to slowly kill us. So you want to dive in all at once. You want it to quickly kill us?"

"Not us. I'm going myself." Yerin didn't want to say it out loud, but she felt like she could keep fighting even once her madra was gone. She would be ground down eventually too, but even if she was left with nothing more than her sword and the strength of her body, she could probably keep fighting for days.

If they kept fighting, Eithan and Lindon would find three bodies and Yerin. And that wasn't acceptable. If Orthos and Mercy died, it would be after Yerin.

Ziel...he was mostly a mystery to her. Maybe he could survive without her help.

"So if we get separated, you're leaving us here?" Orthos asked. He took a casual bite out of the Hydra's meat.

"Guess so," she said, but her grip shifted on her sword. That was the only reason she hadn't dashed up the corridor in the ceiling already. If the labyrinth shifted again and sealed her off, she wasn't confident in blasting her way back down.

And what if more of these Hydras started funneling into the chamber while she was locked away in some broom closet?

Mercy chewed on her lip and looked up, and next to her, Ziel let out another heavy breath.

"We don't have much choice," he allowed.

"Can you take a look and then come back?" Mercy asked.

Yerin eyed the opening in the ceiling. There hadn't been another Tomb Hydra yet, but she could feel power gathering above them.

She had been keeping an eye on how the labyrinth shifted, though. It seemed like the tunnels closed off at the entrances, not in the middle, or they would have been crushed to paste the first time an entrance shifted while they were still in the hallway.

"Better to move quick than wait to die," Yerin muttered. She sheathed her sword and spread her arms wide. "Come here, everybody. Family hug."

Ziel walked over to her, still dull-eyed as ever. Even Orthos hopped from the ground to land on her shoulder. Mercy's eyes sparkled as she joined, wrapping everyone in an eager hug of her own.

"I never thought I'd hear you say those words!"

Yerin was a little thrown off at how easily everyone had joined her. "I'm about to carry you."

"I know," Mercy said, squeezing Ziel with one arm and Yerin with the other. "It's still nice."

Yerin held on to everyone and leaped.

She had expected to have to walk the others through her plan, but since they seemed to be sharper than she'd expected, she didn't say anything.

The second they cleared the inner entrance to the tunnel in the ceiling, Mercy spread out a web of Strings of Shadow and Ziel Forged a hovering circle of green runes. They landed on this Forged platform, and Yerin released everyone.

Mercy gave Ziel and Yerin each one more squeeze before she released. Then she patted Orthos on the head.

The aura above them was growing stronger, and though the tunnel was long—long enough that Yerin wondered if it extended aboveground—she could see the glow of death madra above her.

"Seal yourselves off when I'm gone," Yerin ordered.

Ziel had already started Forging runes over their heads.

Yerin wasn't sure how the platform of madra beneath her

feet would hold up to a full-powered jump, so she hopped onto the wall and then bounced between the inside of the tunnels as she made her way up.

All the time, she had her spiritual perception extended. She regretted it almost immediately.

Whatever was in the chamber above her felt nauseating. Like the Bleeding Phoenix, it had a sense of hunger, corruption, and death. It felt like a ravenous pile of corpses, somehow brought to hideous life.

Her stomach twisted, but she ran her madra through her sword. If she had to end up retreating from the labyrinth, ridding the world of a creature like this would have made her trip worthwhile.

The higher she got, the more the sensation churned her gut, but she braced herself.

She still wasn't prepared when she cleared the upper entrance.

Eyes—glowing with the pale green of death madra—glared at her from every direction. The entire chamber was a mass of disgusting flesh, endless, as far as her spirit could sense. Motion stirred in the distance, and she spotted another Tomb Hydra emerging from a slick bulbous sac.

It wasn't the only thing in here. Dreadbeasts had half-merged into the flesh, melted, as this thing fed.

And its spiritual presence...

It wasn't a Dreadgod. It didn't have the endless sensation of the Phoenix or the Titan, though its corruption was equal.

She would call it a Herald, but it felt more like half a dozen Heralds stitched together and smeared across the chamber. Its spiritual pressure *crashed* over her, and she found it hard to take a breath as every eye in the room focused on her.

Tendrils of flesh snaked across the entrance to block off her retreat, but Yerin wasn't about to let it get its way.

This thing might have been a highly advanced dreadbeast, but it was full of blood.

The Final Sword was difficult to use in the labyrinth normally, because it required aura, and the aura here was all being consumed by hunger. But there was enough blood aura inside this massive body that she wove it together quickly.

She couldn't launch the technique down, or she'd risk killing her friends. So she held on to her shining sword as she fell toward the tendrils of dead, animated flesh.

Then she twisted sideways, unleashing the beam of concentrated silver-red energy horizontally. It scraped the monster away from the entrance and sliced through its huge body, releasing a huge roar that shook her bones as much as her ears.

She continued falling down as the air filled with death madra.

Yerin forced out madra and soulfire, but the hostile will was as strong as her own. It eroded everything she did, and she realized the wave of green madra was going to overtake the others.

She launched a Rippling Sword at the green-and-black barrier Ziel and Mercy had made below her.

It cracked on contact, which was enough for her. She landed sword-first, piercing her way through.

In the instant she crashed into their platform, Yerin saw Orthos, Ziel, and Mercy all staring at her in astonishment. If they hadn't sensed her coming, they would have met her with a barrage of techniques.

But none of them could move as fast as she did. With all the strength she could muster, she slammed a foot down on the Forged madra below.

The explosion of death above her was still coming, and gravity was too slow.

She seized Mercy and Ziel by the front of their robes, scooped Orthos up with her Goldsign, and pulled them down. Yerin twisted in the air, kicking off against the wall and shooting down.

She was sure she was going to make it. The malicious presence of the roomful of flesh was weaker now, and clearly it couldn't follow her. Once they endured this technique, they would be safe.

Then she felt another will barge in. The intelligence that ran all throughout the walls.

A ravenous, desperate will.

Below her, the entrance blurred as the labyrinth shifted again.

Lindon and Eithan passed through the trap-filled chamber after the constructs had exhausted themselves. The air was still blistering with the aftermath of all the madra, but it was simple to protect themselves from that.

Little Blue gave a long, whining note of complaint, but she wasn't in any danger.

"They're still ahead?" Lindon asked. It had taken quite a while for the constructs to exhaust themselves, after all.

"The labyrinth still hasn't shifted yet, which suggests it should very soon." Eithan frowned, running his fingers along the wall as he ran. "I will admit, it is strange," he allowed. "The labyrinth doesn't seem to be working against us. I would have expected—"

They were in the hallway as the labyrinth shifted.

Far ahead of them, the doorway that led onto a chamber filled with flashing machines closed. Lindon felt the overwhelming sensation of space being twisted, though the hallway didn't change.

He suddenly realized why void keys were so difficult to use here. Whatever had authority over the labyrinth was using spatial transmission to move all the chambers around. The usual relationship to space had shifted.

The entrance reappeared in a moment, and while they were still running down the hall, Lindon realized they were about to head upwards.

Someone was falling toward them.

It was Yerin...and she was *dragging* Ziel and Mercy along with her. Lindon felt Orthos' presence, and the turtle was terrified.

Behind them, a massive wave of death madra followed.

Lindon and Eithan dashed into the next room, and his brain twisted as he ran horizontally *up,* and what had a moment before been a vertical wall shifted to become the floor.

Yerin shot toward the ground—toward Lindon and Eithan—and in the split second it took her to reach the floor, the death madra following her would billow out and begin to fill the room.

Lindon thought Eithan would act before him, but to his surprise, Eithan had frozen up the moment they entered the room. He must have seen something through his bloodline power.

So Lindon was the first to act. His eyes cooled as they turned crystal blue, a reflection of Little Blue's, and he projected pure, cleansing madra in all directions.

The death madra poured into his Hollow Domain and wasn't wiped out immediately. It faded as it poured in, like salt poured into a bucket of water.

Yerin landed easily next to Lindon, the durability of a Herald meaning she had no need of a full-body Enforcer technique. He would be far more worried about Mercy and Ziel, who hadn't had an easy trip.

Then again, Ziel had his body thrice-forged in soulfire. He bounced on Yerin's shoulder and then slid off, unfazed by the trip. Mercy staggered as she moved to her feet, grabbing Lindon for support.

Orthos had stiffened up, and Lindon was certain that if his black, pebbly skin could go pale, it would have. The sensation he radiated through their bond was pure shocked terror.

"So much worse," he mumbled. "So much worse to be small."

Little Blue gave a sympathetic chime.

Yerin blew the lock of red hair out of her face and looked up. "Sliced that one a little thin, didn't we?"

"Now that I think of it, staying in the hallway so we didn't get separated was stupid," Ziel commented. "We should have just gotten lost."

"No telling what else we could have run into," Mercy said.

Lindon let his Hollow Domain drop. In fact, the entrance into the ceiling had closed almost immediately after the wave of death madra had reached them. He called his void key open, once again forcing it open with his will.

He had to push more focus and more madra into it this time. Whether it was the hunger aura or the authority of the labyrinth's owner suppressing spatial artifacts, it was getting worse.

He stepped inside, rummaged around for a moment, and pulled out a pill and a sealed case of scales. He handed the pill to Yerin. "You used up a lot of madra there. Are you okay?"

She nudged him with her shoulder before popping the pill in her mouth. "Bright and shiny. Just need to fill my glass back up."

Lindon did not fail to notice that two of her party were covered in fresh bloodstains. He looked to Mercy for confirmation.

"No no, we're fine. We almost had to deal with a Herald-level Striker technique, but Yerin got us out of there." She released him and shifted from one foot to the other to check her balance.

"Herald?" Lindon thought immediately about the possibility of Reigan Shen being in the labyrinth, and he looked up at the ceiling despite himself, though the door had already been blocked.

Yerin waved off his concern. "Bigger version of the dead snakes. Just a pile of meat, so not like it's going to chase us. And we'd feel it coming from a mile off, it's—"

With a blur, the stone wall on the far end of the chamber fuzzed out of existence. It left a hole into a dark tunnel, which sloped downwards. Lindon's spirit rang an alarm at the feeling of ancient, overwhelming death that radiated from the tunnel.

Yerin looked and sounded like she'd just bitten into a rotten fruit. "It's like that. There it is."

"You and I can handle it, if you're ready," Lindon said. "Eithan can come with us. Mercy, can you back us up?"

Mercy frowned at her bow. "I think Suu is getting tired,

but I can use the binding once or twice more. That's a couple more Archlord hits. But it's not like one Herald, it's more like..."

"A bunch of Heralds smeared over some toast," Yerin provided.

That reminded Lindon of the Eight-Man Empire, and he turned to ask Eithan if he knew what that might mean about their enemy.

When he saw Eithan still standing there, an unreadable expression on his face, Lindon realized Eithan hadn't said a word since they'd entered the room.

It inspired Lindon himself to look around.

There wasn't much to sense in the room; certainly nothing to draw his spiritual perception. There were a few small dream tablets here and there, but by and large the chamber resembled a once-crowded workshop or storeroom that had been cleared out in a hurry.

Dust covered the floor, along with bits of grit and undefinable scraps of metal. There were scuffs and indentations in the stone where something heavy had been moved, but with the power of these floors, Lindon would be shocked if any amount of weight would have made a dent on their own. Here and there bolts remained in the walls where something had been suspended, but whatever it was had been removed long before.

High up on the far wall, he saw the thing that must have grabbed Eithan's attention immediately. A giant symbol: a scythe hanging like a crescent moon over the Arelius family crest.

This room had once belonged to the Arelius family Patriarch.

Ozriel.

Lindon was suddenly much more interested in the dream tablets.

Here and there, glittering tablets like cut gemstones were embedded in the wall next to where something must have rested.

Lindon held his hand over one nearby, which hung next

to a pale square of wall that looked like it had once held a painting. He slipped his perception into it.

The intricately carved ivory box is ringed in script so dense he can barely make it out with his eyes, and it carries a powerful will to bind. The bones used to make it are irreplaceable, and come from—

Lindon felt a sudden, blinding headache and was kicked out of the memory. He blinked and held onto his head.

This was what it had felt like when he tried to view a memory too advanced for him. But that was a shock. What concepts couldn't he handle? He thought he could comprehend most Monarch dream tablets now, but evidently not if it trespassed on certain subjects.

"Careful," Eithan said quietly. He still hadn't moved.

[It is only that moment of the tablet that exceeds your authority,] Dross mentioned. [It should be safe to experience if you pick up a moment after you left off.]

Generally speaking, it was hard to view dream tablets with so much precision, which was one reason why they were often attached to projection constructs or control scripts. But with Dross to help, Lindon adjusted his entry point and dove back into the tablet.

In a windy forest, his hands open the ivory box. The scripts activate, and he's proud of their efficiency. They are a work of art in the way they synergize with the significance of the bones and of the box itself.

The device is now designed for one purpose, and it fulfills that purpose before him now. A powerful suction fills the air, drawing spirits closer. Remnants stumble out of the trees. They have been drawn by the hunger aspects in the madra, though the hunger doesn't touch him at all.

One spirit—a water Remnant with minor sword aspects—is the first to fly into the air. It's only about Highgold in density, and it resembles a six-foot praying mantis. At first.

In seconds, it folds like paper as it is packed into the box. It sounds disgusting, like meat and bone being crushed and folded, but this device doesn't need to be pleasant to use.

Most importantly, the dead matter and binding are perfectly preserved. And the box still has plenty of capacity left.

Lindon broke away from the memory. His head still hurt a little from even that momentary thought about the bone, but his thoughts spun as Dross helped him sort out the memories.

As with most dream tablets, there were plenty of thoughts behind the memory itself, lending the scene context. Lindon could tell how much better this device was at catching and compressing Remnants, and how it could wait for centuries with no loss. There had been an idea at the back of the creator's mind: this would be the perfect way to seal a Monarch-level Remnant. It could even have applications for those attempting to advance to Herald.

He expected this to become a much sought-after treasure, and Lindon completely agreed. It wasn't as glamorous as a weapon, but he thought Reigan Shen would pay the worth of several cities for a Soulsmithing tool of this level.

Maybe he was the one who had looted this room.

He moved to another dream tablet as Yerin was pulled away from it. She had a troubled look on her face. "This is your ancestor, Eithan?"

Eithan ran a hand over his head as though wishing for longer hair. "The first of my House, yes."

"I'd pick you over him six times out of five."

Eithan blinked. "That may have been the kindest thing anyone has ever said to me."

"Don't let it swell your head," she muttered.

"This inspires me to compose a poem!"

"Can I pay you to stop?"

"There once was a man from Iceflower..."

Lindon reached out for the dream tablet and let the memory overcome him before he had to listen to Eithan's poem.

The enemy is desperate. He's already bloody and beaten, low on madra, as he has been tormented and kept on the edge of defeat for days now. He raises his axe and swings with a roar, squeezing the last of his madra and soulfire into an echo Forger technique. Phantom axes swing along with them.

Ozmanthus looks down on him in disdain. There is barely any willpower remaining in this technique.

He reaches out with his madra—pure destruction, as befits the Hollow King—and reaches into the Forger technique. With his soulfire art, he weaves destruction aura as well, drawn from all around him.

It takes him a moment of concentration to synchronize his control of madra and aura together, but he dismantles the technique. Before the Forged axe-blades reach him, they dissolve into essence.

He is displeased. With his skill in Soulsmithing, he should be able to separate madra much more quickly than this.

The prisoner tosses his axe to the ground and drops onto his heels.

"Kill me," the man says through a raspy throat.

Ozmanthus gives him a razor-edged smile. "You tried to kill me. You put my children in danger. Why should I show you mercy?"

"Your death would have been clean."

"What a comfort that is to me."

Ozmanthus began a Forger technique of his own, and shimmering black stars hung in the air over his prisoner's head. The Hollow King's Crown.

"Cycle," he ordered. "Restore your madra. Give me practice, and then I will give you mercy."

The memory skipped ahead after that, and he demonstrated his dismantling technique twice more—once on the prisoner's Striker technique, and then again on the man's Remnant.

Lindon committed it to memory, and Dross assured him that with some alterations, they should be able to develop a version of it themselves. Lindon suspected he might actually be better at it than Ozmanthus Arelius had been, at least at the point that dream tablet was recorded. He had three compatible madra types that could be used to take apart the techniques of others, and pure madra was better at taking apart spiritual energy than destruction madra was.

But despite the gains he had made through the memory, he was left with a sick feeling.

The man had an arrogance that permeated his every thought. He was the best, and he knew it. The prisoner really had tried to assassinate him, so Lindon didn't feel much pity for him. But neither was he comfortable with the Arelius Patriarch's callous disregard.

Eithan turned to him, having noticed that Lindon had finished. He didn't say anything, but Lindon got the impression he was waiting.

"I didn't realize the Path of the Hollow King was a destruction Path," Lindon said. That was the safest topic.

"It was less difficult than you might think to adapt it to pure madra. Many of the lesser aspects and fundamental principles were complementary."

"Apologies, but why bother?"

Pure madra had its advantages—Lindon was proof enough of that—but Eithan would have had a far easier time training a destruction Path. At least destruction aura existed.

Eithan busied himself with his clothes, not meeting Lindon's eyes. "No offense intended to the Path of Black Flame, but I found myself...less than comfortable with destruction madra. I have seen the Patriarch's memories myself. His experiences were enough to cause me to develop a distaste."

Lindon could understand that, and he didn't comment further.

Ziel peered down the sloping hallway. "Don't bother hurrying, but the enemy is building up strength."

The tunnel had already been sealed off by three layers of his scripts—this time, the runes were etched onto plates that he'd stuck to the walls, floor, and ceiling of the hall rather than Forging them in midair. The script should be less brittle this way. The first row was powered by Eithan's pure madra, the second by Yerin, and the third by Ziel himself.

"Does anyone else find it alarming that we haven't been attacked by the hunger spirits in a while?" Mercy piped up.

Lindon was examining the display next to the tablet he'd just read. He couldn't tell what had once sat there; he suspected a table and chair. Perhaps a book of some kind.

He spoke as he investigated. "If Subject One can't reach us here, we should use the time wisely. The value of these memories is...I don't have words for it."

Yerin pulled a hand back from a tablet nearby, next to a series of six triangular imprints in the stone. She looked startled.

"Lindon. You...I don't...bleed me, take a look at this."

He hurried over and immersed himself in another memory.

Ozmanthus' black hammer cracked against the gleaming chunk of wintersteel. He poured his madra into it, his soulfire, and his desperate wish for destruction.

His hammer amplified his wish, focusing his will, forming the metal into a perfect tool of elimination.

He could atone for the ruin he'd brought only by causing more, because that was all he could do. This arrowhead would be his apology for what he'd already done. His atonement.

His penance.

Lindon snapped out of the memory, dragging himself out of an ocean of despair. This memory felt much later than the others, and carried sadness like Ozmanthus had just watched his entire world collapse.

From the context of the memory, he knew what had been enshrined here. Not Penance, the prize that the Abidan had gifted to Yerin.

The prototypes. The failures.

Ozmanthus had tried many times to complete his Penance, to leave behind a perfect weapon to repay those he'd failed. But while these weapons might have all graced a Monarch's armory, he had never succeeded. He'd kept them here in the hopes that another Soulsmith might complete his work.

Eventually, he would succeed. But clearly sometime after he'd left this room for the last time.

"Long odds that we'd stumble on the place Penance was made," Yerin said. She was frowning at the spaces in the wall where the arrowheads had once been kept.

Eithan stood by her, looking on them as well. "Not as

coincidental as you might think. He spent many years on that project. Similar failures were once kept beneath House Arelius and in Blackflame City, though they were all used long ago. Anywhere you find his works, you are likely to find an attempt at Penance."

"He was a master of destruction madra," Orthos said from across the room. "Some of these techniques could teach us more about Blackflame." Lindon realized Little Blue was missing from his shoulder, and she and Orthos had found a dream tablet that even they could view.

Ziel firmed his two-handed grip on his hammer. "I like learning from my predecessors more than most, but I prefer to do it when we have *more time.*"

Lindon glanced over to the commotion in the hallway that he'd been ignoring. A Forger technique from the Tomb Hydras was actively clashing against Eithan's layer of scripts. Forged glowing fangs snapped at a barrier of blue-white madra, which flashed into existence every time they attacked.

There were half a dozen sets of jaws attacking, and as Lindon watched, another joined them. The barrier was going to fall soon.

"Can we pry out the dream tablets?" Lindon asked. It would be a real tragedy if they couldn't milk this room for everything it was worth.

"Not unless we can break the walls," Eithan responded. Once again, Lindon suspected he could do that, but it would cost him. And he certainly wasn't willing to flagrantly spend energy and attention with a powerful enemy in the next room.

He sighed. It seemed they really did have to take care of this enemy first.

"Oh, this one!" Mercy said excitedly. "Look at this one!" She pointed to a shimmering purple gem embedded under a set of lines that had once been etched into the stone, but time had wiped away.

Lindon flicked through it, but it wasn't as cohesive a

memory as the others. It was just a series of impressions, thoughts that Ozmanthus had meant to pass on.

Once, it had been a map of the labyrinth.

Dross!

[I have compiled the information, but much of the memory is faded, as this environment lacks a way to replenish dream aura.]

Any information was better than none. And as the labyrinth shifted seemingly at will, a "map" was more like an understanding of the patterns that governed its changes rather than a physical layout.

But there was one thing that stood out even more to Lindon. The wall showed an X scratched into the bottom of what had once been a diagram of the labyrinth. It marked the lowest room.

Ozmanthus' exact warnings and instructions had faded over the years, but his emotions remained. He urged those that would come behind him to make their way to that room.

That was where he had left a test. And a prize for any who proved themselves worthy.

"Eithan, I think—"

Eithan heaved a heavy sigh at Lindon's excitement. "What you're thinking is correct. I formed my reputation with Tiberian on my insight into the first Patriarch's memories, so I understand him better than anyone still alive. He left a Soulsmith inheritance here."

Lindon's heart raced.

"Not his *complete* inheritance, you understand," Eithan hurried to assure him. "He left this one behind long before he ascended. But it is still the legacy of a Soulsmith without peer. If you can win its approval, it would be invaluable."

Lindon clenched his fists. This was what he'd been waiting for.

The outer layer of scripts shattered, and Lindon finally turned toward it with impatience. This was an opponent that deserved his full attention, but it would be tragic if he couldn't find his way back to this room.

Still, he was filled with renewed motivation to proceed. "It's death madra. Can we get rid of it from here?"

"Not with the aura as weak as it is," Ziel put in. "Ruler techniques would be best for such a big target."

Lindon nodded. Mentally, he went over the constructs and dead matter he had prepared. How could they clear this with the least expense?

"This is going to cost us," he finally said. "We'll try to spread it out—"

He was cut off by a roar that shook the entire labyrinth and a flare of spiritual energy. The Forger techniques pushing against their defensive scripts vanished.

Everyone readied weapons.

"Here it comes!" Yerin shouted.

But nothing did.

After a moment of waiting, everyone turned to Eithan. He closed his eyes and extended his awareness.

"It's tricky to get much here," he murmured. "But I don't think its attention is..."

Eithan trailed off, and his jaw hung open for a moment. Then his eyes snapped open.

"Run," he ordered. "Lindon, we need a hole in the wall. Right here." He pressed his hand against the wall in the opposite direction of the Tomb Hydras.

Lindon didn't ask any questions. If Eithan was talking like this, that meant that the time for saving resources had passed.

He focused everything he had into black dragon's breath. Soulfire bathed the technique, and it fused easily with the authority of the Void Sage. A black bar of liquid flame, containing distant sparks of red flame, warped the world as it struck at the stone of the labyrinth.

Lindon felt another will opposing his, but his technique won out. He began carving through the protected stone. The edges glowed red-hot, but there was no molten stone; it had been erased by destruction.

Behind him, even without focusing his perception, he

could feel a presence clashing against the death madra. He couldn't make out its properties exactly; it was like a team of sacred artists of all different Paths had joined forces.

Eithan was still barking orders. "Yerin, guard the tunnel! Ziel, we need veiling scripts now! Mercy, put up the Dream of Darkness past the scripts. Orthos, help Lindon with the wall."

Drilling through the wall like this was far harder than cutting through ordinary stone, but Lindon had almost carved the outline of a human in the stone.

Then webs of hunger madra shot from every direction.

Everyone had to dodge. His Striker technique was disrupted, and everyone's techniques were interrupted.

Lindon and Eithan unleashed waves of pure madra—Lindon a little slower, as he'd been forced to switch from his Blackflame core.

These strands of hunger were more difficult to disrupt than any they'd faced so far. They pushed through the Hollow Domain, carrying a stronger will before Eithan eradicated them with concentrated Striker techniques.

"Too late," Yerin said, and then Lindon felt what she had a moment later.

An overwhelming presence had been unveiled, and it *felt* like the twisting of space. The death madra swelled to meet it...and was battered back.

Then torn apart.

They heard the tearing of meat echo down the hallway, followed by a deafening silence. And all of them knew who was coming.

Reigan Shen.

第十四章

CHAPTER FOURTEEN

ITERATION 001: SANCTUM

On Suriel's screen, Gadrael hovered in the middle of space. A translucent blue wall of force intercepted a planet-obliterating strike without so much as trembling.

"Did Makiel agree with this course of action?" Gadrael asked.

The Titan was a small but athletic man, made of muscle, with blue-gray skin and short horns like swept-back hair. He had perfected his body as he ascended, as virtually everyone did, and among his people his form was considered ideal beauty.

Suriel wondered how they would see him with a broken nose.

Not that she *could* break his nose. Not only was he an infinite distance away, but his cartilage was sturdier than most planets.

She could dream, though.

"Makiel is still in treatment," she told him. Again. "His mind is occupied with potential outcomes, and he cannot be distracted from his management of Fate."

"Contact me again when you have his approval." Gadrael turned, presenting her with the back of his smooth white armor, and readied the buckler on his arm. A vast cloud of black smoke billowed against his barrier, and the wall of order slowly began to dissolve.

Gadrael swept a hand and his barrier vanished. The smoke boiled forward, suddenly unhindered, and Suriel could sense the appetite and corrosive influence it carried. Enough to swallow a hundred planets.

The mundane buckler expanded in an instant, and Gadrael was holding the Shield of the Titan. It was a bulwark of gleaming steel, wide enough to shelter his entire body, and it crawled with red-hot veins like molten metal. She heard a distant roar as its powers activated.

The black smoke crashed over Gadrael in a wave, and her connection to him faded to nothing.

Suriel's hands curled into fists as she stared into her blank wall, and her Presence had to restrict her strength before she crushed everything in her building with the force of her irritation. With every passing day, worry ate away at her soul.

Not worry for Gadrael. He was the closest thing to invincible, and anyone standing behind him was as safe as they could be.

But he would plant himself like a fortress wall in front of someone, declare them under his protection, and never consider whether there was someone else who might need him more. He relied entirely on Makiel to direct him effectively.

Makiel, the Hound, who had refused to lend his support to Suriel's efforts.

She'd fail, he said. She had a far greater likelihood of success by waiting for the Vroshir to leave, as her Presence had told her.

Suriel couldn't accept that.

She had contacted every single one of the other six Judges, and they had all—in their own ways—turned her down. They would be delighted to accept *her* help, but provide their help to a risky venture when they didn't need to? Why? *Their* worlds weren't under threat.

Suriel was starting to see why Ozriel had left.

[You always knew why Ozriel left,] her Presence said. [He was abundantly clear about his frustrations with the Court.]

She held her hand over her eyes, wondering if she should

make herself sleep. Sleep was nothing but a luxury for her now, but it sounded amazing.

She wouldn't, of course. There was too much to do.

"I thought that when things were dire enough, they would change."

[That was never likely.]

"What haven't we tried?"

[Giving up.]

"Other than that." She downed another cup of tea. It really *was* good. It had been Ozriel's favorite.

Her Presence tapped into the power of her residence and teleported another dose of steaming tea into her cup.

[How high of a priority is this request?]

That was an unusual question. Suriel almost responded that it was the highest priority, but her Presence literally lived inside her mind. There was a reason why it had asked.

So she gave the question a moment of thought.

She could point out the number of lives at stake, but that was just as compelling an argument to wait. Every decision she made balanced the fate of innumerable lives. That was what it meant to be a Judge of the Abidan Court.

The Vroshir were coming for Sector 11, which included the strategically significant worlds of Cradle and Asylum. Strangely enough, Asylum was probably safe for the moment. Oth'kimeth, the Fiend inside the Mad King, did not appreciate rivals.

But after the rest of the Sector was destroyed, the corruption would no doubt break open that prison sooner rather than later. It would be a disaster for the Abidan. She could use that looming threat as a card.

In addition, Cradle was the birthplace of the Abidan. The first-generation Court of Seven had ascended from that world.

She had tried to use that as a lever for negotiation already. None of the current generation of Judges came from Cradle, and while they agreed it was a tragedy, the history of Cradle was already thoroughly represented in their archives. They would build it a lovely memorial.

Those were reasons why the Sector might be important to the Abidan, and strategic reasons why the Vroshir had gone to such lengths to surround it.

How important was it *to her?*

She thought of the worlds in the Sector. Asylum, Amalgam...Cradle.

She thought of Wei Shi Lindon, and of Ozriel. She had always known she would see Lindon die someday. Had expected it, in fact. And while Ozriel had left memories all over that Iteration, he *hated* the place. He might have even seen the outcome of the world's destruction and allowed it, though she couldn't imagine him allowing the rest of the devastation the Vroshir had brought.

"There is no reason to extend myself for this Sector," Suriel said aloud. It was lost. She'd made her peace with that.

Or she should have.

[No compelling one,] her Presence agreed.

"But I want to."

It was irresponsible, given the scope of her responsibilities. And far too small in scale. When the entire city burned around you, why try to save one house?

Then again, why not try? The city was already burning.

Her Presence gave her a sigh. [Then go to the Sector yourself.]

They had modeled that, and she couldn't stop the Vroshir advance. Not that she needed a model; the Mad King had torn through Suriel and Makiel together. She alone wouldn't even slow him down.

[Sector 11 is not enough of a strategic asset to mobilize the Court of Seven,] her Presence said. [But Suriel is.]

Suriel's armor flowed around her, and runes spun in her eyes. She looked into Fate; could Makiel see what she was about to do?

Under normal circumstances, he would have seen the possibility years ago. Now, he was watching futures other than hers, and chaos muddied the entire weave of Fate.

But her decision had shifted threads of causality. Makiel

was already starting to trace them back, looking for the cause.

Before he could find it, Suriel summoned her Razor and entered the Way.

She let the flows of pure order carry her between worlds, guided by her intentions. It took time to complete the journey, but she spent it gazing into the future and preparing.

When she arrived, she didn't emerge right away. She sat inside the Way and looked into the Sector.

As always, the space between worlds looked like a tunnel of textured blue, like a cross between light and cloth, but also indescribable in physical terms. But with her understanding of the Way, she could see tunnels branching off, splitting in different directions.

She hovered outside Sector 11, catching glimpses of its Iterations.

There, down that tunnel, was Amalgam. A standard, almost barren world, with tinier balls of color and potential clinging to it like fuzzy moons caught in its orbit. What the locals called Territories.

Up another sloping tunnel, she saw Asylum. This one was sealed off, and she could see the discs of elaborate script-formations set up by a previous generation's Gadrael. The scripts were fragmented and flickering, on the verge of failure, but they had been that way for decades.

Beneath the seals, the world itself was smoky gray, locked against intrusion from the outside. Through that barrier of gray, she could dimly see unspeakable shapes squirming, pushing against the restrictions of their prison. Fiends of Chaos, each powerful enough to contend with Judges. Trapped there by the collective will of ordinary humans.

She looked to each of the other worlds in the Sector, some more notable than others.

Then, finally, she looked to Cradle.

It should have been closer to her than any other Iteration, but the Way grew thin and gray as it approached Cradle. The Vroshir influence. If she tried to enter that Iteration, she would be shunted off to the side, most likely into another Sector.

But even obscured, Cradle shone like a star. She could see the powers that made it up swirling, the powerful—but still mortal—fates that clashed inside.

[WARNING: intrusion detected.]

Her Presence drew her attention up, until she looked into the neighboring Sector Twenty-One.

The Mad King's burning eyes met her own. Around him, blue light crumbled and twisted, the rules and laws of the universe breaking around him.

He wouldn't enter the Way physically for her. No fisherman dove into the ocean to wrestle a shark.

The Vroshir reached out with one bone-gauntleted hand, and that hand clawed for her in the Way, larger than her entire body. Its weight distorted the swirling world of order, bringing with it the crackling darkness of the Void.

Suriel's Razor erupted into its true form, from a meter-long bar of blue steel to a branching tree that sparked with light. It was the ultimate tool for cutting away corruption, and she cut at the Mad King's attack, severing it from existence.

[WARNING: multiple intrusions detected.]

Her enemy wasn't alone.

A chain of shining stars crashed into the Way to wrap around her, a constellation brought to life. From another direction came a thousand hands of blood. From yet another, a wisp of the same dark, corrosive smoke that Gadrael had faced.

She cleansed or severed each one, catching glimpses of the Vroshir on the other side as she did so. A spear crashed down on her like a meteor striking a planet, and she met it with her Razor.

Outside the Way, that would have been a deadly attack. Here, she could meet it, but it took all her focus.

And more and more of the Vroshir were drawn to this spot.

They swarmed around her, and the Way dimmed. Thread

by thread, it unraveled around her, revealing endless darkness specked with distant, swirling balls of color. The Void.

Enemies surrounded her, all attacking. And as they struck, she slipped from one side of existence to the other.

At least it's working, she thought.

Then the Mad King reached out again. This time, she had to bring the full force of her power to bear against the grasping hand, and the clash of forces stretched the Way even further.

The chain of stars wrapped around her midsection, and she couldn't spare the attention to stop it. Bloody hands landed on her leg, and a wisp of smoke twisted around her neck.

Her armor began to crack.

[Arrival incoming,] her Presence said.

A flaming sword burst through the Mad King's hand.

A woman carved through the Vroshir's attack with her sword, her Mantle boiling behind her like wings of white fire. Even her hair was crimson flame, and she severed the other attacks binding Suriel with one more sweep of her blade.

Razael, the Wolf, turned to face Suriel with a furious expression. "I should have let you die!"

Threads of blue light slipped back in as the Way recovered some of its hold. A shimmering orange diamond appeared over Razael's shoulder, sparkling with a different reflected face in each facet.

[My host is relieved she arrived in time,] Razael's Presence said.

A string of twisting symbols punched through the Way again, and Suriel glimpsed a group of Silverlords chanting in tandem. The silver crowns on their heads shone and serpentine runes twined around them as they called on the energy systems of plundered worlds to make their attack.

That working would be enough to rewrite the physics of any local Iteration, but Razael backhanded the ribbon of symbols with an armored fist. The working of the Silverlords shattered.

Razael glared at her Presence. "Plot our retreat!"

[We don't have a retreat,] the crystalline Presence said to Suriel. [She knows that.]

Void beasts clawed their way into being, indescribable horrors slashing their way through more strands of order, drawing them closer to the Void.

"Stop talking and help me!"

[She's happy to be here.]

The Mad King let the Scythe drift off to one side and drew his sword, a length of bone that screamed with the sorrow of a thousand butchered worlds. Suriel's instincts and Presence screamed danger, and she turned her attention to the attacks of the other Vroshir as the Wolf faced down the Mad King.

Another figure marched into the fading blue light, holding his molten shield ready. The Titan blocked the oncoming void-beasts, slapping them back out of reality.

"You will stand trial for this," Gadrael warned Suriel. "But for now..." He set his shield and faced the Mad King. "...nothing will touch you."

The blue light shone brighter, but only for a moment.

Daruman's red-sun eyes blazed as he spoke one word. "Come," the Mad King commanded, and he was echoed by his Fiend.

Their word spread through the Void, echoing among the empty chambers of chaos, and those who dwelled in chaos obeyed.

The world darkened, and once again, the hold of the Way began to slip. Even with three Judges present, the forces of the Void were too strong. Their gravity tugged the Abidan away.

Just when the Way had faded to one thin azure thread, a girl's head popped out.

She looked like she was about twenty, and she glanced around with uncertain eyes. "Quick, let's go!"

Someone else shoved her from behind. A distinguished gentleman whose glasses gleamed. As the girl tumbled out of her tunnel and emerged next to Suriel, he stepped out elegantly, and he even had his weapon in the form of a cane.

"I suppose you're going to insist on making me work, aren't you?" said the Spider, gesturing with his cane.

The Fox, Zakariel, trembled and hid behind him.

"This is not my doing," Makiel said.

The Hound manifested in full battle armor, holding his broad two-handed sword in one hand. He looked completely unharmed, with his dark and weathered skin and his iron-gray hair, but Suriel could see that his existence was still weak.

He gave Suriel a hard look. "But if we are to walk this path, we will walk it together. All of us."

The Ghost blew hair away from her face, and Suriel realized for the first time the woman was standing at her side. Durandiel was the only one of the Seven not wearing armor, instead wearing a dull gray dress that hazed into smoke and carrying a tall staff.

"We're all going to die," the Ghost said.

Makiel's Presence, a floating purple eye, answered her. [We have not seen our deaths.]

"I didn't mean here," Durandiel sighed. "I just thought it was worth contemplating our own mortality."

The Fox tried to slip out through the strengthening Way, but Razael caught her. "Where are you going, Zak?"

The young-looking girl squirmed in the grip of the Wolf. "Don't call me that! Call me Zerachiel!"

Razael glared. "That's not your name."

"At least don't call me Zak!"

Telariel sighed and adjusted his glasses. "This is beneath us all," the Spider said.

The attacks had stopped and the Way was back in full-force, now rippling with strength as the presence of the Abidan Judges reinforced order in the cosmos. The Silverlords and Vroshir backed away as they tore open portals into the Void.

From twisting in Razael's grip, the Fox froze. Zakariel's head snapped in the direction of the opening portals. "Now, where are *you* going?"

The Void portals winked out instantly. Some Silverlords in the process of fleeing were spat back into their Iterations.

Zakariel disappeared from the Wolf's hands, and she flickered through existence. A white-armored hand clapped onto the shoulder of the Vroshir.

All the Vroshir, save the Mad King. All at once.

Each Silverlord had a tiny Judge standing behind them, one hand on their shoulder, a wicked fox's grin on her face. Her teeth gleamed even in no light.

Gadrael braced his shield. "I can't cover all her bodies *and* the King! Durandiel—"

"I know," the Ghost said. She blew another strand of hair out of her eyes, and Suriel had half a mind to just cut it off.

Each Silverlord's reaction was different, but each one had once been a champion of their respective worlds. They responded with lethal force, erupting with workings of every description.

Durandiel tapped her staff lightly on empty space, and everything rippled.

The workings vanished, and the Fox struck.

Blood sprayed across many realities.

The Mad King kept his gaze focused on Makiel, and now the Vroshir held his sword in one hand and the Scythe in the other. His voice was a spear penetrating the Way.

"You make quite a show with the heavens to shield you."

The Judges looked down on the Mad King, and their wills were as one. Together, they slipped into reality.

ITERATION 119: FATHOM

A moment before, this world had trembled under the power of the Mad King.

A soldier arrived with his purple-veined sword, and Fate returned to its proper course. Makiel, the Hound.

A guardian appeared, steadied behind his shield, and the surviving mortal population shook with relief as they sensed they were protected. Gadrael, the Titan.

A gentleman stepped out, cane tapping at every step, and the shroud of chaos retreated, restoring the definition of order. Telariel, the Spider.

A woman drifted in, gray dress and black hair blowing like smoke, and perhaps she had always been there. Something shifted in the inner machinery of the world, but none in Iteration One-one-nine knew exactly what. Durandiel, the Ghost.

A warrior strode forward, ready for combat with sword blazing as bright as her hair, and all existence shone more brightly. Razael, the Wolf.

A healer descended on light like blue wings, and all over this reality, wounds knitted back together and fortress walls reassembled themselves. Suriel, the Phoenix.

A predator slunk behind the other six, and she tossed the still-bleeding head of a Silverlord behind her as Void portals closed and space stilled all throughout Fathom. Zakariel, the Fox.

For the first time in centuries, the Court of Seven manifested together, and the world was healed.

One by one, they met the burning red eyes of the Mad King. He hovered between them and the central planet of the Iteration, stained bone sword in one hand and dark Scythe in the other. His helmet of yellowed bone kept his face in a shadow impenetrable even to their light, and a mantle of hide ran from his shoulders to match their mantles of white flame.

He took not a step back, and his will was firm. He raised his sword to his face in a salute.

"Your courage does you credit," the fallen hero said to the entire Abidan Court.

From the darkness between the stars of Fathom, Fiends slithered forward. Blue flashes appeared in the darkness all over as Silverlords pressed against the outside of the world. They couldn't enter, with the Fox and the Titan both inside, but still they remained on the border. Waiting.

A host of their kind were inside already. Silverlords

floated up behind the Mad King, outnumbering the seven Judges many times over.

Makiel looked over them coldly. "Surrender."

Some Silverlords, those who had served a term in Haven before, shivered. Their wills shook. Even many of the Fiends cringed back like dogs remembering a whip.

But the Mad King did not tremble. "I sought to strike you a blow. Never did I imagine that I could topple the pillars of Heaven," the Scythe ignited in raging darkness, "with my own hands."

In a world called Fathom, between the Way and the Void, war erupted.

第十五章

CHAPTER FIFTEEN

Ziel spoke through gritted teeth. "Why is there a Monarch down here?"

"Same reason we are," Yerin said grimly.

"I know why. That question was for the heavens."

Lindon wrenched open the Dawn Sky Palace. "Orthos. Blue."

Little Blue whistled nervously and clung to Orthos' back. The turtle glared up at Lindon. "If we can fight against the Titan, we can..."

He hesitated. Lindon checked the performance of his right arm while waiting for Orthos to come to the right conclusion.

"...be safe," Orthos grumbled. He carried Blue inside.

Before Lindon let the portal close, he looked to Mercy. She was limbering up her shoulders and wheeling her staff around.

She gave him a forced smile. "Don't worry! He's weaker, I can feel it! My mother would squish him with one thumb if she were here."

Lindon turned to Ziel. "How about you? Can you keep up?"

"No," Ziel said. He hefted his hammer. "But I won't get in the way."

That was good enough for Lindon. He let the Dawn Sky Palace close and opened his other key. Not only could he feel the strain this time, but he could feel the invisible mechanisms of authority inside the key stretching and warping.

If he did this too many more times, he was going to break it.

Yerin had reached into her own key and withdrawn her Heart's Gem. She rolled the ruby of congealed blood onto the floor, where it began exuding billowing clouds of blood aura.

The blood was steadily eaten away by the hunger, but it would fuel her techniques. Swords spread out from her as well, scattered around the floor. They were practically drowned out by the Heart's Gem and the hunger, but they helped.

She stood defiantly in the center of the room. Her sword, robes, and most of her hair were black. Her eyes, Goldsigns, and one lock of her hair shone red.

Yerin was ready. And she wasn't hiding.

Mercy had webbed herself to the far corner of the ceiling, bow ready. The dragon head at the center of the bow glared amethyst beams, and she bit her lip in concentration as she held an arrow half-forged.

Beneath her, Ziel was Forging ring after ring around his hammer and each of his limbs. He must have been exerting himself, and the tips of his horns glowed as green as his madra, but his face was as blank as ever. The gray cloak on his back billowed with force.

Eithan stood next to Yerin in fine pink-and-blue silks. He looked...disturbed. His usual smile was missing, as it had been for most of the time they'd spent in this room, and he smoothed his short hair down though it didn't need it. He looked agitated, which might have made sense in the situation, but it didn't match what Lindon knew of Eithan. The man should have greeted even certain death with a grin and a joke.

Lindon controlled the aura generated by the natural treasures in his void key to send weapons floating out.

Wavedancer wouldn't help much, since flying swords oper-
ated on ambient aura, but he had plenty of other constructs
available.

As the balls of Forged madra flew, crawled, or rolled out
seemingly of their own accord, Lindon steadied his own
breathing and looked to Eithan.

"Are our odds that bad?" he asked quietly.

[Yes,] Dross said, but Lindon hadn't been talking to him.

"I may be making it look worse than it is," Eithan said. "I
was already in quite a mood."

"Good." Lindon strapped three launcher constructs to his
left arm. "Let's take it out on him."

Spiritual pressure rippled out over the entire room, shaking the surface of Lindon's construct. He felt Reigan Shen's
will, and Mercy was certainly right. This wasn't a Monarch
at full power. He must have spent months in the suppression
field, and the power of hunger would have taken bites out
of him.

In a way, that was more terrifying.

Because his will settled on them like the tide as Reigan
Shen strode out of the shadows. He looked like he'd spent
a year living in the desert. The white-gold mane of his hair
and beard was matted and overgrown, and his clothes were
ragged and patched. He had cases, bottles, and containers of
every description belted all over him.

A pair of swords hung at his hips, one huge and shining
orange and one thin as a needle. A shield had been slung over
his back, and a lens covered Shen's left eye.

And in his eyes was all the confidence of a Monarch.

He didn't look like someone who had survived the wilderness. He looked like the wilderness had survived him.

"Eithan! It seems I owe Subject One some thanks. I could
use an Arelius guide." He glanced up to the symbol on the
wall. "Especially here."

At some point, Eithan had recovered his smile. "I'm flat-
tered! I didn't think you'd trust me, given my track record at
guiding Monarchs."

"I was talking about your Remnant."

"I have a suspicion he wouldn't be any more pleasant to deal with."

"I'll find out for myself." Reigan Shen looked to Yerin and nodded. "Uncrowned Queen. Your performance was magnificent, and Red Faith is quite taken with your methods. I'd be more than willing to work with you."

Yerin shrugged. "No blood spilled between us. You want to get friendly, it depends on what you want to do with the Dreadgods."

Lindon, Ziel, Mercy, and Eithan were now spread out to flank the Monarch as Yerin stood boldly in front of him.

Reigan Shen didn't seem to mind their positioning at all. He openly examined Yerin with a sudden interest. "I think we might be able to work together. I intend to finally bring the Dreadgods under control."

"You'd bet that you can?"

"I'm betting everything."

Gleaming red-chrome madra slowly expanded from Yerin, and her sword lifted to point at him. "Love to test the edge of somebody who can hold a Dreadgod's leash."

"Yes. It will be your honor." Reigan Shen surveyed the rest of them with disdain. "Well? If you're going to attack, let's see it."

Lindon wasn't so rude as to turn down an invitation like that.

The three launcher constructs on his arm fired in a set sequence. First, the Web of Silence, a shimmering purple-and-orange web from a strange Path that attacked the mind and the spirit. Then a Starkeeper's Lance, from a Path that compressed sword and lightning madra to the utmost. Finally, the Swamp Fire, a swarm of knuckle-sized poisonous fireballs.

In a blink, all three constructs had launched, timed to land at their target together. From his other hand, Lindon unleashed a bar of black dragon's breath.

The others had struck at the same time.

Mercy—who once again felt like an Overlady—had released a barrage of a thousand Forged amethyst arrows. The binding of Eclipse, Sacred Bow of the Soulseeker.

Instead of swinging his hammer, as Lindon had expected, Ziel also used a simple launcher construct. It looked like a wasp's stinger, and it sent out a series of nails made from force madra.

Three people didn't move: Reigan Shen, Yerin, and Eithan.

A web spread out to devour Reigan Shen, glistening orange and purple. Behind it, a needle-sharp beam crackling with lightning and a spray of green fireballs. Lindon hadn't skimped on these weapons; all of them had been enhanced to the level of Archlord constructs. Meanwhile, a dark beam of Blackflame tore through the air to the side.

Gold-and-gray bolts flew from another angle, strong enough to drive holes through thick city walls. And from above, Mercy's amethyst bolts. Reigan Shen faced techniques from every angle.

A transparent bubble expanded from the shield on the Monarch's back.

All the techniques shattered when they struck the bubble, but Lindon could feel the impact they carried. The construct couldn't hold out—and sure enough, the shield itself broke.

That was what Yerin and Eithan had been waiting for.

Yerin shone white and appeared behind Reigan Shen, her sword shining. Eithan stood where she had before, and he drove a Hollow Spear at the Monarch's midsection. It was so advanced that it actually took on the image of a spear, the triangular head plunging straight for Shen's core.

He twisted, slamming the back of his fist onto Yerin's sword as he swung a kick at Eithan's head.

The force from that simple, mortal movement was hard for even Lindon to comprehend. It was like the Monarch had a Dreadgod sealed inside his body. Just one punch and a kick sent a storm howling through the labyrinth.

Eithan ducked back, avoiding the kick, but Yerin's sword met his fist head-on. Madra from the collision exploded, tearing the air again, and Lindon felt the world itself ripple. The Hollow Spear scraped past Shen's middle, vanishing into the wall.

Ziel's hammer came in a moment later, driven by five layers of Forged script. He swung with his whole body, and while he still hadn't fully recovered, Lindon *felt* the strength of an Archlord from him at that moment.

Reigan Shen still hadn't regained his stance, but he still twisted in midair and stopped the hammer with a palm.

Which was when Lindon, blazing with the Burning Cloak, arrived at his other side. He threw a punch at the back of Shen's head, and the Monarch spoke.

"Stop," Reigan Shen commanded.

But Lindon had felt his authority gathering and met it with his own. Their words overlapped.

"No."

Pain spiked through his head as his will clashed directly with the Monarch's. It *almost* worked. Lindon's fist hesitated for an instant before continuing, but it was enough for Shen to twist out of the way again.

Then Lindon found himself taking a step back again as Reigan Shen fought fist-to-fist with Eithan, Ziel, and Yerin.

Every clash between him and Yerin shook the room, but she couldn't make him take a step back. He didn't ignore Ziel's attacks, but he treated them dismissively anyway, and Eithan...

Lindon found that strange. The fight had only continued for a breath, but Shen had made sure to dodge all Eithan's attacks.

Spiritual attacks, Lindon realized.

[Agreed. I've sorted the appropriate constructs.]

Lindon switched to his pure core as Dross linked him to several constructs. A second later, and Lindon joined the fight again.

A sword of Forged cyan madra appeared in his hand, and he swiped at Reigan Shen, who dodged at the last second. Lindon followed up with an Empty Palm, and Shen was forced to face him for the first time.

That gave Eithan and Yerin an opening, and Yerin began Forging her Netherclaw technique as Eithan dropped stars of pure madra that speared down from the sky.

Reigan Shen blurred as he leaped, cracking even the protected stone of the labyrinth. He created distance, but Mercy had already webbed the top half of the room in soulfire-enhanced Strings of Shadow. As he broke through, a sphere of shadow expanded around him. The Dream of Darkness.

His mind and spirit would be protected from such things, but it should slow him down for a moment.

No one needed a reminder.

Lindon raised both his hands and filled the space with black dragon's breath. Eithan launched a Hollow Spear, Yerin slashed with Netherclaw, and Ziel accelerated his hammer through several rings of script so that it cracked like thunder as it plunged into the shadows.

[Danger!] Dross called to everyone, and Lindon switched back to his pure core. The Hollow Domain erupted from him just in time.

A slash of orange light split the room in half like a sunrise, dissipating the Dream of Darkness. Reigan Shen hovered in midair despite the lack of aura in the room, a misshapen orange sword blazing in his hand. It gave off an overwhelming pressure no less than Shen's own.

A chill ran down Lindon's spine as he felt Dross' alarm focus on spider-thin cracks that slowly vanished in front of Reigan Shen. He had, however temporarily, cut through the world itself.

"I've kept you company long enough," the Monarch said. "I don't like to work so hard."

A green feather emerged from a case at his side, and suddenly the room was filled with wind aura.

None of them waited for him to do as he wished. Striker techniques speared toward him, but slashes of orange light flickered out and struck them down, though his sword didn't seem to move.

A moment later, nine tridents appeared, shining green

with death madra that reminded Lindon of the Tomb Hydras. They hovered in the wind aura, and Lindon's heart sank. The Soul Cloak bloomed around him.

Even by a Monarch's standards, these were no ordinary weapons. They had a powerful will to destroy that resonated with the aura all throughout the labyrinth.

These tridents were *hungry*.

And one flashed at each of Shen's enemies. Dross slowed the world down, and Lindon extended his left hand to the trident spearing toward Mercy.

He could feel the will compelling the trident to seek life, and rather than oppose it, he redirected it.

"To me," Lindon ordered.

The trident swerved and headed to Lindon, but it wasn't as fast as the one that was already about to reach him.

This one, Lindon reached up and caught with his right hand.

Ordinarily, that would have been a fool's move. The Soul Cloak gave him the speed and precision to catch it, but he shouldn't be strong enough to hold back such a weapon.

The strength he'd gained from draining Crusher stayed with him, and now he was strong enough. Physically. But death madra seeped into him, eroding his life from the inside. It was trying to consume him.

So Lindon Consumed it right back.

The power of the trident soaked into Lindon, and he saw a few flickering images, pieces of the weapon's will. It didn't have memories, exactly; not like a living being did. But he pieced together something of an understanding.

These weren't nine weapons made to work together. This was one weapon, and it had one intention. Nine fangs flashing together.

And it wasn't happy about having its energy stolen.

The second trident arrived as the first started struggling to pull back. But Lindon had a firm grip on it.

He swung the first trident into the second.

[It will try to dodge, but it is not a true intelligence. Just a naturally formed will. But it is a very good thing that all nine are not focused on you.]

Sure enough, the trident tried to dodge, but it couldn't keep up with Lindon enhanced by the Soul Cloak. He knocked the second trident out of the air and vented the death madra into the air.

All the while, he watched and thought.

Mercy had used her freedom from the trident to focus attacks on Reigan Shen. Ziel had matched against his trident, Eithan had blasted it from the air and kept his attention focused on the enemy, and Yerin hadn't even been slowed down by hers.

Why *hadn't* Reigan Shen focused all the tridents?

He had kept four back to defend himself, which was certainly more than he needed. If he had sent them all at one person, he would have been able to keep them out of the fight.

[It looks as though he's trying to preserve your lives,] Dross suggested.

Or the tridents, Lindon responded.

And that hunch felt right. Reigan Shen would not waste his prized collection.

With renewed vigor, Lindon adjusted his grip on the death trident and Consumed again. The madra channels running into his arm strained, and he could feel the binding warping under the flow of powerful energy, but he kept it up.

The trident he'd knocked away turned back to him, and Reigan Shen shot him a look of annoyance.

One of the tridents defending him from Yerin's attacks peeled away and shot toward Lindon, leaving Lindon fighting *three.*

Lindon's thrill at having his theory proved right was accompanied by an equal sense of crisis. If Reigan Shen was fighting them while trying to avoid damaging his weapons, that meant he wasn't taking them seriously.

And the moment he did, they were going to die.

Lindon was overwhelmed for a moment, and only with

Dross' help did he manage to keep the three tridents off him. Even Mercy shot one down as it was about to hit him, and he focused soulfire and Blackflame madra into the most condensed black dragon's breath he could make.

With that, he sliced a trident in half.

Yerin and Reigan Shen were clashing in the middle of a visible thunderclap that distorted space, but Lindon still caught the Monarch's grimace. All eight of the remaining tridents flew back to Reigan Shen, almost impaling Yerin until she dodged.

"Enough of this," Reigan Shen said. The tridents vanished. "Engrave this memory into your Remnants. For you are privileged to witness the Path of the King's Key."

Gold-edged portals swirled open behind him. Five of them; one for each opponent.

Techniques emerged from the portals like serpents leaping from the ocean, and these were not the limited techniques that had been eroded by hunger aura. These were true Monarch techniques, and they blinded Lindon's senses.

[Processing!] Dross cried.

The scene seemed to freeze, as it often had before. That gave Lindon plenty of time to see what effects Reigan Shen had summoned from the weapons hidden in his void space.

One was a Forged hand, seemingly made of jade streaked with gold. The madra was so dense that it seemed physical, but Lindon could feel that it was dense energy of life and earth. The hand was reaching out for Ziel, and it was going to flatten him.

An orange-white line blasted out of another portal; this was red dragon's breath, focused to such a degree that Lindon could scarcely believe it. It must have been a launcher construct made from a red dragon Herald, and it shot for Eithan.

Ocean blue tides gushed out of a third portal, with enough pressure that the water itself could crush stone. Inside the depths were glowing, flickering humanoid figures. This was a mysterious water technique headed for Yerin, and it brought an energy of suppression that struck at the soul as well as the body.

A flurry of silver bat-like techniques rushed after Mercy, carrying sword energy complex enough that Lindon couldn't quite identify its makeup. They were possessed by a furious will, like a swarm of bloodthirsty bees. And their very presence shook his senses until he felt like he was going to bleed from the ears.

This was a technique meant to shred Heralds. Mercy wouldn't last a second.

A massive sword, so detailed that its blade gleamed in the light, speared toward Lindon, but he paid it no mind. It was made from dream madra Forged solid, and it reminded Lindon that Reigan Shen didn't know about Dross.

Between pure madra and Dross' support, Lindon should be able to crack that sword like it was made from cheap porcelain. But the others were in danger.

Dross, what can we do about the technique targeting Yerin?

[Inconclusive.]

Do we have enough time to block for Mercy with the Hollow Domain?

[Inconclusive!] This time, Lindon caught a hint of desperation from Dross' voice. That was fair, as Lindon was feeling not a little desperation himself.

What can *you tell me?*

[If we do not intervene, at least three of our allies will likely suffer life-threatening injuries. And I cannot hold on for much longer.]

His hold on Lindon's perceptions was beginning to slip. The dream madra was thin here, and Dross was still weak. Lindon looked desperately from one of his friends to the other. He could throw himself in front of Mercy, but then he wouldn't be able to reach Yerin. And what about Ziel?

With the Pure Cloak, can I make it to Mercy first and then get to Yerin?

[It depends on the exact strength of the techniques and how long Yerin can hold on. Most likely, yes. But that leaves Ziel.]

Eithan's closest to him. Tell him to cover Ziel. Lindon had to assume Eithan had another trick tucked up his sleeve.

[That will be the last significant action I can take.]

Do it!

The world slipped back into motion, and so did Lindon.

He dashed in front of Mercy, the Hollow Domain erupting around him. The world was filled with blue-white madra.

The techniques Mercy was using to defend herself were canceled, and her purple eyes widened in panic as the Strings of Shadow lashing her to the ceiling were wiped away.

The bladed silver bats were *not.* They were so dense and so much stronger than Lindon that they dove into the Hollow Domain and continued flitting for Mercy.

While they weren't destroyed, they *were* weakened.

Lindon slammed an Empty Palm against them, focusing his will and his soulfire on the technique. A Forged palm bigger than his body smashed into the fluttering blades, and they crashed into it like a wall.

But each one pounded against his spirit, and he felt like a window pelted by hail. Each strike left him cracked.

That was when the dream sword arrived. It wasn't as dense as the spirits of sword madra, so it was weakened more by the Hollow Domain, but still not enough. It plunged into Lindon's mind, and his concentration was disrupted as it struck.

The Hollow Domain flickered. Dross pitted himself against the technique, but he was weaker than he had calculated. It took too long.

In the absence of the Domain, the remaining bladed bats flew around Lindon toward their intended target. Mercy called up her bloodline armor as she fell, and it formed before the Domain returned.

Even so, they cut straight through her armor.

Mercy's blood sprayed the floor from a dozen wounds, and she screamed.

Dross finally broke the sword, and instead of rushing toward Yerin, Lindon had to fall toward Mercy. Concentrated pure madra broke the technique, but Mercy's bloodline armor had already shattered. She bled from too many wounds, including one to the neck.

Lindon pressed down on it, pulling out the healing construct he'd withdrawn earlier. A pulsing sac of blood and life madra attached to her wound, feeding her healing energy, and her breathing steadied.

With dread in his heart, Lindon looked up to Yerin.

She was pinned to the wall by a rush of dense water madra, and he saw flickers of red as she battled with the glowing white silhouettes in the depths. He felt her holding her own, and he was encouraged.

Then Reigan Shen lazily raised his sword in her direction.

Lindon's world focused to a single point.

"Stop!"

Reigan Shen froze. He snorted and tugged his arm against Lindon's will as though pulling against stubborn cobwebs.

Pain stabbed through Lindon's head, and his working broke. But he blinked past tears in his eyes to see that it did have *some* effect.

Reigan Shen had turned his sword toward Lindon instead.

[I cannot go further,] Dross said, but there was a little more emotion in his words now. He sounded ashamed. [I am...too weak.]

Me too, Lindon thought.

But Lindon raised his arm and gathered his madra. He would try to Consume some of the power in the attack Reigan Shen was about to use. If it had worked to weaken the Titan's attack, maybe it would work here.

As he activated the technique in his arm, he felt a soul-piercing snap. The binding fell apart.

And his arm fell to his side, inert.

The glowing sword cracked the void as Reigan Shen swung it down, sending spatial cracks to every side like a spiderweb. A slash of orange light rushed for Lindon, and when he felt it, he realized his Consume technique would have done nothing anyway.

Lindon still didn't give up.

He stood over Mercy's body and radiated the Hollow Domain. If he weakened it enough, then maybe—

Eithan appeared in front of them.

Ghostly blue-white armor shimmered over every inch of his body, as though he wore a Remnant over his skin. Archlord soulfire rippled through him for a second, like quicksilver.

Then he was striking forward with a Forged spear.

His will and technique crashed against Reigan Shen's. Deep, black cracks spiraled through the air as the world began to break.

Orange madra dispersed into essence, Eithan's spear broke, and the cracks healed.

A smile tugged at one side of Reigan Shen's mouth. "You've worked so hard to stand before me. I'm almost proud."

"That's not what I was working for," Eithan said. "But I admit...it is a perk."

Lindon felt something. Eithan had reached beyond himself for that attack. His will was dense, and far-reaching. He had tapped into something bigger than himself.

An image began to form at the ceiling, something more real than a working of dream and light. Lindon began to see a shaft of polished wood, projected from beyond reality.

Then Eithan gestured, and the image cut off.

Reigan Shen's head jerked back, and he looked truly shocked. "What are you thinking?"

Eithan pointed another spear of pure madra. "You are not my goal. You're just in my way."

"Very well." The Monarch lightly twirled the sword in his hand and another golden portal appeared behind him. "Die, then."

And the battle between Eithan and Reigan Shen began.

第十六章

CHAPTER SIXTEEN

Eithan's spear grew as it flashed across the room, and Lindon saw that he had projected the Hollow Spear technique from his scissors. It was a perfect blend of sacred instrument and Striker technique, carrying the power of both.

But it was only enough to match the orange energy that Shen projected from his own sword. The entire room shook, spiritually and physically, and Lindon was painfully aware of how little madra he had remaining.

Compared to his normal state, at least. Compared to the others, he was in great shape.

Ziel moved weakly against the wall, half his body burned. His clothes had been singed away. Lindon hadn't seen what had happened to him, but obviously Eithan hadn't been able to save him completely.

Lindon carried the still-healing Mercy away. She mumbled at him that she would be fine—and she would, thanks to the healing construct on her neck—but he needed to move her away from the battle.

Eithan called a rain of stars down on Reigan Shen, and Shen responded by swallowing them all into a portal he opened over his own head.

This time, Lindon noticed that the portals were actually sticking just like the void keys had been. Shen had to spare the willpower to force open his own void space. That had to be a weakness they could exploit.

But another worry overcame him first: Yerin.

She was still inside the water technique.

Every clash between Eithan and Shen shook the surging mass of water that imprisoned Yerin, and every now and again her madra speared out, but her spirit was still flashing inside. She was battling against the spirits inside the technique, and she was weakening.

Lindon sprinted around the wall of the chamber. His pure core had less than a third remaining, and his soulfire was a dim candle, but he had to help.

Dross, what do you have left?

[Not what I should, and that disturbs me. Northstrider once used me to develop a combat report against Reigan Shen.]

Lindon's hopes soared.

[But I am too fractured,] Dross continued. [I can piece together so little of it. Too little.]

Lindon's heart crashed back down. *Let me know if you remember anything. In the meantime, tell Yerin I'm on my way.*

As Reigan Shen hurled Eithan across the chamber and Eithan retaliated with a slash of suddenly-huge scissors, Lindon dove into the side of a raging river like a waterfall suspended in midair.

Suddenly he could feel the pressure of the technique first-hand. He'd been able to sense it from across the chamber, but this was like the weight of the ocean crushing him from every direction. It was a churning maelstrom of water madra on at least the Herald-level, and every drop bore the will to destroy him.

A ghost of soft white light drifted up to him, extending hands out to him as though in peace. The spirit's smile was a black crescent in its face.

Lindon met it with the Empty Palm.

On a human being, the Empty Palm washed their madra channels clean, temporarily robbing them of control over their own spirit. On a spirit, it blasted away the very material of their body.

The spirit dissolved, but its smile only widened.

From the darkness of the chaotic water, two more spirits came for him. They darted in when he wasn't looking, then flitted away when he turned toward them. They were afraid of his pure madra, and Lindon couldn't tell if it was an instinctive aversion or if they'd learned from what happened to the first.

Lindon extended his perception, searching for Yerin, but he found his senses choked off. He felt as though he were adrift in the center of an endless ocean with no surface, and it was only him and these eerie, malicious spirits.

He began cycling for the Hollow Domain, but Dross stopped him.

[This environment is already filled with madra denser than your own. The most you could do is weaken it for a moment, and then your Domain would collapse.]

Then I'll have to try something else.

Surrounded by water, Lindon switched to his Blackflame core.

It wasn't ideal, of course, but the Path of Black Flame was destruction as much as it was heat. And he had more Blackflame madra left than pure.

Lindon controlled finger-thin beams of dragon's breath, fully aware that Yerin might be nearby. He sliced both spirits in half.

They re-formed instantly, still grinning. Four hands extended to embrace his head, and he felt an overwhelming sense of peace. Foreign will pressed in against him, urging him to relax and allow them in. Strangely enough, the technique reminded him about Bai Rou, although the Skysworn's techniques had always felt repulsive.

But such a vague temptation had no sway over Lindon. The spirits were close, now; closer than they would have gotten if he had kept cycling pure madra.

So they had fallen for his trap.

Blackflame retreated, replaced by pure madra, and his eyes turned blue.

They turned to swim away, but it was too late. An Empty Palm caught one, then the Soul Cloak propelled him after the second. He dispersed that spirit too.

And in the instant he projected the Hollow Domain, it lifted the veil the water kept over his senses. He felt Yerin.

He swam in that direction and encountered her in seconds.

She was *surrounded* by spirits, slicing them apart as quickly as they regenerated, but they had no physical bodies. A huge spirit—obviously the leader of the white shadows—loomed over her. Lindon had seen many strange Remnants, but this one resembled something like a soft centipede with human hands instead of legs.

He hated it on sight. Especially as it curled around Yerin and tried to entrap her.

Her eyes fluttered under the psychic attack, and her movements became more sluggish. Lindon didn't know how she'd held out so long.

But she didn't have to last much longer.

The centipede's head swirled around, and Lindon saw it too was disturbingly human. It grinned a black grin.

Then Lindon put his remaining soulfire into an Empty Palm and blasted the head off its shoulders.

Water poured everywhere as the entire technique popped like a bubble. Half of it dissolved to essence, but the ground was flooded with real water as well. Half of it had been actual liquid controlled by aura.

Lindon caught Yerin one-handed as they both fell, and he landed with her in his arm. She coughed and sputtered, taking a deep breath.

"Thought...Heralds...couldn't drown," she choked out.

Lindon wanted to respond, but his attention was drawn to the battle still raging in the center of the room.

Eithan and the Monarch had taken it to another level.

Hollow Spears flashed in a flurry as stars rained from the ceiling. A gold portal opened and released another beam of concentrated red dragon's breath like the one that had targeted Ziel, but it broke on the Hollow King's Armor. An orange slash missed Eithan and broke the stone of the labyrinth as a stab from enlarged scissors did the same to the floor.

It was so fast that it was hard to follow, even for Lindon, though he was sure Yerin wouldn't have a problem. But there was a dimension to the battle that only he could appreciate.

Every move from each of them was a clash of will so profound as to bend reality. While Reigan Shen used no verbal commands, each of his techniques carried enough authority to kill Eithan outright.

And with sheer willpower, Eithan matched and stopped them.

An image appeared over Eithan, a connection to powers beyond this world. An Icon.

Eithan canceled it half-formed.

He peeled aside chains that Reigan Shen summoned, and another Icon began to form. Eithan denied it again.

Lindon asked Dross, *Apologies, but am I seeing wrong?*

[No, I agree with your assessment. It appears he is denying an advancement to Sage.]

Why?

Did Eithan know what he was doing? Maybe he was feeling a foreign influence and cutting himself off for it out of instinct.

But no, this was Eithan. The king of theory that even rival Monarchs respected. He would know what he was doing.

In which case, this must be part of his plan. Advancing to Sage had to hurt him somehow, even if that advancement would bring him advantages.

But Lindon could tell how this fight would end, if it continued as it was. Eithan may have deep madra reserves, but he was facing a Monarch.

Lindon needed to balance the playing field.

His head was pounding, and he found it hard to concentrate. He had pushed himself to the brink already in this fight.

He had enough experience now to understand something about how weaponizing willpower worked. He didn't have a finite amount, like madra or soulfire. Rather, it was more like physical strength, in that by using it he exhausted himself.

And he had already used as much of his will as he ever had.

But that didn't mean he was out.

He focused on Reigan Shen and waited for the right chance. If he wanted to have the most impact, he had to maximize his timing and the connection to his Icon. Meaning he needed to leverage his Void authority to maximum effect.

Lindon's gaze was naturally drawn to the golden portal forming behind Reigan Shen.

"Close," Lindon commanded.

The portal made from the Path of the King's Key led onto a void space, so it was the perfect thing for Lindon to affect with his authority. But at the same time, it was Reigan Shen's personal property, and perhaps might even count as a part of his power. He had authority over it by default.

But Shen was focused on Eithan.

While the Monarch was distracted, his portal closed.

A Hollow Spear caught him through the gut.

He roared in pain as his spirit was scored, and Lindon felt the impact the spiritual damage had on his madra. Reigan Shen's eyes flashed gold, and he *tore* open another portal behind him.

Lindon knew immediately that he had no chance of stopping this one from opening, but he had expected as much.

So he did the opposite, and pushed it wider. **"Open."**

The portal opened easily this time, without the resistance that Shen had pushed through every other time inside the labyrinth. "Greetings from Tiberian," the Monarch said.

Multi-colored lightning thundered out of the portal.

It carried such destructive pressure that Lindon knew it

wasn't the end, but Eithan used everything he had to defend. The stars from the Hollow King's Crown flew down to resist the lightning, Hollow Spears crashed against it, and he poured soulfire into everything.

The many-colored thunderbolt crashed through one star, then another. It broke a bundle of spears, pushed through a river of pure madra, and struck against the Hollow Armor.

Eithan gritted his teeth and pushed. His scissors split the storm madra as the attack peeled pieces of his Hollow Armor away one chunk at a time.

Finally, Eithan wavered unsteadily on his feet. Blue-white essence faded upward as his broken armor faded, but he had survived the attack.

Then a hand emerged from the portal, followed by another. The hands were made from Forged madra of the same aspect as the lightning before; storm madra of many lesser aspects woven together. This multicolored lightning was so dense as to be tangible, and it even reminded Lindon of the Ninecloud Court's royal madra.

A man's face pushed through, and Lindon could make out clear features of his face. This spirit was at least as dense as Little Blue or Ruby, with a similar level of existence. He looked like Eithan's older brother, with short hair and a short beard, and a deeper light crackled in his eyes.

When he emerged, spiritual pressure pushed down on all of them. Even Reigan Shen flinched briefly at the tension in the air.

This was a Monarch without months of hunger aura eroding his spirit. A true Monarch's Remnant.

As its gaze landed on Eithan, Lindon saw a golden collar encircling the Remnant's throat. Runes on the gold blazed with power.

"Eithan," the Remnant said, with a voice like buzzing lightning. "You survived. I am sorry."

Pure grief was not an expression Lindon had expected from Eithan. "Shen...was our grudge really this deep, for you to do this?"

Tiberian's lightning eyes turned to Reigan Shen, and he tried to duck back into the portal.

"**Kill!**" Reigan Shen commanded.

There was a clash of authority so intense that Lindon could feel it, as a weakened Monarch pitted its will against the Remnant of another. The collar flared, and he knew it would turn the competition in Shen's favor.

This was Lindon's chance.

With the last of his will, he issued the same command one final time: "**Open.**"

Reigan Shen's concentration was entirely focused on Tiberian's Remnant, and this time the portal around Tiberian expanded more rapidly. It pushed against the labyrinth, clashing against the authority that prevented spatial transportation until Lindon could hear the two forces groaning against one another.

But the labyrinth's rule was endless. Reigan Shen's authority was not.

With a snap, the portal's structure collapsed.

The lightning Remnant smiled faintly as he let himself fade back into the void space. Shen tried to force the space back open, but the connection between himself and his weapons was now broken. It would take time to repair.

His golden eyes blazed with rage, and though Lindon felt like he would pass out at any second, he gave a smile.

"Apologies," Lindon said.

The Monarch was not amused. Lindon only wished there were something they could do with this opportunity. Reigan Shen couldn't recover his power either, and now he was cut off from his supply of weapons. This was the most mortal they could get him, and he had to be as low on madra and soulfire as they were.

But Eithan was just laughing weakly as he swayed on his feet, his armor still dissolving and scissors held in a trembling hand. His spirit felt like it would be extinguished by a passing breeze.

Ziel had lost consciousness at some point, and the burns

across the left half of his body were still smoking. Mercy was conscious, and contained inside a cocoon of Strings of Shadow, but nothing she could do would defend her from even a casual attack of Reigan Shen's.

Yerin had gathered enough strength, and she rolled away from Lindon to rise up on one knee. Her arm was strong as she swung her sword up, and he was certain she could trade an attack or two with Reigan Shen. But not for long.

Lindon himself was down an arm, he could barely see straight after over-using his authority, and his pure core was mostly empty. His Blackflame madra was actually in decent supply, but his soulfire was completely gone.

He was out of cards.

But Dross wasn't.

[I have made contact,] Dross said at last. [Beware.]

The attention of the labyrinth must have been watching them already, but now Lindon felt it focus on them. On Dross.

Then it swiveled to Reigan Shen.

He casually swiped an orange Striker technique at Yerin, who struggled against it. While she was pushing back his madra, he looked up and shouted.

"You see? I can grant your wish!" Reigan Shen roared. "Bring me to you!"

Lindon felt a moment of consideration. And then a sudden, overwhelming hunger.

The walls blurred, and then there was an opening in the center of the floor. A pit that went deep.

He remembered the impressions he'd gotten from the broken map Ozriel had left behind. Subject One waited in a deep chamber at the center of the labyrinth.

Lindon didn't know if this tunnel led all the way there, but it was certainly the right direction.

Reigan Shen laughed and strolled over to the lip of the hole, sheathing his sword as he walked. "Don't worry, humans. Tiberian will rest in peace."

He paused and looked to Eithan. "Because I will fulfill his dream."

Then he dropped into the abyss.

The floor immediately shifted and closed up around him, the entrance vanishing. Ozriel's workshop was now left with the sounds of failure: groans, harsh breathing, the slosh of water, and the distant hiss of madra dissolving into essence.

But Lindon didn't feel ashamed. He was filled with relief.

They had made it out alive.

He was doubly grateful he had thought to hide Orthos and Little Blue. A glancing blow from that battle would have killed them; he would have been worried about their safety even if they were only exposed to the pressure from Tiberian's Remnant.

[Vermin!] Dross cried. [He flees from us like a coward, little knowing that we may bide our time and seek revenge.]

Yerin shot him a strange look, suggesting she'd heard him.

"Dross?" Lindon asked aloud.

[It is I, the mighty Dross! I have shed my weak former self, emerging from that chrysalis as a spirit with no rival!]

Eithan groaned and sat down. "Oh no."

"Dross, what happened? Why did you...change?"

Dross spun out into the real world, and now he wore a tiny, spiked black crown on his head. [I needed to reach beyond myself, for greater power, but I was pathetic and small. So I became a spirit of true power!]

Dross' boneless arms curled into fists and shook at the sky.

A knot formed in Lindon's stomach. If Dross had been forced to his limit and decided to change himself, he may have done irreparable damage to his own structure.

"So this is what true power sounds like, is it?" Yerin asked. She sounded weary but amused, like this was one of Dross' usual jokes.

Eithan traded looks with Lindon. He understood.

[Every word I speak is the word of supreme dominance! Have you ever heard of a spirit that could converse with the Dread Labyrinth itself?]

Lindon gingerly extended his perception into the point

of his spirit that anchored his connection to Dross. Sure enough, the structure of Dross' spirit was twisted differently. Dross had bent himself into a new shape, and his spirit, body, and mind were one.

"Pardon, Dross, but I'm afraid your new form might be too...intimidating for me. Could you change back?" Lindon tried to stifle his own dread and hope so that Dross didn't feel them.

Dross eyed him coldly. [Evolution, once made, cannot be reversed. And why would I wish to return to inferiority?]

Lindon sank to the ground. Yerin grabbed him and looked into his eyes.

"Is he..." she didn't finish the question.

Lindon shook his head, and she crushed him in an embrace.

"It's not him," Lindon whispered. "And even if I were twice the Soulsmith, I don't know if I could do anything about it."

The longer the changes lasted, the more they would become the true Dross. He didn't know Dross' exact structure, and even if he did, he wouldn't have the time to change him back.

Do you remember how to defeat Reigan Shen? Lindon asked Dross silently. At least there may be some upside to this transformation.

[Why would I need such tricks?] Dross sneered.

Lindon's heart crumbled further.

Eithan pointed to the wall. "Far be it from me to dangle a flimsy hope before you, but it's possible we may be able to bypass Reigan Shen and still accomplish something down here."

Lindon raised his head and looked over Yerin's shoulder. The weathered map, lightly scratched into the wall, had been further obliterated by the battle. But he could still make out the X marking the bottom of the labyrinth.

"Ozmanthus' Soulsmith inheritance," Lindon said aloud. He perked up. With the Soulforge and a Soulsmith inheritance of this level...

"Could we fix him?" Lindon asked quietly. But of course the volume of his voice had no bearing on whether Dross could hear him.

The dream-spirit swelled up to twice his size. [Do not test me, human! I do not need *fixed* any more than the moon needs polished! How do you fix that which is already perfect beyond your comprehension?]

"I'm certain it could be...used to that effect," Eithan said carefully. "But I am concerned about potential changes to your mentality if you inherited his legacy. He was not a kind man. Though not so concerned as I am about Reigan Shen getting it first."

Lindon shivered as he thought of the Monarch falling down the shaft straight toward where the inheritance waited. Would he even care about such an inheritance? He was a legendary Soulsmith in his own right.

Then again, if it *was* valuable to him, then they were about to face a Monarch with the absorbed memories of a weaponsmith who had ascended to become known as the Reaper of Worlds.

That did assume that they were going to continue in the labyrinth.

[Of course we are!] Dross declared. [He has thrown the gauntlet, and we are not the sort of cowards who would fail to pick it up!]

"Pardon, Eithan. But I need to know something first."

Everyone conscious looked to Eithan, even Dross. Eithan seemed to know what Lindon was going to ask, because he planted his hands on his hips and beamed. "You want to know about my Icons!"

"If you don't mind."

"The Icons that almost formed in my fight with Reigan Shen!"

"Yes."

"The very Icons that, when manifested fully, would have made me into a Sage!"

Yerin's red eyes narrowed. "Those shoes'll get dirty if you keep dragging your feet."

"It's very simple: I'm waiting for another Icon." He glanced around and shuddered. "Besides, I don't want to advance *here.* The circumstances of your advancement can affect your relationship to an Icon, and these tunnels are so...dirty."

Dross scoffed, but Lindon was caught by the first part of the statement. "What Icon are you waiting for?"

"The Joy Icon."

Yerin groaned.

"It's real!" Eithan said defensively. "It's just not...very common. To be frank with you, I'd take any number of Icons, just not anything Ozmanthus manifested. I don't want to end up as he did."

"Famous?" Yerin asked. "Powerful?"

"Alone."

That was painful enough to hear, so Lindon changed the subject. "What did he mean about Tiberian's dream?"

Eithan sighed and ran a hand over his hair. "This is another step toward coming clean with you two, I suppose. Tiberian's dream was to rid the world of the Dreadgods."

Yerin's eyebrows raised, but Lindon wasn't too surprised. He suspected she wasn't either. The Arelius crest on the sealed hand implied as much.

"We found a method of doing so, and I encouraged him to pursue the cooperation of the other Monarchs," Eithan said with a sigh. "He insisted on starting with Reigan Shen. *Against* my advice, might I add. You can usually count on Monarchs to avoid open conflict, both because there is rarely a definitive winner and because there are usually several million definitive losers.

"Reigan Shen struck back almost immediately. In the end, Tiberian was not his match."

Eithan began tearing burned strips of his outer robe away as he spoke. "As you are aware, it is not simple to destroy the Dreadgods. No Monarch can defeat one individually, and while the Monarchs could collectively destroy the Dreadgods together...there is a reason they do not. A reason I am forbidden by oath to mention. But..."

He raised a finger and gave a smile. "...I am not forbidden from demonstrating it to you. You will find that reason deeper in the labyrinth, unless I miss my guess."

Lindon looked at the place where the hole in the floor had led straight to the center of the labyrinth. "So is he really going to kill the Dreadgods?"

"There is only one truth I trust about Reigan Shen: he desires weapons. We can't know if he means to kill them and weaponize their bindings, or leash them as forces of destruction under his control."

Eithan's smile faded. "He wants Cradle. All of our world. And he clearly sees the Dreadgods as the way to take it."

Lindon's eyes moved from one opening in the wall to another. He could bring out the hand again, if they were willing to endure the assault of hunger madra that would ensue.

While he felt the weight of every second, he still spent the time to organize his thoughts before he spoke.

"I'm going deeper," Lindon said. "I don't want to go alone."

"Neither do I, Lindon. Neither do I."

Yerin stood up and sheathed her sword. Red lines of blood madra covered her flesh in a crimson web, knitting her together. "Blind me now if I see any reason to stay here, but we've got to move. Cuts me to say it, but we may need to travel...light."

Red eyes flicked from Ziel to Mercy.

Lindon knew she was right, but his heart was heavy. "We need to move fast if we're going to catch up. But I don't want to leave them behind."

"They can't keep up," Eithan said flatly.

Lindon felt the hunger aura all around him. It filled him with greed, with a desire to move forward, with an ambition that couldn't be satisfied. The inert fingers of his right hand twitched. Even now, the aura gnawed slowly away at his madra.

But this time, the hunger sparked something in him.

Anger.

"I don't want to leave them behind. Do you want to leave them behind?"

Yerin shrugged, but there was sadness in her eyes. "Done a lot of things I didn't want to."

"I say the time for that is over."

With great effort, Lindon poured madra into his broken right arm. The hunger madra creaked, and bits of it snapped off, and spiritual pain ran through his channels.

But he clenched his fist.

"If we can't use our power for this, why have it?" He looked from Eithan to Yerin, and he could feel a fire in his eyes even with no Blackflame. "I don't want to win by giving something up. I want it all. I want *all of it.*"

The fury of the Void Icon faded, and he coughed a little in embarrassment. "...if you're willing, of course."

Yerin leaned into him, and her hand snaked up his chest and over one shoulder. "Ought to be grateful you don't talk like that more often," she murmured.

Eithan was blinking back tears, which caught Lindon off-guard.

"What..." Eithan cleared his throat. "What should we do, Lindon?"

"I've been sensing something in the labyrinth," Lindon said. "It feels like echoes of other sacred artists, and I suspect it's a phenomenon of hunger aura."

A look passed over Eithan's eyes that Lindon couldn't identify, but the Archlord nodded. "I know what you mean."

"Can you lead us there?"

"If our captor cooperates." Eithan powerlessly kicked the wall.

"If I'm not mistaken, that would be a great place to train. If the three of us can't help Mercy, at least, advance, then we have no right to all our titles. I suspect we could learn something as well."

"And if it ends up to be nothing?"

"Then we drag as much power out of ourselves as we can before we run out of time," Lindon said. "Then we move."

Eithan nodded, and a delighted twinkle returned to his eye. "I'm just happy to be part of the team."

Lindon had also once dreamed about fighting side-by-side with other sacred artists as an equal, but he wasn't about to mention that now.

"Then let's go," Lindon said. He moved to pick up Ziel, but Yerin was still holding onto him.

"Two and a half seconds," she said into his outer robe. Then she reached up, red eyes blazing, and dragged his head down for a kiss.

She released him and he took a breath.

"Two and a half more," she said, and kissed him again.

When she finally released him and picked up Mercy, he had to catch his breath. He very carefully did not look at Eithan.

第十七章

CHAPTER SEVENTEEN

Mercy woke up coughing, with the taste of pine sap in her mouth.

"Sorry," Yerin muttered. "Not aiming to drown you."

Yerin tossed aside a bottle that Mercy was certain had held a healing elixir only seconds before. Before the bottle could shatter on the floor, Lindon caught it with his hand of flesh and tucked it away into his coat.

His right hand hung limp and broken at his side, which caught Mercy with a rush of memory.

She looked frantically around, and aside from Ziel looking burned, they were all healthy. And alive.

They were all ragged and beaten, but she let out a heavy breath of relief. She shivered when she considered how close they had all come to death.

If Reigan Shen hadn't been so drained of his power, he would have eaten them alive. And if he wasn't notorious for playing with his prey. Akura Malice would never have let them live. They would have died for the sin of standing in a Monarch's way.

At the thought, she realized they were in a totally different room of the labyrinth.

It was a long, narrow oval with a trench at the bottom

266 O WILL WIGHT

only wide enough for one person. Mercy was looking down on it from a slope above; the entire room funneled into the trench.

"Where are we?" she asked.

Yerin crouched next to her. She wore an expectant smile and her red eyes glowed; she looked like Uncle Fury when he had an idea that he would have described as "Really fun."

Mercy had a premonition of disaster.

"Training," Yerin said with relish.

Lindon gave Mercy a look of concern. "Are you feeling all right? The construct was stable, but we had to accelerate your healing."

"Better than new!" Mercy said happily, though that wasn't exactly true. Her madra reserves were still low, and her channels were strained from the destruction of her bloodline armor, but her body was safe.

She remembered Lindon covering for her—twice, no less—and wasn't sure whether her gratitude outweighed her embarrassment.

On the one hand, he had saved her!

On the other hand, he had *had* to save her. She was dragging them down.

Eithan leaned around Lindon, giving Mercy that smile that suggested he could read minds. "Reigan Shen is on his way to the bottom of the labyrinth, where we suspect he intends to use the Dreadgods to kill the remaining Monarchs. We're going after him."

Mercy's breath quickened as she calculated. Could he do it? Of course he could; he had to have been planning this for months, and it matched up with what Fury and her mother had already suspected him of doing.

Did her mother know what he was up to? If not, could Mercy bring her some kind of proof? Only another Monarch could stop Reigan Shen; she was certain of that after facing off against him herself.

Then the impact of Eithan's words fully penetrated the exhaustion of her recovery.

"You're going *after him?*"

"*We're* going after him," Yerin corrected. She circled her pointer finger around the group. "All of us."

Ziel gave Mercy a dead-fish look of exasperation. "I had the same reaction."

"But...you've seen...I can't..." It was surprisingly hard for Mercy to admit that she couldn't match up to someone, even when it was patently obvious. She hadn't thought of herself as a prideful person, but here she was.

Lindon crouched in front of her. "We think that, with our help, you can."

Mercy searched his eyes and found rock-solid confidence in her. It was both flattering and very intimidating. Could she live up to that?

"You will be as clay in a master's hands!" Eithan said, clawing at the sky. "We will mold you into a weapon that—"

Lindon raised his hand, and Eithan cut off. Mercy was surprised the Archlord had allowed himself to be interrupted by his student, but he looked oddly pleased.

"What do you think, Yerin?" Lindon asked.

Yerin snorted. "If she's kept up with us this far, she's going all the way." Then she gave Mercy a wink.

Mercy's eyes filled with tears, and she threw an arm around Lindon and Yerin. It was hard to speak around tears, but she mumbled something about her thanks and how she wouldn't let them down. The words were incomprehensible, even to her, but her feelings poured out of her mouth.

Eithan popped up with a grin. "You know, I can't help but notice that we're wasting—"

Mercy grabbed him and pulled him into the hug too.

"Oh. Hmm. This is nice."

It was Lindon who finally pushed back, straightening his outer robe. "Apologies, but we actually *are* limited on time. The sooner, the better. And I think we have this technique figured out, but it takes me and Dross working together."

Dross spun out, still wearing his tiny black crown. He gave the trench a glare. [For now! But soon, I will have my full power restored, and then I will operate greater devices than this!]

"Yes," Lindon said. "Of course."

Mercy wiped her face with her sleeve, trying to stop sniffling long enough to focus. "All right. What's the technique?"

"It's a hunger Ruler technique." Lindon looked over the room with admiration. "I never thought it was possible, until Dross and I found this room in the labyrinth. But it brings out...I suppose they're echoes, or Forged imitations, of people the labyrinth has fed on."

"Demonstration!" Eithan cried, and Lindon didn't need any more encouragement. He eagerly placed his hand against a script panel on one side of the trench.

Mercy assumed he would use his pure madra to active the technique, since his hunger arm was broken, but she sensed no madra from him at all. She supposed he was using his authority as a Sage, and she felt as uncomfortable as she always did.

Sages were *always* old, even when they didn't look like it.

Yerin noticed her discomfort and asked about it, but it was hard to explain.

"It's not...it's nothing big, but Sages are always old, at least on the inside. A Sage my age is just *wrong*. It's like he's a young man with an old head, you know?"

Mercy had tried to control the air with her soulfire to stop Lindon from hearing their conversation, but the aura was so thin that she was afraid he'd overheard. Especially when he looked depressed out of nowhere.

She desperately wanted to apologize, but what if he hadn't heard her? Then she'd have to explain...

Yerin was giving her an odd look. "Huh. Used to say the same thing."

"What?"

"Well, a baby's head on a man's body," she said, making no effort to keep her voice down. "So not the same; the complete mirror opposite. Been a long time."

She was speaking fondly, but Lindon was slumped against

the panel, and he looked like he was about to collapse in shame and depression.

"I'm so sorry!" Mercy called.

Lindon waved it away.

Yerin winced. "Oops. Should pay off that debt later."

Finally, Lindon caught the unfamiliar technique, and Mercy saw the disgusting white hunger aura begin to swirl. It took on a shape in the center, made all of shades of white and gray, until it looked like a person leeched of color.

A familiar person. A *very* familiar person.

Mercy's breath stopped as she saw the hair, pulled back into a ponytail with strands of sticky shadow madra. The familiar build, the stance, the expression. The bow, made all of liquid black threads woven together, with a dragon's head that hissed. She was sure the woman's bright eyes were actually purple.

As the image had started to form, Mercy had at first wondered if this was herself, but every detail that settled proved that wrong. This was her mother, centuries ago. She looked to be Mercy's age.

[We scoured the memory of this place, and we found that it had fed upon your mother,] Dross said triumphantly. [This is a triumph of great effort and skill.]

"The labyrinth?" Mercy asked.

"What you feed on becomes a part of you," Lindon said. "The energy your mother gave the labyrinth is gone—it was consumed long ago—but the memory of her remains. It's powerless, but we should be able to learn from it."

"I...I never knew she came here."

This was a startling revelation. Mercy knew, of course, that she didn't know everything about her mother. It would take her a hundred years to read all the stories of Akura Malice, and it wasn't as though Malice was very forthcoming about her past.

But she knew Mercy had been here, around Sacred Valley, and she had never said anything. She had even warned Mercy away.

Why?

Lindon pulled open a nearby box, which he must have removed from a void key earlier, and aura gushed out. Instantly, hunger aura swarmed over the natural treasures, and Mercy could sense some of the ghoulish spirits coming nearer. They would be crawling through the floor now.

He began spreading natural treasures around the room, quickly increasing the power of the ambient aura.

Mercy realized what they were trying to do, and she braced herself on Suu. "Do you really think we have time for this?"

"Doesn't take more than a breath," Yerin said. She patted Mercy on the shoulder. "Might sting, though."

Eithan had taken his own handful of natural treasures, and he called out from the other end of the room. "You have four people here who have all successfully completed their Overlord revelation, and you have your own mother to learn from. How could you have a better environment?"

Mercy had grown up with near-constant access to people who had advanced past Overlord, and in one of the richest inhabitable aura locations in the world. If it was that easy, everyone would have done it.

But she still found herself somehow believing it was possible here, now. Why not? She was a peak Underlady, and she was even acclimated to Overlord-level madra and soulfire thanks to her Book. Now that they'd prepared the environment, the *only* thing missing was her own revelation.

With a deep breath, Mercy slid down the slope and into the trench.

Facing the black-and-white image of her mother.

Malice spotted Mercy, and Mercy's heart caught. Malice pulled her own bow—identical to Mercy's—back, and Forged an arrow on it. Mercy did the same.

As they faced one another, dream aura drifted over from one of the natural treasures. It twisted and reacted to the hunger madra, guided by this place.

And Mercy felt something. A taste of her mother's memories.

Malice was down here, in the labyrinth, because no one had fully explored it before. This was going to be fuel for her rise to Monarch.

And she would not allow anyone to get in her way.

Both Malice and Mercy released their arrows. Mercy's passed through Malice as though the woman was made of mist, then embedded itself in the wall at the end of the trench. Malice's struck Mercy and dissipated.

Even that image called up another instinctive half-memory. Malice was more of an archer than Mercy was. Not just a *better* archer. *More* of one.

Another memory surfaced, still not Mercy's, but one she'd seen before in a dream tablet she'd won from the Uncrowned King tournament.

Larian, the famous archer of the Eight-Man Empire, demonstrated her form as she drew back her bow. Her voice had explained what she was doing.

"A launcher construct is by far more efficient than a stick with an elastic string. So why do sacred artists use bows?"

She released an arrow, and it streaked through the air, detonating a mountain-sized tree in the distance. The explosion from the arrow filled the sky with dust and debris.

"A woman with a bow taps into the power of all who have used bows, of what it means *to wield a bow,"* she continued. *"You are not just an archer. You are a fragment of The Archer, the single template of all archery. The bow is one of the deepest symbols of all."*

There was a trace of that concept in her mother's archery. The Bow Icon, The Archer, whatever you wanted to call it.

Mercy had meditated on this concept before. She had even asked her mother to demonstrate, and viewed the dream tablets that she could handle. But somehow, watching it here and now—a version of her mother who hadn't perfected her connection to an Icon yet—caused realization to slide into place.

And slowly, subconsciously, Mercy began to adjust her stance in ways she couldn't even name.

Ziel looked down on the trench. "We don't have time for this."

"In fact, we do," Eithan said casually. "Subject One has closed the way forward for the moment, but he has to fight the nature of the labyrinth to hold it. We must wait for his grip to relax, so we might as well put the time to good use."

"You don't seem worried about the lost time."

"Do you think worrying would help?" Eithan nodded to Mercy. "Besides, if we walk out of here with another young Overlady, I will consider that a substantial gain."

"This doesn't look like Overlord meditation," he muttered. An arrow slammed into the wall, and this one caused the room to shake.

Eithan was leaning on the wall over him. "Even if she doesn't technically advance, this could be a more valuable breakthrough. After all, *we're* not Sages, are we?"

"Don't blow smoke in my eyes."

If Eithan had the resources to perform the Pure Storm Baptism and was insightful enough to give a Monarch advice while still an Underlord, he wouldn't be stuck as a mere Archlord.

Meanwhile, Ziel was happy just having a healthy body and spirit.

Am I? he wondered.

It wasn't that long ago since he had felt something else as he faced down the Titan. Some part of him still wanted more.

There were dream artists who performed mental therapy. He should find one of them. Too bad he didn't have any Lord revelations left; he could have used a nice, cleansing personal revelation.

Yerin and Lindon were moving around the room, crushing hunger spirits with minimal madra expenditure. This was known as one of the deadliest locations in the world, where even Lords could be devoured, and they were treating it like a game squashing bugs.

"It's too bad you don't want to improve anymore," Eithan said. He buffed fingernails against the front of his robes, which would have been more elegant if he wasn't still covered in marks from his fight earlier.

"Yeah, too bad."

"We'd love to have you along."

That irritated Ziel into responding, which itself irritated him further. Not long ago, nothing would have bothered him.

"Why do you want me? We're not friends. There's no connection between us. Are you trying to get me in your debt? What is this?"

"Oh, did Lindon not tell you?"

Ziel remembered the uncomfortably intense stare of the Void Sage and had to focus on not shivering. "I will admit, I underestimated you all. You're freaks, and I say that with true admiration. I salute you. But you're all burning with ambition, and that fire went out of me years ago."

Eithan nodded along with every word. "It did, and it left behind a pile of ashes. But I can't help but look at those ashes and think, 'What a blaze that must have been.'"

In spite of himself, Ziel rested a hand on the head of his hammer. He remembered commissioning this hammer. He had earned the metal himself, designed it, and worked closely with the Soulsmith. He had imagined all the grand deeds he would perform with the hammer.

That hammer had taken the lives of many Dreadgod cultists. He remembered the fury that had filled him. The grief, back when it was an empowering force instead of a blanket smothering him.

"It's too late for me anyway," Ziel muttered, and even he didn't know where the words were coming from. "I don't have what it takes to become a Sage."

"How would you know?" Eithan shot back. "What are you, some kind of Sage?"

Ziel glared at him.

"Besides, if you can reach peak Archlord, you know what it takes to become a Herald? Brute force."

"Brute force as in enough raw resources to choke a Monarch, but you left out the part where you need such a thorough understanding of your own spirit that you and your Remnant can work together."

Ziel gave Eithan a smug look. "Don't think that just because I'm young I haven't done my research."

Just as many sacred artists remained stuck at different stages in the Lord realm because they didn't understand how to pass their revelations, many Archlords remained stuck because they had no one to teach them how to reach Herald.

Often, by the time they *did* find someone to tell them the truth, their spirits were twisted against them. Sometimes because of injury, or broken oaths, and sometimes because their spirits hated them.

Ziel would fall into that last category, he was certain.

Even if his soul was stable enough after the Pure Storm Baptism to advance its level of existence, his Remnant wouldn't work with him. He was certain. He wouldn't work with himself, and that was the same thing.

"You think I underestimated you?" Eithan asked curiously. "Quite the opposite. I think I'm estimating you much more highly than you are."

He waved a hand. "But forget it, then. I can't drag you up a hill toward a glorious future. Instead, why don't you help me? There are some young people here who could use our worldly guidance."

Ziel gave a humorless laugh. "What am I supposed to teach an Overlord Sage or history's first Overlord Herald?"

"I always find it arrogant to assume we know everything that has happened in history, but let's leave that aside. Neither of them are Archlords, and neither of them have ever led a sect before. I believe your input could be very valuable to them."

Ziel grumbled inwardly about it, but he *was* curious to see what these young people could do with such a start.

They had a fire for advancement that burned even brighter than his once had. How far could that take them, if it wasn't snuffed out?

He had to admit, he did want to see it.

The hunger aura was steadily eating away at the natural treasures Lindon had placed all around the room, and the focus of the labyrinth itself was on Lindon. The hunger madra attacks were growing more frequent.

While Ziel and Eithan were talking on the other side of the room, he and Yerin kept the hunger madra under control and watched Mercy.

"You think she's creeping up on Overlord?" Yerin asked.

"I think so," Lindon said, watching Mercy battle the echo of her mother. They had closed to melee combat now—which was strange to watch, as neither could truly touch the other—but this was something like a meditative state.

"I've felt it myself," Lindon continued. "You're working with the memories they left behind as much as anything. But it will respond to what you do, unlike a dream tablet. This should help her work out her own condition."

Yerin fidgeted, pulling on her lock of red hair. Finally, she asked, "You catch a glimpse of my master in there?"

"Apologies," Lindon said, in true regret. "I searched, but there are just too many. But I suspect he is there, if we can find him."

"No, wipe it clean. Shouldn't have asked."

Below them, Mercy had frozen. The image of her mother continued attacking, but she looked as though she'd seen something in the distance.

The cycling of her madra reached a crescendo, and the aura in the room swirled around her.

"I am..." she began, "...not my mother."

The aura didn't react.

Mercy's face fell. "I was sure that was it!"

A ghostly arrow passed through her body.

Yerin hopped down into the trench between Mercy and

her mother, ignoring Malice's attacks. "That was mine. Not my master. Wasn't happy about it."

"I thought I had it..." Mercy scuffed the ground with the butt of her staff.

"Never said you didn't." Yerin leaped over Mercy and landed on her other side, then grabbed the back of Mercy's head and angled her to look at Malice's face. "You're not your mother, okay. Tell me what's different."

"I'm not as...ruthless, as she is," Mercy said, as though admitting something.

Malice sneered at her and loosed another arrow.

"Cut deeper," Yerin said.

"I don't have the same drive. She's willing to do whatever she has to. You know, once she—"

Yerin interrupted. "Deeper."

"Is this what worked for you? I don't—"

Yerin shook her. "You talking to me, or you looking at her?"

Mercy slowly quieted and focused on her mother. Lindon felt the interaction of dream and hunger aura, and he suspected Yerin was bathed in it too, but she didn't react.

The aura trembled, and he rushed over to the panel. The technique was destabilizing, thanks to the imbalance of the aura. He could hold it, but he wouldn't be able to fend off the labyrinth's attacks in the rest of the room.

He waved to the two men across the room, but they were still talking. Eithan waved back without looking.

"I like people," Mercy said. "She's not kind. She's...cruel."

The aura from the natural treasures began to tremble.

"She isn't just callous," she continued. "She likes it when her enemies are afraid of her. Malice is the virtue she's named after; it's the hatred that drives you to be merciless to those who oppose you."

There was a resonance in the aura that even Lindon could sense, so Mercy's spirit must be trembling. She was close.

Now, she was whispering. "I don't want that. I've never wanted that. I want the opposite. I want to be..."

She stopped. Then, she corrected herself. "She's Malice. I am Mercy."

Around the room, the natural treasures ignited. Yerin had to release Mercy as the soulfire inside her went up in response.

As Mercy advanced, the labyrinth reacted.

Lindon had expected *some* kind of reaction from the hunger madra, but the ghouls that clawed their way up from the ground were not simple. And they weren't alone. Forged webs shot toward Mercy from every direction.

He drove his fist through one of the ghouls, his channels filled with pure madra, but it was harder than he'd expected. It took him two blows to crush the living technique, and then he had to exert real force to pull some webs down.

Either the hunger madra was stronger here, or this attack was particularly fierce.

Eithan and Ziel both were roused, but just like Lindon, neither of them were eager to use more of their madra than they had to. Ziel was swinging his hammer without rings of script around it, and Eithan was just using his scissors.

Yerin was fighting the hardest.

Mercy's advancement was taking longer than Lindon's had, most likely because of the aura imbalance here in the labyrinth but possibly because of the interference of the hunger madra. She was helpless as the attention of the whole room was focused on her.

Yerin covered her like a red-and-black blur, her Goldsigns and sword flashing. Both had been Enforced with madra, and she slammed into ghouls and webs alike with the force of a Herald.

Lindon couldn't help but worry. They were running low on elixirs, and while Yerin might not need her madra as much as the rest of them given the strength of her physical body, she would still be in trouble if she ran out.

He could afford to spend more than she could, so he covered Yerin with Blackflame. The webs burned relatively easily, though he had to focus on his will to pierce some of the larger ghouls.

Yerin slowed down, and after not too long, the Book of Eternal Night materialized over Mercy. The Divine Treasure shone as a thick violet tome, and as Lindon watched, it slowly flipped its thick, glassy pages until it rested on the fifth.

Then it faded back into Mercy, and she awoke with a gasp.

As an Overlady.

Her clothes and weapons were unharmed, but Lindon could feel her spiritual pressure. Unfortunately, the transformation had consumed much of her soulfire.

But it would be worth the increase in her strength.

"Whew!" Mercy examined her black-gloved hands. "You know, I didn't think it would make much of a difference, since I've used the fifth page so much already. But it feels good!"

Yerin looked to her amid a rising tide of white sparks: the essence of all the hunger madra she'd destroyed. "Glad you're feeling all fresh and shiny new."

Mercy watched the echo of her mother, which was tracking her with an arrow. She pressed her fists together and saluted the image of Malice.

Malice eyed Mercy with disdain, but she lowered her bow. Then she saluted back.

Her image vanished, and power stopped flowing through the scripts all around the room. Lindon ran his perception through them to make sure nothing had broken, but it seemed like the echo of Malice had cut off the process on her own.

He could activate it again, but...

Around the room, the entrances blurred. Now, there was only one exit from the room.

Lindon pulled out the silver case that contained the hand of Subject One, and eyed the single tunnel. He extended his senses down the hall and sensed nothing, but he prepared to unlock the case.

Eithan stopped him. He had an odd look on his face. "Save the effort, I think. I can see where we're going."

Ziel rested against his hammer. "And where is that?"

"Deeper," Eithan said grimly. "Subject One couldn't keep us out any longer...so it's drawing us closer."

Lindon didn't like the sound of that.

第十八章

CHAPTER EIGHTEEN

A white snake wrapped around the point of Jai Long's spear, and he shattered the shield of his Truegold opponent with one final thrust.

Without the shield to stop him, his spear skewered her into the ground.

He stood panting and bleeding, one eye gummed shut with blood. His mask was torn and ragged. The two remaining Highgolds and remaining Lowgold of the enemy squad cut and ran.

"Remnant!" he called, but there was no need.

Fingerling sprayed destructive pink light over the slate-gray Remnant that started pulling its way out of the enemy Truegold. Kelsa was there in a moment, Foxfire in each hand, which burned Remnants better than it did the living.

He had to help out with a strike or two—the Remnant had come from a Truegold, after all—but they collapsed the Remnant to chunks before it could hit them.

The allied Soulsmiths would be disappointed. They paid a premium for Truegold dead matter, and Kelsa was already wrapping some of the intact bits in scripted cloth, to preserve it for sale. But Jai Long had concerns about their immediate survival.

He signaled his squad to fall back. No losses today—one Highgold and two Lowgolds had died and been replaced under his command already.

The fighting among the Golds wasn't merciless. They were fighting for territory, not extermination. But that didn't mean it was safe.

And he wasn't even sure how it was going.

Granted, their forces were creeping closer and closer to Mount Samara, through the foothills and lesser mountains between the Desolate Wilds and Sacred Valley. But the real battle was being fought overhead.

Thunder and lightning cracked the sky as Underlords clashed in flight. One was a burly, bearded man from the Cloud Hammer sect—his weapon and raincloud Goldsign gave him away. That was the Underlord from the Blackflame Empire.

His opponent was probably twenty years his junior and also carried a cloud over his head. The Ghost-Blade wore gray robes and a veil over his face, and his Goldsign was a hovering spirit of death madra.

He swept a blade of death at the Cloud Hammer, who responded with a force technique and another explosion. They were hundreds of yards away, but the wind ruffled Jai Long's hair.

And that fight was one of a hundred. Underlords fought, firing techniques of incredible scope with Overlords above and between them. Here and there, even Archlords.

As terrifying as that fact was, it wasn't as bone-chilling as the reality that the *real* powers of each side hadn't even moved. The occasional technique that a Herald or Sage sent out shone like sunrise and blotted out spiritual perception all over the battlefield.

Those weren't even attacks. They were warnings.

The battle was being fought on the ground, and Jai Long wasn't certain anything they did would even matter.

He led his squad back to the camp, which was close enough that thunder from distant techniques constantly rolled over everything. He was used to it by now.

After a bath and a meal, he returned to his nightly ritual. He had distinguished himself in combat, earning natural treasures for his own personal use. If he advanced to Underlord, not only would his conditions get better, but he might be able to move Jai Chen and Kelsa to a safer position. Or at least one more suitable for Lowgolds.

As he reached out to the circle of natural treasures around him, he focused on his desire to protect them. It was old and familiar, at least where Jai Chen was concerned, and he was sure that this thread would lead to his Underlord revelation.

Lindon had spoken to Jai Long about advancing to Underlord many times, and often repeated the same phrase: *Follow your fear.* Failing his sister was one of the oldest fears Jai Long could remember.

He had been one of the talents of his clan from a young age, and when he let down the expectations of his elders, he had been terrified that Jai Chen would be implicated with him. Now, he felt that same fear. Would he let her down? Would his lack of ability lead to her death?

The soulfire in his spirit didn't shiver.

That was to be expected. The aura was thick enough, but after so many failed attempts, he had stopped using the most powerful natural treasures he could. This was hardly the richest environment possible for an Underlord advancement, but surely he would still feel it when the moment came.

He strained to sense any change, pushing his spiritual sense as hard as he had since advancing to Jade. The very day he'd advanced and developed his spiritual perception, he had pushed himself to prove his talent. To show the Jai elders that he was worthy of their attention and respect. He had been so afraid to let them down.

The aura around him shivered, and triggered his soulfire.

His advancement to Underlord had begun.

Jai Long was so stunned that he almost forgot to guide the soulfire through his body. That was it? An idle thought? What was the revelation?

But he didn't have time to think about it unless he was

willing to let the soulfire rush through his body unguided. When he shifted his attention to the colorless flame reforging his flesh and spirit together, he discovered a problem.

The soulfire was far too slow.

Panic gripped his heart, and he immediately regretted not preparing all the treasures he could. At this rate, he couldn't know how long it would take him to advance. Days? Weeks?

He had just been trying to sense the resonance of the aura; he hadn't truly intended to advance. After hundreds, perhaps thousands, of tries, who would have thought he would succeed *now?*

The soulfire wasn't painful, but his spirit would be unbalanced until the advancement completed. His madra would be almost unusable.

And his squad had to fight in the morning.

If he had known, he would have waited for more powerful natural treasures.

He controlled the soulfire to focus on his core. Maybe if it finished his spirit first, he could get himself in fighting shape as fast as possible.

A messenger found him within two hours, bringing congratulations from an Underlord and instructions to remain out of the battlefield until the end of his advancement.

His squad, meanwhile, would be returning to battle in the morning. Without him.

Jai Long couldn't go find Jai Chen or Kelsa. Every second he spent doing anything except cycling would extend the time his advancement took to complete.

The next morning, his squad left without him.

His baptism in soulfire had barely begun.

"This is what you get for leaving us in there for so long," Orthos grumbled. "I ate all your plants."

Little Blue whistled her own indignation. She sat on

Orthos' back and crossed her arms, looking away from Lindon.

"I ate the pots too."

"My sincere apologies," Lindon said, "but it's very dangerous. I was concerned that you might have been trapped inside."

Little Blue's huff wavered. She glanced down to Orthos.

"We were still worried," Orthos grunted.

Blue nodded.

"I *am* sorry, but I'm glad you weren't around for our fight with Reigan Shen."

Orthos and Little Blue glared at him together.

"We were concerned about you," Orthos said. "You could have informed us."

Lindon dipped his head and apologized. They should have been able to sense that he was still alive, even from within a separate space, but he should have kept them aware.

Yerin strolled back to meet them and sat on her heels next to Orthos. "Yeah, we fought a Monarch. Got whipped like the slowest mule, but we didn't die. So there's a shiny spot."

They were all sitting around for a while, waiting for another trapped room to die down. While flames of all colors raged in the next room, they sat in the hallway. Eithan paced back and forth, Mercy cycled, and Ziel loudly snored as he slept.

Lindon filled in Orthos and Little Blue about what had happened since they were locked inside the Dawn Sky Palace. They were a rapt audience, eyes glowing as they listened.

When he finished, Orthos thoughtfully chewed on something for a long moment. "That's not a *bad* excuse," he allowed.

Little Blue clambered up Lindon's shoulder, chiming about how glad she was that everyone had made it out alive.

The chimes woke Ziel, who rolled over to squint in the spirit's direction. "Glad you're happy," he muttered.

"Almost ready!" Eithan called from the brink of the next room, and everyone began to busy themselves.

Lindon still hadn't closed the entrance to his void key, so the Dawn Sky Palace hung open.

Mercy brightened and ran over as she saw Orthos and Little Blue, but Lindon addressed them first. "If you stay out here with us, I'm afraid I might not be able to open the key again. You might get hurt. Are you willing to risk it?"

Orthos and Blue traded uncertain glances.

Little Blue gave a whistle, but it wavered unsteadily.

"If you get too weak from the hunger aura, I'll have to send you back," Lindon said, as he let the void key vanish. He didn't add that the same remained true for the rest of them.

Soulfire now burned merrily in all of them; Ziel, Mercy, and Yerin had used up the last of the natural treasures Lindon had brought along. At least the ones that he could successfully balance out to create soulfire.

Everyone's cores were full too, even Lindon's. But they were completely out of elixirs. The only compatible scales they had left were pure or Blackflame.

Lindon and Eithan hadn't needed to refill their madra as much as the others, but at the same time, when they *did* need to recover, it took them more to fill up their cores. They also couldn't restore pure madra using aura, but that disadvantage was shared by everyone down here.

Every second, the hunger aura nibbled away at their power. Anything that they spent now, and any energy consumed by hunger techniques, would be gone for good. Lindon and Eithan were the only ones with scales left.

When the traps cleared, they dashed through and found a hall with a mark that seized Lindon's attention. It was the four-part symbol that had marked the Ancestor's Tomb from the outside.

The mark of the Dreadgods.

They passed beneath it and into a room that seemed to be nothing but row upon row of circular transparent tanks. They weren't made from glass, though, but from some kind of loose fabric like transparent skin.

These tanks, or sacs, or whatever they were had long been empty. Lindon suspected from the scripts and tubes around them that they would usually be filled with liquid, and at that point, the skins would be taut. But this machinery hadn't been operational for centuries.

Dead tanks spread ahead of them in rows, but Lindon studied them in glimpses as he ran past. Dross was responsible for noticing and remembering more details.

[These were nothing compared to the specimen tanks in Ghostwater. So outdated! We glorify the past too much, and we fail to notice the strides we've made in more modern times.]

Lindon tuned Dross out.

They were rushing through the labyrinth as quickly as they could, but all of them slowed when they reached the end of the room.

Four tanks had been removed from the last row, elevated onto a higher platform and surrounded by tools. Lindon didn't need to identify the scripts on the scopes, gauges, and marked sticks to know that these were all measuring tools.

And he had a good guess at what was special about these tanks. One had been stained red, one blue-gold, one a heavy yellow, and one purple-and-white.

Lindon slowed to examine some partial notes that remained on the nearby tables, but he knew what these had to be. The tanks where the Dreadgods were born.

A quick glance through the notes led him to a quick hypothesis. He ran it by Dross, who agreed.

[Yes, these were most likely unremarkable dreadbeasts when they were born. Clearly, this was the facility in which creatures were infused with hunger and then had their growth accelerated. Once the Dreadgods grew beyond their peers, their birthplace was removed and examined more closely.]

Lindon had kept his perception extended for dream tablets or guide constructs that Dross could absorb to understand more of the research, but he'd found nothing.

Yerin stood before the blood-colored tank, looking disgusted. "Feels like rubbing mud in your face."

The sensation the four tanks gave off *was* nauseating, and to Lindon's intrigue, it was more than spiritual. They radiated not just the power of madra and aura, but an ancient authority that he recognized.

Eithan danced closer, then rapped his knuckles on the solid base of one of the tanks. "It's not the whole tank, I'd say."

At Eithan's knocking, a tray slid open in the tank's base.

Within was a...Lindon didn't know what to call it. It looked like a bone, twisted into a shape that resembled a ring. It contained a smooth ruby that had once given off a powerful blood aura, but instead of strengthening over time, it had emanated its power with nothing to replenish it. Now, the once-strong natural treasure only gave off a tiny radiance of red aura.

But it felt *heavy* to Lindon. He was reminded of the pearl necklace and the other items he'd taken from Ozriel's room, but this was in a higher realm entirely. To his senses, it felt as if the weight of this bone ring could warp the world.

He didn't want to touch it—as Yerin had said, this gave off the disgusting impression of the Bleeding Phoenix—but he wasn't going to leave a treasure like this behind.

Ziel and Mercy had pried open the purple-and-white tank belonging to the Silent King, and the treasure they recovered resembled a twisted thighbone with an amethyst randomly fused into it. It gave off a weak wisp of dream aura, but it carried a powerful hunger to dominate.

[A noble artifact,] Dross said. [I will accept it as tribute.]

Lindon was briefly excited at the idea. If he could imbue this level of significance into Dross, how much stronger could the spirit get?

But he discarded the idea immediately. It would only take him further away from his goal of getting the real Dross back, and it wasn't as though such power could be as easily transferred as aura.

Though that thought brought him inevitably to the Soulforge.

Eithan handed the device to him, and Lindon opened the portal to the Soulforge right in front of the tanks. Space groaned as the portal opened, and only a breath later, Lindon forced his personal void key open.

The sound that accompanied the portal's sluggish opening was...concerning. He was certain that his key wouldn't last much longer. But this was worth it, even if the key broke.

He walked out with the broken fragments of Reigan Shen's death-aspected trident, three broken hammers that he'd scavenged, one of his bundles of Soulsmithing tools, and the box containing the Tomb Hydra's binding.

"I look forward to seeing if the Soulforge lives up to its reputation," Lindon said, hiding his excitement.

Orthos spoke from Yerin's shoulder. "How long until the exit opens?"

"Should have a few minutes!" Eithan called back.

Lindon had reached for the case containing Subject One's hand, but he stopped when Eithan spoke. "Are you sure?"

"If I weren't, I would still say this is a risk worth taking. Or would you rather confront Reigan Shen again with the same weapons we used last time?"

Without another word, Lindon headed into the starry world of the Soulforge. He strode out onto the platform, and the others filed in after him.

The blue fire blazed in the altar at the center of the stones, and Lindon sensed that he shouldn't have to fuel it for at least one project. Without consulting with Eithan, he threw the broken hammers onto the center of the altar.

Immediately, the physical wood of the broken hammers' hilts caught fire. Lindon controlled the fire aura to smother the flame, but he shot a startled look at Eithan.

The Archlord gave him a shooing motion. "It's more about the idea of the hammer than the physical form. Natural part of the process!"

If Lindon wanted to complete a project like repairing and

empowering a weapon of Reigan Shen's, he wanted every advantage he could. And Eithan and Ozriel had both emphasized the use of a hammer, so he'd start using one.

Or at least repairing the ones he had.

[Focus as I guide you,] Dross said arrogantly. [I will not steer you wrong.]

Lindon didn't fully trust Dross' new personality, but he certainly had Ozriel's dream tablets. He focused on the power on the altar, letting Dross feed the memories of other Soulsmiths into the back of his mind.

Lindon imagined a hammer in his mind. Not its form, but its purpose. He needed a tool to deliver his will, to shape the material in front of him. One that wouldn't lose out to Reigan Shen's weapons, and wouldn't deform in his hands.

His will started unopposed...then he felt stiff opposition, like he had suddenly tried to lift a heavy weight.

The flames surrounding the broken hammers turned blue, and the material began to rise slowly into the air.

Lindon fixed his concentration, pushing his willpower into the project as he had when he'd torn open space. He could feel the broken hammers; they had once been used to craft masterpieces. He treated that as though it were a new aspect of madra, weaving it into his ultimate design.

The blue light started to congeal into the vague outline of a hammer.

This wasn't enough, and Lindon felt instinctively what he had to do next. Part of that was the intuition he'd inherited from the memories of other Soulsmiths, but part was his own experience.

He needed to invest power of his own into this project. Lindon poured pure madra into the hammer, visualizing as he did the purpose of pure madra in Soulsmithing: its universal compatibility and its ability to purify.

But before the hammer congealed around the pure madra, he stopped. And he switched his cores.

He wanted this hammer to represent his power at its most complete state, so he poured Blackflame into the hammer.

Blackflame added deadly force and destructive intention to weapons, and it too could be used to burn away materials and impurities.

When he had added an equal amount of Blackflame, he stopped pouring in madra and began using his will to guide the forces together. He intended to blend them, but Dross stopped him.

[Stop, you fool! Can't you see they've achieved a balance already?]

At the heart of the blue outline that only vaguely resembled a hammer, two powers swirled: one bright and blue-white, and another darkness outlined in red. They swam around one another like twin fish, and they did indeed feel perfectly in balance.

That was where Lindon's experience failed him. His will trembled as he held the hammer half-manifested.

What do I do now? Lindon asked. He vaguely assumed it had something to do with soulfire.

Just when he was prepared to brute force it, Eithan leaned forward. "Now, bring it forth. It isn't *real* enough yet, like a Jade Remnant that has just manifested. Pull it out until it becomes reality."

Lindon's voice was strained with the effort of keeping the hammer half-existing. "What about soulfire?"

"What do you think *that* is?" Eithan pointed down to the blue flame in the center of the altar.

Aside from the fact that they were both in the form of fire, the flame in this altar had very little resemblance to soulfire. Especially since Archlord soulfire was its highest level, and that looked like quicksilver. Even Ghostwater had been formed with Archlord soulfire, not this...blue kind.

But Lindon's will was at its limit, so he couldn't wait to debate. He pushed one more time, shoving the hammer into reality.

As he did, he had one strange thought: he was pulling something *into* existence, and *out* of nothingness. That resonated with the Void Icon, but he wasn't sure exactly how yet. It was worth examining later.

He got a brief glimpse of a black hammer with a double-sided head: one side blue and one red. Then the azure soulfire consumed it, hiding it for a moment.

When the flame passed, he could see his hammer.

Just sitting on the dark metal of the altar, it emanated a heavy pressure. Its will thrummed against his own, and he could feel its desire to *create* hanging in the air like a musical note.

It was made of a black metal he couldn't quite identify, but that he recognized from the heads of the hammers he'd used to make it. The handle was rough enough that his hand wouldn't slip, and the two halves of the head were very different.

The Blackflame half shone red and gave off a sharp, even savage impression. The pure half was smooth with round edges, and it emanated a soothing air. But when he picked it up, the weight was perfectly balanced. Red and blue lines trailed in the air behind it as he turned to show it to everyone.

"That was...strange," Lindon said. It had felt as much like difficult manual labor as an effort of creation. Without Dross guiding him, he would have needed to fail many times to create such a product, and without the Soulforge the result would have been much lower.

"What are you going to name it?" Ziel asked.

Yerin nodded. "Needs a name."

Everyone had crowded into the Soulforge's platform, and Lindon began to wonder if the presence of so many people here would overburden the pocket world.

"Names *are* said to have an effect on an object's purpose," Eithan said.

Lindon could tell that they were heading into a situation in which everyone shouted out their suggestions for a name, so he turned to Dross instead. That conversation, at least, could be held at the speed of thought.

What do you think?

[Worldbreaker! Father of Weapons! Iron of the Netherworld! Midnight, Cursed Genesis of the Destroyer!]

I don't mind 'Genesis,' Lindon thought.

Dross spat at him.

"Genesis," Lindon said firmly, to cut off the discussion beginning around him.

Ziel shrugged. "Eh."

"Sure," Eithan said.

"Makes things. There's sense to it, and it's not all flowered up." Yerin nodded.

"I think it needs to be longer," Mercy said, running a hand down Eclipse, Ancient Bow of the Soulseeker.

Little Blue waved her hands in the air and cheered the new hammer.

Orthos blew smoke.

"Very good," Lindon said, having gotten enough consensus. He hadn't been overly concerned about making the hammer; the materials he'd used weren't too valuable, and he wouldn't be losing much even if he failed.

But now the blue soulfire inside the Soulforge had died down noticeably, and it needed fuel. And the components... while he'd gotten them for free, and as such wouldn't *really* be losing out if the Soulsmithing created a useless product, he was still afraid to mess up.

Onto the altar went the two broken halves of Reigan Shen's death trident...and the beating, throbbing heart-shaped binding from the Tomb Hydra.

The death madra immediately resonated between the two of them, and some death madra strings—dead matter that were still attached to the heart—began to weave around the trident.

"Better hurry up," Eithan observed. "Looks like it's trying to finish itself."

Lindon gripped the bone ring set with the ruby, the object that had once given birth to the Bleeding Phoenix. He felt its weight on the world and looked back to Eithan. "Are we sure we want to—"

Eithan slapped his hand, knocking the twisted ring into the Soulforge. The circle of bone flew into the flames.

Instantly, the blue fire roared. It swelled to fill the entire interior of the altar, to the point that flames licked out around Lindon's knees. He wondered whether the altar could handle it.

The invisible energy on the surface of the altar grew powerful, and the trident levitated into the air, carrying the death binding with it.

Lindon wasn't sure whether it was an effect of the Soulforge or the materials, but he could sense the hunger aspect of the binding much more clearly than he had before. He pushed only a little, and the physical form of both faded.

They didn't burn away to blue light, like the hammers had. This time, they seemed to fade until they covered one another, like one piece of paper layered on another.

This time, Lindon could feel an easy resonance with the Void Icon. There was hunger in the binding, and a hunger in the trident too; a hunger to destroy the enemy. To bring death.

Lindon spun Genesis in one hand, and he didn't need anyone to tell him to use the red side.

Blackflame focused his will as he slammed it down on the two ghostly images.

You bring destruction, Lindon thought.

The heart squeezed halfway into the trident, and the weapon's physical metal began to shift. The two halves slid closer together.

You bring ruin.

The metal came together, and the binding disappeared into the weapon. Now loose strands of death madra flailed around, and even the steel of the trident glowed an eerie spectral green.

But Lindon wasn't watching its physical shell; he could feel the essence of the weapon in the Void Icon. Having used the Soulforge once before, he could more clearly feel how this process was similar to the Soulsmithing he'd always known.

Normally, he balanced different aspects of madra with his own, while making sure to manually mold its physical shape. Now, he was holding the clashing wills in the weapon, molding and steering them into one purpose.

You bring death, Lindon said.

Dross cackled in his head.

The hammer came down again, and this time Lindon saw—and felt—a clash of red against green, fire against death.

The trident shone, and blue soulfire erupted upward in a roar. It surrounded the weapon so that he couldn't see it, and instead of passing over it, it twisted and disappeared as though it had been inhaled into the trident.

An entirely new weapon hung in the air. A spear. Its shaft was dark, with a green tint to it, and the steel of its blade was a death-green chrome. Spectral green sparks came off the weapon here and there, as though it were still hot.

And its presence...

In Lindon's senses, it pushed against the world so that the air seemed to bend around the spear. It pushed against the spirits of everyone present, eager to be used. Even its spiritual might wasn't at all inferior to the attack of the sword Reigan Shen had used to crack space.

"I don't know that you could quite call it a Monarch weapon," Eithan said, "but a Monarch wouldn't be ashamed to use it."

Lindon wasn't at all embarrassed by the evaluation. He agreed; this could be considered a Herald weapon with added significance. Perhaps one day it would evolve into a Monarch weapon, if someone used it to accomplish great deeds, but even at the moment he would pit it against almost any other weapon he'd ever encountered.

He sent a glance at Mercy's bow, Suu, which was currently in its staff form. Without knowing exactly what the spear's binding did, he couldn't be certain how it stacked up, but in terms of its overwhelming aura, the spear definitely won.

Mercy was looking at the hovering weapon in excitement. "Name!"

"We don't have time," Lindon said, but the others over-rode him.

"Lindon already had a turn!" Eithan shouted. "Who's next?"

After a moment of deliberation, Lindon was left with Midnight, Cursed Spear of the Destroyer. Dross and Mercy had combined forces and dominated the discussion.

He was almost afraid to grab the weapon, even as its creator. If his hunger arm was functional, he would have had more faith in that, but he ended up gingerly retrieving the spear.

Its will to destroy was almost a voice in his mind, and he found himself wishing he could keep it in his void key. But he wouldn't risk opening the key again in the labyrinth unless he had to.

"Good timing," Eithan said, looking out of the portal. "It seems we're due for another shuffle."

Sure enough, as Lindon closed the Soulforge—and slipped its key around his neck—they saw the walls of the labyrinth blurring. The lights flickered as the entrances changed.

New doorways opened up all around the room, but one caught everyone's attention in the first moment. Instead of a gaping cave mouth onto a hallway of stone, this one was a small wooden door leading off of the platform with the Dreadgod tanks. It simply hadn't been there before.

And instead of a symbol over it, there was a handprint. It was thin and skeletal, sunk into the stone, and it had stained the rock white.

Eithan strode forward. "Well this seems like the obvious choice, doesn't it?"

He threw open the door. It was a narrow closet, but there was only one object inside: a tank, just like those that had once given birth to the first generation of dreadbeasts. But none of them wondered why it had been separated from the others.

This one was corrupted and half-melted, turned gray-white. It gave off *waves* of hunger aura, and a level of signifi-cance that at least matched the other Dreadgod pods.

The birthplace of Subject One.

Lindon could sense the Void Icon clearly here, and he longed to stay in the room and meditate on the nature of his Icon.

Instead, he rapped to open up the drawer. This time, instead of a twisted bone, there was...dust. Fine gray sand, or perhaps fine ash.

As with the others, the power had been leeched out of this natural treasure long ago. Lindon swept it into a bag that came with his Soulsmithing supplies, afraid to miss even a grain. As he did, he opened himself up to the Void Icon.

There were reflections on the concept of nothingness everywhere. What was hunger if not a desire to devour, a will to *allow the stranger in and kill me, borrow my powers, start the chain of events that would finally END IT ALL.*

Lindon staggered back. The sudden intrusion of thoughts that weren't his own had disrupted his concentration.

Did you hear that? Lindon asked.

[Clear, firm resolve. You should learn from him.]

That was...

[Subject One, I'm sure. The thought clearly came from below us, which you would notice if you had paid attention. Let's see if we can hear more.]

Lindon reached out again, and the sensation was instant.

He waits in the darkness. He had waited for time beyond counting, hungry for freedom, for power...for everything. He only knew hunger, and the connection to the others of his kind that remained on the surface. Those who had followed him. The Dreadgods.

Finally, a Monarch had come to him. Finally. Finally, one of those who had cursed the world had come to end what they had created.

Subject One welcomed Reigan Shen with open arms. The Monarch was close, and would be here soon. He would close off the labyrinth from the pursuers, so they could not interfere.

For the Slumbering Wraith hungered for all things. Even death.

"Out!" Lindon shouted. He tried to shove everyone out the door, but it had already blurred closed.

They were surrounded by nothing but featureless stone. Eithan had theorized earlier that the labyrinth couldn't lock them in; it had to move on set paths in certain patterns. Ozriel's remaining dream tablet had suggested the same.

But now, the labyrinth had broken its own rules to turn against them.

And they were trapped.

第十九章

CHAPTER NINETEEN

"There's no way this can stay locked for long," Lindon said, as he scanned the sealed room they were crammed into.

If Orthos had been his normal size, they wouldn't have all been able to fit into this room at all. Now, they were packed around Subject One's birth pod, and Lindon had Ziel's hammer jammed up against his jaw and Yerin's back pushing into his.

Orthos and Little Blue had scrambled to the top of his head, and Blue was ringing like a panicked bell.

Eithan nudged Mercy's staff away from his face and spoke. "It's too bad that time is of the essence, because I don't know if the labyrinth can seal us in here for minutes or for days."

Lindon, of course, had no idea either. But it was clear to him that the labyrinth had been twisted out of its natural patterns. Not only did it make sense logically, but he could feel it. The labyrinth's controller had twisted space to lock them here, which couldn't last forever.

He looked to the wall a few feet away. "What does that script do?"

There was a slight indentation in the wall, which held a script at about head-height. Ziel answered him. "It's a spatial transfer script, like the ones on a transport anchor. I'm no

Sage, so I don't know exactly how it works, but it's written like a one-way trip."

Lindon guessed that made sense, and Dross chuckled along with his thoughts.

[Yes, they had to ditch their failures somewhere, didn't they? Those inferior beasts who couldn't properly adapt to the energy must have been shipped off to the surface.]

"At least there's a way out!" Mercy said.

Eithan sat on one ledge of the tank. "If I didn't know better, I would think the labyrinth was trying to kick us out."

They were being rejected, and Lindon knew it. Subject One had chosen Reigan Shen, so it was blocking their way forward. There was nothing for them to do but retreat.

Or...

Lindon tapped the floor with his foot. "It will be difficult, and I can't make any promises. But I think I can break through the floor."

"If that doesn't wring your spirit dry, I'll dig through the next floor with my teeth." Yerin gave him a frown over her shoulder.

Ziel sighed, and leaned his head back against the wall. "What do you think we're going to do to Reigan Shen if we catch up to him and you're out of power? You think Arelius is going to smile him to death?"

"I've done it before!"

Smoke blew down into Lindon's eyes, and he blinked it away.

"Very well," Orthos said solemnly. "I'll do it."

Lindon considered very carefully how to refuse without destroying Orthos' feelings. But before he came to a conclusion, Dross laughed out loud.

[Ridiculous! What can an Underlord sacred beast do to the stone of the labyrinth? Can you sense the layers of aura and authority embedded in this stone? You could not burn away the dust!]

Lindon couldn't see Orthos, but he could *feel* the glare that the turtle directed toward the smug, floating spirit.

"Before Lindon fixes you," Orthos said, "I hope he lets me bite you one time."

[Try it, beast! I am only as physical as I choose to be!]

Even that conversation tied his stomach in knots, because it reminded Lindon that he might *not* be able to fix Dross. But he distracted himself with the problem at hand.

"Orthos, are you suggesting you transfer your power to me?"

"It hasn't been much use since you outgrew me, but yes. I'll lend you what I can, and then you can send me back to the surface."

It wasn't a *terrible* idea. Lindon still had Blackflame scales left, but every source of power would be helpful. And he wanted an excuse to send Orthos back anyway. This was a relief; now, at least, he would be safe.

"Are you sure?" Lindon asked.

Orthos felt the feelings through their bond and let out a heavy breath. "How else am I going to help?"

A little irritation slipped into Lindon's relief. Not at Orthos; at himself.

Hadn't he *just* said that he wanted to use his power to keep everyone together? And now here he was at the first opportunity, letting someone go.

"Next time, we won't have to leave you behind," Lindon promised. "We'll catch you up to us, no matter what we have to do."

"This is nice," Mercy whispered to Yerin.

"Quiet!" Eithan shouted. "They're having a moment!"

Orthos ignored them, and Lindon felt his fondness in his spirit. "There's no need. I'm content just being along for the adventure."

Lindon's feelings firmed. "I'm not."

Without further discussion, Orthos' power began flowing into Lindon. His Blackflame core was already full, so this burning power filled his channels directly. Even wisps of soulfire entered Lindon, though what Orthos contained as an Underlord was much less potent than what Lindon himself had access to.

With the power flowing through his veins, Lindon had no choice but to vent it somewhere. He directed his fury downward, and he guided Orthos' power with the focus of a Sage and the authority of the Void Icon.

"You should move," Lindon said to nobody in particular. There was a shuffling of feet and a groan from Eithan, but then Lindon had a bare stretch of floor to work with.

He sent a liquid bar of Blackflame down into the stone.

It still wasn't easy, even with the support of his authority. The Void Icon was great at removing things, and when the Path of Black Flame melted through stone, there was very little left to melt or burn away into the air. So the small room wasn't filled with the sorts of toxic smoke that would have asphyxiated everyone.

But the resistance on the stone was powerful. Lindon had blazed through all the power Orthos could spare before the turtle released their bond, panting hard.

"I'm sorry," Orthos rumbled from on top of Lindon's head. The hole in the floor was three feet deep now, and wide enough that the others had been forced to back up again.

"No need," Lindon responded. He used his own power this time, and a flame of his own soulfire. "Just a little more."

Sure enough, the next room was only a few more inches down.

They broke through into a hallway that could have belonged anywhere in the labyrinth. Lindon extended his perception through the hole and felt everyone else doing the same...except Ziel, who dropped down without any fanfare.

He called back up: "Good work, Orthos. We'll see you back on the surface."

"Don't throw your life away, boy," Orthos called back. Then he leaped off Lindon's head, landing on the ledge by the transfer circle.

Eithan tapped his forehead. "Good-bye, Orthos. I'll punch the Monarch an extra time in your name."

"And someone bite Dross," Orthos added. Yerin pushed forward to rap her knuckles on his shell.

"Luck," she said.

Little Blue gave a determined whistle, and Lindon realized she had been listening quietly the entire time. She hopped over to Orthos and stood by him with hands on her hips.

She chimed out her resolve to protect Orthos, and looked at Lindon as though expecting to see him object. He only felt relief. Together, they could protect one another.

"Be safe," Lindon said. Then he powered the circle, and the two vanished.

"That's for the best," Mercy said quietly, and Lindon agreed. But he wasn't satisfied.

The rest followed Ziel down the hole after a moment, and Lindon noticed that something was wrong.

He hadn't felt any fury from Subject One when they'd broken through the wall. If it had tried to trap them and failed, it should have sensed as much and been furious. But he didn't feel anyone's frustration transmitted through the stone.

That meant they were still in the trap.

Sure enough, he sent his perception down the hallway one direction and detected another of those rooms that was absolutely filled with deadly launcher constructs.

And down the other direction? The same.

Lindon tapped into Blackflame again and looked beneath them. "Does anyone else have any better suggestions?"

"Yes," Eithan said. "Use the hand. We can still follow the labyrinth when it makes sense."

Lindon wanted to argue, but he could see the sense, and they didn't have much time to argue. He withdrew the twisted white hand from its case and exposed it to the aura in the air. It immediately clawed to their right.

Then Lindon felt the eye of the Slumbering Wraith on him, and he thought he felt a distant smile.

Hunger madra erupted around them, and Lindon realized that Subject One was finished playing with them.

Ghouls clambered out from every inch of stone. When they were slashed with madra, they didn't even dissipate, and Lindon's Empty Palm blew one ghoul in half...at which point its upper half landed on him.

Its white madra burned on contact with his skin, and he shouted as he hurled it away.

In the grand scheme of things, it hadn't taken much, but it had taken a bite out of *everything.* He was noticeably more tired than he had been before, both physically and spiritually.

He erupted in the Hollow Domain, but as the blue-white light filled the hall, he could tell that it wouldn't be enough. The ghouls weakened, but they didn't die, and more clawed at his ankles. He saw Ziel shaking several off, Eithan flipping through a crowd, and Mercy covering her limbs with armor.

Yerin was the best off of all of them, with her six blade-arms and her sword all glowing slightly with her Flowing Sword. Enforcer techniques weren't disrupted by the Hollow Domain, so she was a blurring cage of blades that shredded any ghoul that got close.

These ghouls were tough, as though they had been invested with soulfire. Lindon thought the actual explanation was probably much simpler; Subject One *meant* this attack. It had his full attention behind it.

And his theory was strengthened a moment later when Dross shouted a warning and webs shot from the walls.

He blew through the strands, which were weaker thanks to his Hollow Domain, but as long as he kept the Domain up, his friends wouldn't be able to use most of their techniques. And there were more ghouls coming every second, in an endless tide.

Lindon followed the scratching, clawing hand and dashed down the hallway, the others following. He tucked the hand back into its case.

They emerged into a trap room, but Lindon didn't intend to wait this time. He ran through, keeping the Hollow Domain active.

The traps triggered, but the fogs of venom madra and balls of fire madra melted as they encountered the edge of his protective field of pure madra.

His pure core was leaking madra by the second, but he had plenty to spare and a supply of scales. It was better for him to spend madra than anyone else.

As such, he was confident that they would be able to blast through these traps instantly.

Then the walls blurred, and the exits vanished again.

Dross roared in all their minds as they came up against a stretch of blank stone. [Coward! Come face me instead of leaning on these cheap tricks!]

"It can't keep doing this," Mercy protested. "It's going to run out of energy soon enough."

Eithan nodded even as he evaded a lunging ghoul. "Yes, it is paying quite a cost for this. Even the labyrinth itself may not be able to keep up. But will we?"

Now that the hand was locked away, Lindon wanted to release the Hollow Domain, but he couldn't. It was the only thing holding back the traps. The remaining ghouls were dispatched, but he was dismayed when he swept his perception through the group.

They had been weakened by that attack. Too much.

Dross, how many more attacks like that can we handle?

[Four,] Dross said confidently. [After that, you'll have to start spending resources you can't afford to replace.]

Yerin paced restlessly inside the blue-white dome of the Hollow Domain, clearly frustrated. "How many more rats do we have to clear out?"

Lindon wondered if that was the question that Subject One had been waiting for, because he felt a cruel amusement drift through the walls of the labyrinth.

The traps ran out of fuel soon after—these hadn't lasted long, with the Hollow Domain disrupting their structure— but an entrance still didn't appear.

Something else did, though.

Lindon knew immediately it wasn't a ghoul, despite the white hand that pulled through the stone. Yerin struck at it as the hand appeared, but her sword was deflected by a punch from a thick gauntlet.

The spiritual pressure of a Herald filled the room, and Lindon's heart dropped.

This was another black-and-white copy of an expert from

ages past, but unlike the ghost they'd conjured of Mercy's mother, this one had real power.

Lindon didn't recognize him—he wasn't one of the current generation of Monarchs, and may have died centuries before—but he was a short, broad-shouldered man with thick metal gauntlets on either hand. Another eye hovered over his head, and he met them with an arrogant grin, clashing one gauntlet against another.

Ziel's eyes went wide, and he levered his hammer in position. "Steel Dragon's Mountain!"

Lindon didn't know if that was a technique, a place, an organization, or even a Path. But the echo dashed forward with a punch, and Lindon could feel overwhelming force madra. Yerin matched his punch with her sword, and the entire room shook with their clash.

Space rippled, and it was a measure of the strength this past expert carried that he only took one step back from Yerin.

He grinned at her, and she held her sword up in acknowledgement.

Then Mercy and Eithan struck, without regard for any honorable duel. Arrows landed with the force of the Dark Tide Incantation, and Eithan struck out with the complete version of the Hollow Spear.

The Herald wove through the arrows, his speed a blur, and met Eithan's Hollow Spear with a massive Forged fist superimposing his own: a Forger echo technique.

Rather than the battle, Lindon and Dross were focused on analyzing the underlying technique.

[This application of hunger madra is far outside your meager understanding,] Dross declared.

You think I could learn this?

That would be *beyond* useful, and could perhaps have synergy with Dross. If Dross could comprehend and remember the strength behind other sacred artists, and Lindon could mimic them with hunger madra...

Dross cackled at Lindon's expense. [You don't think

you're a *real* hunger artist, do you? Master Northstrider can copy the wills of those he devours into his techniques, but your use of hunger is simple and crude. Even if you had the skill, you are not on a true hunger Path, and all you can do is manipulate your arm's binding.]

The Consume technique in his arm was indeed the most basic and straightforward use of hunger madra; it was like a fire binding designed solely to burn things. There was nothing subtle or complex about it, but it had limitless applications.

Reluctantly, Lindon abandoned his dream of an army of ghostly sacred artists under his command. *Can we disable the technique?*

[If you're willing to pay the cost, Void Sage.] Lindon could hear the sneer in Dross' voice.

Lindon had been forced to infuse his will into virtually everything he'd done since entering the labyrinth, and it was harder and harder to recover his mental energy. The hunger aura devoured even that.

But he still focused on the manifested phantom of the Herald. He would be defeated eventually—he was constantly on the defensive against his four opponents—but their every exchange wasted energy.

"**Enough,**" Lindon commanded.

The technique was a contained construct of energy, and Lindon ordered that energy to empty out.

It was well within the authority of the Void Icon, and the Herald instantly lost a chunk of strength. Yerin's sword passed through him an instant later, and then Ziel's hammer crushed him.

But Lindon's mind spun, and he had to sit down. That working had taken something out of him, and he wasn't sure how much he could do before he rested.

The same went for the others. Every technique they'd used to oppose this echo was a technique they couldn't use later.

And there was no way this was the only ghost in the labyrinth's arsenal. What if they had to face Malice later, with actual power behind her techniques?

Or even one of the Dreadgods?

When two more exits appeared, Lindon hesitated as he brought out the box containing the hand. "Eithan, can you tell..."

Eithan was already shaking his head. "They both lead deeper, but I can't follow them far enough."

"I hesitate to use the hand. If it Forges more experts, I'm not certain we can handle them."

Ziel let out a long breath. His horns began to glow green, and a circle of runes started floating around the head of the hammer.

"Is the route back still open?" he asked.

"Nope," Eithan said.

"Well that's too bad. Use the hand. Whatever shows up, leave it to me."

Lindon and Yerin traded a look. They didn't want to be skeptical of Ziel's ability, but if the labyrinth could simulate Heralds...

"Orthos had the right idea," Ziel went on. "I can't help here. I can with whatever's going on out there." He levered his hammer up in both hands. "I'll cover you, then you eject me."

Lindon wanted to argue, but Ziel was right. If he spent his energy now, they wouldn't have to waste resources covering for him. It was the best use of Ziel. Lindon just didn't *want* it to be.

In the end, since they were short on time, Lindon pulled out the Dreadgod's hand.

This time, the surge of ghouls that rose from the ground couldn't be counted. It was a tide of animated hunger madra.

Lindon immediately recognized that this couldn't be left to Ziel. No matter how confident he was, his Path wasn't suited to this situation. It was a job for the Hollow Domain, and Lindon diverted his attention from Subject One's authority and started to use his technique.

But Ziel had prepared. The circle of runes spinning around his hammer expanded immediately, taking on the entire room.

He inhaled as he lifted his hammer...then he brought it down.

The entire room *exploded* with force. Even the stone cracked, and Lindon's feet left the ground for a moment, though of course no one lost their balance.

The hunger techniques detonated, sending sprays of essence into the air, and Lindon tucked the hand away. He pointed to the hallway the hand had indicated.

But then another echo appeared. This time, it was a woman spinning a ring around each hand. Each ring was sharp on the outside, and there was another ring floating around her forehead, though this one was clearly a Goldsign.

She nodded at Ziel before hurling one of the rings at him. As it flew, it multiplied in an instant until dozens of rings flew at him.

From the spiritual pressure alone, Lindon wasn't sure if she was a Herald, but this should at least be the echo of an Archlord.

The Forged rings crashed into Ziel, who braced himself for the impact. Four huge runes floated around him, projecting a column of force that cracked and shuddered under every impact.

Lindon cycled Blackflame, but Ziel glanced to him beneath shining horns. His voice was so low that Lindon wouldn't have been able to understand his words over the crashing techniques without the hearing of an Overlord.

"What did I say?" Ziel asked wearily.

Then he exploded.

Green force erupted from him in every direction, blasting aside the rings in the air, and he hurled himself at the colorless woman. She herself was surrounded by several looping lights, which Lindon recognized as some kind of full-body Enforcer technique.

Ziel's hammer crashed against two rings that she held

in her hand, and once again the clash between them was deafening.

Several blades flew out from her—Striker techniques, and Lindon suspected they were propelled by launcher constructs. They swerved to attack Ziel, but his movement blurred, and his hammer shattered every one of them.

Neither moved particularly quickly, at least by Lindon's standards, but each impact was sturdy. Ziel was burning through soulfire, infusing his runes so that his script-circles lasted longer. Therefore, as the fight went on, more and more green rings surrounded his arms, legs, and hammer.

With each exchange, it became clear: he was getting stronger and stronger.

Until this moment, Lindon hadn't been able to estimate how much of Ziel's former power he'd recovered. But based on the density of his madra and the strength of his soulfire, Lindon put him at the high end of Overlord or the low end of Archlord.

His skill, though, would be considered impressive no matter where he was. He was Forging runes with incredible precision and operating scripts with such speed that Lindon wondered if he had a mind-spirit like Dross.

[Not like me! I am one-of-a-kind. If he had me, he would rule the world right now.]

Lindon wondered where Dross got the confidence in his own abilities.

Finally, Ziel cornered the woman with the rings. She was locked inside a script-circle which she could surely break, but there were three others in the air surrounding her, and Ziel was covered in slowly spinning emerald runes.

The black-and-white echo sighed and bowed her head, the sign of a good match.

Ziel triggered all the scripts.

She was crushed by pressurized air from all directions, her madra spraying onto the walls. Ziel let out a breath and looked up at the ceiling.

"Incredible," Lindon said. "I am...truly in awe. I've never seen anyone operate scripts so quickly."

Ziel gave a crooked smile. "Still not a Sage."

Lindon was also impressed by the flexibility of Ziel's Path; all of those rings were effectively permutations of a single Forger technique. He would love to examine such a binding.

But as efficient as the technique may have been, Ziel had spent his power lavishly. His core was dim, and his channels strained; he had been largely remade thanks to the Pure Storm Baptism, but the material of his spirit was still new and tender. Between this and the fight with Reigan Shen, he likely shouldn't have pushed himself so much.

Ziel looked down at himself, a clear expression on his face for a change: frustration. "That's embarrassing. Maybe I *should* try harder."

Lindon focused his authority on the Dreadgod's hand to give Ziel an exit...but he barely had to wish it before the walls blurred and a pair of doors appeared. There were only two openings: one in the wall, leading forward and down, and another in the ceiling.

"I'd feel at ease if you told me that was you," Yerin said.

Lindon shook his head. He stared at the exit, and he wasn't the only one. The spiritual sensations from above were clear. Not only did that lead back, but it led *out.* It was a straight shot back to the surface.

"Huh," Ziel said. "This is probably a trap."

Then he leaped out of the room.

"Good-bye!" Mercy called after him.

They all expected the way out to vanish as soon as Ziel left the room, but it lingered. It stayed long enough that they all felt it when Ziel left, because they got a sudden taste of spiritual power from the outside.

All their expressions changed at the same time, as they all sensed the same thing.

There was a war out there.

Great powers clashed in the world above, so many that it was difficult for Lindon to sort them. Sacred Valley—if they *were* still in Sacred Valley—was no longer a battlefield for Irons and Jades. Heralds fought up there, and Sages.

And Monarchs.

Mercy's face was pale, and she gripped Suu. "That's my mother."

"And she's not playing alone," Yerin said grimly.

"Oh my, it *is* a party." Eithan cocked his head as though listening. "How did the Eight-Man Empire make it all the way here? *And* the Dreadgod cults? If he brought House Shen as well..."

Lindon passed a hand over his face. Of course. If Reigan Shen had come here, he would have brought his forces in reserve.

"How strong is House Shen, Eithan?" Lindon asked.

"I'll put it to you this way: Reigan Shen's decision to compete in the Uncrowned King tournament as the patron of the Dreadgod cults was only unexpected because he had a perfectly viable team before. They're at least the match of any other Monarch faction, but it is...not simple to bring them here. He must have spent quite the fortune."

"We need answers," Lindon said. His perception remained in the still-open passageway to the surface, and he weighed the dilemma in his mind.

Should they all go back?

They could report Reigan Shen's actions to the Monarchs, who were surely more qualified to stop him, and then they could join the fight. At the very least, they could help suppress House Shen, and Lindon was *very* concerned about the fate of the Blackflame Empire.

They were not too far away, in the grand scheme of things. If Monarchs started fighting directly, then the Empire was still within Striker range.

But that meant giving up on the full story of the Dreadgods.

It meant giving up on the potential prizes, like Ozriel's Soulsmith inheritance. That could be the key to fixing Dross.

And it meant letting Reigan Shen do as he wished down here.

"I'll go," Mercy said heavily. "I think I have to."

"They can't make you," Yerin said. "As long as we have a voice, you don't have to do anything you don't want."

Mercy leaned on her staff as she looked upward. "Do you know how bad I'd feel if something happened to the Blackflame Empire while I'm stuck down here?"

Yerin tried to speak, but she was clearly stumped. If Lindon knew her, he suspected she was thinking along the same lines herself.

Mercy gave everybody an encouraging smile. "Sorry I can't help, everyone! But don't worry, I can take care of what's happening up there!"

She leaped up after Ziel.

But Lindon was still connected to the authority of the labyrinth, and he could feel where she went. She was only seconds behind him, but he had emerged miles away, and she was right above them. Was that Subject One's trap?

"And then there were three," Eithan murmured.

[Three humans,] Dross agreed. [...and one almighty mind-spirit.]

Outside the labyrinth, Ziel was spat out into a filthy cave, half-ruined by some earthquake. Or, more likely, the Wandering Titan.

He emerged to feel the chaos of battle all around, and the mobile headquarters of the Dreadgod cults high above.

"Why did he send me so far away?" Ziel muttered.

But there was no sense complaining. For once, he had a job to do. Ziel leaned the hammer on his shoulder and began to hike.

第二十章

CHAPTER TWENTY

The sensations from outside had gone away, as evidently Mercy had sealed the door behind her, but the labyrinth still didn't shift.

"You don't leave the gate open if you want the lambs to stay put," Yerin muttered.

Eithan folded his arms. "I don't like that Subject One seems to have taken Reigan Shen's side. That makes our odds...unfortunate."

Lindon had pulled out the case containing the Dreadgod's hand, but now he just stared at it. Thinking.

He had resolved himself to keep everyone together, to fight together, and not to let the difference in their strengths matter. But in the end, he'd been forced to bow to reality.

"So it's just us," he said aloud. He forced a smile. "Makes sense. We're the strongest."

Yerin gave him a strange look, but Eithan looked as though he understood.

Evidently the labyrinth had lost patience with them, because the walls blurred again. Now, there was only one entrance.

And it led to another overwhelming spiritual presence, like the ones that had birthed the Tomb Hydras. This time, though, the feeling was of unstoppable physical power.

He released the hand, just to see if Subject One had been messing with them. This time, there was no response from the hunger techniques, and the hand indeed clawed in the direction of the one entrance.

"So which costs us less?" Eithan mused. "Fighting with *that,* or carving through the floor?"

Yerin was still watching the ceiling. "You want to run your feet instead of your lips?"

Lindon racked his brains. No matter how he thought of it, he couldn't come up with a way to reach the bottom of the labyrinth with all three of them at peak fighting condition.

And if he didn't, they would have no chance against Reigan Shen.

He might be able to see to himself. There should be an opportunity to extract some unadulterated hunger madra, and then he could get his Consume technique working again. At least for a while.

If he did, then he and Dross would have a way of restoring Lindon's strength even in this aura-less environment.

But that required fighting this massively powerful dread-beast and hoping.

"Let's fight." He began to run, but Yerin stood in front of him without moving.

"Don't duel with yourself," she warned.

Lindon nodded, but he dashed forward.

They ran down the hall...and although the master of the labyrinth had made them face a long hallway, their speed without Mercy and Ziel along was truly incredible. The Soul Cloak was economical enough to use even while sparing his madra, and Yerin's physical power meant that she could literally sprint faster than her physical body should allow.

They reached the end of the hall in a blink, with Eithan lagging behind.

Lindon could see another of those endless rooms filled from wall to wall with flesh. The gorilla-like dreadbeasts that emerged reminded him of Crusher, and there were at least a dozen of them. Their pointed ears twitched toward the group as they arrived, and when they roared, the sound itself counted as an attack.

Right away, now that he could feel the scope of the opponent, Lindon stopped and began to turn. "We'll try digging."

Yerin had her sword and all six sword-arms out. "Better idea: let's make a deal. Think I can get us good terms."

Lindon's heart twisted. She was about to fight. "No! Apologies, I mean, but...without you, we can't...we can't win."

"There's a lot about you that's bright and sharp, Lindon." Yerin smiled, and her red eyes gleamed. "But you think too much."

Yerin's entire body flashed white, and he saw another flare of light as she appeared in the center of the huge dreadbeasts.

Lindon still worried for a moment, feeling that overwhelming spiritual pressure, even though it didn't make sense. The ones who were really in danger here were the dreadbeasts.

He was far away, now, so the chime sounded like a bell ringing softly next to his ear.

As Yerin used the Endless Sword.

Like a thousand invisible soldiers striking at once, blood flew into the air all around the chamber. If the previous scream had felt like an attack, this one rattled Lindon's bones and shook the entire labyrinth.

The gorilla-like guardian dreadbeasts hurled themselves at her, and the Netherclaw technique began Forging over her head. As the three-clawed red hand wove itself into existence out of red strands of madra, Yerin looked at the surrounding monsters in contempt.

She said something, and though Lindon couldn't hear it after having sealed off his ears, he understood the meaning behind it.

"Oh, please."

Her Goldsigns flashed in four directions, and Rippling Swords shot out. In front of her, behind, and to either side.

The shining waves of razor-sharp madra divided the chamber into quarters. Then the Netherclaw technique struck, and Yerin herself launched forward. She darted around for a second, landing delicately near Lindon and blowing her red streak of hair out of her eyes.

The whole room, big enough to house a fleet of cloud-ships, exploded into gore.

"They have blood in 'em," Yerin pointed out. "Well, *had.* Won't get far with me that way."

She was standing in the hallway with the other two, and Lindon felt a formless fury fill the walls. They blurred, and the room vanished. The three found themselves nose-to-nose with a blank rock wall.

But only for a moment. A second later, they were facing another giant chamber, this one empty under an arching dome so high that it might as well have been the sky.

Hundreds of entrances covered every surface so that it resembled the inside of a beehive. And *thousands* of creatures began pouring in.

Lindon was truly shocked by the chaotic presence of it all. The hunger aura was so thick he thought he could taste it, and there were so many monsters here that he could scarcely separate one from another.

[Finally, a deadly move worthy of my opponent!] Dross cried. [He's reconfigured the entire labyrinth to focus the dreadbeasts here. It takes a lot to impress me.]

Yerin, however, was less impressed.

She disappeared again and repeated her show from before.

This time, one Endless Sword meant she was standing in the center of a rain of blood and meat. She controlled the thin aura, so not even a drop splattered on her.

The splatter of blood made a roaring waterfall, and this time Lindon could barely see her. But not everything in the chamber had been a dreadbeast; there were spirits as well.

Briefly.

Rippling Sword blasted through the room, Lindon saw a few flashes of white, and a second later Yerin stood next to him again. Perfectly dry.

She was burning through power, just as Ziel had, but Lindon couldn't help but feel a little awe. How could he compete with that?

Dross made a choking sound. [You can tear a hole in the world! It *stinks* of false humility in here.]

Yerin leaned casually against the wall with one hand. "Oi, I know you've got ears. Give them a road forward, and me a way out, and I'll leave."

The anger that radiated from the walls only increased.

"Fine, we'll take your deal," Yerin said dismissively. "Keep sending meat to the grinder. Maybe when I run dry of madra, you can make my arm sore."

The walls blurred again, but this time the stone wall remained in front, trapping them in the hallway.

"Good. Curious to see what happens myself."

Yerin drew her sword back, and she began cycling the Final Sword. It was an unstable version, but she compensated with raw power.

And then she kept pouring power in.

Lindon initially thought she was bluffing, since the blood aspect of her power now meant that she would do less against stone than against monsters. But as she kept pouring more and more madra into her technique, along with the last of her soulfire, powerful pressure surged off her in waves. He had to take a step back, and Eithan had virtually set up camp at the far end of the hallway.

The air around her was beginning to distort in a way that suggested space was about to crack, and only then did the technique reach its apex.

Before she could unleash it, something in the labyrinth gave in.

A moment later, there were two tunnels. One led directly up, and Lindon could see the entry hall they'd first entered through back in the Ancestor's Tomb. The other sloped down.

And it was marked with a familiar symbol: the crest of Ozriel.

Yerin jerked her chin at the hall sloping down. "The pair of you head in there, go get your Soulsmith tablet, and I'll head out. Fair deal. You see a Monarch, you run."

Lindon removed the Dawn Sky Palace and tossed it to Yerin. "If it tries to trap you, get in there. If the key breaks and you can't escape, I'll come back to release you."

"Sounds like a fast road to getting stuck outside the world," Yerin said, but she did take it. "Now get moving."

Lindon hesitated. "Without you—"

Yerin grabbed him with one hand. "Don't split off from each other," she warned. "Don't fight Shen. Take what you can and get out."

Then she seized Eithan with her other hand and shoved them both down the tunnel.

When they were safely in the hallway, she looked up. "I'll go see who needs killing."

She leaped upward, leaving them to walk down.

Two left.

[The fact that you haven't learned to count me by now proves to me that you are irredeemable and will never amount to anything.]

Only when Lindon had scanned the next room with his perception and was satisfied that Reigan Shen wasn't lurking within did he move forward. Eithan had already strolled down, hands in his pockets.

Lindon had to stop his expectations before they rose too high. This should be the deepest room Ozriel had left behind in the labyrinth, which meant that it was likely to hold his Soulsmith inheritance.

He hadn't sensed anything like that in the room, which didn't necessarily mean it wasn't there. The inheritance could easily be inactive, or sealed, or veiled behind a script, or...

His thoughts crashed to a halt when he entered the room.

The chamber had been raided. Ornate, scripted chests stood open, and Lindon could still feel residual power emanating from inside. Powerful treasures had been hidden there, not long ago.

A nearby projection table had once housed a dream tablet, but it was now broken. No one would view the memory again. A shelf full of labels had once held books and scrolls dating back centuries, if not millennia. Every one of them missing. Some had been sealed away to preserve them, and others had been protected so that their power didn't disturb visitors.

There was another display hanging on the wall that showed triangular indentations—more of Penance's prototypes would have waited here. They were all missing.

But there was one central feature of the room that Lindon had not overlooked. A shrine against the back wall, holding a cut gem the size of Lindon's head. From everything Lindon had read, and heard—and from what he could still sense—this had been a Soulsmith inheritance. Ozmanthus Arelius had left the sum total of his Soulsmithing knowledge for future generations here.

The crystal was cracked. Dream madra still leaked from the fissure, dissipating in the air.

With Dross' help, Lindon could still read a flickering memory here or there. Not enough to form an image; they were mostly impressions, half-formed thoughts, or emotional reactions. They didn't make a clear picture.

Lindon stared at it.

"I can't fix you," he said aloud.

Dross spun out, tiny crown displayed proudly on his head. [What is there to fix? You should be concerned instead that you missed the chance to increase my power!]

"Apologies," Lindon whispered. He wasn't apologizing to this Dross, but to the old one. The real one.

Eithan looked around, hands still in his pockets. Lindon didn't think much of it, but on some level he still found it strange that Eithan wasn't more interested in records of his ancestors. Instead, he looked almost fond.

"Don't give up yet," Eithan said cheerily. "There should still be a way. Reigan Shen, for instance, always carries top-notch loot perfect for any Soulsmith."

Lindon's voice was dull. "Gratitude, but I'm all right. It would have been beyond difficult even if I did get Ozriel's inheritance. By the time I comprehended the techniques and learned to use them, chances are it would be too late."

"The theory is fairly straightforward, if difficult to execute. You have to realign Dross' structure in the same manner as before. Something like this Soulsmith inheritance would make it easier, but that doesn't mean it's impossible."

"I know that. I tried. I looked. I couldn't tell what he was like before."

Even Dross hadn't remembered what his alignment was. As he'd put it, *Have you ever paid attention to the exact order of your own bones?*

"There should be small hints in each piece. It's one of the many areas in which enhanced perception comes in handy." Eithan shrugged. "I'm always reluctant to tear off a piece of my spirit, but once we get out of here, you could Consume from me and borrow my bloodline legacy. I think you could do it."

Lindon looked around the room. There was no exit, and he could feel power gathering in the walls. The labyrinth was going to use its trump card, whatever that was.

He was going to have to use the last of his power to blast a way out, and when he did, they'd just leave. Whatever it was that drove him forward, he had just run out.

"Gratitude, Eithan." And because that didn't feel like enough, Lindon pressed his fists together and bowed. "Thank you."

Eithan lifted his eyebrows. "What was that for?"

"I think I understand how you feel, now." Lindon stared past the broken jewel. "When you're strong enough to move forward on your own, the only thing you can't do is bring others with you."

Lindon began to cycle Blackflame, because the power in the walls was still growing. Whatever the labyrinth was coming up with, it was *strong.*

[This is that echo technique, which you wouldn't need

me to tell you if you ever bothered to pay attention to your own spiritual sense.]

Lindon thought back to the ghosts that Ziel and the others had faced. "How much stronger is this one?"

[It's always a rough estimate, your senses not being precise enough to have a numerical measurement attached, but I would say that if those were an incomplete shell of a Herald's Remnant, this is a real one.]

Lindon even felt ripples in reality that suggested authority was being exerted. He readied the spear Midnight; even if the death madra would be largely useless against a technique Forged of madra, the sheer force in the instrument would help him.

Eithan clasped his hands behind his back, looking... fond. "You know, even as a child, all I ever wanted was people to grow with me. Every extraordinary thing I ever accomplished, I left behind another friend. And the world celebrated.

"That's not limited to advancement, you understand. When you see deeply, to the point that Monarchs clash over your advice, what does another Underlord have in common with you? Your peers are Sages and Heralds, and even they treat you like a stranger."

Hunger madra coalesced in the hallway, and Lindon prepared himself to face it as Eithan spoke.

"I wanted to raise up peers. In theory, it was possible. If you started from the beginning, you can raise a generation of truly unparalleled sacred artists who would never leave each other behind."

"Congratulations," Lindon said firmly. Blackflame materialized in his hands. "Yerin and I, at least, would never leave you behind."

Eithan walked beside him and gave Lindon a brilliant smile. "I know. I've never been happier."

Lindon wondered if Eithan wanted to fight together as the strongest hunger echo finished Forging.

Wind passed through the tunnels. Not a forceful wind,

as Lindon had expected. Nothing violent. A cool, thorough, gentle wind that picked up every speck of dust and carried it away.

A solid, black-and-white version of Ozmanthus Arelius strode out of the shadows. At this age, he looked like Eithan's brother. His hair was bright, his smile small and subtle. And across his shoulders, like another sacred artist might carry a spear, he carried a broom.

There were no overwhelming fluctuations of madra, but Lindon's spirit still trembled. This was a dangerous opponent.

But one still more dangerous waited ahead.

"Leave him to me," Lindon said.

Eithan turned back again, surprise evident on his face. "You want me to face Reigan Shen on my own?"

Ozmanthus didn't take advantage of his opponent's lack of attention, but rather waited politely.

"Apologies, Eithan, but I saw you fight earlier. He's weakened, and you could break through to Sage at any time. Go face your family's killer."

Eithan sighed and held up a hand for Ozmanthus to wait. The Broom Sage looked a little surprised, but dipped his head in acknowledgement.

Then Eithan turned to face Lindon entirely. "Everyone misunderstands me. Reigan Shen isn't the one I'm trying to surpass." He jerked a thumb over his shoulder. "He is."

Ozmanthus Arelius waved.

Lindon felt like the more he learned of Eithan, the less he knew, but he kept his attention focused on the enemy. "Then let's face him together."

"Yes, of course! If you think he'll allow that."

Lindon was about to ask who Eithan meant when Ozmanthus Arelius put a hand on the labyrinth wall.

This echo was far more solid than the others Lindon had seen. It even carried a measure of the original's authority.

Authority over the labyrinth.

Lindon gathered his concentration, but he was too late.

The hallway blurred around him...and he found himself facing a dead end. The ramping hallway sloped down behind him.

Powerlessly, he slapped a palm against the stone. "I think the heavens are playing a joke on me."

Dross laughed uproariously. [Weep! Despair! No matter what you do, you end up alone!]

Lindon turned to face down the hallway. "I'm not alone. I have you."

Dross' laughter faded.

This hall was soaked with was the most concentrated hunger madra he'd ever sensed. The tunnel walls glowed a soft, eerie gray-white. The mummified hand in his pocket pulsed in time with the light, even through the silver metal sealing it off.

Lindon's right arm ached and started to twitch. He forcibly suppressed it and began to walk.

The white light had grown, and the hunger aura was so strong here that Lindon couldn't open his aura sight for fear of being blinded. The stone had begun to turn white and merge together like overgrown skin, corrupted by centuries of hunger madra.

Lindon's hunger arm had begun twitching to the point that he couldn't control it anymore. In his other hand, he held Suriel's marble for comfort.

He stopped in the middle of the hallway and replicated what Yerin had done. He stretched his will into the walls and spoke.

"Pardon, but you must be Subject One. My name is Lindon." He inclined his head to the wall. "You've seen everything that's gone on in the labyrinth, so I'm certain you understand the situation. I am here to negotiate. There has to be something that you want."

Suddenly, the entire labyrinth shuddered.

Lindon felt the crushing will of the Dreadgod. He felt Subject One's anger. Despair. Relief. And a final sense of wistful, unfulfilled hunger.

None of that was directed at Lindon.

[Your words have angered the beast!] Dross cried.

I don't think I had any effect at all. I think this was...something else.

That hadn't felt like a response to Lindon's plea. If anything, it had sounded like a dying man's final breath.

The labyrinth shuddered, convulsing like a swallowing throat. The wall at the end of the hallway peeled away, and Lindon glimpsed an open room filled with a pale, unhealthy light.

A chill ran up Lindon's spine, and even Dross was quiet. Lindon crept down the hallway and came face to face with the Slumbering Wraith.

With Little Blue on his back, Orthos strode up to the stone door that slowly slid open. The door was a massive gateway that would have towered over him even at his true size, but it opened for them alone.

The Nethergate. The exit to the labyrinth.

When he passed the threshold of the door, and the script containing his spiritual perception, he sensed the powers outside.

Then he scrambled back the other way.

Little Blue wailed out a long whistle. Overlords and Archlords were fighting over Sacred Valley, and he had glimpsed a cloud fortress of staggering size carrying even more intimidating powers. There were Heralds clashing here, and he wanted nothing of that.

More importantly, someone had to tell Lindon and the others. Lindon should be able to feel their alarm—assuming the labyrinth didn't block it—but he would have no idea what caused it.

Or what killed us, Orthos thought as two Overlords and an Archlord dropped around them.

All three sacred artists were dressed in robes of red-and-black, sewn with an emblem he remembered. They gave off a sense similar to Yerin, and the two Overlords carried weapons shrouded in Blood Shadows. One a hammer, the other a long chain.

The Archlady, as Orthos now saw it was a female human, had gray-streaked hair and a Shadow in the form of a serpent. The great snake hissed at Orthos, and he had never before appreciated how menacing snakes could be to mice. Usually he was the one preying on snakes.

"I am Emissary Kahn Mala," the Archlady said. She looked as though her skin had been glued to her bones. "Name yourselves or be devoured."

Orthos had been preparing himself to die with blood on his shell and fire in his mouth, so he preferred this alternative. He lifted his head proudly.

"I am called Orthos."

Little Blue gave a chime.

"This is my partner, Little Blue."

Kahn Mala's eyes narrowed. "You are contracted to Lindon Arelius."

Orthos moved his eyes from the Lady to the two Lords. So they were after Lindon. More of his fear turned to anger.

Deliberately, he looked away and scooped up a stick in his mouth. He crunched it while he looked back to the Archlady.

"Who?" Orthos asked.

Little Blue hopped off his shell and stood beside him, arms crossed. The sound she made was among the harshest he'd ever heard from her; it sounded like someone had slapped a cat.

The Blood Shadow in the form of a snake wrapped around them. Not tightly, as though constricting them, but to fence them off. Its head reared up, and skin flared into a hood. So it was a giant cobra. Its jaws parted, and it made a sound that was like a thousand hissing screeches at once.

Orthos had to stop from pulling his head back into his shell.

He didn't blame himself; there was something instinctive about being so small and facing something giant. Similar to what he'd felt against the Titan.

But this was no Titan, and he glared back at the cobra defiantly.

Out of the corner of his eye, he noticed that Little Blue had flinched and taken a slight step behind him. That relieved him. At least he wasn't the only one afraid.

"Besides Lindon Arelius, who else is down there?" the Archlady continued. "We want to protect them as best we can."

That seemed reasonable, and Emissary Kahn Mala looked kinder than she had at first. He had likely been predisposed against her just because she was part of Redmoon Hall, which wasn't fair.

He opened his mouth to respond, then snapped it shut when he noticed what was happening. With the last remaining spark of his soulfire, he blew away the dream aura she was weaving around his head.

She had been using her soulfire to influence the aura of his *mind.* That was terrifying. He had never seen anyone use their soulfire to manipulate minds; at least, not as far as he'd noticed. But she couldn't have been a dream artist. Not only could he feel her madra, but an Archlord-level dream artist wouldn't have been bothered by Orthos' pathetic soulfire.

Kahn Mala's lips thinned further, but now his fury was fully aflame. "Whoever this Lindon Arelius is, I'm sure he'd rather die than receive your *protection."*

He kept her eye as he leaned down and munched on another stick.

Little Blue popped up from behind his shell to lend a ring of agreement.

The Archlady snorted in annoyance and addressed her pair of henchmen. "Keep them contained. I will return if anyone else arrives."

So began a boring period of waiting and eating sticks.

Orthos only knew someone else was coming when the

Nethergate cracked again. The Archlady appeared at his side in an instant, barking orders to her pair of Overlords.

Mercy arrived, hair pulled back into a tail and Suu in the form of a walking stick. She blinked at the sight of the Redmoon Hall Emissaries arrayed before her.

"Akura Mercy," Emissary Kahn Mala announced. "You are under our protection per the agreement between our forces and your mother. Please cooperate and confirm the identity of your companions so we can protect them as well."

Orthos and Little Blue shook their heads.

Mercy beamed. "You found them already! Thank you so much!"

She rushed over and scooped up Little Blue and Orthos, carrying them into a hug that felt for Orthos like being lifted into the top of a tree. Only softer.

Kahn Mala looked over them all. "We know Lindon Arelius and Yerin Arelius are with you down there. What about Eithan Arelius?"

"Nope!" Mercy said cheerily. "I was just here with my friends Orthos and Little Blue!"

Orthos wasn't sure he'd ever seen Mercy's joyful demeanor irritate someone so visibly. "You should know better than this, Akura. If we were hostile to you, we would be using techniques rather than words. Since we are allied for the moment, you will show me the respect I am due and tell me the truth."

Mercy's eyes shimmered slightly, as they did before she called her armor. "You're not calling me a liar, are you?"

Her tone wasn't much different than usual, but Orthos shifted uncomfortably in her arms. She was weak after her time in the labyrinth, and he could *feel* that she was weak, but his spirit still itched like he was in danger.

The Archlady was less impressed. "You can't use your mother to threaten me here."

"I can't? So you wouldn't mind if I called her right now, then?"

"...sit by the others." Kahn Mala put a trembling hand over

her eyes. Her cobra hissed again, and Orthos got the strong impression that the Archlady wasn't used to dealing with anyone without threatening them.

While the next wait was boring, at least it was less so with Mercy there. She chatted easily with them, and even struck up a brief conversation with their Overlord guards. All the while, she kept patting his head or stroking his shell.

That struck him as undignified. If he was his normal size, no one would think of him as a pet.

After time crawled on for too long, the Nethergate swung open again.

Yerin emerged, and she wasn't alone. Eithan walked at her side. Yerin's red eyes widened as she saw Redmoon Hall, and she put a hand on her sword.

Orthos began to laugh.

第二十一章

CHAPTER TWENTY-ONE

ITERATION 119: FATHOM

Spread out among the stars of Fathom, the seven Judges of the Abidan Court did battle with the Mad King and his armies.

Zakariel, the Fox, slid in and out of existence, dodging lightning-strikes that detonated stars and slipping past armies of half-real Fiends that clawed for her soul. Her dagger flashed, and ten thousand kilometers away, an ancient warrior wearing a silver crown grabbed at his chest.

Despite all the protections he could weave, despite oaths and promises and seals older than many worlds, his heart had been pierced by a hidden dagger.

The Silverlord died without knowing what had killed him.

Telariel, the Spider, spun invisible webs throughout the universe. Ten thousand lesser Vroshir sacrificed ten thousand Class Four Fiends to begin a working that would strike a deadly blow. They were confident in their stealth, hidden by shadows they had dredged from the end of time.

He saw right through them, and with a swipe of his cane, he disrupted their ritual. They slew ten thousand of their own kind for nothing.

A fleet of warships was conjured into reality from the stuff of dreams, targeting the population of a distant planet to weaken the world's connection to the Way. Telariel misaligned all their engines at once, and the second they ignited their Void Drives, they all exploded into miniature suns.

The Angler used the chaos of battle to slip into a local stellar landmark known as the Heartbeat Star to steal a horn from the dragon that slept at its core, but Telariel tugged her away with a thread of order to let her know that he was watching. Sulking, she retreated.

None of this took The Spider's full attention. He solved a thousand problems at once, in an instant, without moving a step.

Durandiel, the Ghost, faded in and out of visibility. She strode through a twisted reality that a Class Two Fiend tried to manifest, a warped world of distorted gravity and fleshy trees.

"No," the Ghost said, and the half-formed reality collapsed.

One Silverlord controlled diamond chains with each link the size of a star, forged from the energy of a foreign world and refined in Fathom's own system. The chain crashed like a train through a series of inhabited planets, only to slam to a halt on the end of Durandiel's hand.

"Wrong," the Ghost said. The diamond chain popped like a bubble, leaving the debris of the planets it had destroyed to drift through space.

A four-armed woman gathered up the collateral damage from one of the Mad King's attacks, spooling up spatial cracks like thread, and wove them into text that touched something deep inside the world of Fathom.

Time froze around her. In that space beyond time, she began a subtle but far-reaching working, redefining the mechanisms of Iteration One-one-nine.

Durandiel rose up from behind the four-armed Vroshir and watched.

"Not bad," the Ghost said.

The woman spun around, her backhand trailing energy that could annihilate entire populations, but it was all a function of will and energy, so it faded to nothing before the authority of the Ghost.

The slap landed normally on Durandiel's cheek.

"Ow."

The Vroshir flinched and tried to run, but space was still sealed. The Ghost grabbed her by the collar. "Why don't you come work for me?" She folded the four-armed woman like a piece of paper, but this paper squirmed and resisted, so Durandiel let it unfold slightly and peeked inside.

"It's that or execution," she pointed out.

The woman stopped resisting, and the Ghost folded her up and slipped her inside a pocket. The zone of frozen time vanished as she strode after other rule-breakers.

Several galaxies away, the Mad King clashed in combat against Razael, the Wolf, and Gadrael, the Titan. The unstoppable sword of the Abidan and their unbreakable shield.

Every clash between them devastated star systems, setting even distant planets trembling. Civilizations throughout Fathom begged for someone to save them from what was surely the end of the world.

Suriel, the Phoenix, answered them. Her Razor removed toxic energy, hostile will, and insidious parasites even as she herself constantly renewed the Iteration, keeping it moving toward a state of wholeness and order. Corpses returned to life, shattered planets re-formed and drifted back into orbit, and the explosion of stars reversed.

Over it all, the Hound watched, directing each Judge from one decision to another, guiding Fate toward victory. Futures flashed, were chosen, and sprang into being at his command. In realms unseen, he steered causality around dead ends of nonexistence and pitfalls of chaos.

All passed in one blink of a mortal eye.

To the uncountable trillions of mortals who called Fathom home, this was an incomprehensible nightmare. Only earlier that day, across many thousands of inhabited planets, the universe had functioned exactly as it always had.

Then reality had begun to tear apart. A figure with burning eyes, in armor of bone, had appeared in the sky, some-how visible from every city on every planet at once.

He had unraveled their world. They had seen space crum-ble, time spiral in on itself. Unnamed horrors had sprung forth from nothing, and neither gravity nor reality were reliable any longer. Then the quakes in existence had ceased without warning, and all had been restored to normal. The warped rules had righted themselves, leaving everyone in Fathom to wonder if they had suffered a collective hallucination.

Until the stellar war had ignited. Then planets exploded and were remade seconds later. People were slaughtered, revived, reborn, repaired. Time twisted, slowed, sped up. Space was com-pressed, then stretched. Bloody lightning fell from the sky, fol-lowed by healing rain. Towers sprang from dreams while ruins bloomed into bustling cities that had suddenly always existed.

And Suriel knew that all this was only possible because of the presence of all the Court of Seven. Fathom was the lynchpin of Sector Eleven, with by far the greatest popula-tion and the most stable connection to the Way. The world was so stable that it helped steady all the other Iterations in the Sector, so it had to fall before any of the others could. The Mad King had spent great effort trying to destroy it, even with the Scythe of Ozriel.

Yet, without the seven Judges anchoring its existence, he would have succeeded. That the beings of Fathom remained to experience the battle was itself a stroke of fortune.

While Suriel reached all over the Iteration to correct dis-ruptions and knit the fabric of reality back together, her Presence continually spat communications and warnings into her mind.

[WARNING: incoming attack.]

[Telariel has redirected attack; requests restoration at the following coordinates.]

[Sector Three Control reports an unusual spike in deviations.]

[Temporal deviation detected. Corrected by Durandiel, but requires Phoenix support.]

[Sector Zero Control requests an update.]

It was the Spider and his Presence that handled communication through the Way, so Suriel knew he was enduring a far greater deluge of requests and alarms, but she found herself overwhelmed anyway.

There was a reason the Judges never acted together. There were only seven of them.

While their greatest enemies may have chosen to stand and face them here, this was by no means an exhaustive list of the forces arrayed against them. While they were here, they would lose territory everywhere else. Even Sanctum was no longer completely secure, though it had powerful and ancient protections ready to deploy.

They would certainly win here, but they had to make it worth the price.

Suriel's Presence blared with another alarm, and Suriel knew that this time, the Spider had passed this message to all of them at once.

[WARNING: Haven breached.]

It came with a vision of Haven, the prison-world that looked like an iron prison even from orbit. It flared red in her vision, indicating a spatial breach in the Iteration.

Suriel overheard as the Hound's voice was transmitted to the Fox.

"Zakariel, go."

The transmission was more than mere words; she understood that Makiel had scanned the future and found this course of action acceptable. The Fox was the only one who could breach the cordon around Fathom and return to Haven without being caught, *and* the one who would catch the prey quickly without letting them escape.

Her absence in this Iteration meant that some enemies would be able to flee, and increase the pressure on surrounding worlds, but this was less damage than a full breach of Haven would cause.

But Suriel glimpsed what they would trade for such an action, and her heart went cold.

"Makiel!" she shouted.

The Fox had already slipped out of Fathom and back into the Way, bounding for the prison-world. Only a few prisoners had escaped, those in the least secure layers.

Makiel never turned to Suriel. He continued watching the future.

"It was necessary," he said, as possibility played out before Suriel's eyes.

The Mad King clashed swords with Razael, and the stars quaked. At the same time, he struck with the Scythe at Gadrael, who took the blow on his shield.

A stalemate. Until the Fox left.

As though waiting for this very moment, the Mad King tore open a hole to the Void.

That was still extraordinarily difficult; the Way was powerful here, making it all but impossible to reach out to chaos. But Daruman had been capable of such feats even long ago, much less with Ozriel's Scythe in his hands.

Suriel reached out to heal the fabric of space, and the void portal grew smaller. The Mad King struggled against her, as the portal swirled and flashed, fighting for stability. The longer she held him here, the more time she would give Razael to recover and strike another blow; the Wolf was already gathering power in her flaming sword.

But as Suriel took her focus away from the rest of the Iteration, a crack in Razael's armor grew wider, a wound in Durandiel's side festered, and a planet far away cracked and drifted into oblivion.

The moment of her decision seemed to stretch out before Suriel. She could keep Daruman here, or she could keep everyone alive.

Though it wrenched her heart, she stopped struggling against the Mad King.

Razael's armor flowed back together, Durandiel's injury reversed until she had never been wounded at all, and the broken planet drifted back together.

The Mad King met Suriel's eyes as he drifted backwards

into the Void, and though millions of kilometers separated them, she could hear the laughter of Oth'kimeth, the Fiend, echoing in her soul.

As the portal winked shut, his blazing red eye never left hers.

[Without first removing Fathom, he will struggle to completely destroy any other worlds in this Sector,] Suriel's Presence reported, as though that would soothe her. [His removal from the battlefield will ensure our victory, and it is possible that we will win and escape long enough to preserve fragments of any destroyed world.]

Fragments. The pieces of a world that drifted through the Void after an Iteration had been destroyed.

Unless it had been completely culled by the Reaper's Scythe. In which case no fragments remained at all.

What are the odds that he will change his target?

Her Presence was silent, and Suriel knew why. The Mad King's target wouldn't change. There were more strategically valuable worlds in range, like Asylum. With the state of the cosmos as it was, he could strike even at Suriel's homeworld in Sector Twenty-three.

But he wouldn't. He wanted a victory that was as symbolic as it was strategic, to conquer the Abidan of the past as well as the present. He would send a message by destroying the home of Ozriel, the birthplace of the Abidan, and the place that produced more Abidan-qualified ascendants than any other.

He was going to destroy Cradle, and Suriel was too late to stop him.

Lindon walked onto a chamber that shone with gray-white light that pulsed like a heart. It was another one of those massive rooms filled with flesh, where the truly enormous dreadbeasts had fused into one mass.

Faded off-white meat filled the entire chamber, spilling over the floor and spiraling up pillars. So far, so expected. But there were no other dreadbeasts here, no children or guardians.

The entire room was focused on one figure in the center. One skeletal, desiccated, six-armed man.

He sat half-melted into a growth that resembled a throne, and he leaned on the armrest with one elbow. His skin was dry and papery, and he had no muscle at all. All six of his hands were intact, but some were a slightly different shade than the others, leading Lindon to wonder if one of those was the hand he now held in a script-sealed container.

The man was dead.

Glassy eyes met Lindon's. Largely black, with white irises, they had no life within them. And Lindon could feel the power radiating off the figure slowly dissipating, like the last wisps of smoke from a dead fire.

In the center of his chest, where the heart should be, was only a gaping hole.

[You were too slow!] Dross raged. [Reigan Shen has slain the beast!]

It *had* to have been Reigan Shen, Lindon knew. But there were no signs of battle. He was reluctant to expose the hand he had locked away—in this chamber, it might even bring the Wraith back to life—but he had already figured out how to tap into the authority of the labyrinth.

Focusing on the Void Icon, Lindon extended his awareness into the room nearby. He was looking for a familiar binding, a Forger technique embedded somewhere...

Dross contemptuously pointed it out a moment before Lindon found it himself. The technique that would create a hunger echo.

Without Subject One to wrestle against him, Lindon found this one easy to activate. He still needed Dross to help him sort through the dizzying impressions—the Dreadgod had fed on far too many people—but one presence was clear above all others.

Lindon poured pure madra into the technique. The more he fueled the technique, the more solid the echo would be. Before long, he managed to Forge a black-and-white echo nearby. It was still transparent, but it should be conscious and ready to speak.

It was little more than a ghost, but not just any ghost. This was the manifestation of the Slumbering Wraith itself.

The echo flexed all six of his arms, then looked at his own body that sat next to him. Rage and weariness and longing radiated from him.

"Betrayal is the nature of Monarchs," the Dreadgod said.

Lindon glanced at the hole in his chest. "Pardon, but it looks like he held up his end of the bargain."

"No. He was meant to strike the final blow, then leave this place. He violated his oath." Smoldering black-and-white eyes met Lindon's. "Clever he was, to find a way to break such a bond. But he will pay a price. There is always a price."

"He's still *here?*" Lindon tried to push further into the labyrinth, to find him, but the weight of the labyrinth's authority was old and heavy. He could get no more.

"In my last moments, I cast him away, but he will return. Then you will join me in death."

"Then help me work against him." This echo would have no control over the labyrinth, but he could still guide Lindon.

"What do you hunger for, young Sage?" Subject One asked, and there was a kind of dark humor in the question. He pointed to Lindon's arm. "You put my power in your body, so your desire must be great indeed."

"I am honored that one of your stature would ask about my needs. But I want to grant the wish we share. How do I defeat Reigan Shen?"

Subject One slowly strolled around his own throne. "Yesterday, I tried mindlessly to devour you. But I find that after death, I have control of myself again. At last."

"Apologies, but I feel that every second is vital."

"My nightmare is that I have been trapped here only hours, and that it simply *feels* like an eternity."

"I hope it is a comfort to know that nightmare is only a dream."

"Not entirely. Because it means that the destruction I have seen my successors wreak is reality. The countless lives they have destroyed...the great power they have *consumed...*"

Subject One shuddered, and the white in his eyes flashed, but he re-focused on Lindon. "To foil Reigan Shen, you must know the truth about us. Those you call *Dreadgods.*"

Lindon sharpened his attention, and even Dross didn't interrupt. This was the answer they had come here to find. "How do we kill them?"

Papery lips fluttered up into a smile. "I don't know what the Monarchs have allowed you to know, but it should be no surprise to you to learn that hunger aura isn't a natural force."

Lindon nodded, but it was interesting that the conversation had started with hunger *aura*. Everyone assumed that hunger *madra* was just a corruption of pure madra that had escaped into the wild long ago.

"It is a corruption of the natural order of Cradle," he went on. "A manifestation of ambition, of selfish desire. Created by the presence of the Monarchs." Subject One met Lindon's eyes and spoke clearly. "The Dreadgods will die only when there are no more Monarchs."

There was much Lindon wanted to learn here—How was aura created or corrupted? Was there a mechanism that decided which aspects of aura were allowed and which weren't?—but his time was clearly limited. The white light was steadily fading, and Subject One's presence grew weaker with every word.

Lindon could put more madra into the technique, but Reigan Shen was growing closer. He couldn't waste time.

"What's wrong with the Monarchs?" Lindon asked.

"They are too much for this world. A great weight. Sages like yourself are only half-ascended, which is within the scope of a world like ours. But when your body and your spirit have both grown too great for this world to contain, you must escape to a place that can contain you."

Dread grew in Lindon's heart. "Do the Monarchs know this?"

"They *must* know. It is a fight against the Way to stay in this world at all. And they have stayed not for hours or days, to say farewell to their loved ones, but for *centuries.*" Subject One bared his teeth. "What do you know of the days before the four great hunger beasts roamed the surface? The four... Dreadgods?"

"Apologies. I've never heard of that time."

"Of course not," Subject One said heavily. "The Monarchs would control their records. Hunger aura drifted all over the world, and where it moved, all other aura weakened. It corrupted everything; Remnants, natural spirits, sacred beasts. Even humans. Many of them were powerful enough even to threaten Monarchs."

He took a rattling breath. "*We* came to this labyrinth as a secure location to perform our research. We were looking for a way to control the hunger aura."

That was the least surprising thing Lindon had learned so far. Even he had immediately started thinking of all the ways he could use hunger madra the moment he had learned of it, and one hunger spear had allowed an ancestor of the Jai clan to dominate the Desolate Wilds.

"This site was old beyond memory, even to us. We used it as a trap to focus all the hunger aura in the world. Instead of running wild, it would be concentrated here, controlled by ancient seals. We researched fusing hunger bindings into animals, whose power would be suppressed by the great formation."

He laughed quietly, until Lindon couldn't tell the difference between laughs and sobs. "We thought we had it *under control.*"

[He volunteered to take the hunger binding into his own flesh,] Dross said confidently. [The first test subject. Let this be a lesson to you, Lindon: never volunteer.]

The Dreadgod's cries became laughter again. "The spirit is right." Lindon stiffened as he realized that Dross hadn't just been speaking to him, but Subject One didn't seem to mind.

"I was afraid *not* to volunteer. You understand the allure of hunger madra, I see. Endless power." He gave a humorless chuckle. "We were wrong about virtually everything."

Black-and-white eyes met Lindon's. "Hunger, you see, is all linked. It is one force, one entity, one...existence. As I spiraled out of control, so did our four greatest subjects. They escaped, contained as they were on the surface...but I was locked here."

His attention had drifted off, and Lindon felt the power around him ebb. He had to keep the man focused. "Please, how do I defeat Reigan Shen?"

"Slay the Monarchs," Subject One whispered.

Lindon froze. "No one but the Monarchs can do battle with Dreadgods."

"It is the Monarchs who sustain the great beasts," the Wraith continued. "If they are gone from our world, hunger aura will fade away. And we can finally...rest."

[Fool. That will take decades!]

"How much damage will the Dreadgods cause without the Monarchs around to contain them?"

Subject One gave a cruel smile. "Try to defeat the beasts first, then. That was what the last generation attempted. It was the most awake I've felt in...however long. They crushed the beast of earth, and then they discovered what we did. When one of the beasts dies, the others inherit its power until it is reborn. They become smarter. Stronger. And the hunger takes hold.

"The beasts devoured the rest of the Monarchs, and for a while, I could live through their eyes."

He stared off into the distance, reminiscing, but only for a moment. Then he returned to reality. "But that energy didn't last. As a generation of Monarchs passed, hunger weakened. The great beasts had to sleep more often, and never fully awakened. I lost myself to the long dream...until more Monarchs were raised up, and failed to leave."

Not only was Lindon having trouble reconciling this new knowledge with what he knew of the Monarchs, he was becoming restless. Subject One paced around his throne, looking down at his own body, but Lindon felt a foreign will pressing against the authority of the labyrinth.

"Apologies, but *how* does this help me defeat Reigan Shen?"

"He seeks to replace me." The echo touched his chest, where the hole was in the enshrined body. "To devour the devourer."

Lindon looked to his heart again. "He took your core binding?"

"It will be his path to great power," Subject One said, and each word dripped with mockery. "Such power."

Lindon looked to the throne where Subject One had been imprisoned for an uncounted number of years. His spiritual perception moved throughout the endless room, and he recognized that this was the perfect state of the dreadbeasts. Physical and spiritual had been fused seamlessly, so that it reminded him of the Herald's body.

Subject One suddenly shot forward, his teeth bared. "You stop him by ridding the world of Monarchs! Kill them, banish them, convince them, it matters not! *Make them leave!* If Reigan Shen becomes me, then he will fade into mortality with no Monarchs to sustain him. If he does not..." His grimace turned into a horrific corpse-smile. "...then the beasts will feed one last time."

"I will do all I can to stop him," Lindon promised, and that commitment settled on him. Rather than a promise between him and the echo, it felt like a promise between him and the labyrinth. "But I need a way out."

"As the first child of hunger, I give you my blessing." The authority of the labyrinth softened, easier for Lindon to mold. Now he could feel the script-chains controlling the mundane functions of each room. He suspected that if Subject One were still alive, his blessing would have been more effective, but anything would help.

Lindon focused his will and the walls blurred. Another exit appeared.

Now, for the first time, Lindon felt the ancient authority that bound Subject One here. It was a suction even stronger than the hunger aura, a hole that Lindon could sense through the Void Icon. No matter how much power the Slumbering Wraith consumed, it only weighed him down.

Lindon saw the longing in the transparent black-and-white eyes of the echo. Even with the keys to his prison, he had been unable to escape. He had been trapped here, half-awake, controlled by hunger.

And feeding on those who entered the labyrinth.

Intelligent he may be, a prisoner of a tragic story, but Subject One was still a Dreadgod.

The doorway out was open and waiting, and Lindon made a note of its position. He bowed his head. "Gratitude. May I know your name, so that it can be remembered?"

For the first time, Subject One looked troubled. "I'm...I don't...I don't remember."

"I will tell your story nonetheless," Lindon said.

Then he thought, *And I'll take your arm.*

Once he banished the echo, he would have the greatest upgrade for his arm. Just before he did, though, he plunged his authority back into the labyrinth. "My apologies, but my friend was fighting your projection of Ozmanthus. Is he still...?"

"All such projections would be cut off when I died."

Relieved, Lindon saluted the Dreadgod and bowed. "My gratitude, then."

He let the echo fade, then the Burning Cloak sprang up around him. He reached for one of the dead Dreadgod's arms.

[His information will support a divine purpose,] Dross said. [Mine.]

The script-lights overhead flickered, and the hunger aura howled. Even the wind drifted past Lindon, being drawn behind him as though by a huge indrawn breath.

Without Lindon's approval, the wall blurred.

"Two possibilities," Lindon said aloud. "Either there's no

power going into the control script, so the entire mechanism is resetting, or...the Monarch found his way back."

Dross appeared just to sneer at him. [Which do *you* think it is?]

Lindon pulled the spear Midnight from the haphazard harness he'd made on his back. It was awkward to use one-handed, but the aura was still too thin here, and he had no more suitable weapon.

We're fighting to run away, Lindon sent to Dross. *If you can borrow my authority for the control script, then let us out.*

[If you were stronger, I wouldn't have to do such menial labor.]

Lindon didn't argue. He was focused on the approaching presence, and wondering how long it would take him to burn through the wall and get away.

Then a new figure appeared at the doorway, striding into the room. "Have a seat, Wei Shi Lindon Arelius," Reigan Shen called. "Let's talk."

CHAPTER TWENTY-TWO

The light in Subject One's chamber was thin and gray, and the golden chair that Reigan Shen pulled out of thin air gleamed more brightly than anything else. The Monarch found a mound of flesh that rose higher than anywhere else and perched his chair atop it, so no one was seated above him.

"Apologies for disturbing you," Lindon said, as soon as he entered the room. "I was only on the way out."

Reigan Shen sat down and raised a crystal goblet, studying Lindon over the rim. The lion's eyes were sharp, and the light inside them resonated well with this room. He was a predator of endless hunger, and he ruled over this ancient and ruined kingdom.

His clothes were still worn and stained from months of travel, and Lindon noticed that many of the cases, capsules, and devices strapped to him were now missing or empty. He didn't carry the orange sword or the thin one anymore, but rather had an axe of weathered stone leaning up against the side of his seat.

And he still didn't give off the spiritual pressure of a healthy Monarch. By what Lindon could read of his power, he reminded Lindon more of Yerin. A Herald, but spiritually weaker.

That lifted Lindon's spirits, as there might be a way out of this.

Then again, he remembered the endless weapons Reigan Shen had summoned, and the skill with which he'd fought so many opponents at once.

A skilled wielder could more than compensate for a weak weapon. And Reigan Shen still had Tiberian Arelius' Remnant, the most powerful weapon of them all.

Lindon had strained the connection to that space past breaking, and it was possible that Reigan Shen hadn't repaired that connection yet. At least, Lindon hoped so. If he *could* summon a Monarch's Remnant, then Lindon was a step away from death.

After examining Lindon head to toe, Shen gestured with his goblet to the corpse on the throne. "I see you met the old man. What did you think of his echo?"

"I had great sympathy for him. He was trapped here for so long."

"Yes yes, but otherwise. I presume you understand the origin of the Dreadgods better now, unless Eithan already found a way to tell you."

So Eithan *had* known. He had mentioned being restricted by oath, and it made sense that a Monarch might have forced him to swear to keep their secrets.

"I believe I do have a better understanding of the situation, yes," Lindon said cautiously.

The Monarch leaned back in the chair. "Well then, I won't take the long way around. Swear not to spread awareness, or to tell anyone about me, and I'll let you go."

There was quiet as he sipped from his goblet.

Lindon feigned delight. "Of course! I'll swear as you wish." Dross could tell everyone, and even if he couldn't, there were surely other ways of releasing the information. But that was assuming the promise would bind Reigan Shen.

But twice, now, Lindon had seen evidence that he could slip the bonds of soul oaths. He was only playing along. "Certainly the Monarch factions already know, though?"

"Everyone knows who matters. If you're a Monarch, it's impossible for you not to understand the situation. And for everyone who we think might ascend to Monarch..." He shrugged. "Either they swear, or they don't make it. You would have to swear this oath eventually, to Malice if not to me."

Who is he afraid I'll tell? Lindon wondered. If the Monarchs knew, as did anyone who might advance to Monarch, then he couldn't tell anyone who could do anything about it.

Dross scoffed. [If the rumor spread, the Monarchs would have to kill those who heard it. Surely that would be a pain. Like sweeping up fleas.]

"I swear not to discuss the relationship between the Monarchs and the Dreadgods with anyone who does not already know, nor to reveal details about Reigan Shen's actions in the labyrinth, in exchange for my safety and freedom."

The oath settled lightly around Lindon, waiting for Reigan Shen to answer.

The Monarch studied him again, then drained his goblet. With a faintly regretful sigh, he placed the goblet on the arm of his chair and casually reached for the stone axe.

His spirit flared, and the axe shone as he slashed the weapon through the air toward Lindon. Lines of bladed light flew at Lindon in a net, a complex Striker technique of sword madra, all coming from an Archlord weapon.

Lindon poured soulfire into the Hollow Domain. If he hadn't been expecting this, he would have been too slow.

The madra crashed into his Domain from sixteen different angles and weren't fully wiped away, but were weakened enough for Lindon to strike them all down with his hand.

Reigan Shen stood lazily from his chair. "I knew fools never made it to Sage, but I had hoped. You are young."

"If you weren't willing to let me go, why make me swear at all?"

"Oaths tend to bind Remnants." Lindon felt a powerful will surround him, and the air began to stretch and warp. "I suppose I won't be able to keep yours."

Lindon reached into space. **"Hold!"** he commanded. His working went along with the world, which naturally resisted intrusion, so he remained in place.

But it still strained him. No one who made it to Monarch had weak willpower.

Dross snapped a warning as Lindon's attention faded from the working, and the world slowed slightly as Reigan Shen dashed in, stone axe pulled back for a strike.

Lindon lifted Midnight and used the Soul Cloak. All the strength he could muster went into the weapon, and he didn't strike for the axe; he plunged it toward the Monarch's chest.

Monarchs were incredibly durable, but this *was* still death madra. Lindon was willing to bet his blow would be the deadlier.

Reigan Shen clearly agreed, because he redirected his weapon, striking the spectral green spear aside. Which was when having only one functional arm ruined Lindon.

He could have put twice as much power into the spear, or he could have used dragon's breath with the other hand. But with a dead arm, he was vulnerable as Reigan Shen released the axe with one hand and jabbed at Lindon's ribs.

Lindon threw himself backwards, but even glancing force from someone with an ascended body slammed into him and drove all the breath from his lungs. He was hurled back, and while in midair, he begged Dross for help.

[What would you have me do?] Dross demanded. [I told you, I don't remember him!]

I'll take any help I can get!

Dross hissed. [Fine. But don't blame me if I become useless to you.]

His attention vanished from Lindon's mind. Dross' body—the ball of dream madra at the base of Lindon's skull—began to spin.

The spirit was searching his own memories, but he managed to lend some support at the same time. The entire world seemed to sharpen and slow slightly, as though Lindon had finally learned how to use his senses.

He twisted to land with his feet against the wall instead of slamming into it with his back, swinging Midnight in front of him. He triggered the Striker binding, and a dense river of death madra slashed across the room. Its passage traced a blackened line across the pale flesh that covered the chamber's floor.

Reigan Shen used the broad head of his axe to deflect, not even slowing. He used no Enforcer technique to close the gap, but his body was that of a Herald. He arrived before Lindon landed on the floor, swinging up with his axe as he released his own Striker technique again.

Sixteen blades flew out of the axe-head and struck at different angles while Shen swung up from the ground.

Lindon used the Hollow Domain once more and met the axe with Midnight. But the Striker techniques struck him all over the body.

Weakened by the Domain, they didn't shred him to pieces, but they stabbed into him, leaving him bleeding. Midnight clashed against the axe, but Lindon's strength wasn't enough; his weapon was knocked wide.

Lindon tried his best to defend himself in the following exchanges, but even as Dross' ability to read Reigan Shen's patterns improved, Lindon couldn't keep up.

His own physical strength was beyond anything a Sage should have, and Reigan Shen had his body eroded by months of the suppression field and exposure to hunger aura, but he was originally a lion. His strength was fundamentally different.

He was stronger. Faster. And he had more fighting experience than Lindon and every one of his ancestors put together.

By furious, desperate use of the Soul Cloak and Dross' silent support, Lindon managed to keep the axe from cleaving him in two. But he was still backed against the wall.

He finally deflected one blow and hurled himself away, dragging the Hollow Domain with him as he fled into the open center of the room. He was out of breath and spending pure madra like a waterfall spent water, but he was still alive.

Lindon turned to face the attack he knew was coming, but Reigan Shen didn't bother. He waved a hand, and a gold portal the size of his head tore open.

A red lion erupted from the portal. A spirit Forged of blood madra, launched from some kind of weapon. Lindon kept the Hollow Domain up as the technique plunged into it, and Lindon put all his power into a soulfire-infused Empty Palm.

A huge palm imprint smashed into the lion, which dissolved...but not before it landed a slash on Lindon's chest.

Three claw-marks tore across Lindon's ribs, and he choked back the burning pain as the Forger technique dissipated.

Reigan Shen stood against the wall with folded arms.

Two more portals had appeared in the air around him.

Lindon dropped the Hollow Domain to sweep black dragon's breath at the Monarch, but a silver shield materialized in front of him. He didn't even look.

Dross, what can you tell me? Lindon shouted in his mind.

[Dross, reporting for duty!]

Without manifesting in reality, Dross still popped up in Lindon's vision. He was plumper, somehow cheerier and brighter, with a larger eye and an innocent smile that reminded Lindon of Mercy. [Whatever I can do for you, Lindon!]

Can you give me a combat report on Reigan Shen?

[Hmmm...not quite, but I can give you my best guess!]

Then keep trying!

[But...but I became the helpful version of me!] Dross sounded hurt. [What else could I try?]

How about the deadly version? Lindon suggested, but he couldn't spare Dross any more attention.

From another portal came a series of spheres the size of a human head, each shining a different color and radiating aura. They were natural treasures, sealed in globes, and they flew to scatter all over the room.

Reigan Shen was preparing for a Ruler technique, but Lindon couldn't deal with that yet, because another blood-lion had leaped out of the original portal. Lindon drove black dragon's breath at it, but the technique was at least as powerful as he was; it crashed through his beam, opposing his will with its own.

He had to let the dragon's breath drop and try something else. Without Dross' active attention, it was harder, but he wove threads of pure madra and Blackflame madra together.

Then he reached into the lion, sensed its structure, and dismantled it from the inside.

His spirit burned as he tried it, and it took a little too long, but it worked. The Forger technique fell to chunks of quickly dissolving madra.

Lindon switched back to his pure core and released the Hollow Domain as chains of life madra shot out from the third portal. They looked like shining lime-green roots, but they were unable to break through the Domain.

Reigan Shen was pacing around the fight and back to his chair. "That is how Ozmanthus Arelius dismantled techniques. Not bad. He elaborated on that in his inheritance."

The Monarch reached out, and though his madra had no aspects of destruction or cleansing, his technique was swifter and more practiced than Lindon's.

The Hollow Domain fell apart.

Tendrils of life madra crashed down on Lindon, writhing around him, and he screamed in blinding pain as they tore at his lifeline. The Empty Palm burst one in half, then he switched to Blackflame to tear the others apart with dragon's breath.

As soon as Lindon could breathe again, he tore his void key open.

The key snapped.

The void space still opened, but it would remain hanging there in midair until it eventually faded closed. But Lindon couldn't worry about closing it. He reached inside, now that there was actual aura to work with, and summoned Wavedancer.

It shot out on flows of aura, and Reigan Shen watched it with amusement over the rim of a goblet he'd refilled.

"What a coincidence," he said.

A flying sword of his own emerged from nowhere. Lindon didn't see the portal it had come from. Or had the Monarch kept it in his soulspace?

This one was carved like a dancing flame, and it carried a sense of power and presence no less than Midnight's.

Wavedancer clashed against it and was struck down, but Lindon called Midnight with wind aura. The trident flew into his hand, and he hurled it at Reigan Shen.

A portal opened up and swallowed the weapon.

"It is only right to return stolen belongings," Shen said. "I appreciate that you've taken good care of it."

At the far end of the chamber, one of the already-existing golden portals had expanded into a larger form. Lindon was terrified that Tiberian Arelius' Remnant would emerge, but his earlier theory must have been right: Reigan Shen couldn't summon it since Lindon had broken the portal.

That, or he didn't want to waste energy from a Monarch's Remnant on one Overlord.

A black-armored leg thicker than Lindon's body emerged from the giant portal, and the aura in the room trembled. Lindon realized that he was about to meet the reason why Reigan Shen had scattered natural treasures everywhere.

Shen pointed to it. "This construct does carry a suite of powerful Ruler techniques, but that's not the only reason I brought out the natural treasures. No, I simply prefer the light."

Lindon began drawing in aura of fire and destruction while he Forged Blackflame madra around his left hand.

"You know, this labyrinth should be the perfect environment for you," Reigan Shen called. "I have a bit of a connection to the Void Icon myself. Not enough to call myself a Void Sage, you understand, and I was a Herald first anyway."

The armored figure emerged from the giant portal, and Lindon had finally condensed The Dragon Descends around his hand. Claws of red-and-black madra swirled with aura, a miniature version of the Void Dragon's Dance, and it resonated with Lindon's authority. Even in his senses as a Sage, this attack was powerful.

He dashed forward with the Burning Cloak, clashing against the armored construct's fist as it emerged.

Madra detonated, flames sweeping away warped white flesh. The construct stumbled back, missing a hand, but it hadn't been defeated. Chains of wind aura grabbed at him, and light aura blinded his eyes.

But the last he saw, it was halfway inside the portal.

"Close!" Lindon shouted, and he felt the surrounding aura release.

He fell to the ground, and had to roll out of the way before the smoking front half of the construct landed on him. It had been sliced in half.

"That's exactly why you shouldn't use expensive weapons in battle unless absolutely necessary," Reigan Shen noted. "I have a dozen of those."

Two more portals bloomed to either side of Lindon. These weren't Monarch attacks, like Lindon had experienced before, but they were roughly Archlord level.

Lightning blasted at Lindon from one portal as fingers of acidic liquid reached for him from the other.

From the space of his void key, Lindon summoned a shield to block the lightning. For the liquid, he met it with an Empty Palm.

"As I said, this should be the perfect place for you," the Monarch went on. "Your home turf, as they say. Your den. It's full of hunger, and you're not hungry enough."

Lindon called bombs; explosive single-use constructs he'd created months before. Shining orange-and-red orbs flew at Reigan Shen.

He lifted his chin, and a bright golden marble flew from a pouch at his side. It detonated when it hit Lindon's bombs, wiping all of Lindon's constructs away in an instant.

Lindon held nothing back.

Launcher constructs fired from his void space, and they landed on a Forged silver shield that materialized in front of the Monarch. A cannon drifted into Lindon's hands, and he fired.

With his Blackflame madra and his will joining it, the shot cracked the silver shield in two.

Through that crack, a line of dense white-gold madra shot out and speared through Lindon's arm.

He gritted his teeth to keep from screaming and tried to move his arm, but not only was the arm burned clean through, but even his madra channels were sealed shut.

Reigan Shen wasn't even watching the battle. "I, on the other hand, I want it *all*. I want the Dreadgods, and I want the Monarchs. I want their people, and I want their Remnants. I want this world.

"And I want you, Lindon."

More portals appeared around Lindon, but Reigan Shen stood up again. He walked up to examine Lindon. "You could consider all this a test, if you like. I'm impressed. You almost fight like a real Sage."

"Gratitude," Lindon said through teeth clenched tight against the pain. He was reaching out to the aura around him, following them back to the natural treasures. He wanted more soulfire.

"Swear to serve and follow me in all things, and I will take you out of here." His lips quirked up in a smile. "I will begin the oath this time, if you like. I, Reigan Shen, sole Monarch of the Rosegold continent, swear on my soul and my power to take Wei Shi Lindon safely away from this place in my service and protect him as long as he remains loyal, in exchange for his promise of fealty."

Lindon felt the promise settle on the Monarch, and it trembled in the air between them unfulfilled.

Time seemed to slow, and not because of Dross. Lindon's mind was working overtime. He had played every one of his pieces against Reigan Shen, and they had all been dealt with. The Monarch had clearly never seen him as a real opponent. He hadn't used a single Monarch-level weapon, nor most of his Path's techniques. He had to have more than just portals into his void spaces.

Lindon suspected Reigan Shen could defeat him physically, even without using his Path. Therefore, there was only one option.

He had to swear.

Lindon had gotten this far by doing whatever he had to in order to accomplish his goals. What was one oath? It would naturally end when Lindon ascended, and it still didn't bind Dross. That was an oversight that would one day stab Reigan Shen in the back.

Then again, Reigan Shen had his own way out. He could break the oath whenever he wanted, as far as Lindon knew. It was all about who would betray who first.

But as long as Lindon could make it out of the labyrinth, he'd have a chance.

So, for lack of a better option, Lindon was prepared to make the promise. He didn't really have a choice.

The hunger all around him seethed. His arm twitched.

It was the same reason why he had been forced to leave Orthos behind. The same reason why Ziel and Mercy had escaped: they had no choice. Reality didn't change just because you wanted it to.

Unless you were a Sage.

Lindon felt the hunger all around him, and it resonated with the Void Icon. It shook his spirit. And it awakened something in him.

"I don't think I agree with you," Lindon said politely.

"Oh?" Reigan Shen didn't seem upset. He swirled his goblet. "How so?"

"*You're* not hungry enough." Lindon forced his way to his feet, and though both of his arms were now crippled, he stared into the Monarch's eyes. "You want the Dreadgods? You want to be the only Monarch? You're satisfied with ruling this world?

"Well, I'm *not.*"

Reigan Shen took another sip and then backhanded Lindon's jaw.

His hand stopped an inch from Lindon's skin. Locked by pure will. Lindon trembled to maintain it, but it had worked.

The Void Icon was close, and Lindon could feel its yawning hunger. "This world doesn't have enough for me. I'm going beyond it." He reached through the aura, for the natural treasures that the Monarch had so generously scattered all over the room.

Reigan Shen's will clashed against his. "These are **mine**," Shen said.

"No."

Lindon reached out, and all over the room, natural treasures burned for soulfire that rushed into his spirit. He could feel the aura trembling, especially the hunger aura. He could see his entire journey like a line that pushed forward in the future.

I practice the sacred arts so that I won't be worthless anymore.

"I am not content with this world," Lindon said.

I advance.

"I want more. I want...*everything.*"

And now he felt the third advancement in him. He almost said the words: *I will never stop.*

But the Archlord revelation was all about his future, and this one wasn't to his liking. So he changed it.

"We," Lindon said, "will never stop."

Soulfire passed through him like a warm breeze.

His fading lifeline was restored to a roaring river, and his Bloodforged Iron body reached another level. His flesh knitted together...though his hunger arm crumbled completely, unable to handle the new level of energy.

That was all right. He intended to replace it anyway.

His mind was clearer, his body stronger. Even the Void Icon felt closer than ever, and he stared down the Monarch from inches away.

"Adorable," Reigan Shen said.

His hand flashed out again, and Lindon pitted his will against it. Lindon's willpower was much stronger now, and the world warped all around them as they struggled against one another.

But this time, Shen broke through and his attack landed.

His knuckles cracked against Lindon's jaw, sending him flying.

Lindon called the Soul Cloak as he flew, twisting to land on his feet. He passed Archlord soulfire through the Hollow Domain, which spread out denser than ever.

"Then I'll just kill you," Reigan Shen said.

A Monarch technique thundered through a portal: the water madra filled with shining malicious spirits. It was weakened by the Hollow Domain, but its tide still smashed into Lindon and carried him away.

But Reigan Shen had finished holding back.

Striker techniques flew out like a volley of arrows from every direction except one. Reigan Shen ran up behind Lindon, the water splitting willingly around him, and he held his axe in both hands.

This time, the axe shone with an Enforcer technique.

Lindon struck against it with an Empty Palm, dispersing the madra and borrowing the force from the attack to fly away, but his hand was almost split in half. Even supported by Archlord soulfire, he couldn't face a Monarch's attack.

Dross, I hope you're ready, Lindon thought.

A head-sized ball of purple madra manifested behind Reigan Shen. He was darker than usual this time, almost black, and his crescent grin reminded Lindon of Eithan.

[Information requested,] Dross whispered into Lindon's mind. [Combat solution against Reigan Shen. Beginning report...]

Information flooded Lindon's brain, and time froze.

This time, Dross' voice was soft and papery, almost frightening. [We cannot defeat him, so we fight to flee. Mice before the cat.]

Lindon saw the Burning Cloak spring up around himself. He dashed into the axe, narrowly avoiding the Monarch's blow.

Some Striker techniques hunted him, like sharks in the water, but he could see their trajectory. He had to strike some down with pure madra and dodge others, but he made it over to the wall.

[He will unleash his prized possessions as he sees you slither away,] Dross whispered. [We dance on the razor's edge.]

Lindon saw the things that would emerge from Dross' portal. Spears of blood and storms of blades. Monarch-level techniques that had not yet been eroded by the labyrinth.

The timing would be thin as a fallen leaf, but he saw himself slapping his hand on the wall and exerting his will. The stone blurred and he ran, just in time.

Lindon took in all the possibilities, and he made his decision.

I have a better idea, he thought.

Dross laughed madly, and time resumed.

Lindon followed the path Dross had laid out. He dodged the lion's axe with the speed of the Burning Cloak, dashing through a net of Striker techniques. Gold portals yawned wider as he leaped through the air.

He landed in a crouch on the back of Subject One's throne. What was left of Lindon's broken hunger arm rested on its stone.

"Begone," Lindon commanded.

His authority ran through the labyrinth, but Reigan Shen laughed. His golden portals paused, and he waved a hand casually. "Why don't *you* **begone.**"

In the labyrinth, their wills clashed.

Reigan Shen had spent almost a year living here. He had absorbed the Soulsmith inheritance of Ozmanthus Arelius. He was a Monarch in his own right, and he held the core binding of Subject One. His authority over the labyrinth was strong.

Lindon had grown up here. His Void Icon resonated strongly with the power of hunger in the labyrinth. He was the apprentice of one of Ozmanthus' last descendants. He was only a Sage, but he had the blessing of the Slumbering Wraith. At least, his echo.

He couldn't tell who had the greater claim over the labyrinth, but he could feel the balance tipping.

Lindon, after all, had given his word to Subject One.

And Reigan Shen had broken his.

All at once, space shifted all around the labyrinth. Pressure pushed down.

And the Monarch vanished.

How long will that keep him? Lindon asked Dross.

[Will he batter down our defenses, or will he slip away in shame?] Dross giggled in a way that sent shivers down Lindon's spine. [I can't wait to see. If he does break down our seals, it will not be soon. He will be locked outside, in the cold and hostile world, for at least a few hours.]

"Plenty of time," Lindon said.

Then he tore off Subject One's arm.

第二十三章

CHAPTER TWENTY-THREE

Yerin walked up to the slowly opening Nethergate with Eithan at her side. She couldn't sense anything outside, but she'd left a little madra in reserve just in case she had to fight.

"You left Lindon on his own?" she asked Eithan. He had caught up suspiciously quickly.

"We became separated, but he has the key. I have every confidence in him."

Yerin chewed on her lip. "Can we get back down there?"

"I suspect not," Eithan said. "I only escaped because my opponent was a very reasonable man."

"Only left because I thought you'd be with him," Yerin muttered. "Shame we don't have a key. Maybe we can—"

She was cut off when the Nethergate swung open enough to reveal a man in black-and-red robes, carrying a sword covered by a Blood Shadow. She almost attacked instantly. A moment later, she saw a second man, carrying a Shadow-wrapped chain.

And the third, a woman, stood over a trio of captives. Mercy, Orthos, and Little Blue.

Not a scratch on them, Yerin thought. *That's a bright spot.*

Of course, the thought only occurred to her after she had leaped out of the Nethergate with her blade raised. Her madra was already forming the Flowing Sword around her weapon, and just because she now sensed that the enemy was an Archlady didn't mean she was about to stop.

The Archlady's Blood Shadow, in the form of a cobra, let out a hiss like a tunnel full of snakes all hissing at once. But it was the Redmoon Emissary herself who raised a weapon to stop Yerin. A crystal hand-axe flashed out of her soulspace and into her hand as Yerin's attack landed.

The small weapon stopped Yerin's blow, but it had her full strength behind it.

The Archlady's knees half-buckled and the ground beneath her cracked before she managed to turn the sword aside.

Yerin allowed it and let herself fall to the ground, since neither of the Overlords had attacked or even threatened the captives.

"You've got about a breath and a half before I stop being friendly."

"She's not lying," Eithan observed. "That *was* friendly."

Mercy affected a shocked look. "Oh look, it's Yerin and Eithan! What are the odds?"

The Archlady straightened herself up. "I am Emissary Kahn Mala of Redmoon Hall. I come on behalf of the Sage of Red Faith and the Redmoon Herald to protect you."

Yerin had eyes, and her perception wasn't restricted anymore. She could feel the powers clashing all around Sacred Valley, and could see the four Dreadgod cults positioned over the four peaks. There was a massive battle here, and it looked like the enemy controlled this territory.

Yerin tapped her Goldsigns together, striking up sparks of madra. "Just wants to protect me, does he? That's more kindness than I'd have bet could fit into his dried-up heart."

Kahn Mala flinched and her eyes flicked up, so Yerin immediately assumed they were being watched. "The Sage told us that you would attack when you saw us, so he sent enough people to stop you from killing us but not so many as to threaten you. He asked me to tell you that he knows *exactly* what you saw in the labyrinth, and to remind you that he was a researcher there himself. He requests an audience with you, and said that you have a chance to affect this entire battlefield. Even withdrawing Redmoon Hall is not off the table."

Yerin considered it a triumph of great personal patience that she let a Redmoon Emissary finish that entire speech, and an even greater victory that she considered the message instead of dismissing it out of hand.

"I'll match that bet and raise it a step," Yerin said at last. "I'll meet him in whatever hole he crawls back into at night, but only after you take us back to our people. Can't relax until I make sure nobody's missing."

Kahn Mala looked hesitantly over her shoulder, and then the air buzzed as the Blood Sage's voice was transmitted through aura.

"We need an assurance of your sincerity," Red Faith said.

"Swear on my soul," Yerin responded casually.

The oath tightened, and then snapped into place as the Sage of Red Faith agreed wherever he was. His voice crawled through the air to them again.

"Escort her wherever she wishes to go, as long as you do not put her in further danger."

Kahn Mala bowed to a distant point, and then looked back to Yerin. "Where would you like to go?"

"Can we get back down to Lindon?" Yerin asked Eithan. He shook his head. "Then let's walk the road we've got. Where's the Twin Star Sect?"

"I'll find out," the Archlady responded.

Eithan pointed.

Not all squads returned from the battlefield after dark, but theirs was scheduled to. Jai Long began to worry as the sun set, and that worry grew with every passing minute.

Finally, he went to find the Truegold Skysworn coordinating the Blackflame Empire's forces. The woman was respectful to him, as he was about to advance past her, but she still couldn't help.

"They haven't checked in yet, and a number of squads were pinned down on the eastern slope. There."

She pointed, and it was easy to see what she meant. An Overlord-level battle had erupted involving Emperor Naru Huan himself.

He swept great swathes of destructive green wind madra at his enemy, swinging his Blackflame greatsword in both hands, while his opponent controlled a pair of gold-and-blue serpentine dragons made of madra. A Stormcaller.

Jai Long had seen them in battle many times already, though he hadn't crossed spears with them. It usually disturbed him that his sacred arts were so similar to a Dreadgod cult's, but this time his throat was tight.

Kelsa and his sister were trapped behind *that*. Every Striker technique tore a new path through a forest and broke the clouds apart.

But the soulfire was still crawling through his veins. Slower, it seemed, every hour. There was nothing he could do.

He pressed his fists together and bowed to the Skysworn woman. "Please send someone to inform me when they check in," he said. She gave him a sympathetic look and a pat on the shoulder.

"By this time tomorrow, you'll be an Underlord. You'll be able to take revenge yourself."

Jai Long didn't care what was going to happen tomorrow. He needed results today. And he was still more capable than any Lowgold, even mid-advancement as he was.

So he walked back to his tent, grabbed his spear, and changed into a nondescript outer robe that he stole from an unattended trunk. He veiled his spirit—as best he could, though the soulfire running through his channels meant that he wouldn't stand up to a direct scan—and unwrapped his face.

Jai Long's advancement to Gold had left him with an unfortunate Goldsign: sharp fangs of blue light and cheeks split deeply down his jaw to show them off. Usually, he kept his face covered to both protect his reputation and to spare others the sight.

Usually.

He hoped the advancement to Underlord would fix him, but thus far he'd kept the soulfire refining his spirit, not his body, in order to get him into fighting shape faster. It had slipped into his bones and organs anyway, even some of his limbs, but he'd managed to keep the soulfire away from his face.

While it might fix him, it might instead make things worse, and he didn't want to find out until the last possible second. And, more relevant to his current predicament: no one knew what he looked like.

He strode out of the Blackflame Empire's camp without anyone stopping him. He had to show his rank chip three times to be allowed to leave, but no one questioned a peak Truegold going out to fight.

It was perfect timing, in a sense. An Underlord would be too advanced to leave unquestioned, and a Highgold too weak.

He wouldn't be able to re-enter the camp without a direct scan of his spirit, which would reveal him, but he shouldn't need to hide then. He wouldn't be alone.

Or he wouldn't be returning.

He filled the body with his Enforcer technique. His inconsistently baptized channels meant that the technique was imbalanced, half-powerful and half-weak, so the snaking white lines of madra that covered his skin flickered between the verge of vanishing and shining brighter than ever.

His stride was just as uneven as the technique; he would dash forward, then stumble as strength left him, then shoot off far faster than he intended as his Enforcer technique gave him more of a boost. He kept his perception extended in case his team was on their way back, which had similar drawbacks; the distance and clarity of his spiritual sense varied by the second. But he made progress quickly, and soon he passed beneath the Overlord battle.

Which immediately proved to be a mistake.

The battle was hardly stationary; the two sacred artists were zipping across the sky. Jai Long had balanced slipping past them with staying out of the way, but there was only so much he could do.

A blast of wind from the Emperor tore apart a tree to his right, and he was caught with an enhanced gust of wind that tossed him thirty feet back and peppered him with sharp splinters.

He managed to land on his feet and block his eyes with an arm, but his body was covered with tiny cuts and scratches. If the attack had been a few yards closer, it would have shattered every bone in his body. At best.

Jai Long plunged forward.

Lightning dragons screamed through the sky and hands of wind hurled trees, but he kept his eyes and perception ahead. So he saw immediately when a beam of pink light streamed into the sky at an angle.

Jai Long brightened and kicked off again as soon as he could. That was Fingerling's fire breath; he would know it anywhere. Then the light flashed red, and he felt a sudden surge of overwhelming power.

It was Redmoon Hall. He was certain.

Through sheer will, he squeezed every ounce of speed out of his Enforcer technique. There were no more signs of battle coming from that direction, and he tried not to think about what that would mean. His heart pounded in his throat, and his breath was harsh. He gripped the spear so tight he thought he might snap it.

He crested a hill, and thus saw the source of the blood madra at the same time as he sensed it.

Yerin sat with her arms crossed in the center of a circle of blasted trees, looking sullen, as Eithan danced from one side of a narrow pass to the other at Archlord speed to cut off the retreat of a bunch of Stormcallers. Who looked very frightened.

Jai Long's squad was battered and burned...but they were alive.

Mercy was there, holding Orthos and Little Blue, and it seemed like she was lecturing Yerin about something.

Jai Chen was on her knees, catching her breath, while an agitated Fingerling swirled in the air over her head. Kelsa was nearby, her Foxfire tail lashing. She faced a Lowgold Stormcaller who shuffled from foot to foot nervously and kept glancing behind him.

Jai Long's relief almost disrupted his breathing and cut off his Enforcer technique, but he seized the cycling pattern at the last second and dashed down. It only took him a moment to arrive.

He awkwardly tucked away his spear and wrapped his face as he ran. He wouldn't want to disgust anyone.

"...least he was an Underlord," Yerin muttered. "Not like I threw a Copper into the sun."

Mercy shook her head. "No, I'm not saying your heart wasn't in the right place! But he was as helpless against you as our team was against him."

"They can keep his Remnant, supposing they still want it."

A miniature Remnant version of the Weeping Dragon slunk along the ground, shooting fearful glances at Yerin. Nearby, an unidentifiable pile told Jai Long what had happened to the spirit's body.

"It's very important that we adhere to the rules of fair play!" Eithan called, blocking another escape attempt by the handful of Golds. "Speaking of which, how's the duel going?"

Kelsa gestured to her opponent, who was on his knees. "He surrendered."

"That makes one victory for us! Or...Yerin, do you think your sudden ambush of an Underlord should count as a victory?"

The dragon-Remnant whimpered.

"I don't feel good about this," Kelsa muttered.

Eithan nodded in understanding. "Ah yes, by all means let us return to murdering each other more honorably."

Mercy slammed her staff into the ground, and shadow pulsed out from the base. The Stormcallers flinched back. "There are reasons for this, and you know it! No one wants a slaughter where only the most advanced sacred artists survive!"

"I wish that were true..." Eithan said wistfully.

But he did stand aside and let the Golds rush off. Kelsa's opponent bowed to her one more time before retreating, and the Remnant slithered after him.

"Not lining up to cut Jades into pieces, am I?" Yerin complained. "We'll take your path, then. Who's a match for me?"

Mercy hesitated. Eithan shaded his eyes and made a show of peering around. "You're a bit of an exception, but by common understanding...him!"

He pointed to the battle between Overlords through which Jai Long had just crossed. The fight was winding down as the Overlords ran out of madra, so larger techniques weren't as common as they had been minutes before.

Yerin took a moment to take aim. "Neat and tidy," she said. Then she unleashed a line of bright silver-red madra.

The Stormcaller Overlord had a moment to turn and put up a block before he was obliterated.

Yerin glared at Mercy. "You want me to go fight his Remnant with one hand behind my back?"

"Maybe we should find a new opponent for you," Mercy allowed. "Are there any Archlords out here?"

As though summoned by her words, Ziel flew through the air, his gray cloak fluttering with the wake of his speed. A ring of green runes flashed in the air, stopping him, and he dropped in front of Yerin.

"I felt Stormcallers," he said, and his eyes were unusually bright.

Yerin jerked a thumb in their direction. "Just missed 'em. You can catch up."

"They're just Golds!" Mercy protested.

Ziel's shoulders slumped. "Oh."

Blackflame Emperor Naru Huan raised a hand in Yerin's direction, and she returned it lazily. Then he flew off on wide emerald wings.

Jai Long had walked up to join Kelsa and his sister, and they watched the exchange together. For such a frightening display, it had been disturbingly casual.

He looked to his squad.

"I came to save you," he said.

Kelsa nodded seriously. "Gratitude."

Reigan Shen stalked out of the Nethergate, but not with as much triumph in his heart as he had imagined.

If he were in his lion form, his tail would be lashing. He had the Slumbering Wraith's core binding tucked away in a sealed case, he'd come out with the unexpected bounty of Ozmanthus Arelius' Soulsmith inheritance, and he was about to see the sunlight he had dreamed of for months.

But he had been driven out of his own den.

He would challenge it again soon, but all the time inside the labyrinth had weakened him greatly. Time was on his side, even if the Void Sage ended up taking over the labyrinth. Reigan would gather his strength, and *then* see how Lindon Arelius could stand up to a true Monarch.

The stone door hadn't even closed behind him before the leaders of the cults appeared before him. The Emissaries of Redmoon Hall who had been guarding the door had fallen to their knees as he appeared, but he didn't glance at them, only looking to the Herald and Sages who appeared behind them.

The Blood Sage, Silent Sage, and Storm Sage arrived first, followed soon after by the Herald of Abyssal Palace.

To them, he presented a sealed silver box. "I have succeeded," he said gravely.

All their eyes lit up at once. As well they should. This

binding was the mythical item that their idols had sought since time immemorial.

"The enhancement field is functioning at full capacity," Red Faith reported. "However, with Subject One removed, the hunger aura will exceed our containment at any time. I recommend we hurry."

"We should," Reigan agreed. "I will begin the process. One of you stand guard here."

All four cult leaders gave him a blank look.

"Why?" the Storm Sage asked. He wore his confusion so openly that Reigan wanted to claw his face off.

The masked Herald of Abyssal Palace placated him. "We will place our best sacred artists here."

"No. Yourselves. *Do it...*" He caught himself, took a deep breath, and moderated his tone before these allies. "...because I have requested it of you."

The Storm Sage shrugged both shoulders and sank to the ground, leaning his back against the door and whistled idly. He snatched up a flower and started pulling its petals off one by one.

Red Faith gnawed on one finger as he gazed on Reigan Shen, and as usual, Reigan couldn't tell if the Sage was sizing him up for a betrayal or lapsing into drooling lunacy.

"Do you have a question, Red Faith?" Reigan Shen asked.

He was weakened badly after such a long stay in the labyrinth, and the Sage knew it better than anyone. But one advantage of being Reigan Shen is that no one else knew what cards you had to play.

Even when your hand was empty.

Reigan met the Sage's eyes with complete calm, and eventually Red Faith pointed to the sky with a bleeding finger.

"As I said, it will be for the best if we hurry."

Without waiting any further, Reigan Shen seized the wind aura—it was all but the last of his soulfire—and drifted into the air. He held the silver box aloft, and he projected his voice with Herald lungs. He didn't trust the rest of his soulfire to carry his voice.

"I am the Emperor of the Rosegold continent, and I have

returned in glory. I invite my peers to witness my triumph."

The Eight-Man Empire appeared first, of course; Reigan wouldn't be making a speech if his allies weren't closer than his enemies. Some hovered in the air near him, some lounged on clouds, and some stayed on the ground.

But their presence made it clear that they would defend him when Malice and Northstrider drifted closer.

The two human Monarchs were side-by-side, Northstrider muscled but covered in rags and Malice finely dressed but soft. Neither of their appearances did them justice, in Reigan Shen's opinion.

Malice's voice was carried to him on the wind. "You come to us so boldly, weakened as you are. Tell me, now that you have your prize, how do you plan to leave with it?"

Northstrider simply glared.

"Why do I feel like I have been severely underestimated?" Reigan asked. Now that he was back in his element, with aura nourishing him more at every second and his own spirit restoring his body, he was starting to enjoy himself.

"As I said all along, we could have shared this bounty together. I would have relished your wealth of experience—both of you—and would have been willing to set aside our years of rivalry for mutual benefit."

"Is that what you told Tiberian?" Malice asked.

Reigan raised his eyebrows and looked from one of his peers to the other. "Tiberian wanted us to kill the Dreadgods and ascend. Would you have allowed that?"

Now that he'd recovered some of his power, he could spend a fraction on theatrics. He summoned a goblet and a jar of wine. A construct poured for him.

"I interrupted my work for this," Northstrider said. "I will not come all this way and then allow you to escape."

"Ah, but you see, I don't need to escape."

With one hand, Reigan Shen lifted the goblet to his lips. With the other, he tapped the silver cube in a throwaway gesture. It unfolded, unveiling the core binding of the Slumbering Wraith.

Its authority screamed through reality, warping the world in an invisible vortex. Color seemed to leech from everything, and immediately an image formed in the sky overhead.

A widened mouth full of sharpened fangs.

The Hunger Icon.

The Sages braced themselves against the exposed power of Subject One, but none of the Monarchs batted an eye. The Eight-Man Empire, protected as they were by their armor, looked on only with interest.

Malice's eyes shone purple, and she radiated fury, ready to summon her armor at any second. "If you call the Dreadgods here, you will all perish with us, I promise you that."

Reigan feigned surprise. "Here? I don't need them here. Not yet."

Then he activated the binding in his palm.

Invisible power and white aura thundered out from him, traveling along invisible, metaphysical paths. He had never known this was possible, never gained the insight necessary into the mechanics of reality, until Tiberian gave him the hint.

Then he'd researched on his own. He'd consulted with the Sage of Red Faith, even gathering the Dreadgod cults to gain their knowledge on the invincibility of the Dreadgods.

Ultimately, he'd realized what he needed to do. He would fuse with this binding and become the new Slumbering Wraith, attaining immortality and power beyond the dreams of Monarchs.

He had intended to take over the labyrinth first, then recover his power, *then* become the new Dreadgod. He was doing things a little out of order.

But it would all be worth it. All of it...once the Dreadgods were awakened.

At the heart of a mountain range far to the north of Sacred Valley, the Wandering Titan dug deeper into a chasm of its own construction.

It could have controlled the surrounding aura to make a tunnel, but it didn't bother. Why expend energy it didn't have to?

So with every movement, it burrowed deeper into the earth, and the nation above it split further. A city collapsed over its head, buildings crashing on its shell, and it didn't even feel them. It was digging for something that smelled delicious.

The Titan finally burst through a metal container almost as big as its own rib cage. Inside, there was a structure of interlocking metal swirling with sand that glowed gold. A relic of ancient times; the Titan could smell the ancient aura in every grain of sand.

The device gave off the impression of distant lands, and the will of its creators was ingrained deep. It was meant to birth a city, or maybe revive one, and then carry it to distant worlds through the void.

Not that any of that mattered to the Titan. It took in the details without consideration, tore off a chunk of the ancient metal frame, and shoved the piece into its mouth.

Over its head, sacred artists fled in every direction, but the Titan had already begun feeding. Earth aura flowed into it from miles around, and power of all sorts flooded from the ancient device.

The Titan continued to crunch down on the vessel, but it fed on more than just what entered its mouth. The entire device grew weaker and weaker as it fed, power of all kinds flowing into the Titan. Soulfire, willpower, authority, madra, aura...it all went to fill the empty space inside the Titan.

For now.

It knew that the hunger would return. It always did. But in the moments when it fed, it was content to do nothing else. It hadn't been truly satisfied since its birth.

Then it caught the scent of something irresistible.

Its stone head snapped up, and one of the cliffs around it snapped off and shattered to dust on its shoulder. This was the smell of the original.

The Titan reached up to the surface and began to haul itself up. It was going to return to the origin of this scent, and maybe it would finally be satisfied.

Or so it thought. Until the golden aura on which it had fed flashed white.

Then, at last, it got a taste of what it meant to feel content.

Everything else it had ever eaten was nothing. It was just a lick, while this was a full meal. The aura streamed into it, accompanied by a nourishing will. Its soul swelled, pushing deeper into its body. Its muscles bulged and its skin hardened. Its eyes glowed brighter.

The Titan felt like it did when it awakened from the long sleep, but now it was awakening even further. Now, it was more awake than it had ever been.

With more agility than it had been capable of a moment before, the Wandering Titan slid out of its chasm. This time, it was conscious of all the lives that were lost as the ground cracked and crumbled for miles around.

Marvelous. It was as though it could see everything.

For the first time, the Wandering Titan considered what it wanted beyond its next meal. And as it thought, it wandered.

The Bleeding Phoenix called a rain of red lightning that blotted out the sky, but its fury accomplished nothing. It was only expressing its rage.

It remembered a human, a tiny man with punches that summoned blood dragons miles long. It remembered another, a titan in purple armor.

Those two were prey, but they had dared to harm it. It wanted revenge. It wanted to *devour* them.

Its awareness was scattered, so that at times it felt more

like a council in its own head, but it vaguely remembered a time when it could have found these humans in a moment and annihilated them. Now, it couldn't even come to a decision.

Should it split and gather power?

Should it find the humans and head straight for them, no matter the cost?

Should it sleep?

Thinking was hard. It hadn't always been this hard. After a good sleep and a long session of feeding, then it would know the right thing to do. The many minds and spirits inside of it would be more unified then.

But it couldn't spare the time for that. It needed a decision *now.* It continued unleashing power on nothing, its attacks powerful enough to warp reality, but each blow consumed power it would need to restore.

It hated those humans. *All* humans. At the same time, it had memories from millions of humans. The Phoenix grew very confused.

A moment later, a surge of white power swept through the sky. The Dreadgod's techniques froze, and it fell into a daze.

This was the presence of the original. The final will of its father, its oldest brother, its original template.

This was a gift.

The Phoenix absorbed the power as easily as thirsty soil absorbed rain. The minds of the many spirits within it merged, fusing into one another, and the Phoenix grew larger. Its will grew stronger. And its consciousness was finally, blessedly clear.

It *remembered.*

The male human was Northstrider, a Monarch who had stolen power. Some of the Phoenix's power in particular.

The Dreadgod was irritated at its past self for allowing Northstrider to touch it.

The female human was Malice, Queen of the Akura clan. Her lands were not far.

A moment ago, the Phoenix had plenty of strength, but only instinct controlling it. Now, its increase in power was negligible compared to its *clarity*.

It knew what to do.

Carefully, the Bleeding Phoenix began to dissolve its body. It melted into droplets that fell like rain, each drop an egg that slipped through a subtle spatial distortion.

It spread itself widely, and quietly. The human would not pierce its veil before it was too late. By then, the Phoenix would have devoured its lands.

Beaks couldn't usually smile, but the Bleeding Phoenix was made of blood and madra. It twisted its face into a parody of a human grin.

Then even that liquefied, and the droplets teleported away.

On another continent, the Weeping Dragon tossed in its dreams. It floated on a bed of clouds, and it dreamed of what it always did: the past.

When it had wandered freely. When it had done battle. Even longer ago than that, when it had been confined.

Once, it had been less than what it was. But the process of growing, of *becoming*, had taken something away as well. The Weeping Dragon was technically capable of thinking at a level far beyond the ordinary human, but it had been centuries since it was more than a beast.

Once, the Dragon had thoughts, plans, ambitions.

Once, the Dragon had a name.

The Dragon dreamed of these times, and in its sleep, it wept for what was lost. Rain fell from its bed of clouds, watering the land.

Then its dreams changed.

More memories came: of its predecessor, its form beautiful and white and *hungry*. The one who had infected it with the hunger that could never be satisfied. In its dreams, the Dragon was furious at its ancestor for passing on this curse. Though it knew that the original's fate was far worse than its own, the Weeping Dragon couldn't resist its own anger.

Until it woke, and then its thoughts would retreat back into haze, and it would revert to a predator prowling on instinct. Just food and sleep.

While it dreamed, the Weeping Dragon feared waking. But...not this time.

It found that its dreams grew clearer and clearer. First they were dreams of the past, and then they were memories. And then they were thoughts, realizations, knowledge. Plans.

What it had lost was coming back. And the Weeping Dragon realized that it was becoming whole.

It woke, and this time, it really *woke.*

The Dragon's cry of joy alone killed thousands of people. It was aware of this, though it didn't care.

Distantly, it knew that something must have happened to its predecessor. The Slumbering Wraith had died, or at least released what it had been holding.

The Dragon would check on that later. There might be something to learn.

But for now, it would relish being in control of its own body. It wanted more than just food, it wanted shelter. A domain. Children. Servants. Treasures.

Countless serpents of madra rained from its cloud, crackling with its lightning and carrying its will.

It wanted...everything.

Deep in the jungles of the Everwood Continent, the Silent King crouched in its den.

Unlike its siblings, the King had never lost use of its mental faculties. It would have been impossible to control dream madra otherwise. It was its body that had suffered.

It had never carried as much devastating destructive power as the others, and was only as big as one of these human houses, but for the last several centuries, it could be overpowered even by the average human Herald.

While it was almost always better to avoid dangerous combat, the Silent King still considered this unacceptable. It was a Dreadgod. Except by its own siblings, it should be unequaled in all respects.

The Silent King's mind was rarely focused on its own body. Even now, it tended to its mental web. Its subjects filled the jungle for hundreds of miles. They lived in cities, talked, joked, created art. Remnants crept by newborn sacred beasts and both traded respectful nods. Neither should be as intelligent or aware as they were, but thanks to their King, they could live up to their full domain.

In these lands, there was true peace.

But this was as far as its domain would ever extend.

The thought filled it with fury, and back in its den, it opened its jaws. A waiting sacred artist plunged willingly into its teeth, and the King chewed. The snack helped a little, though of course no amount of food could ever fulfill the curse of its hunger madra.

That was a problem it could solve, though. If only it was *allowed* to.

For the hundred thousandth time, the Silent King ran its spiritual perception around the boundaries of its kingdom. *Roots* stretched all around it, roots under *her* command. Its greatest enemy.

The Silent King knew that its sibling, the Dragon, often lost itself in dreams of the past. But its dreams were...crude. Simple. It didn't know *how* to dream. The King knew, and sometimes its dreams were so vivid as to be indistinguishable from waking.

Whenever it dreamed, it liked to imagine the elaborate revenge it would take on Emriss Silentborn. It dreamed of revenge even more often than it dreamed of plans to restore its power. The only *reason* for achieving its full potential was for revenge.

That, and to spread its peace over all the world.

Satisfying its hunger would be a nice side effect, but it had willpower the likes of which mere humans could not comprehend. It could withstand its own urges forever without losing itself. It wasn't a barbarian, like its siblings. It could endure.

But when the wave of hunger aura passed over it, the Silent King drank it in with absolute delight.

While it luxuriated in the sensation, it never stopped thinking. Who had killed the Wraith? Who could have breached that prison? The Silent King had tried personally, centuries ago, and failed.

Whoever it was, the Dreadgod owed them a debt. One day, if it was so inclined, it would repay that service. Perhaps this mysterious savior would enjoy a continent in thanks.

They had granted the Dreadgod's greatest wish. Its will drew tight, more potent than ever, and the wills of everyone in its kingdom focused as well. Some died of exertion, blood running from their eyes, but most could handle this slight burden of will.

All that willpower focused on the tip of the King's claw. And it slashed once through the air.

The roots wrapping around the kingdom were neatly sliced. The organic script-circle failed, and Emriss Silentborn's madra drifted away like so much smoke.

Finally, the Silent King was free to rule.

第二十四章

CHAPTER TWENTY-FOUR

INFORMATION RESTRICTED: PERSONAL RECORD 5716.
AUTHORIZATION REQUIRED TO ACCESS.
AUTHORIZATION CONFIRMED: 008 OZRIEL.
BEGINNING RECORD...

Ozriel reached out to a shard of his power, created long ago: a beacon left behind in Cradle. It contained a dare, a challenge, an invitation for anyone talented enough to join him.

He changed the message.

He shared the situation of the heavens with them and expanded their viewpoint beyond the world. He included his weariness and his vision for the future.

No longer did Ozriel want descendants who would prove worthy of him. Now, he just wanted help. Someone who could share his burden.

He layered more memories beneath his message. Personal records, to one day be accessed by his heir.

Even so, as the years stretched on, none of his descendants used the black marble. The Court of Seven, again and again, denied his request to recruit. He had started off pleading, then reasoning, and now his meetings with Makiel had become openly hostile.

When their conflict destabilized the surrounding Iterations, forcing the intervention of Suriel, she had made them swear to stay separated.

Ozriel felt somewhat guilty for that.

The longer the situation went on, the more worlds the Reaper was forced to take, and the greater his burden grew. Even so, he continued doing his duty.

Until one day, he realized he couldn't take it anymore. If the Court wouldn't act, he would do it himself.

They had gotten along without him before, and they could do it again.

He looked ahead into Fate and prepared. Ozriel spread false trails throughout existence, so that even the Hound couldn't track him. He even left messages for Suriel, presuming that she would be the one to hunt him.

High-ranking Abidan could see through any disguise, so he would be found eventually, but he needed to make this chance last as long as possible.

The corruption of chaos would devour certain worlds while he was gone, so he set up shelters in the most vulnerable to preserve as much as he could. He would leave the Abidan, temporarily sealing off his powers, and raise up a team of ascendants loyal to him.

Then, when he was taken back by the Court, his team could save worlds.

It was while he was inside Iteration 216: Limit, arranging another of his shelters, that he discovered something odd. A subtle touch of chaos in the future that only he—or a Makiel sitting where he was—could have discovered.

His Presence dismissed it as a distant echo of the Void, but Ozriel took greater notice. If a Vroshir wanted to sneak into Abidan territory, Limit would be the perfect first step.

So Ozriel hid himself in Limit, lying in wait for his prey.

As he waited, he considered which world he should eventually hide in. He planned, he thought, he consulted his Presence. He ran simulations and predictions.

Ultimately, there was only one thing he was certain about: he was never going back to Cradle.

Not only would the other Judges check Cradle quickly, but there were too many bad memories. While it would always be his homeworld, a not-inconsiderable part of him hated Cradle.

He hated it for not being better.

While he crouched in Limit, calculating his hiding-place, his prediction paid off. A being of great power and destruction entered the world, so subtly that they had evaded the web of the Spider.

An old enemy, well-hidden.

SYNCHRONIZATION REQUESTED.
SYNCHRONIZATION SET AT 73%.
SYNCHRONIZING...

Ozriel waited in his shelter beneath the waves of Limit, Scythe in hand. He felt the Vroshir arrive, and was surprised not to recognize them. Judges recognized people by the origin of their existence, by the very essence that defined them, which was impossible to fake.

The world quaked beneath him, so this intruder's power was incredible. How could this person be unknown? How could they have slipped past the Abidan web of detection?

Ozriel intended to find out.

He felt the moment when the Vroshir intruder detected him, sensing an Abidan in the world. The intruder instantly sealed off the world and pounced, a cat on a mouse, eager to find prey.

Ozriel smiled.

When the Mad King appeared before him, Ozriel splattered Daruman's mortal body all over the opposite wall with one swing of his Scythe.

That had been nice and therapeutic, and a memory Ozriel would treasure, but he was still shocked. He hadn't seen Daruman face-to-face in centuries, ever since the Mad King had broken out of the depths of Haven.

It *had* to be him. He was wearing one-of-a-kind armor, and he hadn't changed his appearance at all.

But Ozriel still didn't recognize him. His senses insisted that this *couldn't* be Daruman. It simply wasn't him.

The conclusion was as intriguing to Ozriel as it was impossible. He had found a way to disguise his own existence, even from Judges.

Ozriel stepped through space and into the upper atmosphere, where Daruman had created a new body for himself.

The Judge leaned his Scythe against his armored shoulder. "That's a fine mask you have there. Where did you get it?"

Oth'kimeth, the Fiend sealed inside Daruman, snarled defiance. The red suns that were the Mad King's eyes blazed, and he stabbed out with a bone sword.

Even as a mortal, Daruman had been powerful enough to challenge world-eaters. A blow from him should have blighted the planet.

But he was holding back. When his sword met the Scythe, space cracked and reality warped, but it didn't break.

The Vroshir didn't want to attract attention, which suited Ozriel just fine. He didn't want the attention of the other Judges any more than the Mad King did.

The quiet battle between the two still obliterated stars and left holes in space.

With each exchange, Ozriel became more confident. This was *certainly* the Mad King. There was an extremely short list of individuals who could trade blows with Ozriel's Scythe.

And if this was the Mad King, then he had created something that hid him from the Way. A veil on his existence itself.

Finally, as they drifted back down to the central planet of Limit, Daruman himself spoke. His voice was hollow, echoing with the emptiness of the Void.

"You hide as I do, Ozriel. Let us go our separate ways. Inquire no further into my purpose, and I will likewise respect yours."

Ozriel gave him a mocking smile. "I can let you run...but I can't let you keep that."

He swung his Scythe through the veil that he'd finally isolated. A black cloth, like a delicate weave of smoke wrapped around Daruman's soul.

The Scythe tore it to pieces, and it faded into visibility, drifting down toward the planet as scraps of cloth. They warped and twisted the world as they fell, each scrap more powerful and significant than this entire Iteration. If he left them alone, they would ascend to a higher world just by virtue of their existence.

He wouldn't leave them alone, of course.

The Mad King took advantage of the strike on the shroud to flee, and Ozriel knew the man well enough to know that this defeat would burn his pride. Well, good. He deserved it.

Just in case, he looked into Fate to make sure that this wouldn't prompt the Mad King to ruin his plans. He was certain that it wouldn't. The Vroshir wouldn't discover Ozriel's absence before decades had passed, and the other Judges should keep them locked down.

Ozriel wasn't leaving existence undefended, after all. Makiel and Razael were both able to match Ozriel in battle, at least when it came to open combat.

Only if the Mad King managed to find or create a truly devastating weapon could he be a threat while Ozriel was gone, and that possibility was vanishingly remote. It was only slightly more likely than Makiel disbanding the entire Court of Seven and joining the Vroshir.

So Ozriel put that prospect out of his mind and gathered up the pieces of the fallen veil.

This Origin Shroud would change everything. With that bound to him, he could hide under the noses of the other Judges themselves.

He would need to repair it, so it was a good thing he was the greatest craftsman Cradle had ever produced.

But now, his criteria for a hiding place had changed. He had presumed that he would be discovered in only a few years, but if not...if he could go without discovery indefinitely...

Then this was a chance to start over.

To make a new home.

RECORD COMPLETE.

Lindon desperately wanted to leave the labyrinth, but he held himself back.

He *could* leave. This place was only ever intended as a prison for one being: Subject One. With the Dreadgod's borrowed authority, he could eject himself to the upper layers, and then leave on his own. Just as he had done to Reigan Shen.

But with his senses hooked up to the labyrinth, he could also vaguely sense what was happening above him.

Reigan Shen and his Sages had their spirits unveiled. Northstrider and Malice were there too, and Lindon couldn't sense his friends.

He gritted his teeth and stopped himself from leaving. If he ejected himself from the labyrinth right into Shen's control, he would have accomplished nothing.

[We are perched on the precipice of greatness,] Dross whispered. [Plunge over the edge, and see what you may become.]

Lindon hefted Subject One's arm in his own. "Can the labyrinth get rid of Reigan Shen?"

[It is connected only to itself, but the limbs of the labyrinth are long.] The darker Dross stretched out his own tentacles in illustration. [With no suppression field and no prisoner, it may draw your enemies deep and cast them to the ends of the earth!]

Lindon took that as a "yes."

Subject One's body was still slumped in the throne, which was covered by gray-white growths of flesh. Lindon held a hand over it and reached out his senses.

The humanoid Dreadgod had held dominion over this

entire labyrinth...but not *totally.* It was older than he was, and deeper, made by those with greater knowledge and power.

Lindon had briefly borrowed Subject One's control over the labyrinth. He needed to make it truly his own.

[It's yours for the taking! As long as you can remain you.]

Lindon wrenched the body away, tearing it away from the chair. Flesh flaked away, as Subject One had literally grown *into* the throne over the centuries.

Holding the Slumbering Wraith's severed arm, Lindon fell into its seat.

The accumulated force of the labyrinth challenged his authority. It wasn't conscious—just the pressure of a force so ancient he could scarcely comprehend it.

The source of all hunger, the network of hunger madra that had woven itself through the labyrinth, had developed an identity of its own inextricably tied to the maze. It demanded an answer of him: *Who are you?*

As he had done while challenging Reigan Shen, Lindon gave it an answer, but not in words. In images, impressions, and memories. He was the Void Sage, connected to the endlessly hungry Icon. Hunger madra was a fundamental part of his spirit, and had formed the basis of his power. And he was the one who sat on the throne of the Slumbering Wraith.

The hunger madra reluctantly accepted him. It wanted to devour him, but it would instead allow him to lead it to new feasts in the future.

But the hunger madra was only one aspect of the labyrinth. It was the latest, and perhaps the least.

Before Subject One, a team of Soulsmiths had owned the labyrinth. They sought deep truths here, and meant to create wonders. Their intentions, their wills, had seeped into these walls.

Who are you? The labyrinth asked a second time.

He was a Soulsmith. He was a Sage. He had gained his Iron body in the entrance to their labyrinth, and his hunger arm was a creation of his based on an original weapon of theirs. He showed them Dross, a living construct of his own making who now roamed their own control scripts.

And he was born in Sacred Valley. Some of them had been his ancestors.

Lindon had a right to inherit their authority, and he asserted as much. This aspect of the labyrinth, too, finally bowed to his claim.

But they had not been the original owners of the labyrinth either. Before them had come Ozmanthus Arelius.

Lindon focused his battered consciousness, wrestling against the weight of Ozmanthus' remaining authority. *I'm an adopted member of the Arelius family,* Lindon sent. *I am the apprentice of Eithan Arelius.*

He hoped this would be enough, and strongly wished that he had made it to Ozriel's Soulsmith inheritance. If he'd taken *that,* he could surely be considered an heir to Ozmanthus. Without it, he was worried.

But this aspect of the labyrinth accepted him easily. He supposed being one of the few remaining heirs to the Arelius name helped him.

That left only one remaining aspect of the labyrinth. The oldest and most powerful layer, one that he had only briefly sensed in his journey here. The original creators of the labyrinth.

There were seven of them.

He could scarcely comprehend their power, but they felt like seven pillars of order and structure, intrinsic and *real* on a level that he associated with sensing an Icon.

When these demanded to know who he was, he had no answer.

Who was he, compared to them? Compared to people who represented basic aspects of reality?

Their authority threatened to crush him, and they brought back every scratch and bruise on his body. His consciousness fuzzed.

To steel himself, he grabbed Suriel's marble.

And the labyrinth quieted. In shock, he opened his eyes and brought the marble up to look at it. Only then did he notice that one of the seven founders of the labyrinth felt similar—though subtly different—to the marble. Like pure, unending restoration. Healing that could stitch together the universe.

That presence felt him, felt his connection to this marble, and approved of him. Just like that.

And that simply, the labyrinth was his.

It snapped into place around him, and he could sense every room. He stretched his perception through it, finding corridors snaking throughout the earth for...

His mind boggled at the scope.

Dross giggled softly in his mind. [You see? You see how it stretches to distant corners unknown?]

Spatial transportation was a significant part of the labyrinth's function; he had obviously known that throughout their entire journey. What he *hadn't* known was that only certain pieces of the labyrinth were actually in Sacred Valley itself.

Other branches were far away. Some *very* far.

Now he could not only feel the powers in Sacred Valley, but the script that controlled the surrounding lands. It was his, now. His property. His domain.

But there was one piece still missing, and he looked down, to where a severed once-human arm lay in his lap.

"Mine," Lindon said, and the word was a command.

The arm flowed into his own.

Outside the labyrinth, Lindon doubted whether he could do it. The remaining will of Subject One crashed into his like a stone falling from heaven, and even with Dross' support, he once again came close to losing consciousness.

But the power of the labyrinth was the power of Subject One, and he owned it. Its will was his own.

After only a moment of struggle, his right arm condensed into reality once again. Now it was white-gray, and more physical than ever. Touch returned, and he rubbed his fingers together in wonder; he had almost forgotten what it was like to have ordinary sensation in his right hand.

Unfortunately, the sensation of hunger that ran through

him was too much to suppress. He wanted to devour everything in sight, and it was all he could do not to reach through the still-open portal of his void key and consume everything from inside. Natural treasures, scales, food...everything.

He only had to resist for another moment. For now, he needed the additional support.

Lindon stretched his authority out to the edges of his property, and sensed the intruders. He found it was effortless to separate between those he accepted and those he didn't; if they were connected to him or to the valley, they could stay. If they weren't, they couldn't.

They were no longer welcome.

With an effort of will, conducted by the ancient scripts engraved into the labyrinth millennia ago, Lindon made it so.

Northstrider glared at Reigan Shen as the cat hovered in the air, laughing at the carnage he had unleashed on the world.

Something shifted in the labyrinth below. Something Shen had arranged, surely, but Northstrider was familiar with the labyrinth's functions. It had no weapons, if you didn't count the Dreadgods.

"And with that, we'll take our leave," Shen said.

He was truly arrogant if he thought Northstrider would let him go. "Even with the Empire to escort you, you must travel across our lands. If you can return from here to Rosegold, I dare you to do it."

Shen must have halfway bankrupted his house to hire the Eight-Man Empire *and* transport so many people straight here. If he did it again, he would have to spend such power that Northstrider would find it child's play to topple his Empire.

The lion sneered through his white-gold mane and took another sip out of one of those goblets he was so fond of. "What makes you think I haven't accounted for that already?"

Power swelled from the labyrinth below. Power that Northstrider was more familiar with than anyone in the world: hunger madra.

A titanic script lit all the way around the Valley, and then Shen and his people shone white. They could have fought the authority, pitting their wills against the one who was ejecting them. The one who owned this land.

Northstrider turned to Malice, to see if she had set this into motion somehow...and her smile was wide and crazed, as he had seen it only a few times before. She looked like she had just slain an ancient enemy.

But Reigan Shen didn't die. He and his minions—including the four floating cult headquarters and the eight sacred artists in gold armor—faded to white light and disappeared.

He felt them reappear, but it was far away. Thousands of miles. Reappearing over a distant branch of the labyrinth.

Northstrider's first reaction was jealousy. *He* had tried to take over the labyrinth, many years ago. He had failed.

His second reaction was anger.

"Who is that?" he asked Malice.

"A child," Malice responded.

Lindon. Northstrider knew who it had to be, and the tide of his fury rose. "He dares to cooperate with Shen..."

"Cooperate?" Malice giggled to herself. "You think Shen planned for this?"

Northstrider glanced at his oracle codex, who flashed as it responded to him. [Only a minor chance that this was a plan of Reigan Shen's. Most likely he intended to take the throne of the labyrinth himself.]

As he processed that, Northstrider felt his lips crack into a smile.

Lindon ejected himself from the labyrinth with the last of his strength, but instead of arriving on the surface, he found himself pulled into a world of endless darkness.

The feel of the madra was enough to make it clear whose authority was covering him now, so it was completely expected when Akura Malice glided out of the never-ending shadows. Her hair blended with the darkness, and dark lips were stretched in a pleased smile.

He tried to address her, but his voice wouldn't come out. Now out of the labyrinth, the arm's hunger was too much for his wounded body and spirit. He fell to his knees, the world spinning around him.

One word from Malice washed over him. A word he could feel, but not hear.

Then he gasped. His wounds were gone, healed in an instant. He was still weak, but no longer injured. A black cloth, woven with silver script, wrapped around his upper arm.

"It's always best to suppress your appetites if you want to have a rational conversation," Malice murmured. "After all, whatever would I do if you tried to devour me?" She waggled her eyebrows at him.

Lindon cleared his throat in embarrassment and pressed his fists together. "Apologies for my undignified state. I had not yet recovered from battle."

"But you have certainly enjoyed the rewards." Malice sighed in admiration. "Little did I know that my minor investment would pay off so handsomely. In fact..."

She waved a hand, and suddenly Eithan appeared in the world of shadows. He didn't seem surprised, only raising a hand to Lindon and then bowing to the Monarch.

"Honored Monarch, a pleasure! I appreciate the chance to let Lindon know that his friends are alive and well."

A weight lifted from Lindon's shoulders, and he almost collapsed again.

"My first purpose was to congratulate you both." Purple eyes moved over them warmly. "I see many things in the future, many possibilities, and they very rarely pay off as I wish. But you...I am so glad to have given you my support."

Eithan bowed with a flourish, but Lindon had always wondered one thing.

"Pardon if this is too far, but if you don't mind, would you tell us what exactly you saw?"

She stared into the distance, as though at a fond memory. "I saw a shadow of Eithan Arelius ascending to Monarch. His face was clear, but those of his followers vague. Two Monarchs followed him, or perhaps four. Enough to change the balance of this world, and not in a way that anyone could challenge."

The truth slapped Lindon again, as he realized what it meant that Malice knew. She knew that Monarchs sustained the Dreadgods, and she wanted to raise up more.

Malice must have caught something in his spirit or in a change in his breathing, because her smile grew larger and a touch malicious. "You were down there quite a while. I'm sure you learned much. Yes, the Monarchs in Cradle have reached an equilibrium to avoid letting the Dreadgods grow too strong. We keep each other in check, and the number of Monarchs from becoming too high. If someone reached Monarch independently, then we might allow that. Assuming they cooperated.

"But if one of us managed to raise another Monarch—like my son Fury—the others would turn on them in the name of maintaining the balance. Two cannot face six.

"That was the situation when there *were* eight Monarchs. If you were to raise four Monarchs at once, all loyal to one another...well, you could accomplish whatever you wished."

Eithan's smile could mean anything, but Lindon's gut twisted.

"The Dreadgods...you knew all along, didn't you, Arelius? Tiberian would have told you."

"I worked it out on my own, actually," Eithan said cheerily. "But he did swear me to silence on...certain issues."

Malice tapped the side of her cheek as she turned to Lindon. "So it is only you who remain informed and unbound. How do you feel, now that you know what price we Monarchs must pay?"

Lindon thought it was brazen of Malice to call it a price

she was paying, when she was paying with the lives of thousands of others, but he didn't let that show on his face.

"Overwhelmed," Lindon responded. "I admit, I wondered how the Dreadgods could possibly be such fearsome opponents that the Monarchs couldn't be rid of them."

Malice gave a disgusted expression. "They're fearsome in more than one way. Anyway, this day had to come eventually. Swear not to reveal this to the uninformed, and I won't force you to ascend."

For yet another time that day, Lindon was pushed into swearing an oath. It hung in the air between them, unfulfilled.

He hesitated, but Malice kept speaking. "You're a true Sage now, so it's only appropriate that you take on a measure of responsibility. When any Sage or Herald comes close to the truth, or makes enough progress in their advancement, we make them swear."

"I...apologies, but I feel somewhat...uncomfortable."

"You only contribute to the situation once you advance to Monarch. And you can do nothing to change the situation until you *do* advance. Accepting an unpleasant situation you are powerless to change is not treachery, it is maturity."

She spoke reasonably, and Lindon made sure he looked appropriately relieved. He dropped to one knee to lend weight to his words as he swore the oath.

"I swear on my soul that I will never reveal, without permission, that the Dreadgods only remain alive because the Monarchs will not ascend."

Malice ran a hand over his head before he stood. "Good boy. And don't think I've forgotten about *you.*" Dross was pushed out of Lindon's spirit by the force of her attention.

The one-eyed spirit undulated through the air, his motions serpentine and disturbing to watch. [I have seen ancient secrets, and the truth of them has changed me, muta—]

Dross suddenly plummeted out of the air and slammed to the ground, flattened like a leaf beneath Malice's casual spiritual pressure.

Though Lindon could sense the lack of violence in the Monarch's will, he still involuntarily took a step forward to save Dross before he stopped himself.

"You can speak like a Monarch when you live inside one," Malice said softly. "Until then, swear."

[I...swear,] Dross choked out.

He swore, and Malice released him.

All along, Eithan had stood smiling at the entire scene. Malice looked at him with an expression of playfully exaggerated suspicion.

"If I didn't know better, I would suspect you were up to something, Arelius."

"I'm just enjoying the wonderful weather," Eithan said, looking up into the endless black sky.

"I am a busy woman." Malice's voice resonated. "Swear to me now that you are already bound by Tiberian's oath and therefore cannot speak the truth of the Dreadgods."

"I do swear, have sworn, and will not speak," Eithan said easily.

The air trembled and Malice finally clapped her hands together. "Well now! I will call on you soon. If the Dreadgods have been affected as I suspect...well, dark days are ahead for those not under the protection of a Monarch. But when we do battle against Dreadgods, all who can affect them will be mobilized. Prepare yourselves."

The black sky retreated, and Malice was gone. Lindon stood under a blue sky, on the grassy green side of the mountain called the Greatfather...and Eithan, Ziel, Yerin, Orthos, and Little Blue were standing next to him.

Everyone looked around as though startled to be there. He could feel shock radiating from Orthos and Little Blue.

Yerin stared blankly at Lindon. "Let me give you what just happened, from my perch: Mercy's mother dragged me into a shadow, patted me on the head, then tossed me back out with the rest of you. Am I about to be a Remnant?"

[Our secrets have been bound inside us by a greater will!] Dross said. [Be grateful that you do not share the burden of glorious knowledge, as we do, lest you attract the attention of Monarchs.]

Yerin's gaze turned to Lindon.

"Apologies. We are sworn not to say anything about... whatever it is she wished to speak to us about."

"So something happened with Reigan Shen."

"No, not him specifically." Eithan clutched at his chest. "Alas! I feel the oath tightening around me, preventing me from speaking!"

Yerin looked around at all of them.

"What is this?" Orthos demanded. "Do not keep secrets from us!"

Little Blue gave an offended clang.

When Yerin looked at him, Ziel shrugged. "No clue. But if a Monarch made them swear to keep their mouths shut, they're not going to say anything."

Lindon sighed. "It was actually a more ironclad oath than I expected. I had expected to be able to write you a letter, or give you a dream tablet, but it seems that I can't willingly bring up the subject."

"The majesty of soul oaths," Eithan said wistfully. "It's the spirit of the promise, not the letter."

Yerin continued looking around. "Can we race ahead to the part where you all figured out a way to tell me what's going on?"

Eithan gave a loud, exaggerated cough.

Lindon felt his cheeks go warm. "Apologies. I did try." There was a sound recording construct in Lindon's pocket, but his spirit was restricting him from sending it to Yerin. He had even intended to spill it out of his pocket onto the floor—surely then he wouldn't be *giving* it to her—but the promise was more effective than he had imagined. Now, even if Yerin searched his clothes, he would feel the need to crush the construct.

[You will know in due time,] Dross said mysteriously.

Yerin did not look happy with that answer.

Lindon was the first to notice the person missing. "Where's Mercy?"

Mercy knew as soon as she was drawn into the all-black world that this wasn't going to be one of the fun meetings with her mother.

Malice looked down on her daughter with...Mercy wouldn't call it a *glare,* but that wouldn't be far off.

Mercy inclined her head respectfully. "Mother. You're looking lovely today?" That came out as more of a question than a statement, but the compliment should help.

"You are lucky that your friends are more resourceful than you are," Malice said coldly. "If events had not worked out in my favor, I would have been forced to punish you."

"But they did!"

"Don't be a child." The temperature in the shadow world lowered, and purple eyes glittered. "You *knew* I would want to keep them out of the labyrinth. You meddled with forces beyond you, and you can only thank Fate that you didn't all die."

Mercy shifted her weight. "It wasn't quite so—"

"You were supposed to do as I bid you. That is your role in serving the family."

"I don't think—"

"You lied to me."

Mercy's fear slowly shifted to anger. That wasn't a healthy attitude before a Monarch, but she couldn't help it. "How am I supposed to stop Lindon and Yerin and Eithan from doing *anything*? And why would I want to? You didn't even tell me why!"

"You think weakness *excuses* you? You've had advantages they never imagined, and still they have surpassed you. You couldn't even reach Overlord on your own."

"But I got there! I thought you didn't care how!"

"When you defy my orders, you had better have something to *show for it,*" Malice snapped. The darkness behind her boiled, and Mercy's anger shook, but she held onto it.

"What more were we supposed to do? We made it to the bottom and back out, just like you did! We're not Monarchs! We can't come out with a new Dreadgod!"

"Oh, but one of you did," the Monarch said softly.

Mercy paused. "What?"

"You haven't seen your friend Lindon yet. He emerged with the power of the Slumbering Wraith under control. He ejected Reigan Shen's forces from the valley. In effect, he owns the labyrinth now."

Mercy's anger was replaced by uncertainty. "Wait, but... how is that..."

"I am disappointed in you for many reasons. You disobeyed me, your loyalty to the family is questionable, and you depend on others as a crutch. But most of all, you lack ability." Malice's finger jabbed Mercy in the collar. "You are the daughter of the Monarch who owns these lands. You were born with enough authority to claim the labyrinth, if you had been present when Subject One died. If I were you, I would have been there. And if I could not claim it for myself, I would claim the one who did."

Mercy's face heated up. "That's not your—"

"You think I mean *affection?*" Malice snapped. "I mean *control.*" The entire dark world focused to a point, as though a spotlight had illuminated Malice. Her eyes shone. "I can tell you one thing with absolute certainty: your friends have grown too powerful to remain free. I will shower them in glory and power...

"...but they will be mine."

Lindon sat on the hill next to Yerin, comparing notes as the sun set. They had all asked him for the story of fighting Reigan Shen, and he had gone over every blow in detail. With Dross' help.

Now he had made it to the part where he'd claimed the

throne of the labyrinth. "There was still a deeper layer," he said. "An older one. I thought I was done then, until I pulled out..."

He reached into his pocket and withdrew Suriel's marble. There came a general murmur of appreciation as they saw the blue candle glow.

"Without this, I don't know that I would have been able to claim the labyrinth. It might have cast me out...or even devoured me."

"You would probably have still been granted partial authority," Ziel put in. "At least enough to operate the scripts." The others looked at him, and he shrugged. "Or maybe you would have died."

"Anyway, it recognized me because of this," Lindon went on. "I think they..." He trailed off, staring at the glass ball.

So did everyone else.

"What happened to it?" Orthos asked.

"Shake it," Yerin suggested.

Ziel leaned closer, and Eithan paled.

The flame inside the glass ball had shrunk. Now it was almost nothing but an azure spark.

"I've never seen it like this before," Lindon said. Apprehension crawled into his heart. "I think something might be wrong with it."

The flame trembled, like it was straining to grow brighter.

And then the light of Suriel's marble winked out.

第二十五章
CHAPTER TWENTY-FIVE

ITERATION 110: CRADLE

After the rise of the Dreadgods, Emriss Silentborn had never expected that she would feel something even more frightening on the same day.

Her body, that of a blue-green tree big enough to brush the sky, trembled at what she felt approaching their world. Each of her leaves, each set with a functioning eye, shook as they stared into spectrums no human could see.

Something was coming. And it shook their world like the footsteps of a Dreadgod shaking a tiny pond.

For miles around, aura of all aspects jerked and trembled. It was a disturbing, chaotic dance, and it only got worse.

Emriss looked into the future, and she saw nothing.

Malice staggered in shock.

Her own World of Night technique activated without her consent, and it was as though she'd gone blind, plunged into a black domain.

Only a moment before, she would have seen the shapes of the Dreadgods looming over her in the World of Night, an imminent threat. She had already been gathering her forces and making her plans, ready to fight a second Dread War.

Now those silhouettes crumbled, shattering like statues obliterated by an invisible hammer. Without them surrounding her, she looked into the distance, at the other possible futures that always lingered around her.

One by one, they were smashed to pieces. Disappearing.

She dismissed the technique, and the world returned. It was no less disturbing. Something *behind* the air quivered, like lightning about to strike.

Even Mercy was affected. Tears still streaked her cheeks, but her earlier defiance was forgotten. She looked in every direction, Eclipse ready in her hands, looking for the attacker.

"Mother, what...what's happening?"

Tears rose in Malice's eyes. Her heart broke.

And she wondered what she had been so concerned about a moment before. The feelings of her daughter had counted for nothing next to the value of the future.

But now, there was no future.

She walked forward and gathered Mercy to her chest, wishing only that she had time to find her other children. Where was Pride? Was Fury all right? Or had this disaster consumed him as well?

She should have left Fury with a better good-bye. Their last conversation had been a fight. He had wanted her to leave—wanted *all* the Monarchs to leave. She'd refused, as she always had. And always would.

"I'm so sorry, Mercy. I don't know what I was thinking. It only matters that you're safe."

Mercy's arms tightened, but she leaned back to look into Malice's face. She was so young. "Mother, I'm scared," she said, as she had never said when she was a child.

The Monarch stroked her youngest daughter's head. "Sssshhhh. It's nothing to worry about," Malice lied. "Everything's going to be all right."

The Bleeding Phoenix gave a keening cry and fled like a chicken desperate to avoid the axe.

Northstrider was watching the Dreadgod from far away, but he cut off the vision as he felt the same thing the Phoenix had. Doom, like a thunderbolt to the soul.

The Way itself was trembling, and he tried to step beyond the world, but found he couldn't. It was as though there was nothing beyond Cradle at all.

His oracle codex screamed, the surface of the glossy black orb flickering with texts, and he seized it in one hand.

"What is happening?" he demanded.

The codex was incoherent. It repeated only one phrase, over and over:

[A destroyer has come.]

Reigan Shen grabbed the Sage of Calling Storms and shook him, but the man only stared uncomprehendingly at the sky.

"What are they doing? Are the Abidan coming for us? ANSWER ME!"

His roar was enough to kill lesser sacred artists, but the Sage looked like he had seen every nightmare at once come to life.

Reigan Shen had no skill at reading Fate. He had devices that did as much for him, and now they were screaming all around him. He could barely hear himself think over the sirens, alarms, and blaring screams of his divination tools.

When he tried to figure out why, he couldn't get them to do anything but display the same message: *A destroyer has come.*

Among his subordinates, Calling Storms was supposed to be the best at divining the future, but now that Reigan Shen needed him, the man was useless.

The Sage could only scream.

Lindon was frozen in terror.

"Lindon, what happened?" Yerin demanded. "Who's doing this?"

Her eyes trembled, and she looked to him for explanation, but what he was feeling from the Void Icon was too overwhelming.

There was only one phrase that fit what he was seeing now. "It's the end of the world."

"What do you *mean?*" Tears leaked into her eyes and her voice, and she grabbed the front of his robes. "Is it an attack? Is this...is this the Dreadgods, or...or a Monarch?"

Her voice shook, and rather than shaking him, she sagged powerlessly against his robes.

Lindon ran his hand down her hair. "The stars," he said. When she looked to him for explanation, he pointed up.

One by one, the stars were winking out.

In Lindon's spirit, Little Blue and Orthos were rapidly-approaching spots of pure horror. Orthos galloped up with Blue on his back, running with the speed of the Burning Cloak.

"What are you doing sitting there?" Orthos shouted. "Do you want to be outrun by a turtle?"

When Orthos battered into Lindon's leg, Lindon reached down and scooped up Little Blue. Her trembling sounded like the jingling of glass shards, and he gathered her to his chest.

She should have been even more frightened than he was, but her trembling slowed. Little Blue gave one long flute sigh and embraced him.

Lindon sat down next to Orthos. The turtle was headbutting him over and over, but each one was weaker.

"Run," Orthos mumbled. "We have to..."

"There's nowhere to run," Lindon said. He looked up to the sky and watched points of light wink out, one at a time.

Orthos lifted his head, and Lindon could see the despair in his eyes when he saw for himself.

A moment later, a bar of Blackflame shot up into the sky.

"You never know," Orthos rumbled. "Maybe this enemy can be burned."

Yerin looked at him for a moment before snorting a laugh. She wiped her tears and sat down on Lindon's left side. "Always thought I'd go down fighting."

Lindon took her hand. "I never thought it would end here."

But it was the end. When he saw the stars vanish, he knew the truth without doubt. An ant had a better chance of resisting a boot.

He had to admit, he was somewhat bitter about that. He had set his sights far beyond this world, thinking it was too small for him. He'd fulfilled everything Suriel had promised him, so that even she had descended and met him again.

Now, after all that, he was going to die here after all.

Yerin snapped off a long stalk of dry grass and popped one end into her mouth. "Can't say I'm smiling about ending it like this, but weighing all our options, we didn't have it so bad." She glanced around at their surroundings. "Just think: you could have died in Sacred Valley."

Lindon laughed and looked over at a small sound.

Ziel was weakly kicking a mound of dirt, over and over. He wasn't using nearly the strength he was capable of, but from the expression on his face, he was still taking out some long-held anger.

"Now?" Ziel demanded. "It had to be *now?* I pull myself back together, and the world ends!"

Yerin jerked her head. "Come on, drop yourself down with us."

"Why? Is that the hill that will survive the end of all things?"

"You rather die alone?"

Ziel grumbled, but he trudged over and plopped down, still seething with visible frustration.

Yerin craned behind him. "Anybody clap eyes on Mercy?"

That got Lindon thinking about who they were missing. There were precious few stars left now, and even the wind had stopped blowing. Grass hung still in the night air, waiting, as the buzzing pressure behind the air increased.

He didn't need the Void Icon to tell him that the end was almost here.

You've been quiet, he said to Dross.

[I am ready to face this despair!] Dross cried. He spun out into reality, smile crazed. [If the darkness is to snuff out the stars, I say, let us see what waits on the other side of oblivion!]

Lindon rested his sealed right arm on Dross' head. "Looks like we'll find out together."

The spirit's large eye swiveled to Lindon. [You did not abandon me, so I have nothing left to fear!]

Lindon's heart tightened. Now, more than ever, he wished he had been able to meet the old Dross one more time.

Lindon glanced left and right. He tried extending his spiritual perception, but found that all he could sense was endless death.

"I thought you'd have popped in by now," Lindon said to the air.

No one responded.

"Eithan?"

For some reason, even in the face of the imminent apocalypse, Eithan's absence alarmed him. He untangled himself from Yerin, Blue, and Orthos, and he drifted a short distance away to where he'd last sensed the Archlord.

Eithan was still there, on his hands and knees, heedless of the dirt on his clothes. His fingers tightened on the soil, and his back shook.

It took Lindon a long moment to realize that Eithan was quietly sobbing. Tears plopped to the ground one at a time.

Lindon placed a gentle hand on his back, but Eithan didn't respond.

"Thank you, Eithan," Lindon said quietly. "For everything."

Eithan looked at Lindon in shock. His expression slowly softened, and he rose to his feet. He placed his hands on Lindon's shoulders and met his eyes.

"I'm proud of you, Lindon," Eithan said.

That hit Lindon harder than he had imagined.

The others were looking over to them, and Eithan swept towards them. Uncharacteristically, he didn't wipe his face or brush his clothes clean.

"I had hoped we would have many more years together," Eithan said, in something approaching his usual tones. "I wanted to see the sights beyond this world with you. All of you."

A distant scream of terror echoed in Lindon's mind, and he looked up. He was just the first. The others looked up a second or two later.

The sky was completely black now. Empty, except for one figure.

He was only the size of a human, so he should have been invisible at that distance, the man in the bone armor. But Lindon could see him clearly.

His eyes blazed under the shadow of his helm, balls of red fire. He wore a full suit of armor that had been carved from yellowed bone, and a pelt of ancient fur fell from his shoulders. Lindon shuddered as he sensed the power emanating from the figure.

It was depthless. Boundless. He twisted the world just by *being* here.

In both hands, he held a Scythe so black that its darkness stood out even against the empty sky. As he stared at that Scythe, Lindon knew he was staring at the end. An apocalypse given form. It was like seeing his own death.

Eithan snapped his fingers, and Lindon realized that he had never looked up at all.

"We don't have much time left. If this is going to be the end, then remember one thing from me: I loved every second with you all. I really, truly...had so much fun."

Yerin met his gaze for a moment and then threw her arms around his ribs.

"If there's another side, we'll catch you there," she said.

He smiled fondly and placed a hand on her head. "Yes, I suppose you will."

The earth seemed to *snap*. Not like an earthquake breaking open a canyon, but as though someone had slashed through a painting. Not long now.

Lindon looked around from face to face, and there was too much he wanted to say. Yerin slid away from Eithan and went back to Lindon. He looked deeply into her red eyes and searched for the right words.

But apparently Eithan wasn't finished. He cleared his throat. "It seems like I'll be leaving a little sooner than the rest of you. I'll miss you all when I'm gone. Tell Mercy for me, will you?"

The figure in the sky was now the only thing that seemed real. Spatial cracks spiraled across the black sky, as the entire world crumbled just as Ghostwater once had.

Well, Lindon thought, *at least I'll see beyond this world after all.*

Then he realized what Eithan had said.

"Eithan...this is it for us," Lindon said. "We're all gone."

Eithan brushed off his hands and wiped his face clean with a cloth. He let the cloth fall, and all trace of his tears was gone. He held out his right hand, and revealed that he had been holding something else.

A black marble.

"No," Eithan said, "just me."

The marble cracked.

Eithan looked into the sky as he held out the black marble. "Remove restraints and release authority. Authorization zero-zero-eight...Ozriel."

⬡

The world stopped shaking.

Northstrider stared into the reflective black surface of his codex. The turmoil calmed, and the message it had displayed—[A destroyer has come]—now flickered out.

It was replaced with a new message, and if the previous one had brought with it the chaos of panic, this one came along with the silence of the grave.

White letters on a black surface declared:

[The Destroyer has come.]

The screams from the Sage of Calling Storms choked off just as all the sirens and alarms around Reigan Shen stopped blaring.

The man jerked up, taking a deep breath.

Reigan Shen had long since given up and slumped into a chair. "What now?" he asked, with little hope.

"He's here," the Sage whispered.

Reigan wasn't much interested—he figured they were all dead either way. He sighed. "Who?"

"The Reaper."

Emriss Silentborn had earned her title for two reasons. First, she had a long history with the Dreadgod known as the Silent King. Second, trees were notoriously quiet. She was used to reading meaning in silence.

This silence that covered the world was even more frightening than the trembling had been. It was like an axe poised to descend on her branches.

But it was still a relief.

The axe wasn't aimed at her.

With Mercy in her arms, Malice's eyes rolled up into her head.

She found herself back in the World of Night, the technique once again activating without her conscious intervention. She looked across the endless darkness, and instead of a field of smoky statues, she saw only one.

The armored figure in the sky. He held a sword in his left hand and a scythe in his right, and he brought destruction.

Even with the world crumbling around her, she felt irritation. Why show her this? She already knew she was going to die, so there was no point in rubbing her nose in it.

A curved blade swept in from the darkness and sliced the armored figure in half.

It was so sudden that she was shocked, and so quick that she lost track of the blade. As the statue's top half fell, it crumbled to dust, so that it burst on contact with the ground. Even the bottom half of the statue dissolved like salt in water.

And the other statues returned. The imposing Dreadgods, the statue of Mercy sitting at the head of the Akura clan, half-formed scenes between Malice and the other Monarchs. They all formed slowly, remaking themselves out of particles of dust.

She felt something behind her and turned.

There, looming over her, was a new statue that she had never seen before. It was far larger than anything else, towering even over the Dreadgods. A long-haired figure with a familiar face and a scythe propped up on his shoulder.

Always before, the statues had been motionless and made all of one color.

This statue's lips stretched, and its smile was blinding white.

Eithan ran a hand along his hair, and it grew out. Long and golden...but as it grew, it got paler, until it was pure white. A veil slid out of his spirit like cloth made from smoke. *The* veil, the ultimate concealing item. The Origin Shroud, made by the Mad King and repaired by Ozriel.

It dissolved into nothing now, its purpose fulfilled and its conditions broken.

He didn't want to look back at the others from Cradle. He didn't want to see Lindon's uncomprehending eyes, or Little Blue trembling in terror before his true power.

So he focused on the man in the sky.

"You ruined everything," Eithan said, and his rage wasn't as cold as usual.

Through the cracks behind the Mad King, even the Void quivered in fear.

"How?" Daruman demanded. "How are you here? You couldn't have known!"

Eithan hadn't known.

"I *always* know," Eithan said.

Armor flowed through the Way, black liquid slithering around him and covering him, seamless and smooth. The Mad King saw him protecting himself and struck.

With his scythe.

The Iteration split in half as he cut at the fabric of existence, but Eithan held out a hand. The slice in reality stopped exactly at the edge of his palm.

Eithan laughed. "A poor choice of weapon."

Who could have more authority over Ozriel's Scythe than Ozriel?

Not that this was the true Scythe, just a thin imitation, but Ozriel still had full claim over it. Eithan simply wished it, and the scythe disappeared from the Mad King's hand and appeared in his own.

He examined the weapon for a moment. "It's a crude toy,

but not bad craftsmanship. Iri's work, I think, and someone else's. Someone who should have known better."

Oth'kimeth snarled and stretched out from Daruman's body, and for a moment, Eithan saw the Fiend and the man separate. One was a demonic figure with horns arranged into a blood-tipped crown, with eyes of burning crimson ambition. The other was an ancient king, burdened with power.

The Fiend wanted to fight, furious. The man spoke.

"You left the Court behind already, Ozriel. There is no need to return."

Eithan took a deep breath as his armor settled around him. The Mantle of Ozriel had been sealed in Sanctum, in the treasure vault of another world, and even now it shattered through its seals and came for him.

"Come with me," Daruman continued. "Tear down the system and build it anew. Without you, the Judges are worthl—"

Eithan interrupted him. "You should have known I would come for you."

The Mantle of Ozriel emerged from the Way. It settled onto Eithan's shoulders, boiling shadow streaming out behind him.

"Maybe I *have* been away too long," Eithan continued, "if you thought you could destroy my home and walk away."

Oth'kimeth and Daruman merged again, and once more the Mad King looked down from the sky. "I assumed you had seen the truth and left."

"The truth? Here is the truth you deserve. You do not decide who lives and who dies." Eithan levered the scythe up onto his shoulder. "That's my job."

With the speed of the Fox, he moved.

He disappeared from the surface of Cradle, appearing behind the Mad King. He struck with the power of the Wolf.

The Mad King swung his sword back, and the clash between their weapons would have ruined the planet.

But the planet was under the protection of Ozriel. The damage struck a blue shield covering the entire central planet of Cradle, and the barrier held with the defense of the Titan.

The Mad King dashed away, but Eithan had once been declared the heir of the Spider. His awareness expanded to fill...everything.

Nothing could hide from him.

Somewhere in the stretch of empty space in Iteration One-one-zero, Daruman came to a halt. Bloody claws emerged from nowhere to either side of him, manifestations of his will.

Eithan drifted up next to them, and with the touch of the Ghost, he wiped those powers away.

He looked into the future, seeing and arranging Fate. With the vision of the Hound, Eithan twisted his destiny.

He and Daruman traded hits, and after every exchange, chips of bone flew off to return to the Void. But so did gleaming black metal.

Eithan's fake scythe couldn't keep up with his power, and in truth neither could he. Too much of Eithan's strength had faded as he stayed under the Origin Shroud for so long. His armor was chipped and cracked from hits that he'd missed.

Red eyes blazed as the Mad King noticed. "You are not what you were."

Eithan readied his scythe and focused his power.

Color vanished in the entire Iteration. Darkness and emptiness gathered on the edge of his scythe as he finally unleashed the power of the Reaper.

"Would you destroy your home to kill me?" Daruman asked quietly.

"Daruman, the Mad King!" Eithan shouted. "Oth'kimeth, the Conqueror! By the authority of Ozriel and the Court of Seven, I condemn you to die. No matter the cost."

Eithan drew back his scythe, ready to swing, and the power of annihilation reached its peak.

Daruman had every intention of standing and facing this strike, Eithan was sure of it. But the Fiend within him had other plans.

It clawed open a rift into the Void, and Eithan allowed it. Oth'kimeth dragged his human vessel behind.

Daruman vanished before he could call Eithan's bluff.

Eithan let out a breath and released the power of death that had gathered in his weapon. Color raced back into the universe. It was a good thing the Fiend had bought his act; unleashing a strike powerful enough to break the Mad King's defenses while in Cradle would indeed have destroyed the entire Iteration.

And he wasn't willing to do that. Not anymore. Still, he left wounds behind. Scars in space, missing stars.

Eithan had no power to heal them.

He let himself drift through the Way, the flows taking him down to the surface where he had started. Another piece fell from his armor, and his scythe creaked in his hand.

With an irritated flex of his will, he unmade the weapon. It was a crude imitation anyway.

That fight had taken more out of him than it would have, once. He had been veiled too long, and it would be some time before he could face the Mad King without fear.

If the Court ever allowed him to regain his power. They would have felt this clash and would be on their way. At least, someone would be.

Eithan hoped it wasn't Suriel. He still owed her a debt, and he was feeling enough guilt as it was.

He blinded himself to the stares of hurt and shock on the faces around him, and he focused on the one-eyed spirit floating nearby.

"I couldn't fit everything of...myself...inside a mortal vessel," Eithan explained, without looking Lindon in the eye. "My Soulsmithing was one thing I left out, and I am now bound by the—an ancient pact. I am sorry, but I cannot repair Dross unless it would prevent further damage to the world. But with the labyrinth, you should be able to do it, if you act quickly."

Lindon looked down to his own marble, his Abidan beacon. A fire from the Way now burned merrily at its heart once again.

"Who are you?" Lindon asked, and Eithan flinched. That was the question he'd always dreaded.

"My full name is Ozmanthus Tiberian Mereithan Arelius. Always hated it. Such a mouthful. My mother called me Eithan." He looked from one face to another. "My power was restricted, but I was still...me. It was real, I promise! I—"

He cut off and looked down as Little Blue stared up at him. Then she threw her arms around his shin.

His eyes filled with tears again. He hadn't cried as Ozriel... maybe ever. His Presence could tell him for certain, once he recovered that from Abidan lockdown.

"Don't know why you made such a secret about it," Orthos grumbled. He tore up a bite of grass and began chewing. "We wouldn't have known who you were anyway."

[Give me your secrets!] Dross whispered. [Let me taste your power!]

Ziel looked Eithan up and down. "Can you tell me how to get to Sage?"

"I think you're more likely to reach it on your own than anyone here," Eithan said honestly. "Except Lindon, of course. That cloud has already drifted away."

Then he looked to Lindon and Yerin.

Yerin's left eye twitched. "Did you really...you...bleed and bury me, you let me think we were finally going to catch up to you."

Eithan tried not to smile. It was a serious moment.

"It's not too late," Eithan said.

Lindon struggled with himself for a moment, then he stepped forward...and extended his Dreadgod arm.

"See you soon," Lindon said.

Eithan clasped Lindon's hand in his, and they shook. A handshake wasn't a tradition from the Ashwind continent, but from Rosegold. Where Eithan had been born.

Something pulled at his gauntlet, and Eithan caught Lindon trying to Consume his power.

Lindon coughed and averted his eyes. "Apologies, it's a... new arm."

CHAPTER TWENTY-SIX

The sky was still starless above Lindon, and a ragged scar in the world ran from distant eternity all the way down to the ground, where Eithan had stopped a cosmic attack with the palm of his hand.

Lindon remembered Suriel reversing time and bringing the dead back to life. Could she have returned stars to the night sky?

Eithan saw him looking and his smile turned sad. "Someone will be along to fix that in just a moment."

Yerin shifted uncomfortably, and Lindon saw questions writhing in her. She settled on a casual tone: "So we'll see you on the other side, true?"

"It may...be a while," Eithan said hesitantly. "I'm certain you will eventually! But for the Mad King to arrive here, in a world that should be protected, that means something has gone terribly wrong in my absence. I may find myself in quite a bit of trouble."

The Mad King. Lindon stored that name away for future reference.

"You have to report to a superior even in the Abidan, do you?" Ziel asked.

Eithan tossed his long white hair. "Who do you suppose is

superior to me? No, these are my *peers* who might imprison me for eternity. My peers!"

Before anyone could ask further questions, a subtle blue light slid over the scene. Lindon looked up to find sapphire energy spreading across the sky like a blooming sun.

"And it looks like you'll get a chance to meet them now," Eithan said. Some of the energy seemed to have gone out of him.

From the spreading blue light, seven figures descended. And as they did, Lindon felt *everything* change.

The world felt steadier around him, calmer. He found himself relaxing in their presence, like a child held in his mother's arms. That trembling sense of chaos behind the world, and the otherworldly stillness that had come at Eithan's transformation, both faded away for a sense of *rightness* like comforting music.

The ragged slash in reality nearby began to slowly crawl backwards, broken earth slid together, and even the snarling presence of Lindon's hungry arm quieted.

But Lindon was only aware of those things as distant details. His attention was fixed on the seven newcomers armored in white.

He had seen Suriel twice before, of course, and caught images of the rest of them in the vision trapped inside Eithan's marble. But in person, their radiance took on totally different meaning.

A weathered man with gray hair, dark skin, and merciless eyes drifted to the front and descended to the ground. "Ozriel. You have much to answer for."

Eithan looked him up and down, dismissed him, and looked to the other six. "You sent him to speak for you? You knew I wouldn't talk to him."

"You look different," a woman in ghostly gray said in a dreamlike voice. She was the only one not wearing smooth armor, and she vaguely gestured to him. "It suits you."

"Thank you, Durandiel. You see? At least one of you is friendly."

Blue lightning cracked across the sky, and anger pressed down on Lindon from every direction. A woman with hair of white-and-red flame glared at Eithan. "Do you know how many lives your absence cost us? Do you have *any idea?*"

"I know how many would have been lost if my predictions were accurate," Eithan said calmly. "I never foresaw the Mad King getting his hands on a new weapon."

A straight-backed man wearing glasses and a cane snorted. "Then your sight is not as flawless as you pretended."

"It was *your* weapon!" the flaming woman shouted.

Eithan's eyes drifted over to the stone-faced man in front of him. "Was it?"

"All will be answered for," that man said with icy calm. "You have cost us enough time already. Gadrael."

The strangest-looking of the seven, a short man with blue-gray skin and horns for hair, raised a hand. Spinning discs of intricate script surrounded Eithan from head to toe, and aside from feeling alarm for Eithan, Lindon immediately asked Dross to remember anything of the runes he could.

Eithan coughed out a breath as though he'd been punched in the stomach. "That's uncomfortable. You could have used a softer touch."

The blue-gray man, Gadrael, gave him an icy stare but said nothing.

"Zakariel, take the prisoner," the stone-faced man ordered. "Let us convene the Court and put an end to this farce at last."

He turned and stepped into a flash of blue light, then vanished.

A girl appeared behind Eithan. She might have been ancient, but Lindon could only think of her as a girl; she looked younger than he was. She gave Eithan a razor-edged smile.

"Good to have you back, Oz."

"I have missed our charming dynamic, Zak."

The girl stamped her foot, and space rippled. "Call me Zerachiel!"

"Maybe old age has altered my memory, but I don't think that's your name."

"I've changed it!"

They vanished a moment later...but Eithan seemed to linger a fraction of a second longer than the girl. He met Lindon's eye and gave him a beaming smile.

"It was fun," Eithan said.

Then he disappeared.

The other Abidan strode away one at a time, without a word for the mortals. Except for one. Suriel lingered, bright green hair drifting behind her as though she floated underwater. Her eyes were bright purple rings of script, and lines of smoke ran from her hand up to the back of her skull.

It had only been a few months since he'd seen her again, and when she was the only one remaining, Lindon bowed deeply to her.

"Pardon, but I never expected to see you again so soon."

"Lindon..." She breathed out a sigh. "I don't know what to say to you except that I'm sorry."

Blue light streamed from behind her, like the wings of an azure phoenix, and the stars winked back into existence one by one.

"Ozriel hid himself well, and I couldn't foresee his actions. When the two of you intersected, it caused...great changes. I fear that my actions in your home have had disastrous results."

Lindon's stomach tightened. "Not for me."

"Not yet. But your fate is far beyond reading, now. And Cradle is still in danger." Stars continued to reappear, and spatial cracks sealed themselves, as Suriel said, "Right now, the heavens lie in ruins. Perhaps Ozriel's return will allow us to fix some of what has been broken."

"Apologies, but what's going to happen to him?"

Her expression became complicated. "He will be tried in the Abidan Court. His actions are in violation of our laws, and have resulted in great destruction. But he is still an irreplaceable asset, which is what led to this problem in the first place."

Lindon was silent for a long time, chewing on that information, and Suriel continued weaving the universe back together.

Unexpectedly, she went on. "Did he tell you what role he played in the cosmos?"

Lindon exchanged looks with Yerin as they remembered the vision in Eithan's marble, and Yerin was the one who answered. "Seems to me like he put down worlds that were too sick to go on. Uh, honored...queen?"

"That is an accurate summary of his function, but it is not one he would have chosen. He left us, abandoning his mission, in an attempt to raise up people who could replace him. To cut away infected tissue before the infection spreads."

Suriel eyed the group before her, and deliberately said, "He was looking to raise up a new Reaper."

Lindon's Dreadgod hand involuntarily curled into a fist.

[We need that title!] Dross cried. [Let's ascend at once!]

He was tempted. Not only did Suriel seem to be suggesting that they could help Eithan, but Lindon had now seen the difference between him and the most powerful beings in creation. Lindon couldn't unmake stars.

There was no pursuing power like that while stuck in Cradle.

"Can he wait a little longer?" Lindon asked. "We have unfinished business here."

The Dreadgods were still here, and stronger than ever, with no one left in the world who could oppose them. And those who knew the truth wouldn't do anything about it.

When Lindon advanced, he intended to drag the Monarchs with him.

Suriel searched his eyes...and then gave him a grin that reminded him of Eithan.

"Repairing a broken system is a worthy goal. But you'll be on your own. We've interfered far too much already, and anything further could break Cradle beyond recovery. And you should know that you will find more enemies than allies."

"Even so, I'd like to try." Then honesty compelled him to add, "And I would hate to leave the world behind without getting everything I could out of it."

"Then I will await your arrival in the world beyond," Suriel said. She surveyed the group and added, "All of you."

Then, in a rising tide of blue light, she vanished.

Lindon and the others remained on a flawless grassy hill, with no evidence left behind to prove that anything had happened.

Yerin stretched. "Well that shook my spine, I'll tell you true."

"We have stared into the abyss and lived to tell the tale," Ziel said. "I'm going to sleep."

Malice broke her way out of the World of Night and found that everything had been restored to the way it was before, but her memories remained.

She wondered if that was an oversight on the part of the Abidan, or if they had been unable to wipe the memories. If *she* had intervened in such a public and global way, she would have made sure that the native inhabitants remembered nothing.

But she remembered the figure she'd seen. The one who dominated the future with his broad smile.

"That was Eithan Arelius," she said with certainty.

Mercy sat on the floor at her feet, trembling. "No, it can't be. Eithan's not...he isn't...*terrifying.*"

Malice begged to differ. And it made her take a closer look at those Eithan Arelius had chosen while he was here.

That *thing* had been close to her daughter.

"What about Lindon and Yerin?" Mercy asked suddenly. She paled. "Are they still...they're not hurt, are they?"

Malice swept out her spiritual perception. She had gone blind during that brief apocalypse, but now she could feel everything she usually did.

Those under her authority were easy to sense, and Lindon and Yerin had fought in her name for a long time. They were easy to find.

"They are unharmed," Malice said, and Mercy let out a relieved breath. Malice was not so pleased. "It's enough to make you wonder: why?"

Reigan Shen sweated so much that his mane was matted to his skin.

"That was Eithan Arelius."

"That was Death himself," the Sage of Calling Storms said in awe. "We have seen the divine!"

"That was *Eithan Arelius*."

Reigan shuddered with his whole body. He had plotted against Eithan, had taunted him, had slain his mentor. No, he now realized, he had slain Eithan's *descendant.* Or rather, descendants.

Only recently, Reigan Shen had merged with the Soulsmith inheritance of Ozmanthus Arelius, and he knew how that man would respond to such treatment.

If Reigan Shen had been allowed to live now, it was only for some more gruesome death later.

"His students," Reigan suddenly realized. He felt another chill as he thought of the boy with the Void Icon and the hungry arm. "He left them behind...for us."

The Sage of Calling Storms wore a crazed smile. "Then I will meet Death on my feet!"

The Monarch was less eager to meet his fate than the Sage. If Eithan's students really had been left behind by their master, he would have to force them to ascend.

Reigan Shen looked at the hunger binding in his hand. By any means necessary, he had to get those Lords out of Cradle.

Or he was dead.

THE END
of Cradle: Volume Ten
Reaper

LINDON'S STORY CONTINUES IN

CRADLE : VOLUME ELEVEN

ΛΠD ΠOW THIS...

"Eithan...this is it for us," Lindon said. "We're all gone."

Eithan brushed off his hands and wiped his face clean with a cloth. He let the cloth fall, and all trace of his tears was gone. He held out his right hand, and revealed that he had been holding something else.

A black marble.

"No," Eithan said, "just her."

He dropped the marble.

Little Blue caught it in both hands. "Remove restraints and release authority," she chimed. "Authorization zero-zero-eight...Ozriel."

The marble cracked, and the darkness within formed a teeny-tiny scythe.

Reigan Shen beckoned to Lindon. "Come here, Wei Shi Lindon Arelius. Let's talk."

Lindon summoned a device from his soulspace. The

weapon he'd crafted for this very battle.

He squeezed the trigger of his spray bottle and spritzed water onto the Monarch's face. "Down! Bad kitty!"

Reigan Shen hissed and ran.

Reigan Shen hissed and ran.

Where do you put our odds of survival? Lindon asked Dross.

[It's impossible to accurately calculate odds of survival without a statistically significant number of prior examples.]

This isn't cheering me up.

[Was that the goal? Then kick Eithan.]

Lindon did. Eithan let out a yelp as he was booted out the door of the Ancestor's Tomb, rolling to a halt outside.

Naru Gwei, Captain of the Skysworn, appeared out of nowhere. "My turn next."

"Now hold on just a second," Eithan protested. He was cut off by the soft sound of a portal opening, and Yan Shoumei walked out, shrouded in her Blood Shadow.

"I'm after him," she whispered.

Eithan looked in all directions. "Who's bringing all these people?"

"Me," Northstrider said. He reached out a hand and showed a line of people stretching off into the horizon. "And I'm first."

"Why haven't you advanced yet?" Lindon asked Jai Long.

Jai Long stopped himself from saying something he would

regret. Lindon could talk like advancing to Underlord was so easy, but it was a barrier that stopped virtually every sacred artist in the entire Blackflame Empire.

"I have not received the necessary insight," he said stiffly.

Lindon rubbed his chin. "Hmmm...well, for me, part of what spurred my advancement was pressure. What are you doing in about a year?"

Jai Long began to sweat.

"Is your calendar open for a duel to the death, do you think? It does wonders for motivation."

Jai Long licked his lips. "Uh, Lindon..."

Lindon eyed one of Jai Long's arms, then the other. "Which hand would you say you like the most?"

Eithan blinked. "That may have been the kindest thing anyone has ever said to me."

"Don't let it swell your head," Yerin muttered.

"This inspires me to compose a poem!"

"Can I pay you to stop?"

"There once was a man from Iceflower—"

"Wait a second," Lindon interrupted. "That reminds me. I found this in Ozmanthus' workshop." He held up a small black book. "I thought they might be Soulsmithing secrets, but they seem to just be poems."

Eithan made a choking sound.

"Might be it runs in the family," Yerin said. "You read any?"

"I don't see what good that would do. This one says his pain is 'a bottomless hole in the night sky of the soul,' which...I'm no poet, but that can't be very good."

"May I see that?" Eithan's voice was strangled.

Yerin took the book before Eithan could. "This is mud and

rot. Did nobody teach him about meter?"

"Did you see the one that says, 'My Remnant aches with longing to see your face'?"

Eithan slapped the book out of Yerin's hand and set it on fire.

Elder Whisper sat on his haunches, tails waving as he regarded Lindon and Yerin.

"So how do we kill the Dreadgods?" Lindon asked.

Whisper leaned forward. "Attend me closely, for this is ancient knowledge. There is only one thing that can kill the Dreadgods: *points*."

Lindon gasped. "I *knew* it!"

"Ozmanthus Arelius, the original Patriarch of our clan, was known as the greatest Soulsmith of his day," Eithan explained. "Perhaps in history. Famous for his great power, his wisdom, and his long, flowing hair. I'm no expert, of course, but from what I hear, he sounds like a wonderful fellow. Kind-hearted, keen-eyed, with flawless skin and the most spectacular clothes."

Yerin gave him a strange look.

"Alas, his handsomeness was too much for this world!" Eithan cried. "If only we could all have been so fortunate as to bask in the presence of such a statuesque Adonis!"

"This is you, isn't it? You're talking about yourself."

"*What?* But how could it be me? It's true, I can see a certain resemblance in his carved musculature, his perfect bone structure, his fatherly yet mischievous smile—"

"Yeah. It's you."

WILL WIGHT lives in Florida, among the citrus fruits and slithering sea creatures. He's the New York Times and #1 Kindle Best Selling author of *The Traveler's Gate Trilogy*, *The Elder Empire* (which cleverly offers twice the fun and twice the work), and his series of mythical martial arts magic: *Cradle*.

He graduated from the University of Central Florida in 2013, earning a Master's of Fine Arts in Creative Writing and a flute of dragon's bone. He is also, apparently, invisible to cameras.

He also claims that *www.WillWight.com* is the best source for book updates, new stories, fresh coriander, and miracle cures for all your aches and pains!

Made in the USA
Middletown, DE
10 November 2021